Party Chicks
&
other works

by Natalie McKelvy

The Dunery Press

Other Books published by the Dunery Press:

Odin the Homeless & Other Stories, four novellas and a short story by Charles McKelvy (1990)
My California Friends and Other Stories, four novellas by Natalie McKelvy (1988)
Holy Orders, a novel by Charles McKelvy (1989)
Chicagoland, four novellas by Charles McKelvy (1989)

Party Chicks & Other Works
Published in 1990 by
The Dunery Press
P.O. Box 116
Harbert, Michigan 49115
Phone: 616/469-1278

Cover photograph by Gerald Losik
Cover design by James Green
Illustrations by Mike Sova

Library of Congress Catalogue Card Number: 89-051334
ISBN: 0-944771-04-1

For Judy and Charley,
who taught me how to live

Table of Contents

Party Chicks   1

Black   125

Divorced   231

Fired!   337

Party Chicks

Chapter One

Mary Frances had been wild in high school.

When she got out she was out of control.

The autumn after she graduated she moved into a slummy apartment on the north side of Chicago with two friends and enrolled in the Belvedere School of Beauty Culture. Every weekend she partied — hard. She careened through the streets at 4 in the morning, drunk, her body entwined with that of the latest man she'd picked up at the singles bars.

She usually went for salesmen. It was the law of averages: there were more of them at the bars than brain surgeons.

Tonight she hung on the arm of the sales manager for the Great Lakes region of Zarconda Precision Tool Company, in town for a convention. He was about 35, well-dressed, with a small gut pushing up against the walls of his French-cut shirt. He kept trying to get her to come back to his hotel room.

"I don't think so," Mary Frances said, twisting her fingers through a strand of her hair. She was a compact woman, about 5 feet 4 inches, with thick blondish hair permanented into loose waves.

"I'll do unspeakable things to your body," the tool man whispered. "Just give me a chance." His eyes were bleary with drink.

"No," she said.

He leaned back against the bar, then pursed his lips and leaned over.

"I'll pay."

"I've got to go," she said, grabbing her purse.

"Have it your way." He turned back to his drink.

She pushed through the crowds to the door and hailed a cab. All the way home she burped up shrimp scampi from the dinner the tool man had bought her.

Mary Frances kept on partying; she just stopped doing it in bars.

* * *

The Belvedere School of Cosmetology and Beauty Culture spread over two floors in a decrepit office building downtown. The cracked linoleum floors had faded from black to gray; yellowing fluorescent lights flickered. Fifty-five young women – and 13 men – labored over the haircuts of 26 young women who were too poor or too cheap to go to a real beauty salon.

More than one would regret it.

The Belvedere was perfectly integrated: half-black, half-white with a sprinkling of Hispanics, mostly shy women who spoke to each other quietly in Spanish and brought their lunches from home.

Mary Frances thought they were all stupid. The Belvedere was not at the high-end of the beauty school spectrum. With half the school black, they spent a lot of time un-kinking black hair and discussing skin cleansers that wouldn't turn black skin gray. Half the black girls braided their hair into corn rows with bands of bright-colored beads woven through. It took so long to do, they only washed their hair once a month.

Some of them smelled.

"If I were you, I'd cut the whole mess off," Mary Frances told Corinthine, her only black friend at school. Corinthine had a well-beaded collection of corn rows.

"Girl," Corinthine said. "You don't know shit."

"You *look* like shit," Mary Frances said.

"And you look like some kind of brillo pad," Corinthine said.

Mary Frances laughed. "You're a fool," she said.   She and Corinthine didn't talk for two weeks.

Such was the extent of interracial communication at Belvedere. It was two separate schools with the Hispanics wandering in bewilderment between them.

Mary Frances swore she'd never have black customers. Their nappy hair broke at the roots. They shouldn't wear it longer than 1/2 inch, yet they were always pouring goo on it, trying to coax it into long, flowing waves. It ended up looking like stiff boards, stuck at right angles to the sides of their heads.

Mary Frances had started complaining about the Belvedere from the moment she arrived. Her mother wouldn't listen. Kathleen Barton had selected the school; she wasn't spending a penny more.

"Blanche went there and she turned out fine," she told Mary Frances. Blanche was Mary Frances's 45-year-old aunt. She worked 12-hour days in a storefront beauty salon in a Polish neighborhood on the far northwest side of Chicago. As far as Mary Frances could see, Blanche was cutting the same haircuts she'd learned in 1961. She half expected her to show up at Sunday dinner some time with a pixie cut, a tiny blue velvet bow nestled in her fluffy bangs.

"Mother," Mary Frances told her mother over the phone one night. "Blanche is paleolithic."

"Don't swear," Kathleen said.

"They aren't teaching me shit at that place."

"Don't swear, dear."

"I don't want to cut nigger hair."

"Don't use words like that."

"I want to go to another school. I'm not learning a thing except how to straighten nigger hair and smear it with brillantine. That's not where the money is in this business."

"Racial slurs are unbecoming to a young woman."

"You're not listening."

"I'm listening. You want to leave school and play around, just like you did in high school. I won't have it. You're learning a profession. Being a beautician is a good job for a woman. It will serve you in good stead when you marry and have children."

"I'm not getting married," Mary Frances said.

Kathleen laughed. "Young girls never change," she said. "I used to talk like that before I met your father."

Mary Frances's father worked at a John Deere dealership on the far edge of Kankakee. He drank a lot and was never home. Mary Frances thought it might have been a good idea if Kathleen and John Barton *had* never met.

Of course, then she and her three brothers and four sisters would never have existed. With the exception of her and Colleen, that might not have been such a bad idea either.

"I've got to run, Mom," she said.

"Eat right, dear."

That night Mary Frances and her two roommates got very drunk.

* * *

Mary Frances graduated from beauty school in June. Her classmates giggled and kissed each other. The blacks disappeared into the vast network of black beauty salons spread through the south and west sides of the city. They'd spend their lives straightening and tinting hair with cheap chemicals at $20 a shot. They didn't seem to mind.

The white girls went home to their mothers.

Mary Frances had other plans.

"I'm going to work at Guillaume-Larson," she told Colleen over lunch soon after graduation. Mary Frances and Colleen were the only Barton children to leave Kankakee. A skinny woman, Colleen piled her hair in ratted curls on top of her head. She was a student at the Art Institute of Chicago.

Guillaume-Larson was the most avant-garde and expensive hair salon in the city.

"They don't do black women's hair," Colleen said.

"Very funny."

"They'll never take you. Not from Belvedere. No way." Colleen bit crisply into her tuna sandwich; tuna juice and mayonnaise ran down her chin.

"No harm in asking," Mary Frances said.

"You like embarrassing yourself in public?"

"Don't be a bitch."

"Don't be an idiot. You think they want some kid from Kankakee who's done 10 permanents in her life?"

"Eleven. I've done 11."

"Eleven, 12. Who cares? You're dead meat." Colleen wiped the mayonnaise from her chin.

"So what am I supposed to do?" Mary Frances said. "Roll over and die?"

Colleen shrugged. "I dunno." She bit into her sandwich again.

Mary Frances glared at her and stood up.

"Thanks for the support."

"Don't mention it," Colleen said, her mouth filled with tuna. "See you Saturday." They were going to a party together Saturday night.

Mary Frances finished her Coke and headed home.

She put on a tight red miniskirt, teased her hair into a stylish nest, and painted her eyes. Then she took the subway downtown and walked over to Guillaume-Larson.

The salon was located in a bubble of glass and chrome floating on top of a rehabbed factory building. A glass-brick wall separated the entryway from the main shop. Synthesizer music drifted through the air.

A woman with a severely short haircut, styled into three stiff, purple-tipped spikes, sat behind the reception desk. She shifted in her chair and looked up from her work. Her metal bracelets clanked.

"I'd like to see the manager," Mary Frances said.

The receptionist picked up a microphone. "Mr. Larson, please come to reception." Her upper-class British accent rolled over the synthesizer music and out the public address system through the shop.

Mary Frances sat in an uncomfortable chair made of leather and chrome and stared at a violently red painting that took up the entire far wall. It looked like a two-dimensional side of beef.

A few minutes later a small, balding man in a leather apron came from behind the glass blocks. He hurried to the receptionist who nodded at Mary Frances.

"I'm Bill Larson," he said. "Can I help you?" He seemed to be dancing on his feet, a hummingbird quivering in place.

Mary Frances stood up. "Mary Frances Barton," she said. "I'd like to work for you."

He smiled slightly.

"I've just graduated from beauty school," she said.

"Which one?"

"Belvedere," she said, her voice dropping in embarrassment.

His smile drooped.

"I'm sorry. . ."

"I'll do anything: shampoo, sweep, clean the coffee pot."

"I don't have time to train people."

Her face fell.

"I am sorry. Now if you'll excuse me. . ." And he flitted off behind the glass wall, narrowly missing identical twins in black minidresses. Their blonde hair was swept up and shellacked into cones on the tops of their heads. One of them had a tiny paper umbrella stuck in it.

Mary Frances cursed Belvedere and her mother, then left.

* * *

She stopped at a McDonald's, bought a cup of coffee, and pondered her options. Money was running out. She either got a job immediately or moved back with her parents and looked for a job from home.

The thought made her sick. Her divorced sister Lindsay was already there with her two kids and a dog. Her retarded brother Patrick had never left home. Younger sister Gloriana was doing drugs and driving Kathleen crazy.

Plus they lived in Kankakee.

She lit up her last cigarette and watched the poor and hungry mixing with the well-to-do as they all waited in line for their hamburgers. A black clerk snapped her gum so loud Mary Frances could hear it. She drank her coffee and left.

The subway was to the left but she turned right, the direction of the expensive beauty shops clustered among the boutiques of the Gold Coast.

She walked into the first one she hit, "Georgio Sorti: Precision Hair Stylists." It was one of a big chain of hair salons, started in Italy and now worldwide.

Mary Frances had seen articles on it in *Hairdressers Weekly* as well as a photo of the founder. He was a short, lumpy little Italian, the son of a Neapolitan laundress. He wore a baggy suit in a tiny checked pattern and a tie with a fish on it. His hair was a mess: it looked like gobs of cotton wool stuck to his skull.

The salon was another chrome and glass concotion, just like Guillaume-Larson. But the furniture was cheaper, the paintings had more pastel colors, and the carpet was worn in front of the receptionist, a young, blonde girl with a head of permanented curls.

She looked just like Mary Frances. Mary Frances stared; they could have been twins.

She asked to see the manager.

"Are you looking for a job?" the receptionist asked in a flat Chicago accent.

"Well. . .yeah."

"You'll want Miss Phillips then. Take a seat."

Mary Frances sat down in a chrome and leather chair. Two women in business suits and dirty running shoes came out, their hair permanented into floppy curls that bobbed above their shoulders. They looked like cocker spaniels.

A Mexican girl in an ill-fitting pink uniform walked by. She pushed a cart piled with boxes of hair chemicals. Mary Frances waited 15 minutes, thumbing through hairstyle magazines and watching the clientele.

Most were younger women; nearly all were having their hair permanented into curly mops. The smell of ammonia hung heavy in the air despite the giant vase of dried eucalyptus by the door. The two smells fought with each other; Mary Frances got a headache.

She was fishing in her purse for an aspirin when Miss Phillips appeared. She was a young woman, small and bottom-heavy. Her hips pushed out against the sides of her shiny black jumpsuit like wings trying to unfold. She had beautiful eyes which she had lined in iridescent blue. Her shoulder-length red hair was permanented into a frizz. She introduced herself in a girlish voice, then sat down next to Mary Frances.

"So, you want to be a stylist here?" she said.

"Yes."

"Where did you go to school?"

"Christian D'Or." Mary Frances didn't blink. Christian D'Or was the best and most expensive beauty school in the city.

Miss Phillips screwed up her beautiful eyes and looked at her closely.

"I teach there Tuesday and Thursday evenings," she said. "I don't think I've ever seen you."

Mary Frances felt her heart grab.

"I was a day student."

Miss Phillips smiled. "That explains it then."

They chatted about trends in hairstyling. Miss Phillips told her about the salon: "Fifteen stylists, three shampoo girls, and five aides. Mr. Pierre runs a tight ship. We work hard."

Unfortunately, they had no openings.

Mary Frances left her name and phone number.

"We'll call if anything comes up," Miss Phillips said.

Out on the street again, Mary Frances fumed. The woman had wasted her time. She felt like a piece of meat.

She pulled down her miniskirt and hiked to the next salon, two doors down, "Charles Piquet, Hairdresser." They had only two stylists and no openings, the receptionist said. She hardly looked up.

"Mr. Charles" needed no one.

"Frederick Ungaro" was closed for two weeks for remodeling.

"Hair Fantasia" hired only experienced stylists.

"The Carmody Brothers Hair Circus" imported its stylists from its own school in New York.

Mary Frances got giddy. She told one salon owner she'd gone to the Cordon Bleu Hairstyling Academy in Paris.

"I thought they only trained chefs," he said.

"Oh no," Mary Frances said. "They have a famous hairstyling school."

He looked at her. "Get lost, kid," he hissed.

After 15 salons, she'd worked her way through all the expensive salons in the city. She dragged herself home on the subway.

She called her mother that night.

"I can't find a job," she told Kathleen.

"The city is full of beauty salons," Kathleen said.

"Not any I want to work in."

"I'll talk to Blanche."

"No!"

The phone was silent a few moments.

"So what do you want me to do?" Kathleen's voice was angry.

"I don't know. Don't do anything. I'll think of something."

And she hung up.

Chapter Two

Colleen picked up Mary Frances for the party at 8:30 Saturday night. Colleen wore a blue chiffon cocktail dress from the 1950s, black leather jackboots, and cheap gold bracelets up and down her skinny right arm.

It was a warm night in late June.

Mary Frances looked at Colleen's boots.

"You're going to be hot," she said.

"I'll be fine," Colleen said. For an art student, Colleen wore the ugliest clothes Mary Frances had ever seen.

The party was in the loft of an art student Colleen had met in Life Drawing at the Art Institute. Colleen and Mary Frances took the bus to a slum on the near northwest side of the city, then walked the six blocks to the loft. A band of young Puerto Rican men followed them to the door, hooting in Spanish and whistling.

Outside was urban Spanish ghetto; inside was urban starving artist. The artist had painted the dark brick walls of his space with giant white lilies. Six-foot canvases splashed with violent oranges and reds hung on three walls. The fourth had a small table pushed against it with a cooler full of beer on top and two bowls of pretzels. An expensive stereo system boomed loud rock music. It was stifling hot.

The artist himself was a dirty 20-year-old with a long shank of greasy hair and paint-spattered blue jeans. He came from a good family in an expensive suburb. His father was a lawyer with a big firm downtown.

"I'd kill for space like this," Colleen muttered, admiring the big grimy windows overlooking the street. Colleen worked out of a studio apartment in a neighborborhood of black dope dealers and mental patients of all colors.

This neighborhood was a step up.

The party was full of art students, all of them looking more or less like Colleen, and one well-groomed refugee from corporate America. He looked neat and bewildered in his creased pants and light shirt, wondering where the hell he was and how he would find the expressway.

The male art students talked baseball; the females talked about the males, and clothes. Everyone was stoned; most were drunk. Colleen lit up a joint and grabbed a beer. Mary Frances poured herself an orange juice from the refrigerator and sat down on a paint-spattered chair in the corner of the kitchen.

Why did she come to these parties?

Colleen's friends drove her crazy. They couldn't talk. When they weren't painting and sculpting, they waited tables. Paint tubes, chisels, and beer cans littered their apartments, which were usually covered with plaster dust or dirt.

Uniformly, they were slobs. Most were broke. From what Mary Frances could see, none had the talent or drive to make it as a professional.

Why were they wasting their time?

A tall young man in raggy cutoffs shook a beer, opened it, and sprayed the wall over the table. Everyone laughed, a drifty, stoned-drunk laugh interspersed with high-pitched shrieks from a particularly drunk young woman.

Mary Frances frowned. She was getting too old for this. She'd partied all through high school in Kankakee with afternoon drug, booze, and sex sessions at her friends' houses. Everyone's parents worked; big double beds in the town's old Victorian houses were in heavy use every afternoon.

She knew no girls over the age of 15 who were still virgins, at least in her crowd. She'd lost her virginity at 14 to a stone-drunk 19-year-old who worked at a gas station, played rhythm guitar in a local band, and wanted to be famous. She bled all over his mother's best bedspread. He hadn't even bothered to wash the stain out.

"I'll tell her I cut myself shaving," he'd said.

He promised he'd love her forever. Would she come back tomorrow?

She didn't.

Men and boys were cheap and easy.

So was she. Everyone wanted to lay her. By the time she'd finished high school, she'd slept with at least 26 men, including 10 whose names she couldn't remember. She had counted them up once.

Kathleen yelled and fought with her. She once called her a slut and a disgrace to her sex. Mary Frances looked at her mother's lumpy body, sad eyes, and ratty housedress. She was *glad* to be a disgrace to her sex.

After graduating from high school, Mary Frances branched out. She wanted to conserve her savings so she lived at home that summer. But she managed overnight trips to Chicago, usually with a different man each time.

She couldn't understand why anyone would voluntarily spend the rest of her life with one man.

"The thrill is gone in three weeks," she had told her friend, Carol. "Why stay?"

That summer, Carol got a job as a secretary in Chicago. She asked Mary Frances to move in with her and her sister, Carlisle. Carlisle was 24. She was a paralegal and made real money.

Mary Frances was thrilled; her mother had a fit. Apparently, Mary Frances could whore from home, where she inhabited a cute, doll-like room under the eaves with the stuffed animals of her childhood heaped on her twin bed.

But the idea of her living in a grimy apartment with a double mattress on the floor and rock music throbbing through rooms filled with drug smoke drove Kathleen wild. The fact that her daughter had slept in all the clean white beds of the women in her bridge club, their oversexed sons arched over her, never crossed Kathleen's mind.

Actually, it had crossed her mind. She just never let it stay.

Her daughter wasn't a slut; she was just high-spirited.

But she put her foot down about Carol's apartment.

Mary Frances moved anyway, in August.

"I'll disinherit you!" Kathleen screamed at her.

"Fine," Mary Frances said, packing her suitcases.

"How will you support yourself?" Kathleen croaked.

"I'll wait on tables, I don't know." She looked at her mother. "What do you care? You're disinheriting me." She snapped a suitcase shut.

"What about beauty school?" Kathleen viewed beauty school as Mary Frances's salvation.

"I'll go when I get the money."

Kathleen couldn't think about how Mary Frances would raise the money.

"Suit yourself," Kathleen said and left the room.

Carol, Carlisle, and some young man Kathleen had never seen came and picked up Mary Frances that afternoon.

She left all her stuffed animals.

A week later, Kathleen wrote her:

Dear Mary Frances,

Here is a check for your first semester tuition at Belvedere. Blanche says it's a good school. It's so reasonable. Be sure to enroll soon. School starts in October.

The other check for $150 is to help on your rent. I'll send you another in two weeks.

Be a good girl.

Love,
Mom

Mary Frances spent all the money on drugs. She promised herself that Kathleen's next checks would go for tuition. Instead, they went for food and rent.

Panicked, in early October Mary Frances asked a stockbroker who'd taken her out four times and slept with her each time to loan her some money.

"How much do you need?" he asked. His wallet was fat with bills.

"$600," she said. "For tuition."

"You're going to college?" he said.

"Yeah. . . sort of. . . beauty college."

"My daughter was going to beauty school, I mean college, when she died."

There was a silence.

"I'm sorry," Mary Frances said.

He shrugged. "Shit happens." He opened his wallet and drew out six, $100 bills. "You go for her," he said, handing her the money.

She never saw him again.

The next day she registered at Belvedere, counting the crisp bills out in the clerk's office. Class started the day after.

* * *

Where had it gotten her? She leaned back on the chair in the artist's kitchen and stared at a big water spot in the ceiling. She was just another unemployed hairdresser from a third-rate beauty school wandering the streets looking for a job.

Someone turned up the music. It shrieked in her ears. A drunk couple stumbled over looking for the bathroom.

"Is it thith way?" the woman said, the man holding her up with his arm around her waist.

"Yeah," Mary Frances said, pointing. "That door over there."

The couple shuffled through the door. Thirty seconds later, Mary Frances heard vomiting.

She swore under her breath, grabbed her purse, and told Colleen she felt sick and was leaving. She took the bus back to her apartment. Carol and Carlisle were out; they hit the singles bars on Saturday nights.

Mary Frances laid down on her bed, smoked a joint, and fell asleep.

* * *

Monday morning she pulled on her miniskirt and went to salons again.

This time she pursued the second-string shops in the nice but cheap neighborhoods. No one was hiring. She was starting to think she would have to learn Polish and work with Aunt Blanche when she walked into Mr. John's House of Beauty.

Mr. John's was in a run-down neighborhood filled with tired frame buildings and Pakistanis. On one side of the shop was the Cozy Inn Restaurant; a sign in the window announced that it served grits all day. On the other side was the the stairway to the Fun and Frolic Adult Book Store, one flight up. Mr. John's was in the storefront below.

In the window stood a big photo of a young woman with streaked blonde hair pulled into a French twist. The photo looked about 20-years-old. Next to it was a line of black-and-white photos of pouting young men, their hair slicked back in a variety of swirls and swoops. The windows were still lined with Christmas lights; this was late June.

Inside, the salon was simple: four chairs for cutting, two chairs in a small waiting area upfront, and a screened-off section in back. The only people in the place were a terribly pale young woman cutting a little boy's hair and a middle-aged man rolling up a fat blonde's hair in curlers. A beat-up radio on a ledge oozed "easy-listening" music.

Mary Frances stood for two minutes in the waiting area while everyone ignored her. Finally, the young woman glared at the other stylist, hrumphed loudly, and walked over.

"Can I help you?" she said.

"Is the owner in?" Mary Frances said.

The woman turned toward the rear of the store and yelled: "Johnny!"

A moment later, an immense man with a head of brown, frizzy hair and a huge stomach waddled from behind the screen at the rear of the store. He wore wrinkled white linen pants and a flowing pink caftan top that floated over his stomach.

"I'm coming, I'm coming," he said in a soft, feminine voice, hurrying toward the front of the shop.

"Yes, yes, what can I do for you?" he said, stopping in front of Mary Frances. He was panting from his walk across the shop.

She stared at him. Maybe she should have become a a grocery checker at the Kroger's in Kankakee?

She inhaled quickly.

"I'm just out of beauty school, I'm looking for a job, are you hiring?" she said, looking at her feet.

"What sign are you, honey?" he said.

"Pardon me?"

"What astrological sign are you?"

"Cancer. I mean Leo. Yes, I'm a Leo."

He looked at her carefully.

"Sandy," he called to the pale woman. "Can we get along with a Leo?"

The woman paused a moment. "I think so," she said tentatively, touching her comb to her chin. "Just so she isn't a Virgo. We'd scratch each other's eyes out; she'd probably stab Petey." The middle-aged man rolling up the blonde's hair chuckled.

Johnny turned to Mary Frances.

"OK," he said. "You're hired."

Mary Frances stared at him in disbelief.

"When do I start?" she said.

"Tomorrow. Come around 1:30. I have some free time then." He turned and walked back toward the screen before she could say another word.

"Bye, honey," the middle-aged man said, waving his comb at Mary Frances. "See you tomorrow."

They didn't even know her name, much less where she'd gone to school.

* * *

That night Mary Frances called Colleen.

"What are they paying you?" Colleen said. Mary Frances could hear small scrapings and thuds. Colleen was eating ice cream out of a container.

"I don't know," Mary Frances said.

"How can you take a job and not find out what they're paying you? You some Mexican grapepicker or what?"

"They'll pay me what they'll pay me."

Colleen smacked her lips, then burped.

"You're letting life run you over."

"I'm just trying to get a job. Get off my case."

Colleen ignored her. "You've got to hustle. Hustle, hustle, hustle. That's the name of the game."

"What game?"

"The game of life, you idiot. You hustle or go nowhere. You end up waiting tables the rest of your life."

"Like you?" Mary Frances snickered.

"I'm still a student," Colleen sniffed. "Wait until I'm a famous painter." Colleen hadn't really decided what she'd be famous at yet. Last semester it had been fashion design.

"You going out tonight?" Mary Frances said.

"I'm going to the G-String with Lennie." The G-String was a cheap hillbilly bar, currently a favorite with the art-student crowd. Lennie was a goggle-eyed teacher of oil painting at the Art Institute. Colleen had been sleeping with him for four weeks, a longevity record for her.

"I'll come with you," Mary Frances said.

"I thought you didn't like us anymore." She was referring to last week's party.

"I didn't feel well."

"Tell me another."

"Fuck off."

"We'll pick you up around 9."

* * *

Mary Frances hung around the G-String until midnight, sulking in the corner over a flat beer, and watching Colleen's friends drink. Lennie tried to cheer her up, his goggle eyes bulging as he talked. Loud country-western music twanged in the background.

"Everyone's first job is for a lunatic," he said. "Think of how camp it will be."

He stroked her back possessively. Sleeping with Colleen, he seemed to think he had an option on Mary Frances — sort of a sexual two-for-one sale.

"It's not camp, it's disgusting," Mary Frances said, glaring at him. She threw back her shoulders; his arm dropped.

He smiled. He'd have to get her in a better mood to score tonight.

"The guy who runs the place is a fat slob," Mary Frances said. "The customers are geeks. I'll probably get stabbed walking there from the bus."

"Look at it as a growth experience," Lennie said. He gave her his best profile. "How about another beer? Or something stronger?" he said hopefully.

She stood up and yanked her red miniskirt down. "I gotta' pee," she said.

The ladies' room was a tiny closet in the back. The door was locked. She banged on it.

"Just a minute," a woman yelled. It was Colleen.

"Open up. It's me," Mary Frances said, pounding on the door. The door opened.

Colleen stood there in a faded, 1940s housedress, her frizzy hair puffed out at the sides of her head, her eyes lined in deep black. She sniffled and rubbed her nose. A tiny woman behind her, clad completely in black, sniffed loudly. They were snorting cocaine.

"You have any for me?" Mary Frances said.

"I think Ginger just did the last line," Colleen said.

"No, there's another," said a tiny voice.

Mary Frances gave her sister an imploring look.

Colleen sighed.

"I'll be so glad when you're working," she said, handing Mary Frances a tightly rolled dollar bill. "You can buy me some drugs for a change."

Ginger left; Mary Frances came in and locked the door, bumping elbows with Colleen in the cramped space. Then she bent over and snorted through the rolled bill. The line of cocaine on her sister's pocket mirror disappeared up her nose.

"That asshole Lennie is hitting me up again," Mary Frances said, standing up. "Would you get rid of him? He's a fucking embarrassment."

"I think he's cute."

"He's a dirtbag. He'll sleep with anything that moves." Suddenly, Mary Frances felt a surge. She closed her eyes. She was flying over rooftops, far away from Mr. John's House of Beauty, on her way to Paris! She sighed.

She looked down to see the Eiffel Tower. Instead, she saw a rotten wood floor. She was standing in a pool of water spreading from the leaking toilet.

"Shit!" She jumped back from the water, forcing Colleen against the wall. Colleen yelped; Mary Frances pushed open the door.

Two rednecks in billed caps leered at her from the end of the bar, undressing her with their eyes.

She swore under her breath, walked out of the bar, and hailed a cab.

When she got to her apartment, her roommates were already in bed. She slipped into her room and cried herself to sleep.

Chapter Three

The next day, she arrived at Mr. John's at 1:15. The pale woman wasn't there, but Petey labored over a fat old woman with champagne-blonde hair. He finished twisting her hair over a forest of small, pink rollers, then escorted her to an ancient beehive hairdryer. She looked like a overfed Nefertiti under her crown.

Just as Petey was getting her a cup of coffee, Mr. John himself came in, the white linen pants now topped with a blue caftan. His arms were full of boxes.

"Sweet pea," he said, breezing by Mary Frances. "Get the rest, would you? They're in the car."

A late-model Chrysler stood in front, its curbside doors flung open. Mary Frances picked up some cardboard boxes labeled "Jackson-Turner Co., Human Hair" from the backseat. They were very light.

She followed Mr. John into the salon and behind the partition where she was surprised to discover another room. It was lined with wooden booths hung with half doors, just like the stalls in a public bathroom. She peeked into one: there was a chair, a small table, and a long mirror on the wall.

Mr. John was on the phone already, adding and erasing names in his big appointment book. She wandered back into the main salon where Petey was sweeping hair from underneath his cutting chair.

"What's with the back room?" she said.

"Hair transplants," he said. He patted his toupee. "It's not my bag, honey, but Johnny does a brisk trade."

As if on cue, a young man in a suit with thin mousy hair walked in the door. Without a word, he walked back toward the partition and disappeared behind it.

"Har-ry!" Mary Frances heard Mr. John say. "How good to see you!" His voice dropped slightly. "It looks good, very good! I think it's really taking, don't you?"

Harry's reply was inaudible.

Mary Frances went back out to the car and brought in the rest of the boxes. She piled them in a corner of the back room. Mr. John and Harry were already in one of the stalls. Mr. John's massive shoulders, clad in a white lab coat, were visible over the top of the half door. He lifted a plastic-gloved hand; it held a plug of human hair and had blood on it.

She gagged, then hurried back to the main salon where she stood, hesitating, by the door. Petey was still sweeping hair off the floor. He didn't look up.

"You might as well come over here and I'll show you your station," he said. "Johnny will be a while."

"What's he doing back there?" she whispered.

Petey kept sweeping, staring at the floor.

"You put these little hair plugs in the scalp," he said. "They die and fall out a few weeks later. Then you put more in. At $150 a shot it's easy money."

He looked up.

"By the way," he said. "What's your name?"

"Mary Frances Barton."

"Petey Powers." He nodded to an old green cutting chair on his left. "You can work next to me. You get the walk-ins."

Mary Frances nodded.

He set his broom down and walked over to the old lady under the hairdryer. "Well, Mrs. Davidson," he said in an sugared voice. "Just how are we doing?"

Mary Frances sat in her cutting chair and stared at herself in the mirror. She looked pale. She twisted a shank of her blonde hair against her skin. How would she look as a redhead?

Lousy.

She got up and wandered over to the waiting area where she sat down in a chair with blue plastic cushions and picked up a battered copy of the *Ladies' Home Journal.* She was reading a story about a baby born with one lung and a rare bone disease, who, through the superhuman efforts of his mother and modern medicine, survived to become a world-class gymnast, when the young man with the thin mousy hair came out from the back.

Mr. John followed.

"We'll see you in two weeks, then?" he said.

Harry grunted.

Mary Frances stared at his head as he went by. Other than every strand of mousy hair was hairsprayed to lie carefully across the top of his head, he looked the same as when he had come in.

Mr. John disappeared in the back again.

Petey retrieved the aged blonde from under the hairdryer and took out her curlers. Tight little sausages of brilliantly blonde hair covered her head.

A middle-aged black woman with huge hips waddled in the door. Petey went over to talk to her. Mary Frances stared at her. Her black dress had grease spots down the front. The back seam over her rump was splitting.

"Mary Frances," Petey said. "Mrs. DuPont here is a new customer. She's on her way to a funeral. She needs a quick wash and set."

Mary Frances froze her face into a smile and nodded.

Mrs. DuPont huffed over to Mary Frances's cutting chair. She could hardly fit between its narrow arm rests. They both stared wordlessly into the big mirror facing the chair, Mary Frances's mop of blonde curls perched above Mrs. DuPont's gray-black head.

Her hair was a greasy mass of frizzed clumps; it smelled of bacon fat. Mary Frances couldn't run her hands through it.

"Jez put a leel bounce in dem curls and I'll be on my way, gurl," Mrs. DuPont said.

Mary Frances nodded.

She led the woman over to the shampoo station, squeezed her into the chair, and began washing. Every time Mary Frances ran her hands through the woman's hair, a bigger glob of it came out in her hands, along with several bobby pins.

"Your hair is very fragile," Mary Frances said.

"Say wha'?"

Mary Frances turned off the water.

"I said your hair is coming out in my hands," she said.

Mrs. DuPont looked alarmed, then a big chuckle gurgled up from just above the top fold of her stomach. "Doan you worry about dat, gurl," she said. "Dat's jez Rosie's rats."

"Excuse me?"

"My sister, she dun save all her hair from her comb then she stuff it back up inside."

Mary Frances looked at her blankly.

"To give it dat body, gurl!" Mrs. DuPont said, as if Mary Frances was as stupid as mud. "I jez furgot to take 'em out." Mrs. DuPont flapped her feet ineffectually, trying to sit up from the basin. Mary Frances pushed her, then came around and pulled her up by her arm. Mrs. DuPont ran her hands through her wet hair and pulled out a clump of hair. It looked like a hairball spit up by a monster cat.

"You can tell dey not mine, child," she said, showing Mary Frances the hair clump. "Dey be a different color."

Mary Frances stared at the clump; it was the same gray-black as Mrs. DuPont's.

"Is that all there are?" Mary Frances said.

Mrs. DuPont fished around in her dripping hair. "I doan rightly know now, honey," she said, her huge arms lifting as she searched through her hair. "Dis damn water be runnin' down my neck," she said angrily. "You be ruinin' my dress, gurl!"

Mary Frances grabbed a towel and wrapped it around the woman's neck, apologizing in mumbled tones.

Mrs. DuPont kept rumbling her displeasure.

"If you done spotted my bes' dress, I ain't gonna' be too happy, gurl."

"I'm sure it's fine," Mary Frances said.

"I ain't sure of nuttin', gurl." She fished out another clump of hair from the mess on her head and handed it to Mary Frances. Then she slid down in the chair and laid her head on the rim of the basin again, sighing contentedly.

Without her "rats," Mrs. DuPont's hair was thin and limp. Apparently, someone had last cut it with a hatchet: every strand was a different length. It took three washings to get out the smell of bacon fat.

Mary Frances toweled Mrs. DuPont's hair dry, then led her to her station. Petey had gone out for a sandwich. She could hear Mr. John singing to himself in the back room.

Mary Frances set Mrs. DuPont's hair on little pink rollers while the woman dozed in her chair. Then she lead her to a hairdryer. Her hair cooked dry while Mary Frances packed the "rats" in a plastic bag she found under a sink.

Mrs. DuPont's hair came out nice, but its natural curl drove the "flip" hairstyle she wanted into a close helmet of tight curls.

"Wha' kindda' flip is dis, gurl?" she asked Mary Frances, examining her hairdo like a movie star about to go on screen.

"That's as close as you can get without straightening your hair first," Mary Frances said.

Mrs. DuPont snorted her disgust.

"I dun have my hair dun by Mr. Bruno on Kenmore. He dun always make it flip."

Mary Frances shrugged helplessly. She took off the towel around Mrs. DuPont's neck.

The neckline was wet.

Mary Frances said nothing. She hurried to the shop's reception desk. A yellowed schedule of prices was taped to the top.

"That's $7.50 for a wash and set," she said.

Mrs. DuPont puffed out her big cheeks like an angered blowfish. "You dun wet my dress. You turn my hair into some mess. You wash out my rats. And you gonna' charge me money? You some crazy white gurl."

She pulled herself up, clutched her purse, and walked out of the shop.

Mary Frances stared at her a few seconds then started yelling.

"Come back here and pay up, you fat cow!" she screamed. "I'm going to call the cops on you."

Mrs. DuPont looked alarmed and scuttled down the street.

Mr. John came running out from the back.

"My God, what's going on out here?" he said.

"This fat pig just stiffed me on a wash and set."

Mr. John was all action.

"Which way did she go?"

"Left. She's a fat black lady in a black dress."

John mumbled some obscenity about "damn niggers" and headed out the door. For a fat man, he moved fast. Mary Frances followed him out and watched him run Mrs. DuPont down at the first cross-street.

The woman waved her arms, pointing at her hair and the neckline of her dress. Mr. John waved his arms back. Then he set his hands on his plump hips and yelled at her. Mary Frances could hear the low rumble of his voice. His neck and face strained in rage.

Mrs. DuPont waved her arms again.

A few people on the street stopped to watch.

The screaming and arm-waving went on for several minutes. Finally, Mrs. DuPont opened her ragged little purse and handed him some money. He grabbed it and turned back toward the shop, yelling some parting salvo at her over his shoulder.

Mary Frances followed him back inside.

"She gave me $5," he said, opening the little drawer in the reception desk and stuffing the bills in the cash box. "I threatened to break her arm."

He smiled. "She never intended to pay."

He picked up a peppermint candy from a little bowl that stood on the desk and started unwrapping it.

"What's your name, honey," he said.

"Mary Frances. Mary Frances Barton."

He popped the candy in his mouth and studied her.

"What are we paying you?"

She shrugged.

He laughed. "I can only afford $150 a week base. Bring in some business and we'll split the proceeds 50/50."

"On those wages I'll have to."

He looked at her. "Bring in the bodies; it's the name of the game."

Mary Frances looked at the worn furniture; the high tin ceiling dripped with leaves of peeling paint. She wouldn't tell her friends she worked here much less ask them to bring her their business.

She just shrugged again.

Mr. John patted her back with a big hammy paw and headed toward the back room.

"By the way," she said, calling after him. "How often do we get stiffed?"

"Couple of times a month," he said. "But they pay up." He pounded a fist into the palm of his other hand and smiled pleasantly. "I just threaten them with mutilation."

He disappeared behind the partition.

Mary Frances picked up the bag of "rats" by one corner and threw it in the trash.

* * *

Business was slow. Mary Frances sat in her chair and toyed with a comb. She twirled herself around and made herself dizzy. Petey came back about 3; a woman brought in three little boys under the age of 8. He trimmed their dark hair into smooth caps, the bangs fringing the brows over their blue eyes.

At 5:15, the rush started. Two men with thin hair and wearing business suits hurried in and went toward the back. Mr. John gurgled his happy welcome: "Mr. Sor-kow, To-ny, what a pleasure to see you again!"

A thin, tired-looking woman of about 50 wearing a mustard-colored suit walked in and plopped down in Petey's chair. Her hair was a faded red, almost pink. Rigid with hairspray, it looked like cotton candy.

"Just the usual, Petey," she said, slumping in the chair.

He draped her shoulders in a plastic cape, pulled on rubber gloves, and started squirting red dye on her hair, rubbing it in with his fingers. The dye made her face look powdery and lumpy, like a tray of white rolls from a good bakery.

Another pair of young, business-suited men came in. They looked embarrassed. One had the usual thin thatch carefully coaxed and glued with hairspray across the top of his head. The other was completely bald; a thin ruff of hair fringed the sides of his head. Mary Frances stared at him. What could Mr. John do with a completely bald man?

The bald man looked at her nervously.

"He's in the back," she said, nodding toward the partition.

Both men smiled and nodded then headed back to the transplant room. The familiar gushings of Mr. John drifted over the partition. "Mr. Hennison, Frank, how *good* to see you. It looks *good,* Frank, don't you think so?"

How could Mr. John do plugs on four men at once? She envisaged him running among them, his hand full of bloody hair plugs of all colors, sticking one of each in the men's heads. They'd look like balding Indians bedecked for war, multi-colored sprigs of hair sticking up like tiny waterspouts all over their heads.

Mary Frances slouched down in her cutting chair. Petey combed the red dye through the tired woman's hair. She talked about her son, a young man who was a runner on one of the trading floors at the Board of Trade.

"He gets home at 2 in the afternoon and just lays around," she said. She pursed her lips into a pout; valleys of deep lines shot away into her puckered mouth.

"I should ship him down to his father on the south side, but he's 26-years-old. You can't tell him anything. No sirree. He has all the answers. He's a Mr. Smarty Pants."

She shook her head gravely. "He's turning out no good, just no good."

"Maybe this new job will be good for him," Petey clucked diplomatically. He struggled to comb the dye through her hair. Finally he braced one hand on her head and just yanked, jerking her head.

She didn't miss a beat.

"New job, old job, what difference does it make? He *had* a good job at the mattress factory. They would've made him a foreman in five years. But he thinks he's going to be rich!"

She snorted and shook her head; red dye splattered the plastic cape. "Rich! A messenger boy for a bunch of Jews! What kind of job is that? What kind of rich is that?

"I mean his father was stupid, but not that stupid. Thirty-three years he's been with Ford, 33 years in the painting department. He'll get a good pension. What will his worthless son get?"

She kept raging, a cloud of acrid disappointment hanging over the chair. Petey nodded and combed, nodded and combed. Finally he set his timer and led her to another chair. There she would sit for 45 minutes while the dye soaked into her hair. Petey handed her a fashion magazine with "Spring KAPOW!!!!! Best Fashion Answers EVER!!!!!!" printed across the bottom of the cover. On the cover was a photo of a perfect, blonde, 18-year-old model with a manic smile.

The woman formed her mouth into its lined pout and stuck her face in the magazine.

Mary Frances wondered about the sex life of 26-year-old men who still lived with their mothers. It made her tired.

Petey's next customer was sitting in the little waiting area, her eyes bugging out. A young woman, her hair hung like dull boards and frazzled ropes down to her waist. Three-foot strands flew away from the sides, trapped in static electricity.

"Just a little off the ends, please," she said. "Not more than 1/2 an inch, please." She emphasized the "please" with a pathetic tone suggesting she was certain Petey would chop her hair off at the roots.

Petey carefully cut 1/2 inch off the dried ends. It took him two minutes.

"Done!" he said brightly.

The woman smiled with relief, opened her purse, and gave him a dollar.

"See you in a month," she said, happy to be leaving.

Mary Frances understood the urge; she caught Petey's eye. He looked at the wall clock.

"Why don't you take off," he said. "Can't do everything in a day."

She grabbed her purse from under one of the shampooing sinks and was out the door in 15 seconds.

Chapter Four

That evening her roommates Carol and Carlisle announced they were moving.

"To Los Angeles," Carol said. "Carlisle met this lawyer at Murphy O'Grady's who promised her a job as a paralegal in Laguna Beach."

Murphy O'Grady's was a singles bar.

"Anaheim," Carlisle said. "He's in Anaheim."

Carol and Carlisle were sisters. Carlisle was the older and prettier one with long legs and blonde hair. Carol was Mary Frances's age. Her brown eyes drooped at the outside corners. With her thick brown hair hanging to her shoulders, she resembled a bloodhound.

Mary Frances threw her purse on the floor and sat with a thud on the sofa.

"So what are you going to do in L.A.?" she asked Carol.

"I'm going to be on TV. This guy, the lawyer, said I'd be perfect for the part in this sitcom he's producing with another bunch of lawyers. They're going to sell it to TV."

"Really?" This sounded more interesting than curling hair. Mary Frances kicked off her shoes and stretched her toes.

Carol nodded solemnly. "In the meantime, I'm going to work the switchboard at his office."

Mary Frances made a face.

"Well, they have to raise the money first, you know," Carol said. "You just can't run out and produce a show without backers. That's how they do things in Hollywood."

She and Carlisle looked at each other, nodding in agreement, then at Mary Frances.

"So when do you move?" Mary Frances said.

"Next month," Carlisle said.

"Next month!" Mary Frances shrieked. "What am I supposed to do for roommates?"

"Carol has some friends from work," Carlisle said. "We'll ask around."

"You guys are on the lease."

"I know a girl at work who needs a place," Carol said.

They were silent a few moments.

"There's always Colleen," Carlisle said.

Mary Frances glared at them. "I lived with her for 19 years. I've had enough Colleen."

"Her money's as green as anyone else's."

"Buzz off."

"Call her."

So Mary Frances and Colleen became roommates, along with a friend of Carol's from work, Janeen Thomazcek, a quiet, 22-year-old bookkeeper with a featureless face. Mary Frances and Colleen looked at her as part of the furniture.

She thought of them as whores. Besides, Mary Frances and Colleen were always shrieking at each other at 2 in the morning. Two months after Janeen moved in, she moved out.

Colleen and Mary Frances replaced her with Kikki, a part-time cocktail waitress who was "discovering herself" in oil painting. Kikki was Bohemian and from the south side; her father was an ironworker at Inland Steel. A plain woman heavily daubed with eye makeup, she rivaled Colleen in the bizarreness of her dress. She always wore a black leather collar studded with metal around her neck.

Colleen had met Kikki in "Oil Painting 2B – Advanced Brush Techniques." They immediately hit it off: it turned out they were both sleeping with Lennie, the instructor.

He was immensely pleased when they started rooming together. It was a much shorter commute between beds. One night when both women were out and Mary Frances was watching TV, Lennie came over. He sat on the beat-up easy chair across from Mary Frances and fixed his goggle eyes on her.

The guy was insatiable.

Why not? she thought, leading him into her bedroom.

Lennie thought he'd died and gone to heaven.

* * *

The weeks dragged on at Mr. John's. Mary Frances ordered hair chemicals, swept floors, rolled up old ladies' hair in curlers and did more blue rinses then she cared to remember. It seemed that a good percentage of Mr. John's clientele were poor old women from an adjacent decaying neighborhood. He gave them a break on blue rinses every Thursday. A rinse and set for $5.00, $3.00 off the regular $8.00 price.

The old ladies flocked in; Mary Frances did most of them. It was like assembly-line work: frazzled old women in shabby clothing and greasy hair walked in: frazzled old women in shabby clothing with blue-tinted greasy hair walked out.

The rest of the week, she cut unimaginative haircuts and did permanents with cheap chemicals. To keep his prices down Mr. John only bought the cheapest materials. She was learning nothing.

Twice a week in the evening, Lennie came over and slept with Mary Frances, Colleen and Kikki – all at once. Colleen and Kikki thought it was funny; Mary Frances was starting to feel like Lennie's concubine.

One time Kathleen called while the four of them were sitting nude on the living room couch, stoned. They were just getting warmed up. Kathleen was thrilled her daughters were rooming together; if they weren't going to live at home, it was the next best thing. She viewed their apartment as an extension of the familial homestead, a sort of Kankakee-North.

Mary Frances picked up the phone.

"How are you, dear?" Kathleen said.

"Fine, just fine, Mom."

Lennie and the other women suppressed snickers. Then Lennie crawled over and started licking Mary Frances between her legs as she stood. Kikki and Colleen laughed.

Mary Frances glared down at him.

He looked up, an obliging troll with immense brown eyes, and began stroking the inside of her thighes.

"Easter dinner is at 3 this year," Kathleen said.

"Yeah, Mom."

Kikki and Colleen tittered.

Despite herself, Mary Frances was getting aroused.

"I gotta' go, Mom," she said. "I gotta' meet someone."

"Is Colleen there?"

"No, Mom. She's out."

"Be sure to tell her about Easter."

"I will, Mom."

"Well, good bye, dear. We'll see you Easter."

"Bye, Mom."

Mary Frances plunked the phone down loudly, pulled out the plug, and jumped on the couch, to the squeals of Kikki and Colleen. Lennie came galloping after her, a bug-eyed satyr, his huge penis ahead of him like a charging lance. He plunged it into Mary Frances from the rear, to her great discomfort, and started pumping wildly. He came in 30 seconds, then lay on the couch while the other two women rubbed and licked him.

Mary Frances sighed, stood up, and went into the bathroom to take a shower. The running water drowned out the gurgles and squeals of her roommates. She slipped into her clothes, grabbed her purse, and walked through the living room to the front door. Kikki, Colleen, and Lennie were laying on the floor like a human chain: Kikki's mouth was on Lennie's dick, Lennie's mouth in Colleen's cunt, and Colleen's mouth on Kikki's cunt.

"Where you going?" Colleen said, looking up from her work.

"I'm going to get some pizza."

"Bring back a large pepperoni," Lennie mumbled through Colleen's pubic hair. "And a diet Coke."

Mary Frances nodded and left.

When she returned with the food, they were all watching reruns of "Love Boat" on TV and smoking dope.

Mary Frances knew she'd hit bottom.

The next morning she called in sick to work and went looking for another job.

***

This time she tried the Gerrard Herrand Salon; it had just opened on a side street off the best part of Michigan Avenue.

Herrand had hit Chicago with a bang. Straight from the continent, via L.A., he had built himself a five-story building, with the entire front made of glass. The bottom three floors he rented to expensive leather and clothing boutiques; the top two floors were his huge hair salon. A confection of glass and chrome, they topped the building like a crown.

At night, from the street, the salon looked like a two-storied set from a movie, the occupants moving around in the brightly lit rooms with the blackness of the city's night sky as a backdrop.

A diminutive glass elevator took Mary Frances to the top floor. It opened to mayhem. A dozen clients jammed the chrome-trimmed waiting room. Hairdressers ran back and forth to the receptionist checking appointments. The phone was ringing. Herrand had underestimated how popular his salon would be. Open three months, he was already running out of room. His handpicked staff were strained to breaking.

Moments before Mary Frances walked in, Ellie Mae, the head shampoo girl, had quit. A big black woman with hands and arms like a professional wrestler, Ellie Mae had a 14-year-old daughter who was having her first baby. The girl's 12-year-old sister had called from the High-Risk Pregnancy Center at the exclusive private hospital down the street. Cassiopia was in labor and calling for her; was she coming?

Ellie Mae had been elbow-deep in shampoo suds; her sink had just backed up. Six women with towels around their necks glared at her, waiting in line to be shampooed. The other three shampoo girls leaned over their basins, sudsing heads with vigor.

Ellie Mae had stood up slowly, wiped her hands on a towel, and gone to her supervisor.

"My baby's in labor, Mr. Ricky," she said. "I gotta' go."

Mr. Ricky was a middle-aged man with a rumpled linen suit and a tie shaped like a fish hanging by its tail. He was at the receptionist's desk calming four women who all had the same appointment with the same stylist.

"No way you leave," he hissed at Ellie.

"But my baby could die," she said loudly.

"She's not going to die. She'll be fine."

"I leavin', Mr. Ricky."

"Leave now and you're not coming back."

"Dat's OK," Ellie Mae said loudly. "She goan get her guvernment check. We doan need you." She untied her apron and let it fall to

the floor. Two women in the back of the reception area started
applauding. Mr. Ricky glared in their direction.

The elevator doors opened and Mary Frances walked in.

"I don't suppose anyone here knows how to shampoo?" Mr.
Ricky said loudly to no one in particular.

"I can!" Mary Frances yelled instinctively, pushing through the
crowd to Mr. Ricky.

"Ask for Leatrice," he said, nodding in the general direction of
the shampoo room.

Mary Frances bounded out with the joy of a young woman
picking spring flowers.

Leatrice turned out to be a young white woman, not much older
than herself, standing at the far sink.

"I'm the new shampoo girl," Mary Frances said.

Leatrice looked at her in surprise.

"What happened to Ellie?" she said.

Mary Frances shrugged. "Got me."

Leatrice wiped the sweat from her forehead on the short pink
sleeve of her uniform.

"It's the sink over there," she nodded. "Two shampoos, one
conditioner, one toner. Shampoo's the pink bottle, conditioner's
blue, toner's in the beige spray thing. Towels are in the cabinet
overhead." She went back to her shampooing.

Ellie Mae's sink was filled with water covered with a grey oily
film. Four women slumped in waiting chairs. Mary Frances pulled a
rattail comb from her purse and unplugged the drain.

"Now," she said, "who's next?"

The women perked up. One with short-cropped gray hair sat
down at her sink. Mary Frances finished her off in seven minutes
and moved on to a brunette with a grown-out permanent. The
shampoo and conditioner felt good on her hands. It was Gerrard
Herrand's own brand with a minty, expensive smell to it.

She washed, she conditioned, she chatted with the clients and the
other shampoo girls.

She felt like she'd come home.

The customers were generous. Everyone tipped her at least a
dollar. She washed 18 customers before lunch and pocketed $26 in
tips. That was almost as much as she made in a day at Mr. John's.

By 7:00 that night she had washed 54 customers, collected $73 in tips, and made friends with the three shampoo girls. Leatrice lived with her punk-rocker boyfriend. Jennifer was halfway through beauty school and a divorce, and Palmyra, a black woman with a head full of tight curls, lived with her mother and worked on her G.E.D. at night.

They had all hated Ellie Mae. "A lazy nigger," Palmyra had called her when the white customers were out of earshot. "And dat daughter of hers, whooey. She'd git down on anything dat moved."

Mary Frances went home that night, happy and exhausted, her hands red and smelling of mint.

* * *

Kikki and Colleen were appalled.

"You washed hair all day?" Colleen said. "What did you go to school for? You knew how to wash hair when you were 13."

She and Kikki laughed, the heavy metal bangles in their ears clanking as their heads moved.

"Maybe you should wash cars instead; there's more money in it," Colleen said.

Mary Frances glared at them and went to her room.

The doorbell rang and she heard Lennie's voice. He was getting greedy; this was the second night in a row he'd come over.

She made herself a peanut-butter sandwich for dinner and locked herself in her room. Lennie left about 1 am. She stormed out to her half-naked roommates, sprawled in front of the TV on an old blanket.

"That dirtbag is out, Colleen, and I mean out!" she yelled at her dazed sister.

Colleen hiked herself up on her elbows.

"What's your problem?" she said.

"I'm not having that sleaze in this apartment."

"Buzz off. I live here, too."

Some guy came on the TV and started selling wall-to-wall carpeting.

"Get rid of him or I'm moving," Mary Frances said.

"So move," Kikki said.

Colleen elbowed her in the side.

"I move out," Mary Frances said, "and you'll never find another roommate. Who's going to move in here and put up with the three of you crawling in and out of each other's crotches? Wise up or I'm gone."

She turned on her heel and left.

The next morning they didn't talk. Colleen twisted her nest of dry hair into a tight bun and went to school. Kikki trundled off to the coffee shop where she waited tables every Wednesday and Thursday from 10 am until her sculpture class at 2.

Lennie never came around much after that. And when he did, he always kept his clothes on in the living room.

* * *

The next morning, Mary Frances pulled on her leather miniskirt and was at the salon by 7:45. The guard in the building's main lobby wouldn't let her in.

"I work here," she said.

"Where's your ID?" He was a small, suspicious black man with a head of salt and pepper wool.

"I just started," she said.

"They give you a special paper when you start." He leaned forward in his beat-up chair. "Where's your special paper?"

She stood aside as two young women came by, one in tiger-striped tights, the other in a leather jacket. They waved at the guard and walked toward the elevator. Following them were two men, a tall thin man and the man who had hired her yesterday morning.

She ran up to him. "Excuse me," she said.

"Yes?" He looked tired.

"I'm your new shampoo girl."

He looked at her again, then smiled with recognition. "Oh yes. From yesterday morning. Thank you for pitching in like that," he said, stepping toward the elevator.

"I'd like the job permanently."

He looked at her, all eager and happy and ready to work. She was a definite improvement over Ellie Mae.

"You been to beauty school?"

"I graduated."

He nodded and didn't ask which one.

"Well come on then," he said, motioning her toward the elevator. She stepped in, followed by him and his companion. Tiger Tights and Leather Lady were already in. Everyone mumbled polite "good mornings."

"This is Alex," the man said, indicating his companion. "He's our creative and educational director."

Alex looked about 30. He was pale and bony with brown wavy hair down to his shoulders. He was as tired-looking as the first man.

"Pleased to meet you," he said, smiling and extending his hand. Mary Frances shook it awkwardly.

"I'm Rick," the first man said. "Business manager for Mr. Herrand here in Chicago."

"Mary Frances Barton," Mary Frances said, smiling and nodding.

"Mary Frances replaces Ellie Mae in the shampoo room," Rick told Alex.

"Oh really?" Alex said.

"But what I'd really like to do is style hair," she blurted.

"Do a good job in shampoo and we'll see what we can do," Rick said offhandedly.

Mary Frances beamed. Alex looked at her and suppressed a smile.

The elevator lurched toward the top floor; the door opened to the salon's main lobby. It was empty and dark; the EXIT signs glowed. Rick stepped behind a door, flicked some switches, and the room jumped with lights and rock music.

Mary Frances jumped with surprise. The main salon stretched ahead of her, brilliant and stark with its white walls and white tiled floor. The two men and two women disappeared into the room, wending their way through cutting chairs and mirrored walls.

The rock music driving through the loudspeakers heated her blood; 8:00 in the morning and she was ready to boogy. She examined every work station carefully. The photos, the pinups of hairdos, the postcards from clients. One had a vase of 12 half-dead red roses on it. She read the card: "To Joe, much love always, Tom."

In a far corner, a 5-foot, naked, inflatable plastic man hug over someone's cutting chair. The ventilating system came on: the doll's oversize inflated penis bobbed up and down in the light breeze.

Mary Frances went to the shampoo room, ran water over her hands in her basin, and waited for her life to begin.

Chapter Five

Mary Frances worked as hard that day as the day before. The next day she worked harder. Gerrard Herrand Coiffures packed the women in.

They were mostly young or in their 40s. A few women spiked their hair or curled it under into pageboys, but most adopted the poodle-dog look. Their hair hung to their shoulders in a mass of tight, permanented curls or poufed out to the sides in frizzy clouds.

Many of the customers worked in offices. They hurried to the salon dressed in pastel suits, ankle socks, and worn running shoes, their eyes constantly on the clock. Those who were secretaries studied the price charts carefully. At $60 a haircut, $75 a permanent, and $65 for hair color, they could easily drop two days' pay on their hair.

By the end of the week, Mary Frances was bored with shampoo. Her arms hurt, her hands were sore and red, and she was stiff from bending over her basin.

On Friday, she asked "Mr. Ricky," as everyone called Rick, when she could start cutting hair. He told her she could sit in on Alex's class, but it took six months to go through his course, assuming Alex decided she was good enough to stay. Maybe then they would let her cut hair, just maybe.

Classes met in the main salon after the shop closed, four days a week at 10:00 at night.

Mary Frances was the first one there Monday night.

* * *

Fifteen students milled around: five from the shop in Chicago, Mary Frances, and another nine who were going to start the new Gerrard Herrand Salon in Atlanta. The class was equally divided between men and women. The men looked thin and homosexual; the women wore a lot of eye makeup and had strange-colored hair, nearly all of it some shade of red. Red was the "in" color that year.

Mary Frances stood next to the only normal-looking woman in the group, a sad-eyed girl with olive skin, bags under her eyes, and black hair who introduced herself as "Marilyn." She looked Italian.

Promptly at 10:00 Alex strode in, followed by the guinea pigs — people who'd agreed to have their hair done by the students at six dollars a shot. Mostly women, they gawked at the expensiveness of the place like a stream of peasants being shown Versailles.

The "pigs" filed in front of the cutting chairs and sat down. The students arranged themselves behind them and opened their little cases of scissors and shears. Mary Frances got a long-haired girl of about 16. Her blonde hair hung to the middle of her back. With a pinafore and a blue ribbon in her hair she would have been a dead ringer for Alice in *Alice in Wonderland.*

"I just want a little trimmed off the ends," she told Mary Frances.

"Tonight we're working on layering," Alex announced to the class. In front of him in a cutting chair was a woman pig. Her dark brown hair hung in a shapeless blob to her shoulders. He sprayed her hair with water, then started pinning it up with big aluminum clips. The students herded over to watch, pushing around the chair to see.

He pushed the hair up from the nape of the woman's neck and tilted her head down.

"Now, look at the hair line here," he said. Everyone stared at the nape of her neck. "Her neckline is nothing to crow about so let's leave some length here."

He picked up his scissors in one hand and a shock of hair from her nape in the other. He fanned the hair between his fingers and snipped two inches off the ends in one fast movement.

Then he took off. He fanned and snipped and fanned and snipped, emitting constant instructions, his hands darting around her head like nesting swallows.

"Taper away from this worl."

"Don't fight cowlicks."

"Watch the length by the ears. Cut it wrong and she'll look like a goat."

Snip, snip, snip.

The shapeless blob gave way to a shiny brown cap with a tufted crown.

"Let's give her a feathered bang over one eye," Alex said. "She has a high forehead and can carry it off. Most women can't."

All the banged women in class brushed their bangs back self-consciously.

He cut several long, separate strands over the woman's left eye. Then he flicked on his blow dryer and blew her hair dry, running his fingers through it for lift.

"See how this finger action gives her hair height?"

Her feathered bangs floated over her left eye at a whimsical angle. She looked lighter, brighter. The hairdo was far too good for her, Mary Frances thought, like a crown of jewels on a cow.

"Voila!" Alex said, turning the woman around theatrically in the chair. The students applauded enthusiastically, the other guinea pigs shifted in their chairs, and the woman stared at herself in the mirror. She tugged at a curl over one ear.

"Don't touch it!" Mary Frances almost screamed. But the woman nodded politely at Alex and crawled out stiffly from the chair.

"OK," Alex said, clapping his hands. "Let's cut!"

The students hurried excitedly back to their chairs. Fear rose in waves from the pigs.

"I really only wanted a little edge cut around the left side . . ."

"Could you just leave it long in the back. . . "

The stream of excuses started up from each chair. The stylists-to-be ignored them. For their $6 bargain price, the pigs had agreed in writing to let the students do what they wanted with their hair, with the caveat that the hairdos would be "presentable" when finished.

The students meant to collect. The sound of snipping scissors mixed with the fading bleatings of their victims.

Alice in Wonderland turned around and looked at Mary Frances.

"You'd look great in short hair," Mary Frances said.

"I like it long," the girl said.

"So what are you doing here?" Mary Frances said. She was dying to cut this girl's hair, anybody's hair. The scissors itched in her fingers.

The girl shrugged stupidly.

"My mother sent me. She was tired of trimming my hair herself."

"Get your ass out of here then," Mary Frances hissed. "I don't need this."

The girl got up quickly and left. Mary Frances leaned over the back of her chair and swore. Fifteen students, 15 pigs. She had no one's hair to cut.

"What's the matter here?" She heard Alex's voice at her side.

"My customer discovered she was born to have hair to her ass and cut out," Mary Frances said.

"Excuse me?"

She turned and looked at Alex. He stared at her.

"Aren't you. . .?" he started.

". . . the shampoo girl, yes."

"What are you doing here?"

"Mr. Ricky said I could sit in."

"He didn't ask me. This isn't a home for vagrant shampoo girls."

"I'm not a vagrant shampoo girl. I'm a licensed stylist."

Alex sniffed. "Lots of hair butchers have licenses."

Mary Frances cocked her hip and looked at him. "What are you trying to tell me?"

"You're supposed to test to get into this class. I've got 35, no 37, people waiting on two continents to be here and Rick lets in shampoo girls he picks up off the street. What are you doing, banging him in the afternoon?"

It was Mary Frances's turn to stare.

"You heard me," Alex said.

"Are you always such an asshole?" she said softly. "Do you practice at night in front of a mirror? This isn't a school for brain surgeons. You're teaching a fucking class on how to cut hair. You've got nerve cocking me around."

Alex looked at her like she was a strange animal.

"Get out," he said.

"Sure," she said. She picked up her scissors and stuffed them in their pouch.

He picked his up and moved to the next station where Marilyn the Normal manueuvered her way through a young man's flattop.

"That's right, dear," Alex said sweetly, stepping next to her and running his hands through the man's hair. "Very nice," he mumbled. "Take a little more off the left side over the ear."

Marilyn nodded happily. Alex glared over his shoulder at Mary Frances and moved on to the next station, where a young man with a pompadour was fanning and cutting a woman's hair, just like Alex had done.

Alex took him aside. They conferred quietly, then Alex demonstrated his own technique, pulling the customer's hair up to its full six-inch length and chopping it in half.

The young man nodded earnestly and went back to work. Alex moved on to the next student; he was the picture of professorial concern.

Mary Frances stared at him with hate. She zipped up her scissors case and left.

The next time Alex glanced in her direction, he was disappointed to see that she was no longer there.

* * *

When Mary Frances got home, Colleen and Kikki were just leaving for Mr. K's, another arty bar in another bad neighborhood.

They didn't invite her along. Their fight over Lennie had created bad blood.

"Wait for me," Mary Frances had said.

Surprisingly, they did. But they ignored her on the bus, cutting her out of their conversation.

Mr. K's was in Humboldt Park, the meanest Puerto Rican neighborhood in the city. Mary Frances knew the owner, Kale Cahners, from some party. She couldn't remember if they'd ever slept together or not. Kale had picked the location for the cheap rent, but after four robberies, a shooting, and a drug ring operating out of the men's room, he was seriously considering moving to a more genteel location.

The artists came to Mr. K's because it was cheap and convenient. Lots of artists lived in Humboldt Park. The women learned to swear in Spanish to drive off the gangs of hooting men; the men hunched down when they walked and tried to look inconspicuous.

The gangs soon discovered they had no money and left them alone. Occasionally they'd rape a woman for sport.

One day a reporter from a trendy local magazine dropped in at Mr. K's. He'd heard through the grapevine that it was an art-crowd hangout. And it was: the walls were covered with the splashed and smeared canvases of the expressionist minimalists who frequented the place. Tiny price tags at the corners of the paintings announced their hopelessly ridiculous prices: $550, $800. A particularly gaudy canvas had a hunk of mud stuck to it with a piece of bent aluminum molding sticking through the fabric; it was the top dog at a price of $1500.

No one ever bought the art. No one with any money ever came there. In addition to the artists, the bar was popular with indigent blacks and old Puerto Rican janitors on their way home from work. But the artists had hope. They changed the exhibits every six months.

But when the trendy reporter showed up one day, nervous in his blue jeans, denim jacket, and ostrich cowboy boots, the world changed.

He wrote about the bar in the trendy magazine!

A week after the magazine came out, white people with money appeared! They drove in from the suburbs and pricey city neighbhorhoods, adorned in casual, expensive clothes and driving expensive foreign cars – which usually lost their hub caps, radios, and front grillwork until Kale began paying the gangs protection.

The rich white people clustered in small groups at Kale's lopsided little tables. They talked in low voices, sneaking looks at the artists drinking in the corner or leaning over the torn green surface of the bar's wobbly pool table.

The white people would order Perrier, white wine, and imported beer. Kale started carrying expensive English ale. They sipped their drinks and wandered the room, staring at the art on the walls and talking quietly among themselves.

One day, one of them, a fat man in a racoon coat and a meticulously trimmed beard, asked Kale where he could find the artist of the $1500 mud and aluminum concoction.

He wanted to buy it!

Kale broke into a cold sweat. By coincidence, the artist was in the bar. Marvin Nugelheim, a small Jew from Hackensack, N.J., worked nights sweeping floors at the Central Wire Company's distribution center on South Ashland Avenue. During the day, he smeared mud on canvas in his small apartment and roamed the alleys looking for old aluminum; mud and aluminum were cheaper than paint.

Kale called Marvin to the bar and introduced him. The man wrote Marvin a check for $1500, said he'd have someone come by and pick up the work next week, and asked to see Marvin's studio.

"Right now?" Marvin said. His small brown eyes were nearly rolling out of his head like loose marbles.

"Whenever's convenient," the man said.

"Tomorrow. Tomorrow at 2." Marvin scribbled his address on a bar napkin and handed it to the man.

"You'll have to excuse us," the man said. "We have other stops." He turned and nodded to his companions, a woman completely dressed in fringed-leather deerskin and another in a business suit. They got up and walked out.

The entire population of the bar ran to the front window. The threesome crawled into a green Mercedes and drove off.

Marvin turned around, waved the check in the air, and started doing a little hornpipe, screaming: "The drinks are on me! Let's party!" The entire bar cheered, including the swing-shift janitorial crew from the Clearwater Laundry and Uniform Service up the street.

Marvin got stinking drunk.

Two weeks later, every artist in the area was working in mud and aluminum.

That had been six months ago. Since then, the artists had sold $18,325 worth of art, mostly mud and aluminum. Then several commodities traders looking for watercolors showed up. Everyone switched to watercolors. The bar was now lined with pastel scenes of Italian villas and olive trees overlooking a deep blue Tyrrhenian Sea.

No one had been to Italy. They painted from *The Pictorial Guide to Italy* by Frances Guidon, recently borrowed from the Humboldt Park branch of the Chicago Public Library and ripped to pieces to give everyone a shot at making some money.

The commodities traders bought 14 watercolors.

When Mary Frances and her roommates walked in, a scrawny man was selling an earnest fellow in a tweed jacket a foggy seascape of Crete.

"I walked this beach every day for a year," he said.

He'd never been east of Indianapolis.

The man bought the painting.

Kikki and Colleen saw some of their friends and ran off to a corner table to sit with them. Mary Frances found a quiet table by herself. She perched on the bar stool, ordered a beer, and brooded.

Why couldn't she keep her mouth shut? Now she was out on her ear, at least from the cutting classes. Her mother had always said charm was the way to a man's heart.

She had no charm; all she could offer was sex.

Alex was an asshole. Imagine accusing her of screwing her boss? If it would have helped her cause, she probably would have eventually. But to come right out and say it . . .

She sipped her drink, looked up, and scanned the bar. A handsome blonde man in a beautifully cut, double-breasted suit was walking toward her, carrying a beer in one hand. He looked in his 20s. He had a fresh, creamy complexion and cornflower-blue eyes.

"Hi," he said. "Are you an artist?"

"No."

"Can I sit down?"

"Sure." She wished he'd go away.

"My name's Robert Burke."

"Mary Frances Barton."

"Pleased to meet you."

"Sure."

She concentrated on her nearly full glass of beer.

Someone put a quarter in Kale's jukebox. Out came some slow-paced, lonely-hearted ballad of the sixties. Three couples moved to the tiny square of a dance floor near the back of the bar and clung to each other in X-rated embraces.

"Would you like to dance?"

"Sure."

She slipped off her chair and walked behind him to the floor. He turned to her, put his arm around her waist, and pulled her to him like they'd been married for 15 years. Her nose barely cleared his shoulder. The grey wool of his suit smelled clean and expensive, as did his lemony cologne.

She felt his erection against her leg.

This wasn't dancing; this was foreplay.

"I'm a banker, you know," he said, turning his lovely blue eyes on her.

She thought of the tellers at Kankakee Trust and Savings. She was not impressed.

"I'm in international lending at Citibank," he said, swaying to the music. "They're sending me to France next year."

"How nice." She wished he'd loosen his grip; she didn't even know the guy. She started sweating.

"What do you do for a living?" he said coolly, as if they were sitting four feet apart at a business luncheon.

"I'm a hair stylist."

"Sounds entertaining." He pulled her closer to him and nuzzled his handsome face into her shoulder. "You'll have to cut my hair some time," he said, whispering into her ear.

His embrace pushed her face further into his shoulder. He ran his hands lightly down her spine, resting them just above her hips. Mary Frances waited for them to move down over her buttocks. Surprisingly, they didn't.

They swayed on the floor, hardly moving, for what seemed an eternity. The music finally ended; they went back to the table.

"You have a lovely body," he said.

She didn't have to put up with this.

"I'm not interested," she said.

He laughed, his broad face breaking into a big smile.

"You're friendly tonight."

"I've sworn off picking up men in bars."

"That's unhealthy."

"It's very healthy. Last time some guy picked me up he wanted to pay me to come back to his room."

"How stupid."

"I thought so."

"Why should he pay for something he could get for free?"

She looked disgusted. "Get lost."

"I don't give up that easy."

"Are you doing this as part of some dumb fraternity joke? 'Pick up and lay some chick in a bar in one evening?'"

He looked offended. "I graduated three years ago. Do I look that young?"

"You look like you're 12."

His face fell.

"There's a mirror in my purse. See for yourself."

She leaned down to get her purse from the floor. Instinctively, he put his arm around her waist so she wouldn't fall. It felt good.

She hauled up her purse, a huge sac of worn black leather, with an "Iron Maiden" button stuck on it, and started rummaging.

"You like heavy metal?" he said.

"Sure. Rock, jazz, fusion. I like it all."

He smiled as if he had just discovered they had something profound in common.

She pulled out a cracked mirror from the bottom of her purse and held it up to him.

"See," she said. "You look about 12."

He looked right into her eyes.

"So how old are you?"

"Twenty next month."

He laughed a kind of wild laugh. Then he took her hand, opened her palm, and kissed it.

"Come my child," he said solemnly, leading her by the hand.

"Where are we going?"

"Where we can find some real music."

* * *

Robert led her to another table where two well-dressed young men in suits sat with two women in full professional garb. One woman wore a print wool dress, the other a suit.

The women stared at her without interest, as if she were a waitress.

"Let's go to the Chic," Robert said.

The foursome at the table got up wordlessly, like a commando team that moved together — a commando team of dancing bankers.

Car keys jingled, the professional women smiled and talked softly to each other, and they all filed out to various new automobiles parked down the block from the bar.

Robert's car was a shiny new Porsche — bright red and spotlessly clean.

"This guy is rich," Mary Frances thought, crawling into the leather seat on the passenger side. With the exception of the stockbroker who had given her the $600 for beauty school, she'd never had a lover with money. She thought of Lennie and shuddered; maybe it was time to start.

Robert slipped into the driver's seat, smiled at her smoothly, and started the car. He threw it in gear and inched carefully out of his parking place. Then he punched the accelerator, speeding up so fast that she was thrown against her seat. They weaved through the city's post-midnight streets, a one-man road rally in a deserted city.

The "Chic Discoteek" was in an old theatre in another bad neighborhood. Noise and throbbing music spilled out on the street. Inside it was dark, lined with mirrors, and packed with people. Pink and blue lights strobed on and off; a mirrored ball spun slowly overhead throwing splashes of light over everything.

The music howled through huge speakers hung on the wall. A skinny young man in a tuxedo sat in a little glass booth and changed records. People hopped and writhed on the dance floor; he yawned.

The Chic was expensive to get in; cover was $6 a head. Robert and Mary Frances lost the commando team in the crowd. They dumped their coats at a tiny table and headed for the dance floor where they hopped and writhed with the rest of the crowd, Robert giving her occasional sultry looks.

When they returned to the table, he was very direct.

"Let's go to bed," he said.

Why not? she thought.

"OK," she said. "Let me finish my beer."

His apartment was a small studio lost in a back corridor of an expensive highrise downtown. He probably paid as much rent for the apartment as he did for the private parking place with his name stenciled over it in the building's indoor garage.

The apartment had one broad window which stared directly at the backside of another highrise. He had no furniture except a stereo with two four-foot-high speakers standing on the floor and a rumpled double bed.

He didn't even offer her a drink. As soon as she walked in the door, he started removing her clothes.

"You don't waste time, do you?" she said.

"I have to get up early tomorrow," he said.

"It's already 2:00."

"If I get three hours sleep I'm alright."

He led her to his bed half-dressed, pulled off his own clothes and jumped on her. He pumped and moaned for five minutes, came, and rolled off her. It was over before she knew it had begun. She rolled over to complain but he was already asleep, one arm thrown over his head like a tall blonde child in sleep.

She got up, put on her clothes, and rummaged through the pockets of his suit coat. His wallet had $63 in it.

She took it. For *that* sexual performance, he had to pay. As she slipped out, the door locked behind her.

Chapter Six

Mary Frances went through the next day in a fog. Her head hurt, her feet ached, and she was so tired she forgot what she had said moments after she'd said it.

She didn't care what Alex would say.

All day — when she could remember — she worried that he would come in and fire her. But he didn't. He never came near the shampoo room that day; she saw him walking by the doorway several times, running from one end of the salon to the other. He never looked in.

She just kept washing: 43 women and a friend of one of the stylists, a Tamara Something-or-Other, who was getting a free haircut from her friend. At noon, Mr. Ricky came through looking for an extra pile of towels. He smiled at her as he hurried through.

Clearly, Alex hadn't made a stink to anyone.

So, Wednesday night, when class time rolled around again, she showed up, scissors in hand. Alex did a double-take when he saw her back in a corner chair, trying to be inconspicuous.

"You again?" he said.

"Yeah," she mumbled.

To her surprise, instead of throwing her out he just mumbled under his breath and continued on to the next work station. Probably just a matter of time, Mary Frances throught. She kept cutting. The woman in her chair was in her 20s with the thinnest, baby-fine chestnut hair she'd ever seen. Lifeless and dull, it drooped between Mary Frances's fingers as she cut it.

The woman wanted her hair long and feathered to her shoulders.

"It won't work," Mary Frances said.

"But I want it long," the woman said.

By the school contract, Mary Frances could force her to cut it short or ask her to leave, but she didn't want to lose this guinea pig like the last one.

"Your hair doesn't have enough body to it," she said. "I can do something nice with shorter hair over the ears."

"Yes, but I want it long."

Mary Frances sighed. "OK."

She started to cut. The woman's hair would look terrible long.
Alex came bustling by.

"What's going on here?" he said, eying Mary Frances's timid
handiwork.

She stepped aside.

"You can't cut hair like this that long," he whispered to her. "It
looks awful."

"I know," she hissed out of the side of her mouth. "It's what she
wants."

Alex turned to the woman. "You really must cut your hair short,
Miss," he said. "Your hair can't hold a longer style."

He smiled with charm. "You *do* have such a lovely face. I'm sure
you would look just *super* in short hair."

"You think so?" she said looking up hopefully, as if cutting her
hair would release some previously hidden source of beauty.

"Oh *yes*," Alex said. "*Absolutely.*"

The young woman looked in the mirror in front of her, looked up
at Alex and Mary Frances, then smiled.

"OK," she said.

Alex smiled like an idiot; Mary Frances rolled her eyes to
heaven.

"OK," Alex said to Mary Frances. "Do something high on the
crown, smooth back the side, and trim off the neckline long with
texturizing scissors." He ran his hands through the woman's hair
with a swift, light touch.

"Lord almighty," he whispered to Mary Frances. "Some women
were born to have their heads shaved."

To the woman he said. "We'll do something very nice with a
feathered crown," he said, smiling smoothly. "You just let, uh . . . "

He looked at Mary Frances.

"Mary Frances," she said.

"Yes. You just let Mary Frances here take care of you."

The woman smiled happily.

Alex turned to Mary Frances again.

"How about a drink after class?" he said to her under his breath.

She stared at him, open-mouthed, her scissors hanging loosely
from one hand.

He laughed. "I'll see you after class." He walked to the next chair, where a small young man in baggy pants and gym shoes gingerly trimmed a huge head of red hair.

"No! No!" Alex shouted. "Be brave, Carlos." He grabbed Carlos's scissors, pulled a wad of wiry red hair from the pig's head and chopped it off at the base.

"Hair like that shouldn't be allowed to exist," he said to no one in particular.

The woman in Carlos's chair shrank down into her seat.

Mary Frances decided Alex was going to can her.

She gave her pig a very nice haircut, with a lovely wave over one ear.

* * *

After class, Alex took Mary Frances to a dark, expensive bar in a big expensive hotel on Michigan Avenue. They sat on leather banquettes at a dark oak table; a half-naked cocktail waitress served them rum and Cokes after carding Mary Frances. Mary Frances had pulled out her forged I.D.

"So how old are you really?" Alex said when the waitress had left. He was in a relaxed, friendly mood, smiling and almost debonair. His long hair was pulled back in a pony tail at the nape of his neck, making his thin, worn face look even more tired.

"Twenty next month," Mary Frances said.

He looked at her softly. "How charming," he said.

Mary Frances shifted uncomfortably on the thick leather seat.

"Why are we here?" she said looking at the overstuffed conventioneers sitting in the bar's overstuffed chairs.

"Can't I take a student out for a drink?" he said.

"Monday you scream at me. Wednesday you're sweetness and light. What's going on?"

"I'm a man of moods."

"You're an asshole," she said.

He smiled and leaned toward her.

"I like it when you talk dirty," he said.

"'Asshole' is dirty?"

"Dirty enough."

"Why didn't you throw me out of class today?"

"I had a change of heart."

She looked at him. She was sure he was going to fire her. What did she have to lose? She scooted to the end of the banquette and stood up.

"I'm leaving," she said.

To her surprise, he grabbed her arm and pulled her back down with a thud.

"No you're not," he said.

"Look, why don't you just fire me?"

He looked at her as if she were talking another language.

"What made you think I was going to fire you?"

She stood up again.

"Sit down," he hissed. She sat down.

"I know I was a little difficult the other night. I'm sorry. I really would like us to be friends."

He looked at her over his drink, smiling his charming smile.

Mary Frances looked at him suspiciously. She had no male "friends." You were either her lover or a stranger.

"There's a lot better-looking girls at the salon," she said.

"But they don't have a mouth like yours."

"I'm not that kind of girl."

"Sure you are. That's why I like you."

She stared at her drink a few moments.

"I suppose you want me to go to bed with you?"

"Yep."

"I don't want to sleep with you."

He shrugged. "So don't."

"You've probably got AIDS."

"Maybe," he said, sipping his drink. "My brother died of it last year, but I never slept with him."

She stared at him. "I'm sorry."

"Don't be. We weren't close. He was very gay. A real "pouf" as they say back home."

"Back home?"

"Birmingham. . . England."

"So you're gay, too?"

He shook his head. "I like the ladies too much," he said. "That's why I became a hairdresser. You run your hands through their hair and stare down the fronts of their dresses."

Mary Frances laughed and bolted her rum and Coke.

Alex hailed the waitress and ordered two beers.

"So tell me about yourself," he said.

"Not much to tell," she said. "Small-town girl comes to the city to make good and doesn't do too well." She looked up, her thick blonde hair framing her face.

"If you'd kicked me out of your class I don't know what I would have done. Nobody wants to teach me how to cut hair and I can't afford to pay the big schools."

"Sleep with me and there'll be no problem," he said.

"Excuse me?"

"Sleep with me and you can stay in the class."

"Give me a break."

"I am. If you weren't reasonably good-looking I would throw you out. If you can't come up with money you come up with ass. It's a universal medium of exchange. Nontaxable, I might add."

"You're so romantic."

"More so than you. What if you have AIDS?"

She looked offended.

"All the beds you've probably been in and out of. I'm taking a real chance. You could snuff out my young life in a hurry," he said.

"We could always get AIDS tests," she joked.

"I'm planning on it. I'll make the appointments tomorrow."

She stared at him, surprised. "So I suppose you don't want to sleep with me tonight?" she said.

The waitress came back and slipped two beers on the table. Alex pulled out his wallet to pay her.

"No," he said, counting bills into the waitress's hand. "Not tonight. I want to be sure you're clean."

The waitress looked at Mary Frances with no expression on her face and walked off with her money, wobbling on her terribly high heels.

"You done this before?" Mary Frances said.

"Once or twice. No, three times. I forgot Allison. She tested positive for AIDS." He sipped his beer. "Such a pretty woman, too. Poor thing.

"The other two women did well. Clare's now a big-deal hair designer for Sassoon in London. Susan is moving up in our L.A. salon."

"I suppose they make enough money to pay their own way without peddling their asses?"

"I suppose."

He put his glass down and looked at her, irritated. "Look," he said. "No one's forcing you to do anything. It's a business proposition. You might as well get something for what you now give away for free. I can turn you into one hell of a hairdresser, if you're not stupid enough to throw it away."

"You're sick," she said.

"So are you — and stupid."

They looked at their drinks and stared at their hands.

"Alright," she said sullenly. "What do I have to do?"

"Very simple. Be around when I want you."

"Nothing kinky?"

He looked at her solemnly. "Straight missionary position with occasional trysts in the shower. Nothing more, I promise."

"Do I get spending money?" This might as well be profitable.

He laughed. "Why don't you ask about health insurance and pension benefits?"

"I could use some health insurance," she mumbled into her beer glass.

"I thought full-time staff got it."

"Not in the shampoo room. None of us have it."

"I'll talk to Rick tomorrow about it. I didn't think we were that tight on money."

He looked at her with his big brown eyes and worn, hang-dog face, accentuated by the dark stubble of his beard. He was not an attractive man. And so thin.

For a moment she felt sorry for him.

"Shall we go?" he said.

He walked her out to the front of the hotel, had the bellman hail her a cab, and stuck $10 in her hand for the fare. She got into the back seat. He leaned inside and gave her a not-unpleasant, beery kiss.

"Sleep well, my dear," he said. "I'll see you tomorrow."

She smiled weakly.

She was certain he would forget the whole ridiculous scheme by morning.

* * *

When she got home, Kikki and Colleen were up drinking whiskey, smoking hash, and watching the late movie.

"You got a phone call," Colleen said as Mary Frances walked through the living room. "Some guy. Said his name was Robert."

Robert? Robert? Not the blonde from the Chic?

"He says you can call him at the bank tomorrow." Colleen and Kikki started to giggle. "Are you really fucking some banker?" Colleen said. "Have you sunk so low?"

Mary Frances moaned. She remembered she had given Robert her phone number.

"He wanted to know where his money was," Colleen said. "You could tell he was pissed off."

Mary Frances went to her room, slammed the door, and went to bed. Robert's face alternated with that of Alex in front of her eyes.

She sure knew how to pick them.

She rolled over and buried her head under her pillow.

Chapter Seven

Alex hadn't forgotten. The next day he waved and smiled at her when he passed the shampoo room. Later, he took her aside.

"Your appointment's at 10:15 tomorrow morning," he said, handing her a slip of paper with an address on it. "They'll take a blood sample. You'll know in a week." He smiled. "I'm looking forward to a big weekend next week."

Mary Frances felt her stomach turn over.

Alex gave her a lot of attention in class that night. Apparently, she was doing everything wrong, from the way she held her scissors to the way she pinned up a customer's hair so it wouldn't flop in her way while she cut.

"No, no, no!" Alex said. "Don't pin the hair at the base, but in the middle, with a loop." He twisted the pig's hair around his fingers in a sharp turn and stuck it in place with a long silver clip. His clips looked glued to the woman's head; Mary Frances's hung from loose curls like silver pendules.

"I thought you went to beauty school," Alex hissed.

"I did," she hissed back.

"You didn't learn shit."

"That's right," she said loudly. "That's why my body's yours."

The woman in the cutting chair turned and looked up at Alex. He looked embarrassed, glared at Mary Frances, and moved on to the next student.

When Mary Frances got home that night, there was a note from Colleen tacked to her bedroom door: Robert had called again.

"Call him!!!!" Colleen had written, underlining the words with slashes of black magic marker.

Mary Frances pulled the message off the door, threw it out, and went to bed.

* * *

The next morning she went for her blood test. The Grantwood Medical Clinic and Laboratory was in a seedy storefront in the heart of the city's gay neighborhood. When the area was filled with old

Jewish ladies, Glenwood had specialized in high-blood pressure tests. With the homosexuals, it was AIDS.

The clientele was young, multi-colored, and male. The lab technicians were young, Filipino, and female. A tiny woman expertly poked a needle into a vein in Mary Frances's arm. She was done in seconds, with a promise of results in the mail in one week.

Alex was nowhere to be seen; he must have gotten his test earlier.

Nor was he at the salon when Mary Frances rolled in just before lunch.

But Robert was. He was standing in a corner of the reception area, fidgetting under a neon wall scuplture. In daylight, he looked younger than ever, his peaches-and-cream complexion and light blonde hair making him look like an over-tall choirboy.

"There you are!" he called as soon as Mary Frances stepped out of the elevator.

"How did you get here?" she said.

"I took a cab. Isn't that customary?" He gave her a wide, lazy grin.

"Did I tell you where I worked?"

"I got it from your roommate."

Mary Frances vowed to kill Colleen.

"What do you want?"

"I want my money back."

"What are you talking about?"

"The money you stole from my wallet the other night. I want it back."

"I didn't take it."

"I had money when we went to bed. It wasn't there when I got up. The mice didn't eat it."

She shrugged. "Maybe you misplaced it."

He looked right through her. She shifted uncomfortably.

"Let's go dancing Saturday night," he said.

"I've got plans," she said, surprised at the abrupt change of subject.

"Friday?"

"Busy."

"Then next week, say Tuesday?"

"Can't."

"Don't you have any free time?"

"For you, no."

He looked at her, taken aback.

"Well, that's that, I guess," he said. He turned and picked up a thin briefcase, lying on the reception-room couch, and walked to the elevator door.

"Good bye," he said, turning as he stepped in the elevator.

She waved, smiled, and went back to work.

* * *

The week went by quickly. Alex was as good as his word: she learned more in two days of classes with him than she had in nine months at Belvedere. His class adored him. Their eyes followed his every move as he cut and lectured — and spent a disproportionate amount of time with Mary Frances.

"Alex seems to have a thing for you, sweetie," one of the gay hairdressers said to her after class Friday night. "You women get all the breaks."

Alex hadn't asked her out for drinks since their bargaining session earlier in the week. Nor did he ask her out for the weekend. He just waved at her Friday night, giving her a friendly "see you next week," like everyone else, and left. Apparently, all he wanted from her was sex.

Mary Frances and Colleen went home to Kankakee that weekend for their niece's First Communion. Tracy looked so cute in her starched, white First-Communion dress. Kathleen kept talking about how Tracy looked just like Mary Frances at *her* First Communion. She pulled out a family album and found the photo. A small blonde girl gazed pointblank into the camera, a huge pouf of white veil sprouting from the top of her head. Kathleen had insisted Mary Frances wear her grandmother's antique First-Communion veil. She looked like a child bride.

They all sat around the living room and ate jello salad and baked ham from a big buffet Kathleen had made.

"Mary Frances works at Gerrard Herrand's," Kathleen told all the relatives. "She's going to be a great hairdresser."

Colleen sniggered. "She washes hair, Mom," she said.

Kathleen ignored her.

"It all comes from good training," Kathleen said. "We gave her the best. We sent her to Belvedere."

Mary Frances excused herself. She went to the bathroom and felt sick.

* * *

The next Thursday she got her AIDS test results: they were negative.

She ran into Alex in the hallway by the bathrooms.

"I got my results," she said.

He looked at her as if he didn't know what she was talking about. Then he remembered. "Oh yes, yes," he smiled.

"I'm clean," she said.

"Good," he said. "I'll pick you up Friday night."

"For the whole weekend?" Mary Frances said.

"I thought we'd start out with a bang. Bring your party clothes."

Mary Frances gave him a limp smile.

"Cheer up," he said. "It's not the end of the world. It's only the weekend with me." And he smiled sadly.

She wondered how long it would take him to teach her all he knew about hairstyling.

* * *

Colleen couldn't believe it. "You're spending the whole weekend with this guy?" she said as Mary Frances packed underwear, pantyhose, and birth-control pills in an old gym bag. "It's so . . . so premeditated."

Colleen was a great believer in spontaneity in love. She and Lennie had fallen in love at first sight. The fact that he had also "fallen in love" with Mary Frances, Kikki, and half the female population of his Wednesday afternoon painting class didn't phase her.

Mary Frances shrugged. "At least Alex can cut hair," she said.

Colleen huffed up. "Lennie's a very good painter."

"Lennie's an asshole. If he didn't have a diagram he couldn't find his dick," she dropped her voice, "much less your cunt."

"At least we have romance. I don't charge him an entry fee."

"Shut up, Colleen." Mary Frances zipped up her bag and went down to the apartment vestibule to wait for Alex.

He came by exactly at 7. He picked her up, took her to his apartment, and made love to her, all within two hours. He was as organized in his lovemaking as he was in his business life. He licked one of her nipples, then the other, fondled one side of her then the other, rubbed her undercarriage efficiently with one hand until she was juicy enough, then plunged in — straight missionary style, as he had previously announced.

He pumped away for 7-1/2 minutes until her cries of orgasm then came himself. Afterwards, he laid on top of her for 3-1/2 minutes then rolled off on his side. He smiled at her and propped his head up with his arm.

"That was nice," he said.

"That was *fast,*" Mary Frances said.

"Get in and get out. That's my motto." He looked at his watch on the nightstand.

"Time to go or we'll be late," he said.

"Late for what?" She felt like sleeping.

"For Millicent's birthday party." He was already up and on his way to the bathroom.

"Who's Millicent?" she asked.

"My landlady."

Alex lived in the top floor of a two-story apartment building in an expensive neighborhood near downtown. The outside of the building was all gingerbread, stained glass, and charm. The inside was a boxy collection of white walls and cheap wall-to-wall carpeting — "sand beige." From the inside, the apartment could have been any new, cheap apartment complex in any new, cheap suburb.

It reminded Mary Frances of an apartment building on the edge of Kankakee. She felt depressed. She wandered the apartment while Alex showered.

He had done nothing to the place: a bed, two nightstands, and a bureau sat in the bedroom. A white cotton sofa and a big, new TV stood in the living room.

Alex had no taste.

Suddenly, he appeared in the living room, dripping wet with a towel around his middle.

"I almost forgot," he said. "Let's take a shower."

She followed him into the bathroom. He turned on the water, picked up her substantial breasts, and nuzzled his face into them with a contented gurgle. Then he ran his hands over her ass and pulled her close to him, pushing his mouth against hers in a toothy kiss. He pushed himself inside her and came again.

"Sorry to be so quick," he said. "We're running out of time."

He soaped her back while she lathered her hair, then he slapped her playfully on the rearend.

"Let's go," he said, stepping out of the shower.

She rinsed her hair quickly and followed, dripping water on the floor and dragging a towel behind her into the bedroom.

"Look at you," Alex said. "You're such a cupcake I could eat you." But he stood in place and finished knotting his tie, a bright pink-knit cloth with a purple sailboat stitched on the end.

She smiled. She felt like she'd been married to this guy forever — and she didn't even know who he was.

* * *

Millicent was a faded woman of 45 who lived down the street in an elaborate brownstone. She had redone the house to its Victorian glory. Lights blazed through the leaded-glass windows, heavy drapes hung over the windows. The inside was a mishmash of overstuffed furniture, chandeliers, and fringe. It looked like an 1890s bordello, to the red-flocked wallpaper in the bathroom.

Millicent wore a rose chiffon dress of such a light shade that it faded into her skin, which hung around her eyes in papery folds.

She was delighted to see Alex. She pressed his hand and kissed him on the cheek. "Hello, darling," she said.

She gave Mary Frances a distinctly cool look.

"And who's this?" she said, smiling. "An unknown daughter?"

"Mary Frances," Alex said, "Millicent Herschel."

The women nodded.

"Mary Frances works at the salon with me."

"How nice," Millicent said. "How's Margaret?"

"Fine."

"And the children?"

"Justin's just got his first tooth, I understand."

"How lovely. Do give her my best. When is she coming out again?"

Alex shrugged. "In the fall. She's very busy."

"I look forward to seeing her. Make yourselves some drinks," she said, smiling. "I must mingle." She walked toward the far corner of the room where a group of people were standing and talking. She had a light step; her chiffon dress bounced as she walked.

"Who's Margaret?" Mary Frances said.

"My wife," Alex said. He stepped over to a sideboard topped with liquor bottles and started making two bloody Marys. "She lives in L.A. I live here. We've two little boys. They stay with their mother." He turned to Mary Frances. "We've got a very open marriage. It's much more convenient that way."

Mary Frances nodded. She'd met lots of men who cheated on their wives but none who did it with their wives' consent.

Alex handed her her drink. She turned and surveyed the room.

Everyone was at least 20 years older than her and the women 20 pounds heavier. Two frumpy women chatted in a corner. A clump of people stood by the buffet table in the dining room, wine glasses in hand, talking and laughing. The women wore arty clothes with flounces, drapes, fringe, and buckles. One had on a white turban with a big gold brooch hanging off one side. Another had draped a mauve scarf the size of a tablecloth over one shoulder. She had long, shiny-red fingernails. Mary Frances could see them gleam 10 feet away.

Compared to the women the men were of a decidedly duller plummage. They favored pastels — pale pink shirts, khaki pants, and mint-green cotton sweaters. Several men wore gold necklaces or bracelets. Alex fit right in. In her red miniskirt and tight black top, Mary Frances looked like a slut or someone's high-school daughter.

Glasses clinked; some soft-toned synthesizer music plinked and murmured in the background.

Suddenly a chubby man in a khaki jumpsuit, with a mint-green sweater tied over his shoulders, raised his glass.

"Happy birthday, dearest Millie," he called out. Everyone raised their glasses and mumbled "happy birthday" then the whole group lurched into an off-key rendition of the song.

Millicent climbed onto a straight-backed chair and made a little speech about how she'd be 39 her whole life. She hoped they liked barbequed salmon. She'd bought 30 pounds of it.

Two young men in white shirts and pants came out of the kitchen. Each carried a whole salmon on a silver platter. To everyone's oohs and aahs, they set the platters down among the salads and breads already loading the dining-room table. Plates in hand, the guests crowded around, spearing vegetables, snatching thin slices of cocktail rye bread, and hacking at the salmon with heavy silver serving forks.

Mary Frances lost Alex in the rush. She had just pushed her way to the salmon when someone jostled her into the cotton-sweater-clad shoulder of the man in front of her.

"Excuse me," she mumbled.

The man turned around.

It was Robert.

They stared at each other. Robert smiled.

"Hi," he said.

She smiled back. "What are you doing here?" she said.

"I know Millie's ex-husband from my French class. He's here somewhere," Robert said, looking around. "What about you?"

"I'm here with a friend."

Robert nodded.

"I've got to go," he said. He took his plate and disappeared into the crowd.

"Who was that man you were talking to?" Alex said, stepping up behind her. He'd appeared from nowhere.

"Just a friend," Mary Frances said.

"Don't get yourself too many friends," he said. "I need a lot of your time."

Then he turned and disappeared into the crowd himself.

Chapter Eight

The party dragged on. Mary Frances found herself next to Millicent's ex-husband, who was very drunk and slandering his ex-wife.

"She likes young boys," he said. "That's what broke us up. I found her in bed with the 14-year-old son of the man across the street. I could be cuckolded by a real man but not by some little shit whose balls were still stuck halfway up his stomach."

Mary Frances excused herself and went to the kitchen.

Robert was there, talking with Alex.

"Mary Frances," Alex called. "I met your friend."

Both Alex and Robert smiled uncomfortably at her.

"Robert's very knowledgeable on foreign-currency fluctuations," Alex said. "We've been discussing the fall of the English pound."

"Time to trade out," Robert said. With his smile and boyish good looks he made Alex look like a ghoul.

They stood in the kitchen for 45 minutes, Alex and Robert talking about the English pound, the French franc, the trade imbalance, and the federal budget deficit. Mary Frances felt like she was eavesdropping on the monthly meeting of the President's Council of Economic Advisors.

It was preferable to the drunken tales of Millicent's ex-husband, so she stood around, shifting from one foot to another, chewing her lip, and wondering how she ever thought being Alex's mistress was going to be exciting. He'd probably ask her to give him a back rub that night before he went to sleep.

In fact, when they went back to his apartment that night, he asked her to rub his feet, too. She did. He fell asleep within minutes spread-eagled across the bed.

She went into the living room, turned on the TV to the late movie, and got herself a beer from the refrigerator. About 2 am, Alex appeared in the hallway clad in a pair of worn pajama bottoms that nearly fell off his thin hips.

"What in the hell are you doing?" he said.

Mary Frances took a swig from her beer. "I'm watching TV," she said.

"Get back in here. I want my money's worth."

"You were asleep. You want me to just lay there watching you?"

"Of course."

She sighed and turned off the TV. As she passed him in the hallway, he patted her bottom. She groaned.

"How long is this going to go on?" she said.

He grabbed her around the waist and pulled her close to him.

"How long does it take you to learn to cut hair?" he whispered.

"I'm a fast learner."

"Get in there and take your clothes off."

She did, shedding each piece slowly and letting it drop to the floor, like a young child reluctant to go to bed.

Alex made love to her that night — in straight missionary position — with his arms entwined behind her back, pushing himself into her.

"Don't be pissed," he said, huffing and panting over her. "Think of it as your part-time job."

"Do I get days off?" she said.

"Oh. . . Mary Frances," he moaned, coming into her.

After he had rolled off and fallen asleep, Mary Frances lay awake wondering how the late movie had turned out.

* * *

The next morning he made love to her again. Then he sent her home at 11 am. He had to be at the shop by noon.

"I'll pick you up at 7 tonight," he said. "We're having dinner with our bankers." He smiled and gave her money for cabfare.

She went home on the bus and saved the money.

"You look like shit," Colleen said as Mary Frances walked in. Colleen was sitting at the kitchen table, wrapped in a cheap, red-rayon kimona and drinking coffee.

"Thanks," Mary Frances said, dropping her bag on the floor. "I went to bed at 3 this morning and he got me up to fuck again at 9. I feel like some kind of machinery."

She spoke as if she'd just clocked out of the night shift at the Macon Precision Tool Company down the street after a hard night of pulling finished parts off the line and packing them in boxes.

Colleen poured her a cup of coffee.

"I'm working three jobs," Mary Frances said, flopping down in a kitchen chair. "I wash hair all day, cut hair half the night, then screw my instructor into the early morning. The guy's insatiable."

"Young love," Colleen said. "He'll get over it."

"Where's Kikki?"

"She picked up some art dealer at Mr. K's last night. She's probably had more coke up her nose in the last 12 hours than we've had all year."

They both stared at their coffee.

"Do you ever feel like your life is going nowhere?" Mary Frances said. "Like you're destined to be a nobody, do nothing, and be poor forever?"

Colleen looked at her with her big green eyes. "No," she said, "Not really."

Mary Frances sighed. "Colleen," she said. "You're brain-dead."

She turned and stared out the kitchen window. It looked into a maze of telephone and electric wires running into the house. She finished her coffee, went to her room, and took a long, long nap.

* * *

Dinner that night was at an expensive steak house with Mr. Ricky and a trio of pleasant young bankers smelling of men's cologne. Mr. Ricky brought his girlfriend, a wholesome-looking young woman of about 25 in a pink linen suit. She had huge breasts.

Mr. Ricky did a double-take when Alex and Mary Frances walked in together, then introduced them to the bankers. Mary Frances immediately forgot their names, referring to them in her mind throughout the night as "Tic, Tac, and Toe."

But she remembered the name of Mr. Ricky's girlfriend — Delores. Delores wore her name molded in gold and hanging from a chain around her lovely neck. She was an account supervisor in corporate accounts at the phone company, an accomplishment she impressed on Mary Frances all evening.

"I supervise all the account executives for the northwest sector of the southeast quadrant of the west Loop," Delores said. "I oversee 13 people. I got promoted last year."

Mary Frances smiled politely. The men were talking about Gerrard Herrand's expansion plans. Mary Frances strained to listen, but all she could hear was Delores.

"The phone company promotes from within, you know," Delores said. "You become an account executive right after training. You can make $15,000 a year starting, plus benefits."

". . . Alex can run the L.A. salon," Mr. Ricky was saying. "Hawley can take over . . ."

"The pension plan is great. My aunt retired last year and they gave her a gold wristwatch with 'AT&T thanks you for your loyalty' engraved on the back. Isn't that nice?"

". . . a New York salon next year, with one in Dallas the following year, possibly expanding the Paris . . . "

"The people are super. Not pushy at all. Real pleasant." Delores nibbled on a roll from her bread plate. "And so what do you do?" she asked.

Mary Frances stared at her.

"I want to cut hair, but right now I just wash it," she said flatly.

"Oh," Delores said. Clearly, she couldn't think of a thing to say. She concentrated on her green beans.

". . . so Alex would go back to L.A. next year," Mr. Ricky was saying. "How's that strike you, Alex?"

Alex shrugged. "Fine. I'm just here to get the salon up and running." He laughed. "I miss my kids. My youngest has a new tooth, you know."

The men chuckled appreciatively. One of the bankers leered at Mary Frances.

"I'll be seeing Gerrard next week in Atlanta," Mr. Ricky said. "I'll clear all this with him then." He cut another chunk from the huge T-bone lying on his plate. "So," he said. "I see the Cubs are on a winning streak. What did you think of Dunston last night?"

And to Mary Frances's great frustration, the men's conversation drifted into sports. The women's continued its downward path: Delores gave her a complete rendition of the benefits to a business of having a WATTs line. "You can make as many phone calls as you want," she said. "And you just pay one charge. Isn't that great?"

"Are you really moving to Los Angeles next year?" Mary Frances asked Alex when they were leaving in his car.

"Yes." She could see his profile in the darkness.

"When?"

"January, February. I don't know." He paused, then turned to her. "Why don't you come with me?"

She looked at him in surprise.

"Think about it," he said. "Excitement. Interesting people. More money. No snow. And me, of course."

"What about your wife?"

"What does she have to do with it?"

"Why do you stay married to her?"

He looked at her. Even in the dark, she could see the surprise on his face. "What a silly question," he said. "I can't believe you're asking that."

"You don't like her."

"I do like her. I love her." He paused. "It's just that I love other people, too."

"You spread your love around pretty thin."

"And you're some saint?"

"I've never spread my love around at all. You just have my body."

"I see." She could feel him smiling at her in the dark. "Do I get it tonight?"

"I suppose," she said, staring out the car window. "You're paying."

He stopped the car with a lurch.

"I've had enough bitching," he said. "You don't like our arrangement, you can leave."

She shifted in her seat and refused to look at him.

"Do you understand?" he said.

She nodded, her face wooden.

They drove back to his apartment in silence, the only sound the windshield wipers as it started to rain. That night in bed, he pinned her to the mattress with his body and pushed into her, her face under the pillow.

The next morning, he made love to her again.

She decided if she was going to get this much sex, she might as well enjoy it. While Alex pounded away at her body, she thought of one of her favorite high-school lovers, a blue-eyed track star with a foot-long dick and a penchant for practical jokes. To Alex's delight, she had an orgasm.

"That's better," he said, rolling off her. "I thought you were frigid."

She just laughed.

They breakfasted that morning at a greasy deli around the corner from his apartment. She grilled him on the proper technique for doing permanents on color-treated hair.

She had a lot to learn in the eight months before he left town.

* * *

Alex and Mary Frances got into a routine. He'd sleep with her once a week after class, then on Friday night. Saturday night was for Christina, his other girlfriend.

Mary Frances learned about Christina when she answered the phone early one Saturday morning.

"Is Alex there?" a woman asked. She had a strong, deep voice.

"He's sleeping. Can I take a message?"

"Tell him Christina called. He should come to my place tonight. Rachel's with her father."

"I'll tell him."

And the woman hung up.

Mary Frances scrawled a note on a piece of scrap paper and pasted it on the mirror to the medicine cabinet. Then she went and made herself some coffee and turned on the Saturday-morning cartoons on TV.

Twenty minutes later Alex wandered into the living room in his ratty pajama bottoms.

"Come back to bed," he said groggily. He was getting used to rousting his mistress from in front of the TV.

"Batman is just about to rescue Clarice," Mary Frances said.

"Forget it," he said, walking over to the TV and turning it off. Then he came over to the couch, where Mary Frances lay wrapped in his bathrobe. He smiled at her, bent down, and slipped his hands through the top of the robe. He fondled her breasts, kissed the tops of them, and was about to kiss her on the lips when she turned away.

"Who's Christina?" she said.

He looked up.

"A friend," he whispered, licking her ear.

"A friend you sleep with?"

Alex sighed, withdrew his hands, and sat down next to her.

"It's none of your business, but yes."

"Is she a good lay?"

"Mary Frances . . ."

"Well?"

"Yeah . . . she's OK. I've known her a long time. She's Margaret's best friend. Moved here from L.A. three months ago."

"That's sick," Mary Frances said.

He shrugged. "Margaret slept with my best friend. I'm only repaying the compliment."

"I thought you believed in open marriage?"

"There are limits. Climbing into Tom's bed was no fair. It made life too complicated."

He twisted the ends of the drawstrings on his pajama bottoms and stared at his hands sadly.

"Did you make Christina get an AIDS test, too?"

"No. But then she's not a slut like you."

Mary Frances bristled.

"I didn't mean it like that," he said.

"How did you mean it?" She was ready to slap him.

"She hasn't slept around much. She's a mother, has a daughter."

"A good, upstanding woman."

"Yeah. Something like that."

"That you seduced to get back at your wife."

Alex looked at his hands again. "Yeah. Something like that."

To his surprise, Mary Frances started laughing. "You can't keep your dick in your pants, can you, Alex?" she said. "Always whipping it out to show the ladies. We ought to put you in a little box on a street corner with a sign: 'See Alex's dick, five cents.' For 10 cents they can touch it."

He looked up at her. "Shut up," he said angrily.

"And they can fuck you for free," she yelled.

"Shut the fuck up!" he yelled back. He grabbed her by her arm and shook it.

"I suppose you want to fuck me now?" she said.

He glared at her.

"Come on then," she said, getting up, his hand still clenching her arm. They sidled into the bedroom like two fiddler crabs locked together by their giant claws.

They tumbled onto the bed. He pulled the bathrobe down from her shoulders. She ripped his pajama bottoms getting them off. They made love like two animals, scratching and biting at each other.

Then they slept entwined for an hour.

Alex took her to breakfast at the greasy deli where they had become Saturday-morning habitues. They talked happily about techniques of hair layering.

"I'll put Christina off," he said over coffee. "Stay with me tonight." She smiled more.

When she came home late Sunday night she told Colleen she was in love.

Chapter Nine

Mary Frances started getting good at cutting hair. To the immense jealousy of the other shampoo girls, Mr. Ricky pulled her from the shampoo room in September and gave her her own cutting station, a small chrome chair with brown leatherette cushions in a far corner of the salon. The shampoo crowd started the rumor that she got the chair because she was sleeping with Alex.

That was true, but she had also worked hard. She'd attended every one of Alex's classes, labored over her pigs, and shanghaied all of Colleen's and Kikki's friends into getting their hair cut. The student crowd at the Art Institute had never looked so well-barbered. She even cut Lennie's hair. He told her to take a little off the sides. She gave him a modified crewcut with a forelock, making him look more like a satyr than ever.

The only holdout was Colleen. She drew up her frizzy hair into a knot on the top of her head and refused to let Mary Frances touch it.

"My hair is my personal statement," she told Mary Frances one night over an afterdinner joint. "If I cut it I lose my artistic powers."

Mary Frances just inhaled dope smoke and smiled.

The front desk at the salon started sending her the walk-ins, usually out-of-town women looking for a quick trim. If she ever had a problem, Alex was there. He cruised the salon. A pause, an imploring look across the floor from one of his stylists, and he'd appear at his or her side. He'd murmur suggestions, smile at the customer, and pat the stylist on the back with a few words of encouragement. A compliment from Alex was like a blessing from God. Mary Frances felt like an apprentice in the studio of the hairstyling version of Leonardo DaVinci.

They started spending more time together. He took her to parties, gave her cocaine, introduced her to his hairdresser friends, and fed her sushi at a never-ending collection of Japanese restaurants. Their sex life improved, or rather it turned from near rape to something approaching mutual affection. Grinding away in bed with Alex, Mary Frances stopped thinking of the blue-eyed track star and started thinking of Alex—the bumps and angles of his bony body, the thick brown hair he wore to his shoulders or pulled back in a tail at the nape of his neck.

He was so homely. Mary Frances was not beautiful, but next to him she looked like a starlet or a lovely bird accompanied by its gaunt keeper.

They fought about everything: his habits, her friends, Colleen. Alex hated Colleen. Then they'd make love afterwards.

It was great fun.

She told him repeatedly she was in love with him.

"I'm just in lust with you," he'd say.

She'd get angry. They would fight then hit the bed.

She hoped it would never end.

Then, one weekend in October, Margaret appeared with his two boys.

The day before she arrived, Alex took Mary Frances to lunch and told her about it.

"Why didn't you tell me sooner?" Mary Frances said, angrily smearing mustard on her corned-beef sandwich. "You're ruining my weekend."

"I forgot."

She bit into her sandwich and glared at him.

"Why don't you just leave her?" she said, her mouth full. "You haven't seen her since April."

He opened his eyes wide.

"I love Margaret," he said. "She's the mother of my sons."

"And what am I?"

"You're different."

"The piece of ass you play with on the side?"

He smiled. "It's not like that," he said.

Sure, she thought, I'm the woman you can really talk to.

"You're the woman I can really talk to," he said.

Her jaw dropped.

"Is something the matter?" he said.

She stared at him. "Nothing," she said. "Nothing at all."

She shot him another death ray, then took a huge bite of her sandwich. He lit up a cigarette and stared out a window. Finally, he started talking salon gossip. He prodded her into responses and she picked up the thread reluctantly. They finished lunch amicably, laughing over who was sleeping with who.

After class that night, he invited her to spend the night with him. She turned him down and went home. It felt good.

At 11 pm, the phone rang. It was Robert.

"Long time, no talk to," she said pleasantly.

"Yes. . . well. . . how've you been?" he said.

"Fine."

"Look," he said. "I know I haven't talked to you for awhile and this is very short notice, but I just got these tickets to a benefit Saturday night. I wondered if you would like to go."

"What's it for?"

"The Field Museum. We're dancing among the dinosaurs."

It sounded ghastly.

"I'd love to," she said.

"Great." He seemed surprised. Mary Frances's name must have been on the last page of his little black book.

"It's a formal dance. Do you have a full-length dress?"

"Sure." She had a pumpkin coach, too. She and Colleen would rig something up. She gave him directions to her apartment.

"I'll be by at 8," he said. "There's a buffet dinner, too."

"How nice," came her uninterested reply.

"I've got to run," he said. "I'll see you Saturday."

And he hung up.

She crawled into bed that night humming the "Beautiful Blue Danube."

* * *

Mary Frances didn't speak to Alex the next day. Nor did she hear from him on Saturday, which was just as well because she spent the entire day with Colleen, jerryrigging a ball gown. After a morning of bickering, they went out and bought five yards of black cotton knit, which Colleen pulled around Mary Frances in a tight black tube. Colleen ran a seam up the back, pulled some elastic through the top, and added a shoulder strap from left front to right back. She stuck a big black cloth flower behind her sister's right ear, drew smudgy blue-grey lines around her eyes, and painted her lips red.

Mary Frances looked like a chanteuse in an expensive hotel bar.

They were immensely pleased with their handiwork.

"I should hand you in as my project for my fashion-design class," Colleen said, smoothing her frizzy hair up into its topknot. "The bitch who teaches it *loves* black knit."

They smoked three joints and awaited Robert's arrival. At precisely 8:00 he appeared, one white gardenia in hand.

"It's perfect, just too perfect!" Colleen shrieked when he was halfway in the door. She grabbed the flower from his hand, pulled the black one from Mary Frances's hair, and slipped the gardenia in its place.

"You're Billy Holiday!" she screeched. "It's just too retro for words!" She clasped her hands together and danced around her sister.

"Robert," Mary Frances said. "This is my sister Colleen."

Robert nodded. Colleen bounced up and down.

"You look lovely," Robert said to Mary Frances, staring down the top of her dress. The thin material covered only half her cleavage. Standing next to her in his tuxedo, with his boyish face, he looked like a boy on the way to the senior prom with a New York call girl.

Colleen laughed out loud when she saw them together.

Mary Frances shot her a nasty look; she stopped abruptly.

"Have a nice time," she said sweetly, closing the door behind them.

***

In his spotless red Porsche, Robert and Mary Frances spoke only of trivia—the weather, the traffic, the ball, how nice her dress was. The bank—source of all good things in Robert's life—had given him tickets. His boss would be there.

"I'm so glad you could come," he said.

She nodded and stared out the passenger-side window. She imagined Alex and Margaret entwining themselves into a passionate knot on his bed—*her* bed.

"I know we haven't been the best of friends for several months," she heard Robert say.

"As I recall, I told you to fuck off," she said.

"Yes. . . well. After I accused you of taking money from my wallet, I could see why you'd be put out. I am sorry."

"Don't be. I took it."

He cleared his throat and concentrated on the road.

"You were a lousy lay," she continued, looking out the window again. "I felt I needed to be paid for my time."

He downshifted abruptly; the Porsche sped up.

"Technique isn't your strong point," she said.

"How kind of you to bring it up now," he said coldly.

She shrugged and turned to him. "You were so quick off the mark I couldn't get a word in edgewise."

"You've certainly corrected that now." He wove the Porsch between two cars and cut off a station wagon. He was doing 65; the limit on Lake Shore Drive was 45.

"Don't mention it," she said. She put her hand on his arm. The three joints she'd smoked with Colleen were having their effect. "You could have had opening-night jitters," she said. "Maybe I'll give you a second chance tonight."

"Je-sus," he muttered staring straight ahead.

She let go of his arm, lay back in her seat, and closed her eyes. She'd get back at Alex. She'd give Robert the lay of his life.

She slipped the dress strap off her shoulder, pulled her dress down to her waist, and unhooked Colleen's strapless bra, borrowed for the occasion. Her breasts fell out in a rush of honey-colored flesh and dark nipples.

"My God!" Robert said. "What the hell are you doing?"

She leaned over and began kissing his ear.

"Let's ditch the party and go to bed," she mumbled, picking up one his hands from the steering wheel and putting it on her right breast. She could feel his hand quiver, then squeeze her breast.

"My boss will be there," he said weakly. "I've got to go."

"Just a quickie, then," she said.

His hand tightened on her breast. He veered right over four lanes of traffic, turned onto Monroe Street, and headed for the Grant Park Underground Garage. He sped through its endless,

nearly empty acres, finding a deserted corner in a sub-sub-
basement.

He grabbed her, pulled her to him, and nuzzled her breasts while
trying to pull off his pants. Mary Frances laughed with delight.

This time, he approached his lovemaking like a craftsman
corrected by his foreman. He was careful that she got her fill.

She'd get Alex, she thought. To Robert's amazement, she came
and came under him. One hour later, they were on their way to the
benefit, laughing and ready to party.

* * *

Robert told his boss they'd had a flat tire on the way.

"Had to call a tow truck. . . took forever. . . didn't want to get my
tux greased up," he mumbled quickly and with great deference.

Then he turned to Mary Frances. "This is Mary Frances Barton.
Mary Frances, Jim King."

Mr. King gave her a little string of a smile. "How nice to meet
you," he said politely. "My wife, Elizabeth." Elizabeth mumbled
some pleasantry.

King was a tall, thin man of about 45, elegant in a tuxedo of fine
black wool. With his watery blue eyes, horn-rim glasses, and wispy,
carmel-colored hair, he looked like the product of inbreeding
between two long lines of New England Puritans. Elizabeth was his
duplicate, minus the horn-rims and tuxedo. Her blue satin dress had
a high neck and wide lace collar that draped her shoulders, like a
doily hung over the back of a couch.

Another couple was with them, shorter and dumpier, the woman
in a purple sequined top that rustled when she moved. Mary
Frances immediately forgot their names. The six of them chatted
pointlessly about the benefit.

They stood in the Museum's main lobby, a vast space open
through two floors to a skylight and surrounded on the first floor by
a ring of white marble columns.

In the dim light, the marble glowed like white skin. A fountain
splashed in the center of the lobby, and a stuffed elephant, about 20
feet tall, loomed over the conversationalists. A few yards from it was
the skeleton of an equally tall and murderous-looking dinosaur. It

had foot-long teeth. Mary Frances looked up at the monster and shivered in her thin dress.

The lobby was filled with couples in evening dress. At the far end a 20-piece orchestra worked its way through a tinny version of "New York, New York."

Mary Frances nudged Robert. He and the dumpy man were talking about the benefits of different gas grills for barbequing salmon.

"Let's dance," she whispered.

Robert finished his comments on the Home-Dynamo Grill-O-Matic then excused them from the group.

"When did you become an expert on barbeques?" Mary Frances said as he led her through the crowd.

"It's important to the customers, so I keep up. I play golf, too."

Mary Frances laughed. The idea of anyone under the age of 50 playing golf seemed absurd.

"My boss is a real mover-and-shaker at the bank," Robert continued. "If I stick with him I've got a great future. International banking is big at Citibank. They're sending me to France next year, you know." He looked at her and nodded knowingly.

She smiled back. He was so eager, like a boy showing his cousin his butterfly collection.

They reached the crowd of people swaying and dancing in front of the orchestra, which played a limp rendition of "Satin Doll." Mary Frances screwed up her face in disgust. Robert took her in his arms and they began a stiff fox-trot around the floor. She hadn't fox-trotted since a wedding she'd gone to as a sophomore in high school. An uncle had taught her the step.

The crowd jiggled sedately around the floor. She and Robert were among the youngest there. Most were far older, the women with stiff pageboy hairdoes or flips that didn't move because of the hairspray. By and large, they wore severely cut gowns that covered nearly everything, although Mary Frances saw a goddess in an off-shoulder red satin dress with a big bow on her hip sway smoothly by. There were lots of pearls – single and double strands – hanging around the sedate necklines of the women's black and pastel dresses.

The men wore black tuxedos and were indistinguishable from one another.

With few exceptions, everyone was thin.

Robert stared happily down the front of her dress as he wheeled her around the floor. Her breasts were practically popping out of the top. Her bra had underwiring that lifted her already ample endowment higher, presenting them to the world like a pair of plump chickens on a platter. She enjoyed watching him drool.

"I can hardly wait to dive back in there," he whispered, leaning forward to get a better look and rubbing the back of her neck with his hand.

She was about to laugh when she saw *him*.

It was Alex.

He was dancing with a short, mousy woman in a cream-colored dress. His hair was pulled back in a tail at his neck; he wore a black tux with a red cummerbund. With his pale bony face and dark eyes, he looked like a Spanish grandee.

He saw her and his eyes went wide. Then he grinned at her — from ear to ear.

She mouthed a curse at him, just as Robert was telling her how he planned to lick every part of her body and keep her going all night. He was a fast-learner when put on the right track.

"There's someone we know," she said, nodding in the direction of Alex.

Robert turned around and stared at Alex. Alex waved at them.

"Who is it?" Robert said.

"Alex. From that woman's birthday party. Remember? You met him."

"Oh yeah. Yeah. The guy from Millie's party."

"I work with him. At the salon."

"Yeah. Right."

The music ended. Alex and the woman were applauding politely and talking when Mary Frances hurried over, pulling Robert behind her by the hand.

"What a surprise," Mary Frances said, looking at Alex. "Imagine meeting you here."

He gave her a bemused smile.

"This is Robert," she said. "You met him at that birthday party, remember?"

Alex and Robert nodded at each other, mumbled their names briskly, and shook hands.

Mary Frances put her arm around Robert's waist. Pleasantly surprised, he put his arm around her shoulders. Alex's eyes flickered angrily, then went blank.

"This is your wife, Margaret, I suppose?" Mary Frances said.

Alex shot her an irritated look.

"Actually, I'm Sondra Clemens," the woman said, in a lovely light voice. "I'm Margaret's sister. She's dancing with my husband, somewhere." Sondra stood up on the tips of her cream-satin pumps and scanned the crowd, like a delicate gazelle standing on tiptoe in the African veldt and sniffing the air.

"There she is! With David." She waved a thin little arm. A woman in a brilliant blue dress nodded back and waved. It was Margaret. She came over.

Margaret was a dark-haired, delicate creature of fragile beauty. Unlike most of the women at the benefit, her dress was cut off the shoulder, showing her graceful neck and translucent skin to best advantage. Mary Frances was not a large woman, but next to Margaret she felt like a moose.

"Margaret," Alex said. "This is Mary Frances."

Margaret extended a small white hand with a huge amythyst ring on one finger. "How nice to meet you, dear," she said, pleasantly. "Alex has told me so much about you."

Mary Frances smiled awkwardly and shook Margaret's hand.

"I understand you're one of my husband's star pupils," Margaret continued with a luminescent smile. "In fact, I understand you're a star to Alex in more ways than one. I'm so happy you keep him amused. He's in such good spirits these days."

She turned to Alex, who was standing slightly behind her, and stroked his cheek possessively. He smiled, took her hand, and kissed the palm.

Mary Frances just stared.

The orchestra started up again, some slow moody piece Mary Frances couldn't place. Alex walked up to her.

"May I?" he said with great gallantry.

She stared at him woodenly as he took her in his arms.

Picking up the hint, Robert asked Margaret to dance. And out of the corner appeared a short man, Sondra's husband, who took her in his arms and danced her off toward the other end of the floor. Paired off with her short husband, Sondra looked like half of a dancing-dwarf act.

"I'm so glad I ran into you," Alex said, tightening his grasp around her waist. "You look lovely." He stared into her cleavage and smiled happily.

"You shit," she muttered. She stepped on his instep. He stumbled painfully then resumed his step.

"What's your problem?" he hissed.

"What's yours?"

"I have no problem. I'm here with my wife. My sister-in-law the lawyer had tickets to the benefit and invited us. So what?"

She looked straight ahead over his shoulder. Margaret was smiling and dancing with Robert, one thin white arm resting gracefully on his shoulder. They looked like the romantic leads from a dreamy B movie.

"Did you hear what that bitch said to me?" Mary Frances said. "What have you told her?"

He smiled. "Everything, of course. We have an open marriage." She just stared.

"Margaret and I have no secrets," he said.

"You know about her boyfriends?"

"A few. She hasn't had many. She's still shy about picking up men. But I've taught her a few things; she's getting better.

"Her current delight is a young Hawaiian, some surfer going to school in Santa Barbara. He's quite sexually insatiable, I understand." He lowered his voice, "Just like you."

She glared at him.

"The problem with you," Alex said, staring over her head, "is that you're too possessive. I'm not monogamous. I'm an artist. I need to feel passion, to express myself."

"Aren't you jealous of some slanty-eyed Hawaiian banging your wife?" Mary Frances said.

"No. Jealousy is a primitive emotion."

They danced quietly for a few moments, the violins in the orchestra sawing away at some smarmy passage.

"I guess we should have no secrets either," Mary Frances said.

Alex smiled. "Of course not."

"You're not jealous of me seeing Robert?"

"Of course not."

"You want me to keep you up-to-date on my sex life, don't you?"

"Certainly."

"I mean, we *do* have an open relationship, don't we?"

He stumbled over her foot.

"Yes, of course."

"And your other girlfriends, they have open relationships with you, too, I suppose."

"Yes." He paused. "What the hell are you driving at?"

"Well," she said, digging her fingernails into his shoulder, "with all these open relationships, you must need a program to keep all your women separate. I mean if I told you Robert and I had a big fuck in the Grant Park underground before we came here and that the guy's a hell of a lay, you could keep it straight from the stories of your other girlfriends, couldn't you?"

He coughed. "Yeah, sure."

"Good." She smiled, then started humming to herself. "Lovely music they're playing. A bit on the slow side, but okay."

"Did he really fuck you in the Grant Park underground?" Alex whispered.

"Oh yes. I pulled my clothes off on Lake Shore Drive and fast-thinking boy that he is, he headed straight for the garage." She sighed. "There's something so luscious about him, I just can't resist."

Alex jerked her sharply to the left in order to get a better look at Robert. Robert saw him and smiled. Mary Frances shot him such a dazzling look that he actually gave her a small wave.

She sighed deeply.

Alex stared straight ahead.

"So what are you doing Wednesday night?" he said gruffly. "You want to go out with Dennis and Maria?" Dennis was the creative director at some big ad agency downtown; Maria was his third or fourth wife. Of all Alex's friends, they were Mary Frances's favorites.

"I can't," Mary Frances lied. "I'm going out with Robert."

"Next Friday?"

"Sorry," she lied again. "Robert and I are going to a play."

He screwed up his mouth in a pout.

She shrugged. "You know how it is when you're first in love. You have to do everything together. You can't stay out of each other's pants." She leered at him. "You know."

Alex coughed again.

"I could pull our contract on you," he hissed. "I have first rights on your body, remember?"

Her eyes went big. "Now Alex," she said. "You wouldn't want to do *that*."

"Sure I would. Why not?"

"Because then I might tell you to go fuck yourself."

He chuckled. "We have a deal."

"The deal is off."

"You want to go back to the shampoo room?"

"I've learned enough to cut."

"You've learned shit. You need at least another year of work."

She bit her lip. "You're just saying that to get into my pants."

"Probably. But it's also true." He smiled again. "Wednesday night — my place. And don't talk to me about loverboy. I'm making the rules, not you."

It was at that moment she decided to keep sleeping with Robert.

* * *

Alex, Mary Frances, and their group danced and chatted together for another two hours, interspersing their trips to the dance floor with trips to the buffet. Margaret was always talking or dancing with other men. She was supposedly shy and hadn't seen her husband in months. Now she was spending the evening avoiding him.

The next dance Mary Frances had with Robert, he looked around nervously, then pulled her close to him. "That Margaret is one strange bird," he whispered. "She's propositioned me three times this evening."

Mary Frances threw her head back and laughed so hard Robert looked at her in alarm.

Chapter Ten

That night Robert brought her back to his apartment. They were so tired they just went to sleep, Mary Frances's pale arm thrown across the thick blonde hair on his chest. They awoke at 10 the next morning then dozed and made love until 1 in the afternoon.

He offered to take her to lunch.

"In this?" she said, pointing to her slinky black dress.

He laughed and took her home where she changed clothes. Then he took her to a local coffee shop and told her all about Paris, where, he told her for the umpteenth time, the bank was sending him next year.

"How do you know so much about Paris?" she said, munching on a sugary slice of raisin toast. "You ever been there?"

"No, but I read a lot," he said, all boyish eagerness.

"How do you know you'll like it?"

"Compared to Chicago? Come off it!" he said. "And the French women. Oh-la-la. I have a friend who worked for Lehman Brothers over there. He had a blast. The Algerian women were the best. He told me that they liked to fuck like monkeys, hanging from bed posts, draped over chairs. Real contortionists."

"Really?" she said as if someone had just told her it had started raining.

Robert became suddenly silent and hacked at his stack of pancakes. She shifted in her seat and started fussing with the tail ends of her shirt.

He started.

"What's the matter?" she said, tucking her shirttails into her jeans.

"I thought you were going to take your clothes off again." He smiled nervously and looked around.

"You want me to?" she said, undoing the top button.

"No! No. Not here. I have to eat breakfast here every morning."

She toyed with her second button.

"Why don't we go back to your apartment and play around some more?" she said softly.

His blue eyes widened again. "Sure."

They finished lunch, went back to his apartment, and made love all afternoon, with time out for a phone call from Robert's mother in South Bend. Mary Frances sat between Robert's legs as he stood over her at the phone. She toyed with his balls as he talked—little pink-purple balls covered with a light coat of wirey blonde hair. They looked like strange, overripe seed pods. She mouthed one, then the other. He gasped.

His mother asked if he was all right.

He told her he had hurt his foot playing tennis that morning and it was bothering him.

She told him to ice it and got off the phone.

He hung up and turned around with a grin on his face. He picked Mary Frances up from between his legs, slung her over his shoulder, and carried her—yelping—back to the bedroom. He flung her down on the bed and jumped on top of her. He pumped away and she dug her fingernails into his back until she came and came.

Then he began tickling her. She screeched and rolled around, her breasts bouncing and flopping like jello.

Then he pulled the top sheet over his head, slipped his head down between her legs and announced: "Let's play doctor."

He began licking her cunt. She moaned and laid back on her pillow.

"Robert, I'm tired," she whined.

"You just lay there. I'll do all the work," came the voice from between her legs. His tongue felt so smooth and quick that within minutes she could feel herself trembling again, a light wave of orgasm tingling down to her toes.

She rolled her eyes to the ceiling and just laughed.

She went home that night at about 11, sore around the edges.

She told Colleen she was *really* in love this time.

Colleen was sitting at the kitchen table reading *Avant-Garde Art News* and eating frozen yogurt out of the container. A frizzy strand of purple-tinted hair hung down one cheek. She was in her "blue period."

"You're in love with the baby-faced banker?" Colleen said as Mary Frances plopped down at the table. "He's so young-looking they'll get you for child molesting." She spooned another tablespoon of frozen yogurt into her mouth. "I thought he was a lousy lay," she mumbled with her mouth full.

"He's picked up some tips."

"Maybe he's practicing on someone else."

"Probably. I haven't seen him in a couple months."

Colleen scraped the bottom of her yogurt container with her spoon.

"What about Alex?" she said.

"He's 'work' love. Robert is 'play' love."

Colleen nodded as if that made perfect sense.

Suddenly Mary Frances stood up on tiptoe, twirled around with her hands over her head, and danced little slipping sidesteps toward her bedroom.

"See you in the morning," she called back in a drifting voice, closing the bedroom door. She dropped her clothes in a pile on the floor and dreamed of Robert all night.

* * *

Seeing Alex the next morning at 9 was a shock. He looked uglier and more monkey-like than ever. He pinched her ass in front of everyone in the reception area. That night at class, he gave her more attention than ever. Mary Frances felt like everyone was snickering and looking at her.

"Come on over tonight," he said, pulling her over after class. "I need to see you."

"What about your wife?"

"She and the boys are staying with her sister tonight. Girl-talk time."

She looked at him in disgust. She'd been looking forward to washing her hair and doing her nails.

They drove to his apartment in silence.

"So, you having fun with Robert?" he said as he unlocked the door.

"I thought we weren't talking about Robert," she said.

"We are now." He went to a cupboard in the kitchen and pulled out a mason jar full of dope and some rolling papers. He began rolling a joint. "What is it that you like about him so much?" he said.

She shrugged and stared at the kitchen sink. "He's a nice guy."

"That's it?"

He lit up the joint, inhaled deeply, and passed it to Mary Frances. She shook her head "no."

"Smoke it!" he said.

She gave him a disgusted look, took the joint, and drew on it.

"I want you to stop seeing him," Alex said.

"What?"

"You're sleeping with me, not with him. You're my woman, not his."

"That wasn't part of the deal," she said, her voice rising.

"It is now."

She threw the joint down into the sink. "Bullshit. You can't run my entire life because you're teaching me to cut hair. When I'm not with you my time's my own."

"Not any more. *All* your time is my time. Besides, I don't want some jerk dipping his wick in my honey pot. You want to give me AIDS or something?"

"Alex!"

"You don't like it? Go somewhere else and cut hair. You'll end up giving frizzy permanents to old ladies in Berwyn. I'm offering you the best, the absolute best, and you want to stick it to me. Don't you know what you've got, what I'm offering you?"

He paced around the kitchen, pounding his fist into the palm of his other hand.

"I've got connections. In L.A., all over the U.S., in Europe. I could build you a clientele you'd never believe. You'd be set for life."

He leaned against the sink and folded his arms. "And all you've got to do is spread your legs for me for a year. So why don't you just take off your clothes and let's get on with it. I don't have all night."

He looked at his watch, like a man impatient for the next commuter train, and drew another drag on his joint.

Mary Frances sighed and began unbuttoning her blouse. She let her clothes fall to the floor at her feet. When she was naked, she stood there and glared at him.

His eyes lit up. He dropped the remains of the joint into the sink and came over to her. "Oh baby," he mumbled softly, running his hands down the curve of her hips and around her stomach. He pulled her in toward him, his erection hard against her stomach.

He led her into the bedroom, took off his clothes, and laid her down gently on the bed. Then he crawled in next to her.

She wanted to crawl out.

"Come on, baby," he said, toying with her nipples, "give me a little love."

She glared at him, her face stony.

"OK," he said, "be that way." He grabbed her, pushed his way into her, and pumped away. She lay there like a dead fish and reviewed the techniques of layering a wedge haircut, which he had shown them that night in class.

Alex pumped and pumped.

"Come on," he said, panting. "Can't you be more enthusiastic? You feel like my wife."

"Enthusiasm costs extra," she said.

He stopped. "What?"

"I mean if you want me to be enthusiastic it's going to cost you more."

He leaned on one elbow and looked at her. "You used to be a real sex kitten on this bed. I couldn't keep you down. Now you're like the living dead and I'm supposed to feed you quarters like a parking meter." He lowered his voice. "You used to tell me how much you loved me."

"Not any more," she said.

"Why?"

"Her name is Margaret."

Alex moaned.

"I wouldn't want to screw such a happily married man," Mary Frances said.

"Who said I'm happy?"

"You're still with her. You must be happy with her."

"She's the mother of my sons. I divorce her, her sister the lawyer will make sure I never see my boys again."

"You hardly see them as it is."

"But I could if I wanted. I like the option."

"Hire a nasty lawyer and dump her."

Alex sat up in bed and pulled the sheet around his shoulders. His penis wilted. "You certainly know how to get a man out of the mood," he mumbled. "If I divorce Margaret she will clean my clock. I won't have two dimes to rub together and I'll be sending her every penny I make. She's a real American girl: she'll stop at nothing."

"Doesn't she get every penny you make now?"

"No. She's living with several other women in some communal house in L.A. This year, thank God, she's into peace and love and living on very little. The boys look a little thin, I must say. Too much granola and not enough red meat. She says she can live without much money now. But I mention divorce, and she'll bleed me dry."

"Doesn't she get upset about your girlfriends?"

"She doesn't care. She's got her own lovers — of both sexes. All she wants is a different lay every week, my money, and her children — in that order. And she doesn't want a divorce. She thinks it covers her in the community for all her fooling-around. She's a fifth-grade teacher, you know."

Mary Frances thought of Miss Pickett, her fifth-grade teacher. A dumpy little woman with a perpetual frown, she certainly wasn't a bisexual nymphomaniac with an obsession for propriety like Margaret.

"Alex, you're a wimp," Mary Frances said.

He smiled. "Do I get the sympathy vote?"

She smiled back. "No."

"Can't you at least fake some passion? I need it."

"It'll cost you a dinner at Franklin Chang's." Chang's was an expensive Chinese restaurant that Mary Frances adored and Alex hated.

He grumbled. "Alright."

She smiled, closed her eyes, and lay back. He climbed on top of her and she started to moan and writhe.

"That's better," Alex said.

He came in five minutes, rolled off her, and went to sleep.

It wasn't much work for a $50 dinner. She fell asleep dreaming of Peking Duck and Robert.

Chapter Eleven

Mary Frances fell into a pattern. Tuesdays and Thursdays she'd sleep with Robert. Monday, Wednesdays, and Fridays she'd sleep with Alex. The weekends were a tossup.

She developed a ravaging case of vaginal itch, but otherwise she was very happy.

Robert ran her around the bedroom, took her to fancy disco bars, and slept with other women on his nights off.

On his off-nights, Alex slept with a stylist he'd met at the annual hairdresser's show that fall. In addition, he had several other girlfriends and, apparently, a few boys. One night, Mary Frances found a love letter on his night stand. It was from Alfred, a young hairdresser at the salon. She asked no questions.

For her part, Mary Frances took up with the black drummer for an eighth-rate jazz group that played at one of the arty bars on weekends. He was a heroin addict, the father of several illegitimate children, and had an aversion to baths. He also had the most tightly muscled ass of any man Mary Frances had ever had.

Colleen liked him best of all Mary Frances's boyfriends.

"He has soul," she told her. "There's a man you can really get into."

Then he started beating her. Mary Frances dropped him, soul and all.

In December, Alex announced he was moving to L.A. the following month and that Mary Frances was coming with him.

On Christmas Eve, she told Robert. They were sitting in bed eating ice cream and watching some smarmy TV special with little pointy-eared elves singing Christmas carols.

"I'm moving to L.A. with Alex next month," Mary Frances said.

Robert looked at her, surprised and hurt. She'd never mentioned a word about it.

"Well, you're going to go to France," she said hurriedly. "This little show had to break up some time."

He stared at his ice-cream bowl. "I had hoped it wouldn't be so soon," he said. "I had no idea you were planning to leave."

"You're leaving for France in June. I just hurried up the process a bit," she said, irritated. "You're just mad I'm leaving you before you left me."

He sulked.

"Come on," she sighed. She set aside her ice-cream bowl, took him in her arms, and made love to him with a long, lingering technique. By the time she was done, she didn't want to go to L.A. either. But she swore she would. What could Robert do for her in France? He'd screw Algerian women and she could get a job washing hair in a French salon. She'd never improve her hairstyling techniques, especially her color work.

She needed more color work. All her blondes were turning out brassy. Last week, one even had a green cast to her hair. That would never do.

"I'm really going to miss you," Robert said. His eyes were misty around the rims.

"I'll miss you, too," she said. Maybe if she added more toner to the new blonde dye Alex had just gotten in? She resolved to try it next week.

She fell asleep, thinking of possible mix ratios for color rinses, her body entwined with Robert's.

He was a nice boy, but the world was filled with nice boys.

* * *

When they found out Mary Frances was moving, Colleen and Kikki asked Lennie to move in with them. Mary Frances was disgusted, but what did she care? She was going to be hanging out with a higher class of people now. Alex was a big deal in L.A. He was going to run the flagship salon for Gerrard Herrand and Mary Frances was going to be a full-fledged hairstylist. She'd still take classes, but she would have her own regular customers.

She was very excited.

Her mother was very upset. She cried all through Christmas. With eight children and 14 grandchildren, Kathleen Barton certainly had her maternal needs covered, but she acted as if Mary Frances were her only daughter.

Mary Frances ignored her.

Moving day approached and Alex became more and more preoccupied with affairs at the office. So she spend three days in a row with Robert. He acted like a child who had taken swim lessons and was now about to be tossed into deep water for the first time. That is, he panicked.

"I'm going to ask the bank to transfer me to L.A. instead of Paris," he said.

She looked at him like he was crazy.

"That's nuts," she said. "You've been dying to go to Paris."

"I can't live without you," he said.

"Don't be melodramatic."

"I thought you loved me."

"I do. But I love other people, too," she said. Robert was making her nervous. "Besides, you've got other girlfriends."

"I don't feel about them like I do about you. I can talk to you. I just fuck them."

"I didn't think we were big on conversation," she laughed.

"Stop it. You know what I mean."

"No, I don't. We've had some good times. I'll always be fond of you. We'll always be friends. But I'm going to L.A."

"With Alex."

"Yes, with Alex."

"He doesn't love you like I love you."

"Really? It never bothered you before. You still slept with half the women in the city."

"What about Armando!" he yelled. Armando was her black jazz drummer. "I never complained about him," Robert said. "I felt it was something you were going to grow out of."

"I suppose you were going to grow out of sleeping with everything that moved?"

He looked at his hands. "That's different," he mumbled. "Men have different needs."

"You need to sleep around and I don't? What do you think I am, a virgin martyr?"

He looked at her and his eyes went cold.

"You're a slut, Mary Frances," he said. "Just a slut. You can get out of my bed."

He planted one foot on her rearend and pushed. She rolled out on the floor in a naked heap. Enraged, she crashed a bedside lamp on the floor, threw on her clothes, and left.

She never saw Robert again.

* * *

Alex and Mary Frances moved to L.A. the second week in January. It was 20 degrees and snowing when they flew out of O'Hare and 70 degrees and smoggy when they arrived in L.A. Everyone wore summer clothes. Mary Frances threw her winter coat in a trash can in the airport. She decided she was going to like L.A.

She'd brought her life savings with her, tearfully cashed out from a series of U.S. government savings bonds by her mother after a ferocious screaming match.

"That money's for your wedding," Kathleen had pleaded, tears streaming down her face.

"I need it now, Mom," Mary Frances had said.

"You'll never be able to pay for your wedding dress," Kathleen had said.

"Give me the fucking money!" Mary Frances had screamed.

Her mother had looked at her in shock and redeemed the bonds. Mary Frances got the check in the mail, stuck in a dingy off-white envelope and folded in a piece of yellow, ruled paper. There was no note.

Alex paid for nothing on her big move to L.A. He did give her a map.

"Stay out of this area," he said, circling an area on the map with a stubby pencil. "They eat nice white girls like you for breakfast."

She bought a 10-year-old Datsun for $500 and found a cubicle of an apartment on the edge of Beverly Hills, a short drive from the salon. Her apartment was a tiny studio with one narrow window overlooking an alley and a tangle of telephone wires.

She found palm trees amusing, regarding them as giant plastic props stuck in the ground for effect. She peeled bark from one and crumbled a dry leaf in her fingers before she believed the trees were

real. Otherwise, L.A. reminded her of Chicago — except the weather
was better.

* * *

The Gerrard Herrand Salon was on a busy street in Beverly Hills,
sandwiched between two exclusive clothing boutiques with bright
awnings that arched over the sidewalk. The salon blended in with its
upscale neighbors: it was fronted in marble and had heavy glass
doors trimmed in gold-finished metal. Mary Frances felt like she
was walking into a bank.

Everyone looked rich: the customers, all tanned and blonde and
draped in gold jewelry; the stylists, with their bright clothing and
offbeat haircuts. Even the girls in the shampoo room looked
well-to-do. Tanned and blonde like the customers, they looked like
they'd just stepped off the beach for a few hours of shampooing hair.

A dreamy collection of flute and sythesizer music tinkled through
the loudspeakers, reminding Mary Frances of wind in the trees or
lapping mountain lakes. It was very soothing.

The salon was twice the size of the Chicago operation and twice
as luxurious. The towels were thicker, the wallpaper more detailed,
and the hanging planters of ferns fuller and more numerous.

The prince of the whole shebang was Alex.

He'd "gone Californian" overnight. He wore cream-canvas
espadrilles, white linen pants, and white linen shirts left open
halfway down his chest. A clump of gold chains and snaggle teeth
always glittered on his hairy chest. Somehow he'd gotten a tan.

"I got a tanning lamp," he confessed when Mary Frances had
inquired. She went out and got one the same day. Two weeks later
she had bronzed up quite nicely.

In the Chicago salon, Mr. Ricky had run the business while Alex
handled the stylists. But in L.A., Alex ran everything and got a cut
of the salon's profits. Consequently, he followed every dollar from
the moment it came into the salon from a happy, newly-blonded
customer, to the time it went out to pay Peterson Cosmetics
Wholesalers for a case of Gerrard Herrand's custom-mixed hair
conditioner.

He was a cheap son of a bitch.

Within six weeks, everyone at the salon hated him, with the exception of the janitor, who was paid by the building management. And because Mary Frances was clearly his main girlfriend, everyone hated her, too. She wanted to tell them she got no cut from Alex's money. The only thing he did for her was to take her to more expensive versions of the sushi bars they used to frequent in Chicago.

And he made love to her on more expensive sheets in a more luxurious setting. Margaret refused to move out of the communal house she shared with several aging hippies, so Alex bought a beautiful, four-bedroom house in Newport Beach just for himself. It had a tiny kidney-shaped pool with a big fence around it.

Ever one for a gimmick, Alex immediately started screwing Mary Frances in the pool at all hours of day and night. He would perch her on the stairs leading down into the water and jab away at her, the water slurping and splashing around them. One night he fell backwards and got water up his nose. Dignity injured, he led her back into the house: they went back to straight missionary position on designer sheets.

Mary Frances was not pleased with the arrangement. She had hoped that when they had moved to L.A., he would make up with his wife and move back in with her, leaving Mary Frances to link up with richer and more useful men. But Margaret was living with the granola crowd and Alex was hornier than ever.

He also spent more time with his sons. Once a week, he'd bring them home and let them frolic around the pool while he fixed hamburgers on the grill and barked at Mary Frances to bring out the mustard and pickles. Mary Frances felt like she was 35 and had been married 10 years to an insurance salesman.

She missed Robert. Actually, she didn't miss *him*. She missed his dick, his car, and all the bars where they used to go dancing.

Her solution to Alex's demands was to bury herself in her work. She practically lived at the salon. She cut, colored, and permed career women, bored teen-agers, and lots of tiny rich Jewish women with perfect figures and bushels of wavy, mousy-brown hair — dyed blonde, of course.

Once she gave a perm to a customer's dog, a small straight-haired mutt the customer had force-fed Valium before bringing it into the salon. Before she poured a chemical on the limp animal's head, she had stormed into Alex's office.

"I don't care if she wants you to straighten her pubic hair," Alex had said. "The customer is always right."

Mary Frances later heard the dog had died of a cocaine overdose.

Her customers were like that.

They had money, they knew what they wanted, and they tipped well. Within six months, Mary Frances was able to buy a couch for her apartment, a thousand dollars of summery California clothes, and a hood ornament of a naked, male surfer for her car. With her blonde hair, tan skin, and artfully exposed cleavage, she looked like she had lived in California her entire life.

Alex became obsessed with her. He had his other girlfriends and boyfriends — he was going through a Latino phase — but she had risen to top dog. She knew how far she had climbed when he brought her home one night in June, made enthusiastic love to her, and announced over cognac on the couch that he wanted to have a child by her.

"You're out of your mind," she had said, setting her cognac down on the coffee table with a slam. "We're not even married."

"Don't be so Midwestern. Think of how beautiful our child would be."

"Alex!"

"Blonde curls, those blue eyes of yours. He'd be ... "

"Alex, you *have* two sons. You also have Margaret — and a lot of little friends."

"You're perfect breeding age," he said dreamily, swirling the cognac in its beaker. "So young, so firm. . . "

"Alex."

"He'd be gorgeous. A regular Adonis."

"Alex, I don't want children now."

He looked right at her. "So what? I'll pay."

"What?"

"You have the baby. I'll get a nanny to raise it. It will be my boy."

"What if it's a girl?"

"I'll sell her on the black market. White girl babies command big bucks out here. I know a guy who paid $85,000 for his." He shook his head thoughtfully. "All the cash he's laid out on that kid and she's not even three yet."

Mary Frances looked at him in awe. He was serious.

"You're going to pay me $85,000 to have your kid?" she said.

He eyed her over the edge of his glass. "I thought maybe you'd do it for free—out of love."

She stood up suddenly, cognac in hand. "You're a cheap son of a bitch," she hissed. She went into the kitchen and glared out the window. The pool glittered in the streetlight overhead.

"How about $25,000?" he said, following her in.

"How about dropping the whole idea."

"No. No, I'm serious."

"Where are you going to get that kind of money?"

He laughed—a musical, relaxed laugh. "Money's no problem, my dear. I can get a home-equity loan."

She turned and leaned against the counter. "Let me get this straight. I'm supposed to have your child, a child you can sell for $85,000 on the street, probably $100,000 nine months from now, and I'm supposed to get $25,000?"

"$35,000."

"Alex, I wouldn't consider it for less than $75,000."

Alex moaned. "Come on, baby, I'm taking a big risk. The kid could be born deaf, dumb, and blind."

"And I could have permanent stretch marks. $75,000. I'm still giving you $25,000 off the going market price when he's born. Plus it will be a boy. They're worth more money."

"Mary Frances, honey."

"Fuck you, Alex," she said, tossing the dregs of her cognac in the sink. She was halfway out the door when he finally agreed.

They shook hands and went to bed to celebrate their deal.

* * *

Later that night they ordered out for pizza.

"Why are you doing this?" she said, her mouth full of pepperoni.

"I want a son," he said.

"You've got two."

"They're not mine. They belong to Margaret."

"They like you well enough."

He shrugged. "She's working on them. She's going to turn them into fags. I can feel it. They won't be my boys." He brightened up. "So I'm going to buy one of my own that no one can ever take from me. I put up the money; I keep the goods."

"That's nuts, Alex," she said, licking up a string of cheese hanging from her mouth.

He shrugged. "That's the world, kid."

Chapter Twelve

Two weeks later, they went to the lawyer and signed a contract.
Mary Frances would have the baby and Alex would pay all expenses
related to her pregnancy. At birth, she'd collect $75,000 for a boy
and $60,000 for a girl. If the child was a cripple, she'd get $10,000
for the effort and they'd put it up for adoption. They would try
again — at the mutual consent of the two parties.

Alex put $75,000 in an escrow account and began interviewing
nannies. Mary Frances went off the pill and they began screwing
four or five times a week. Within three months, she was pregnant.

Her whole body went up for grabs. She became moody, her face
broke out in pimples, and she threw up every morning for six weeks.
She lost 10 pounds from dehydration, which she put back on by her
fourth month.

The obstetrician said she was doing fine, Alex walked around like
the proud poppa, and Mary Frances felt terrible. Four months into
her pregnancy she tried to talk Alex into an abortion.

"No way," he said, eating a hot dog from the grill. His sons were
over for their weekly barbeque.

"I feel like shit," she said.

"You're doing fine."

"This is awful."

"You're almost halfway there." He smeared more mustard on his
hot dog and smiled. "Think of how rich you'll be in five short
months."

She moaned. "I don't want this baby."

"Don't worry," he said. "It's not yours. Let me get you a glass a
milk."

She moaned in disgust. Alex was always pumping her full of
milk, making her eat green vegetables, and inquiring about her
health. He loved to lie in bed and stroke her stomach. She felt like
her body had been taken over by renegade ghosts. She no longer
lived there; she would only return after the baby's birth in April — if
there was anything left.

She started having nightmares about childbirth. One night she dreamed a giant doctor with a huge pair of scissors was cutting her up the middle of her stomach.

She awoke screaming.

Alex made comforting noises and brought her a big glass of milk.

The weeks plodded on. She put on more weight and Alex started dragging her to natural childbirth classes.

"Forget it!" she said. "I want to be knocked out."

"It's in the contract, remember?" he said.

"What?"

He showed her: paragraph 5, section c.

So she put on her basic black maternity dress and went to the hospital for Lamaze instruction in natural childbirth. She breathed and panted and relaxed with 15 other young mothers— all of whom were delighted to be pregnant. They spoke among themselves about "after the baby came" as if their lives would be completely changed and they would be reincarnated as fairy princesses.

"After the baby comes, this relationship is over. No more sex for hairstyling instruction. Paragraph 4, section e(2)," Mary Frances said one night as she panted and Alex counted.

He winced.

"Right?" she insisted.

"I sort of hoped you'd want to stay with me and the baby."

"You trying to save on wet nurses or what?" she snorted.

"Actually, I hoped you'd marry me."

She nearly gagged. "Are you serious?"

He nodded. The Lamaze instructor glared at them; their talking was throwing off everyone's concentration. They lowered their voices.

"Why the hell would I want to marry you?" she whispered. "You screw around, you're married already, and when Margaret gets done with you, you won't have a pot to piss in."

He shrugged as if he had just suggested they go to a movie and she had suggested dinner instead. "Just forget it, then," he said. "I just thought it would be nice for Nicholas to have a mother. You know, family life and all that."

"Nicholas?"

"My grandfather's name."

"You're naming him Nicholas?"

"I like it. He's my son."

"It's an old-man's name."

"Shut up and pant," he hissed. "I'm sorry I asked."

They joined the eager parents of tomorrow in a final and energetic round of rythmic breathing.

* * *

Nicholas Alex Thompson was born April 11th at four in the morning after 12 hours of labor. Mary Frances screamed and howled all through it, Alex by her side in the delivery room, trying to remain calm and urging her to pant.

"Fuck you!" she had yelled, her face red and covered with sweat. She grabbed at his shirt, nearly ripping off the breast pocket. "I want a shot and I want it now!"

"It will hurt the baby," he said.

"Screw the baby!"

"Push harder."

"Al-ex!"

"Nurse, give her the injection," the obstetrician mumbled, his hands covered with Mary Frances's blood.

"But it will hurt my baby," Alex said, his eyes wild.

"It's hurting your wife more," the obstetrician barked.

The nurse pushed by Alex, needle in hand. Mary Frances looked at her like the angel of relief.

"No! Don't do it!" Alex yelled, trying to grab the nurse's arm. "Think of my unborn son!"

"Get that asshole out of here," the doctor said to the tiny nurse to his left. She shuffled quickly to the operating-room door. Twenty seconds later, two orderlies hurried in and grabbed Alex, one under each arm.

"Wait a minute! Wait a minute!" he yelled as they dragged him out. He pointed at the doctor. "That man is killing my son!"

Alex was kicking one orderly in the shins when the drug took effect and Mary Frances blacked out.

* * *

She awoke in a private room with a huge bouquet of irises and baby's breath on the window sill. A bottle of intraveneous solution dripped into her arm from a bedside stand. A nurse was shaking her by the shoulder.

"Wake up, Miss Barton, it's time for your walk," she said.

A hot sun beat from behind the pulled shades. "What time is it?" Mary Frances said.

"Noon," the nurse said. "Come on, honey." Not much bigger than Mary Frances herself, she pulled Mary Frances forward and levered her onto her feet before Mary Frances could stop her. Mary Frances wavered, swaying gently from side to side. Then she shuffled forward in her terrycloth slippers, pushing her I.V. stand before her.

Everything below her waist hurt, including her feet, which ached and shot pains up her legs as she shuffled forward.

"Oh. . . shit," she mumbled under her breath.

"You're doing just fine, honey," the nurse said, as if Mary Frances had just made some polite comment about the weather. "You'll feel better soon. The first day is always the worst."

Halfway down the hall, Mary Frances remembered to ask. "Is it a boy or a girl?"

The nurse looked at her in surprise. "A boy. No one's told you yet?"

Mary Frances shook her head. A boy, a girl, she didn't care just so long as it was over.

They made their way to the nursery window. The nurse pointed out Nicholas Alex, a scrawny, sleeping bundle in a crib in the back row.

"Isn't he lovely," she said helpfully.

Mary Frances thought Nicholas Alex was the ugliest little animal she had ever seen. What a woman had to do to raise a little cash, she thought. She stared at him for 30 seconds, then turned around abruptly.

"I want to go back," she said.

The nurse looked at her, surprised. They shuffled back down the hall without a word.

Mary Frances shuffled and daydreamed of her $75,000 check. Money. Freedom. No more Alex. All that in exchange for that little

animal in the nursery, dribbling greenish goo out of its unformed
intestines.

Alex had really gotten the bad end of this deal.

She smiled to herself and pushed the nurse's hand away gently.

"Thank you," she said, smiling softly. "I think I can make it back
on my own." And she walked slowly and unsteadily back to her
room, one hand holding on to her I.V. stand like John the Baptist
leaning on his staff and heading out into the desert.

* * *

Alex thought the baby was beautiful, Mary Frances was beautiful,
and the world was beautiful. He visited her around 2 that afternoon,
a bouquet of pink tea roses in hand.

The creature was at Mary Frances's breast, nuzzling and
mewling. She felt like she was nursing some furless little creature
from the zoo. Her breasts ached already.

Nicholas Alex laid back savoring his first breast-fed breakfast.

"He's beautiful, doll, just beautiful," Alex said, letting the baby
grab his finger in its tiny fist.

The nurse came in and took Nicholas from her. Mary Frances
covered her breast with her dressing gown.

"Look at that cleavage," Alex said, leaning over her breasts.
Filled with the milk to come, her already ample breasts were a full
size larger. "How about a little taste of mother's milk?" he leered.

"Is it in the contract?" she said.

"Of course not," he said, laughing lightly. "I just thought that . . . "

"Then forget it." She pulled her robe around her more tightly.
"We're playing straight by the book."

"When did you get to be such a hard-ass?" he said, sitting down in
a stiff hospital chair. "I thought having children mellowed women."

"Yeah, look what it did for Margaret. Did she eat your dick for
breakfast before she had kids?"

He glared at her.

"When do I get my money?" she said.

"You stay at my house a week. The pediatrician certifies
Nicholas is healthy. Then I'll pay you." His voice was hard.

"Good." She scrunched down into the bed. "Now, if you'll excuse me, I'm tired. I'd like to sleep."

He leaned over to kiss her good-bye, but she turned her face away and stuck out her hand.

They shook hands.

"It's a pure business relationship now, Alex," she said, smiling.

He smiled back. "Wasn't it always?"

And he left.

* * *

The week she spent at Alex's with the baby was the longest week of her life. She wandered the house, nursing Nicholas all hours of day and night, and changing his diaper nearly every two hours.

Sometimes she sat in the big rocking chair and rocked him to sleep, crooning lullabies she remembered from her childhood. The kid would never go to sleep. He seemed to be always fussing and throwing up his meals.

She felt like she was 17-years-old and on the longest baby-sitting job of her life.

Alex was very happy. He cooed at the baby, kissed them both good-bye when he went to the salon each morning, and came home by 6 each night to take Mary Frances to dinner. Wednesday, Gabriela, the 18-year-old Guatamalen nursemaid, moved into one of the spare bedrooms. Mary Frances got the distinct impression that if Gabriela had her way, Nicholas would soon have a darker-skinned sibling to keep him company. Gabriela adored Alex and doted on his infant son. She wore her hair in a long dark braid down her back and never spoke unless spoken to.

Alex must have had enough of smart-mouthed women.

Thursday, Alex took the baby to the pediatrician, who pronounced him healthy and strong. Friday morning, they went to the bank and Mary Frances got her $75,000 cashier's check.

She and Alex returned to his house. She was supposed to pack her bags and leave.

"I don't need you to come with me," she said. "I can pack myself."

"I just want to make sure you're alright," he said. Actually, he wanted to make sure she didn't steal the baby. He'd read all those articles about birth mothers who ran off with their newborn children just after they'd been asked to turn them over to the parents who'd paid for them.

He needn't have worried. Mary Frances could hardly wait to get out of his house, back to her apartment, and back to work.

The cab she had called pulled up. She was just lugging her suitcase to the door when the mailman slipped a sheave of letters through the mail slot. An official-looking envelope addressed to her slid to the floor. Without thinking, she stuffed it in her purse. Then she opened the door, and dragged her suitcase outside.

"Alex," she called back to him. "You could at least give me a hand." But Alex was standing with his arm around Gabriela, both of them gazing enraptured at Nicholas, who was sleeping in Gabriela's arms. With Alex's white skin and Gabriela's dark beauty, they looked like the perfect biracial couple posing for the cover of a UNICEF Christmas card.

"Al-ex!" Mary Frances yelled.

He looked up. "Oh yes," he said, waving distractedly. "Good-bye. See you at the shop." Then he went back to cooing to Nicholas.

Mary Frances could have been the departing cleaning lady instead of the mother of his newborn son.

She shut the main door to the house with a ferocious slam and climbed into the cab. She could hardly wait to get home, do her nails, and contemplate how she was going to spend her $75,000.

With its one window closed, her apartment was like walking into a vacuum-sealed bottle sitting in the sun. In the last two weeks, she'd barely been home. She threw open the window, put some ice in a glass, and poured herself a Diet Coke. Then she lay back on her couch and stared at the telephone wires outside her window.

She was rich now. Not rich rich. But rich enough compared to where she had come from. She sipped her drink.

Best of all, she was free of Alex. Her apprenticeship was over; no more sex-on-demand. As of Monday she would be a full-fledged, Gerrard-Herrand stylist. She could go anywhere with those credentials and make good money. Alex had promised her a raise to $25,000 a year. With experience, she'd earn more. Eventually, she could even start her own salon and create her own hairstyling dynasty. She could be a rich woman then.

And she had $75,000 right now, just for popping out Nicholas Alex Thompson.

She sipped her pop and touched her breasts. They ached with milk. The pill the hospital had given her to shut off her milk production had not yet taken effect. She got up, rummaged through her suitcase, and found her breast pump. She pumped her breasts then poured the thin white liquid down the sink.

Alex had wanted her to pump her breasts everyday and ship it back to Gabriela to feed Nicholas. Mary Frances had axed that idea in their second negotiating session.

"I'm not a cow," she had snapped.

"But it's better for the baby. . ." Alex had started to say, then shut up when he saw the cold look in her eye.

He had dropped the issue.

Now she had money, time, freedom. She patted the loose muscle on her stomach. In six weeks, she'd have her figure, too. She resolved to join the Beverly Hills Workout World Figure Salon. Alex had given her a week off with pay. She could join Workout World today!

She got up from the couch and headed for her bureau, where she rummaged through a drawer and unearthed a pair of green nylon shorts and a tee-shirt. She was digging through her purse for her car keys when the letter she had picked up at Alex's fell out. It was from the hospital.

Damn it, she thought. Another bill she should have given Alex. Angrily, she tore it open.

It was a photocopied form letter with her name and social security number typed in by a computer printer. The letter was signed by a machine: Dr. Marc Singer, director of clinical services.

"Dear Ms. Barton," the letter began. "Recent blood tests taken at our facility indicate that you have tested positive for the presence of the virus responsible for Auto-Immune Deficiency Syndrome (AIDS). While this does not mean you will necessarily contract the disease, it is a strong indicator of a high degree of risk and indicates that you can spread this disease to other parties through sexual relations and other modes of communicability.

"Although it is not required, we request that you come in for an immediate counseling session . . ."

The letter dropped from Mary Frances's hand. She started to tremble.

AIDS.

She was going to die of AIDS. Everyone who tested positive for the virus got sick and died. They never told you that, but it was true.

She was a dead woman.

She staggered back to her couch and fell back into it. She gazed out at her telephone wires, the wires she had been happily staring at only five minutes ago when she had her whole life ahead of her.

Now her "whole life" was a hell of a lot shorter.

Two years? Seven years? Who knew how long she had.

They must have made a mistake. This was crazy. She was only 22-years-old.

She picked up the letter off the floor. No. It was her name and her social security number.

Her skin crawled. She could see her body decaying before her eyes. She'd get weak, she'd get fevers, she'd curl up and die in some ratty little hole of an apartment, without money, without friends, her body covered with sores, her sheets stinking of her own excrement.

Like this apartment. She looked around at the sickly green walls and the waterspot on the ceiling over her dying asparagus fern. What an awful place to die, staring up at the waterspot, her life slipping away. She closed her eyes and imagined herself dead. She started to cry.

Stop it! she told herself.

Who could have given her AIDS?

Only old fags and bisexuals got AIDS.

Alex. He slept with men.

He'd probably given her the damn disease. That meant he had it too.

And so did Nicholas Alex.

Her heart stopped.

When Alex found out, he'd want his money back. He might have gotten his letter already. "Dear Mr. Thompson, we regret to inform you that your son, Nicholas Alex Thompson, recently born at this facility, has tested positive for the . . ."

Maybe they hadn't run tests on Nicholas's blood yet. Maybe they wouldn't.

But Alex would find out. That idiot pediatrician who had said Nicholas was healthy would eventually test the kid's blood. Alex would rage; he'd demand his money back. He'd fire her from the salon. Who'd want to work with an AIDS carrier?

She couldn't let a soul know about this. Her life would be over.

Her life was over already.

At least let her live out the several years she had left.

Maybe they'd discover a vaccine? Maybe there was a cure?

Maybe the cow would jump over the moon.

She shouldn't panic. No. Don't panic. Sweat dripped down her armpits.

That bastard, Alex.

She crumpled the letter into a ball and dialled Colleen's number. Colleen was the only one in the family who knew she'd had a baby much less sold it. Colleen had thought it a great idea; she wanted to know if Alex wanted one by her, too. Maybe he had a friend? They had laughed about it.

The phone rang at Colleen's, but no one answered.

Mary Frances opened her closet and stared at herself in the full-length mirror. She saw a tired-looking, pretty young blonde with eyes red from crying. She didn't look like someone ready to contract an incurable disease and die from it.

"You're not dead yet," she whispered to the mirror. "Not by a long shot."

And she put on her gym shoes, got in her car, and drove to Workout World.

But instead of joining the club, she just paid for one class.

After all, she was leaving the country tomorrow.

Chapter Thirteen

The travel agent got her the last seat on British Airways' 4:30 flight to London the next day. Mary Frances booked it under her new name, Rocket Caswell. Rocket had been a girlfriend of Colleen's. A singer in a rock band, she had overdosed on heroin one night in Denver at the age of 19. Rocket had had great hair. Naturally pale blonde, she had dyed it orange trimmed in black.

"I want to look like Halloween," she'd said.

Mary Frances liked that. The "Caswell" was more of an accident. Mary Frances had closed her eyes and picked a name out of the phone book. After rejecting Cazouletti, Czernaksizki, and Chang, she'd hit on "Caswell" with relief.

The airplane was crowded and smelly before it even took off. The woman to her left by the window had a baby on her lap. Twelve hours she intended to hold him there. To Mary Frances's right was a teen-aged boy tuned into a Walkman. He had bad earphones. Mary Frances could hear the tinny drums and high-pitched squeals of the singers. They sounded like a trained flea circus playing inside a bottle. Maybe they had tiny little costumes, too. Tiny leather pants, tiny guitars, tiny manes of wild blonde frizzy hair fluffed out around their flea heads like cotton candy.

Flea rock stars!

She giggled. The mother next to her gave her a disapproving look.

Mary Frances was very stoned. She'd gone to her workout, booked her flight, and smoked all the dope she could handle without passing out. The rest had gone down the toilet. She couldn't risk getting caught with drugs.

Then she had withdrawn all her money from the bank, in cash. The bank gave her a hard time. A clerk with a gravy stain on his tie made her show him every piece of identification in her wallet, then fill out some form for the IRS. She scribbled gibberish on the form, converted $500 into British pounds, and stuffed the money in her flight bag.

She nestled into her seat and thought of London.

Her mind went blank. She'd never been there in her life; in fact, she'd never been east of Cleveland. She once thought she would go to Paris, the summer after she finished high school. On a whim, she'd gotten her passport.

But the urge had passed. It had been part of a two-week fling she'd had with a homesick Frenchman, stuck in Chicago on business for six months. He had spoken beautiful English. He had assured her the French spoke — French.

So she was on her way to London. They spoke English, it was out of the country, and Vidal Sassoon had a big salon there. She'd walk in and ask for a job. They wouldn't care who she was as long as she could cut hair.

Maybe she'd need a work permit? Maybe they'd confiscate her money at the airport? Maybe they'd do blood tests at the airport, find out she was an AIDS carrier, and throw her out of the country?

Maybe they wouldn't find out shit and she'd live happily ever after.

Maybe this AIDS business was a colossal screw-up. Hospitals were always sending people the wrong forms with the wrong information. She pulled her compact from her purse, popped it open, and looked in the mirror. Other than the black, druggy pupils of her eyes, she looked fine. She took her lipstick and smeared a pink line across her mouth.

She'd be fine; this AIDS thing was a lot of hooey.

She felt so good she gave a big friendly smile to a businessman walking down the aisle to his seat. He smiled back in surprise.

The stewardesses filed up the aisles and began their ritual dance with seatbelts and oxygen masks.

Ten minutes later the plane was in the air. Twenty minutes later, the stewardesses passed out earphones. Mary Frances plugged into the rock music channel on the airplane's stero system and fell asleep. When she awoke, they were refueling in New York. But they took off again without letting a soul off the plane.

* * *

The sun set and rose over the Atlantic in three short hours, and on a beautiful, clear morning they descended to London's Heathrow

Airport, coasting down over neat, intensely green fields. Heathrow reminded Mary Frances of a more diminutive and beat-up O'Hare.

She recovered her battered plastic suitcase, told customs she was a tourist, and found the train to the city. On a whim, she got off at Paddington Station, following a cluster of American students who got off there, too. The area was filled with cheap rooming houses, Indians from India, and tiny foreign cars. After the spaciousness of Los Angeles, London's neat, narrow streets and cheek-to-jowl buildings reminded Mary Frances of a toy town filled with full-size people.

Exhausted, she rang the bell of the first rooming house she found, a narrow, four-story building with two defaced statues of lions crumbling on the front porch. A heavy women with bad teeth and a worn, flowered apron answered the door.

Rooms were $50 a night, including breakfast, with a bath down the hall.

Mary Frances was appalled. She could get a weekend package at the Hollywood Stardust Hilton in off-season for $65 a night. "Rowton House," as this dump was called, had nothing but peeling paint, worn carpets, and wobbly formica furniture. It smelled of stale cooking oil.

She'd find something better later. Right now she needed sleep. The fat woman led her to a tiny unheated room with a coin-operated space heater in the fireplace.

They didn't even give you heat in this cheap country.

Mary Frances paid for her room and fed the heater some coins. It made a grinding noise then started up. It threw off a fair amount of heat.

She lay back on the bed and felt like she was going to go through the floor. It was the softest mattress she'd ever laid on in her life. The springs must have been a foot apart.

She fell asleep and woke at five that afternoon with a backache. She went downstairs to the small living room that served as a lobby.

"I'd like to call America," she said.

The pale young woman behind the counter pointed wordlessly to a pay phone on the wall and exchanged Mary Frances's paper money for coins. After four operators and an eternity of clicking and wire-crossing, Colleen's phone rang.

"Hullo?"

"Colleen?"

"A collect call from Mary Frances Barton. . ."

"Mary Frances?" The phone dropped with a thunk, then Colleen came back on. "What the hell . . ."

"I'm in London."

"London? London, England?"

"Will you accept the charges?" the operator interrupted.

"Sure. Sure. Mary Frances?"

"Go ahead, please." The operator clicked off in a haze of static and they were left alone on the wire, a slight hum in the background.

"I'm on vacation," Mary Frances chirped.

"Vacation? It's 9 o'clock in the morning here. You know I work until 2 Friday nights."

"Sorry." Mary Frances was silent a moment. "Actually, I'm in deep shit."

The line was silent, with only the hum in the background.

"I think I have AIDS."

The line was silent again.

"You take the test?"

"I tested positive."

"Testing positive isn't having it. Half my friends test positive. None of us is sick."

"You positive, too?"

"I never took the test." Mary Frances heard Colleen's lighter click as she lit up a cigarette. Colleen inhaled deeply. "Everybody carries that damn disease. I wouldn't worry. We'll all go out at once."

"Easy for you to say. You don't have it."

"I might." She inhaled again. "But I don't care. I'm still here. I'm still painting. I could be hit by a truck tomorrow." Mary Frances heard her exhale deeply. "So how's London?" Colleen said, as if they had just been discussing Mary Frances's tour of the lake country.

"Fine. Fine. I just got here."

"How long you staying?"

"Forever."

"What?"

"I can't come home. Alex will be looking for me. When he finds out his baby is AIDS-positive he'll want his money back."

"Don't be such a chicken."

"I'm being a realist. Don't tell anyone you spoke to me and know where I am, not even Mom."

"You're being paranoid."

"I'll write you when I'm settled." She peeled a long strip of green paint off the crumbling wall. "I have a new name, too. I'm calling myself Rocket Carswell."

"After Rocket Grotowski?"

"Yeah."

"Rocket wouldn't like that. She was very possessive of her name. Everybody was trying to rip off her name, it was so awesome."

"She's dead. What does it matter?"

"Well, it *was* her name."

"Yeah. Right." Colleen was giving her a headache. "Remember, don't tell anyone you know where I am. I wouldn't put it past Alex to come after you looking for me."

"Don't worry. I'm cool." She giggled. Mary Frances wondered if Colleen was smoking dope instead of cigarettes.

"Are you high?" she said.

"A little."

"Aren't you ever straight anymore?"

"No."

Mary Frances muttered a string of obscenities under her breath. "I'll write soon," she said. "Good bye."

"Bye," Colleen giggled.

Mary Frances hung up the phone and leaned against the wall. She felt sick in the pit of her stomach.

She'd never felt so alone in her entire life.

* * *

The next morning Mary Frances put her flight bag of money in the hotel safe. Then she worked her way through her first English breakfast—one thin runny egg, two slices of white toast, and strong tea—all served in the basement of the house, a dreadful, blue-painted room with a view of feet walking along the sidewalk, viewed through the grillwork over the basement window.

Mary Frances booked her room for another night then asked a different pale young woman behind the desk how to get to Vidal Sassoon's hair salon. She had never heard of it, but the fat lady in the flowered apron had. She gave Mary Frances such complicated directions, Mary Frances wrote them down.

It took her an hour after getting off at the wrong "tube" stop and wandering down crooked streets to find Sassoon's. The salon was in an expensive area filled with pricey boutiques and trees. The inside of the salon resembled Gerrard Herrand's — all chrome, glass, and abstract prints. The women stylists had cut their hair into clumps and patches rigid with some mud-like substance. The men were all gay and thin and wore narrow leather ties and silver hoop earrings in their right ears.

She asked at the desk for the manager.

He was out; the head creative man came out instead.

Mary Frances gawked. Tony Hendricks looked like a red-headed version of Alex.

"Where you from, dearie?" he asked.

"Los Angeles."

"Where'd you train?"

"Romeo Carlucci's." Carlucci's was one of Herrand's big competitors in L.A.

"You know Oscar there?"

"Yeah. Yeah, sure," she said. Who the hell was Oscar?

"A good man. A genius with shape."

"Yeah."

Tony chattered on about Oscar for another two minutes then shifted gears. "You have a work permit?" he said.

"No."

"No problem. Come back tomorrow at 10. We're cutting walk-ins for the school then. We'll see what you can do."

She headed for the street, exhilerated. With nothing to do for the rest of the day, she took a bus tour of London, ate dinner at a bad delicatessan, and sent Colleen a postcard.

She was back at Sassoon's the next morning, ready to cut. She gave some acne-ridden girl from Cheapside a Lady-Di hairdo with flying wing bangs, spiked the hair of four young men, and gave an American tourist an asymmetrical bob.

Tony was impressed.

"You can start Wednesday," he said. "We open at 10. 150 quid a week, plus tips. Everybody likes Yank hairdressers. You'll do great."

She shook his hand vigorously, went back to her rooming house, and took a long nap on her lumpy bed.

Wednesday, she cut seven heads and dyed two women red.

Thursday, Tony took her to dinner.

Friday, he took her to bed.

She should have told him she was an AIDS carrier, but one thing led to another. Before she knew it, he was inside her, pumping and groaning and she was pumping and groaning back.

The announcement would have ruined the moment, not to mention her career.

He probably would have pulled out, scrubbed his dick with laundry soap, and called a doctor – or the police. She'd be fired on the spot. And he was really a nice man, much nicer than Alex, and more muscular. Alex had been too scrawny.

Besides, she wasn't an AIDS carrier. The hospital had confused her records with someone else's. She was fine, she thought, admiring her lovely white body in the soft light of Tony's bathroom.

Not fine enough to chance going back to L.A. It could take months to clear her medical records. Alex would want his money back. He'd ruin her reputation and the world would treat her like a leper – just based on the rumour that she carried AIDS.

It wasn't worth it.

She had everything to live for in London. Tony was falling hard for her, she liked the salon, everyone spoke English. Next year she could even chance a visit to L.A. to pick up some clothes and tour around.

Colleen would come over this summer for a few weeks. They would wander Europe, smoke Moroccan dope, and pick up German schoolboys for casual sex.

They'd have a blast.

Two weeks after her arrival in London, she collected her first paycheck. The week after that, she began sharing a flat in

Kensington with a girl from the salon, a fat little woman named Margaret with a heavy Scottish burr.

She decided she liked London.

Chapter Fourteen

Mary Frances progressed up the salon pecking order. Two years after her arrival in London, she was one of Sassoon's best stylists. Her customers were wealthy women from the upper class with pale blue eyes, fine skin, and thin, exquisite figures. She cut lots of pageboys and did lots of long, loose permanents.

She took up with a crowd from the salon that frequented punk bars and dyed their hair in splotches of purple. She dyed a green streak in her hair, started wearing black stockings and metal studded bracelets, and triple-pierced her ears. Her customers, clad in their conservative tweeds, loved it.

One with a daffily open attitude toward the lower classes even invited her to a garden party, where she was a hit with the older men. She started sleeping with a low-level viscomte in the House of Lords, the delegate from some backwater suburb south of London.

At the same time, she kept sleeping with Tony from the salon. In her constant jockeying back and forth between their apartments, she was reminded of her simultaneous affairs with Robert and Alex.

Time had softened their hard-cut images in her mind. She thought of them fondly now. They had been her "American phase."

Alex had indeed called Colleen looking for Mary Frances. Colleen had been drunk when he called and couldn't remember exactly which country Mary Frances had gone to.

"I think it was Mexico," she'd told him.

"It's just that I would like to see her again," said Alex. "Tell her Nicholas is doing well." He'd sent a photo of the healthy, blonde-haired baby to Colleen, who forwarded it to Mary Frances.

Mary Frances was surprised to see her own eyes looking back at her from out of the photo. The kid had her squarish face and compact features.

But she was most interested in his blooming good health. Clearly, the kid didn't have AIDS. Those idiots at the hospital really got their signals crossed. She ought to sue them.

She contemplated bailing out of London with its fairy-tale buildings and winding streets for the broad, open greed of L.A., but she was doing so well. She liked the British at the salon; no one worked too hard and they liked to drink and do cocaine. With just a little initiative and skill, she was moving up. She got a job offer from a competitor at 400 quid a week; Tony started talking about making her assistant creative director and offered her 425 a week to stay—both to keep her at the salon and in his bed.

"You're completely mercenary," he'd told her one Sunday over breakfast.

"Yes," she said, smiling, "of course. Isn't everyone?"

After three years of living in London, Mary Frances decided to visit L.A. She was homesick. Maybe she'd even stay. Someone might offer her a good job, especially as she was now assistant creative director at one of the best salons in London.

Three weeks before her trip, she came down with a bad cold. She thought nothing of it until one day she could hardly get out of bed. She was really sick. Alarmed, she called Tony. He had one of the shampoo girls take her to the public clinic where she sat for four hours, dizzy and nauseous, in a waiting room of fat, gray-skinned women, whining children, and a few decrepit drunks.

The doctor, a young Pakistani with luminous brown eyes, told her she had the flu and sent her home with the pills. He promised she'd be better in a week. She took her pills religiously four times a day and proceeded to get worse. In four days, an ugly red rash started appearing on her legs and torso. She could hardly answer the phone when Tony called.

"Hello?" she rasped.

"Rocket?"

"Yeah?"

"How are you?"

"What?"

"Are you all right?"

"Who is this?" she said. Suddenly her hand lost its strength. She dropped the phone.

"Hello? Hello?" she could hear Tony's voice coming over the phone as it banged against the side of the bedstand. She lay back against her pillows and fainted.

Twenty minutes later, Tony banged on her door. Awakened, she managed to stagger to the door and open it.

He looked at her in horror.

"Hi ya, Tony," she said. "Did you just call me?" Then she fainted again. He caught her just as her head reached the level of his knees. He dragged her to her bed and pulled her into it. She had a high fever.

He picked up her phone, called his private doctor, and insisted that he or one of his staff meet him at the hospital. The doctor clearly thought he was overreacting, but agreed. Tony wrapped Mary Frances in a blanket and carried her to his car.

She was partially conscious again, but kept pulling on his shirt in delerium and saying, "Hello, sweet Tony, did you just call?" Then she'd smile and lay back in his arms.

At the hospital, an orderly came out with a cart and wheeled Mary Frances into the waiting room while Tony straightened out the paperwork with the admitting office. Then the orderly wheeled her to a private room in a back wing of the hospital. A nurse took Mary Frances's temperature, and the resident on duty dropped in to see his latest charge.

He immediately started her on an I.V.

By that evening, they decided she had a severe form of influenza. But they couldn't figure out the rash that was now spreading down over her legs, an ugly collection of raised bumps and flat expanses of red. They started tests.

The doctor tried to get a medical history out of Mary Frances, but she was nearly always unconscious or delirious. Two days after she'd arrived at the hospital, she came to long enough to press the nurse's call button.

"Tell them I tested positive for AIDS," she said, grabbing the tiny Pakistani nurse by her belt. "AIDS. Tell them it's AIDS," she said, then she fainted again.

The nurse immediately called her supervisor who called Tony's doctor who ordered more tests.

Twenty-four hours later they knew.

Mary Frances had some strange, opportunistic infection that was ravaging her body.

They pumped her full of some antibiotic, the rash started receding, and she regained consciousness. She could even sit up for awhile. She'd lost 12 pounds in 10 days. She felt giddy and light-headed. She started coughing up green phlegm from her lungs.

All the nurses and doctors started wearing gloves and masks around her. They moved her to an even more remote floor.

Tony showed up that night, pale and nervous, a bouquet of flowers in hand. The doctor had told him.

He looked at her, an I.V. coming out of one arm, tubes coming out her nose, and a collection of pans, kleenex, and bottles on her side table.

He was next.

"You knew all along, didn't you?" he said.

She nodded.

"I thought so."

"I brought these for you," he said, throwing the flowers on the bed. "I hope you rot in hell."

He walked out of the room and went downstairs to admitting, where he announced that he would no longer pay Mary Frances's medical bills.

Within five hours, they'd stripped her of her tubes and bedding and shipped her off to the public charity hospital where they gave her a lumpy soft bed in a ward of 25 people. The noise was awful. She could never sleep.

Nevertheless, she improved.

Two weeks after her attack they sent her home in a cab. She stumbled up the stairs to her small flat and collapsed on her bed, exhausted. She had been living alone for two years now and her first impulse was to look around her apartment in relief. The paintings of flowers on the wall from Colleen, her big wide bed with its blue-flowered spread. Tony had had one of the girls from the salon straighten the place up in her absence.

Mary Frances tottered to a big overstuffed chair and collapsed into it. The four walls were starting to close in on her.

This was her coffin, not her home. She was too weak to work, too weak to shop for food. She'd have to have someone come in and help her. The social worker at the public hospital had given her the number of a local AIDS support group.

She dialled the number; no one answered.

She felt faint and lay down in her bed. She stared up at the peeling white paint on the high plaster ceiling, then fell asleep.

When she awoke, she was able to get up and find some crackers in her kitchen. She ate them slowly. They were the last food she had, other than some breakfast cereal.

She dialled the AIDS group again; no answer.

She hobbled back to bed and fell into it.

She never got out of it again. She fell into a coma, a peaceful nothingness.

Two weeks later she died.

The landlady found her three weeks later when the tenants next door started complaining of a bad smell. The landlady screamed, called the janitor to open the windows, then called the police.

An enterprising fellow, the janitor went through all Mary Frances's things before the police arrived. His eyes nearly popped out when he found her flight bag and its $75,000 in cash still stuffed under the bed. Mary Frances had been saving it for a rainy day.

He wrote a note that another tenant in another building had complained about a backed-up toilet. He had to go take care of it.

Then he taped the note to the door and left.

He was never seen again.

The End

Black

Chapter One

Harry Davis's great-grandmother had been a slave in Alabama.

His grandfather had been a sharecropper, his father a porter for the railroad, and his mother a cleaning lady at the 433 W. Clayton Street Office Building in Gary, Indiana.

But he had topped them all. He was a postal supervisor for six post offices in Gary with 36 people working under him. A wirey little black man, he wore a neat postal uniform to work everyday, read books on power management, and had reached a federal civil service ranking of 17, thus bringing his salary to $35,499 a year, plus benefits.

At 45 years of age he had 20 years of service with the Postal Service. He planned to retire at age 55 when he had 30 years.

Harry had a modest blue house in Horton Beach, a suburb of Gary, a lovely wife of 21 years named Millicent, and two children in college. The boy was going to be an electrical engineer; his sister, a teacher of retarded children.

College was a strain on the family budget, even though both kids went to Purdue's North Central campus near Michigan City and lived at home. They needed cars and clothes and books and tuition. He couldn't let them work; they needed the time to study.

So, once again, Millie's salary saved the day. For 10 years, she had commuted every day to Chicago, working downtown in a highrise office building as a secretary. Now her $21,500 salary went to pay for the kids and taxes. He found it depressing how much they paid in taxes but Millie bore it all cheerfully.

"Think of all the social security and pension benefits we'll get when we retire," she'd say as she trudged off to the train at dawn in some freezing rain. "We're doing well."

Millie's mother had been a huge black woman named Esmeralda. She had worked in a cafeteria her whole life, opening huge cans of cooked green beans and shlepping big boxes from a warehouse. Millie had an indoor job with no heavy lifting; she was doing much better.

Harry Davis also had a brother, Mike.

A wiry man like his brother, Mike was 10 years younger but had gone even further in life. He worked for IBM as a sales manager in Chicago. He had 24 salesmen reporting to him, made $70,000 a year plus bonuses, and lived in an expensive house in Naperville, a white suburb of the city. He sent his two kids to the local all-white high school.

His wife, Elizabeth, had joined the Naperville chapter of the American Association of University Women and spent her days attending luncheons, going to lectures on antiques and interior decorating, and campaigning for money to expand the local library.

A tall black woman who was losing the battle of the waistline, Elizabeth acted more white than white people. She was always the only black at any event she attended, her dark skin immediately drawing the observer's eye. She even spoke like a white woman, down to an upper-class Boston accent, a vestige of her childhood in that city.

It was hard to believe that her father had been a short-order cook in south Boston, her mother a teacher's aide, and that she had picked up that accent at night, remembering the words she had heard well-dressed white people say during the day and rolling them over and over again in her mouth as she went to sleep.

Now, she could turn the accent on and off, waltzing into it on command and out of it into the hard singsong black accent she had learned on the Boston streets.

But she *never* did that. Her husband would not approve.

Elizabeth thought Millicent below her and liked to snub her.

Millicent thought Elizabeth a "stuck-up nigger" as she once told Harry in a fit of rage after Elizabeth had told her her slip was showing at a dinner party. Elizabeth had waited until the room was filled with guests drinking cocktails and then announced it so loudly that Millie had blushed and left the room.

Millie swore she wouldn't speak to Elizabeth again, a threat Harry had almost agreed to as a good idea.

Harry Davis didn't like Mike or his wife; he was jealous of his brother's success and found Elizabeth obnoxious. But he was a strong believer in the family. Families had to stick together, especially black families.

"We have to be role models for the children," he lectured Millie. "They need to see a strong presence of adults in their lives."

"Let them see it with some other relatives," Millie said. "That woman is a complete bitch." Then she stomped off to the kitchen and her cooking before her husband could respond.

Harry sighed and turned on the TV to the Bears game. Christian charity, that's what Millie needed. A deacon in the Mt. Olivet Missionary Baptist Church of Horton Beach, Harry sang and prayed every Sunday with fervor, thanking God for all He had given him and praying that He would give him more. Another climb in the civil service rankings would help. They could use another $5,000 in income. His old Chevy was starting to break down and he needed a new one.

Instead, God sent him his nephew and his niece.

* * *

One Sunday evening in late October, Elizabeth and Mike were killed in a car accident coming home from a charity auction for the Episcopal church in LaGrange. Harry and Millie were the children's only relatives north of the Mason-Dixon line. Harry had never liked Mike but he would have never sent his nephew and niece back down South to live with their grandmother. He hated Alabama more than he hated his brother.

So, one moment Harry was watching "The Sunday Night Movie," sprawled out on the couch eating popcorn, both his children in their rooms studying. Five minutes later, a telephone call from the state police sent him grabbing his coat, running for the car, and yelling at Millie to come with him.

They suddenly had two more children to raise.

* * *

As befitting two children who had just lost their parents, Pamela and Edward Davis were a mess.

For six months after she moved in with her aunt and uncle, Pamela, the 14-year-old, kept breaking into tears for no apparent reason. A big-boned, wide-hipped young girl like her mother, she would be sitting on the couch in Harry's family room watching the weeknight sit-coms with the family. Suddenly she would start sobbing, big tears glistening on her dark cheeks, her eyes red and swollen.

They were sympathetic for the first three months, turning off the TV and huddling around her. The fourth month, they started getting annoyed, the fifth only Millie, driven by maternal pity, came to her side. By the sixth month, they ignored her. By the seventh month she had stopped crying entirely and had become sullen and reserved.

Pamela's older brother, 16-year-old Edward, was more self-possessed. A tall boy with his father's bony build, he sobbed uncontrollably the week of his parents' death, then lapsed into a state of quiet shock. He ate his meals, went to school, did his homework, and smiled all the time — a sad little distant smile.

The kid was distantly polite and acted like a gracious houseguest, constantly concerned that he was putting someone out on his behalf and trying to make himself as inconspicuous as possible.

It drove Harry crazy.

"You know, Ted," he told the boy bluntly one night while they were watching TV, "you're my son now just as you were your dad's son before. You have two fathers."

Ted winced and smiled his sad smile.

"Yes, Uncle Harry," he said, "I know. Thank you for taking me and Pamela in."

"But this is your home. This is where you live."

He smiled another sad smile. "Yes," he said again. "Thank you." And he sat stiffly in his chair and watched TV as if he were in an airport waiting room waiting for his plane to start boarding.

Needless to say, other than the occasional sobbing confessions of misery from Pamela during her crying fits, neither child saw fit to confide in their aunt and uncle about what was bothering them in their lives. They just went to school every day, came back, and locked themselves in the bedrooms they shared with their cousins until dinner.

Then they came out, ate, and went back to their rooms where they listened to music and supposedly did their homework.

Harry continued to worry about them. He confided his fears to his 20-year-old son, Franklin.

A gregarious little man with a patch of red in his close-cut hair, Franklin was busy blundering his way through Purdue's civil-engineering program. He had originally started out in electrical engineering, but to Harry's dismay, it had proved far too difficult. Now Franklin was barely passing civil engineering and talking about becoming a lawyer.

His father was appalled. The only lawyer in the family was a cousin of Millie's who had defrauded the government of some urban-housing grant money and run off to Costa Rica with his English mistress, a blonde-haired white woman 20 years his junior.

Franklin told his father that his cousin Ted was "a stuck-up Uncle Tom" and it didn't pay to worry about him. "He'll always land on top," he said, bitterly, "he's whiter than white people."

In fact, Ted did bring in good grades and was well-liked by his teachers. As for Pamela, Franklin shook off his father's fears with a shrug. "She's just a girl, Dad," he said. "Wait until she finds a boyfriend. She'll be doin' real fine then." He leered at his father and winked.

Harry started worrying that Pamela would become an unwed mother. She brought home mediocre report cards. Her teachers never said anything about her. And Harry's 18-year-old daughter, Lavonne Rae, didn't like her at all.

"She's stuck-up," she told her father six weeks after her cousins had joined the household. And Lavonne had left the house, slamming the door behind her. Her heavy bottom in tight jeans swung from side to side as she walked.

Harry decided his children hated their two cousins.

* * *

He pinned the blame on overcrowding. He was housing four teen-agers and two adults in a three-bedroom house with one bathroom. Within two months of moving in, Franklin was already screaming at his ever-smiling cousin Ted to "get his fat black ass out of that bathroom" when the entire family descended on it in the early morning hours.

Harry had solved that by drawing up a schedule of who got to use the bathroom when.

But he couldn't solve the problem of the children sharing bedrooms. Harry's house dated from the 1950s. A boxy little saltbox, it had only 1200 square feet of space and three tiny bedrooms.

It was bad enough when Franklin and Lavonne had their own rooms. They complained constantly of their tight quarters. Now that their cousins had moved in, Harry had been forced to install bunk beds. Franklin had just glared at him, but Lavonne had cried for a week when her pink-ruffled bed piled with fluffy stuffed animals and flounced pillows had been sold and replaced with an austere set of bunks.

"It looks like a prison cell," she had sobbed in her mother's arms. "I can't live there."

But she had.

Harry wondered if they should have just kept Lavonne's fluffy pink bed and let Pamela sleep on the floor. The girl didn't seem to care about anything, including where she laid her head at night.

But the real problems in the family began when Ted and Pamela went to school. Products of a school system in an affluent white suburb, they found Horton-Gary High School confusing at best. From a high school of 1,200 students where they were two of 24 blacks, they went to one of 1,500 students where 1,300 were black. The remaining 200 were mostly Slavic whites with broad faces, foul mouths, and no aspirations to be much more than secretaries and janitors.

Ted wanted to be a doctor; Pamela had thought of being a fashion designer. But everyone at Horton-Gary seemed to have no goals beyond getting laid, finding drugs, and having money to buy cars.

The black girls were continually getting pregnant and dropping out of school. They announced their pregnancies to their girlfriends in the bathrooms, the school's social centers. Their delighted shrieks and giggling spilled out into the corridors.

The boys were a rough lot. Six gangs fought for control of the hallways and the principal, an old white man with a perpetual scowl, called in the police twice a month to keep the gangs and drug dealers out of the halls.

One day the principal called a surprise search of the boys for weapons. The shocked teachers found enough knives and guns to form foot-high piles of weaponry on five trays from the cafeteria. One boy carried three knives and a snub-nosed revolver.

Considering the source of the student body, none of this behavior was surprising. Most were poor, black, and from broken homes. Horton had a proud little enclave of middle-class blacks and some whites who refused to leave, but it was surrounded by poor blacks.

The little town was getting overrun. The poor blacks moved into the cheaper, rundown houses, let their children run wild, and brought in their nasty friends from the seedier parts of Gary. Horton Beach had been nice when Harry and Millie had moved there 20 years ago; now they avoided many streets. They couldn't afford to move again, especially with Ted and Pamela to watch over.

Harry had hoped that his brother would have left some money for his children, money that could be used for their education or to move the entire family to better quarters.

But Mike's estate was a ruin. Mike and Elizabeth Davis had lived beyond their means. They had no savings and the proceeds from Mike's profit-sharing at IBM went to pay off their $37,832.46 in credit-card debt. The profits from the sale of their house paid off their $50,000 home-equity loan.

Mike had no life insurance. His policy through IBM had lapsed; he'd stopped making payments for the last eight months, apparently to meet other expenses.

The children ended up with $10,000 from the sale of the house and the family's furniture. Pamela got her mother's fur coat and a few pieces of fancy jewelry.

Otherwise, they were indigent.

Harry prayed hard every Sunday, asking God what to do, but He didn't respond. So he put the $10,000 in a five-year CD at the Horton Beach State Bank and brought home his premium – a pink electric blanket with dark pink-ribbon trim.

It was the only material benefit he ever received from taking in his orphaned niece and nephew.

Chapter Two

Their first weeks at Horton-Gary High sent Ted and Pamela into shock. Within the first two weeks, three black girls corralled Pamela in a bathroom and burned cigarette holes in two of her nice wool skirts. One tried to rip her favorite pink cashmere cardigan off her back.

Pamela broke into tears and reported the incident to her gym teacher. The woman took her to the administration office to fill out a complaint. Since Pamela didn't know the full names of her attackers and was afraid to find out, she couldn't complete the form.

She went home, put away her lovely wool skirts and sweaters, and started to wear the jeans and sweatshirt she had used for yardwork to school every day.

Ted was more obstinate. He wore neat buttoned-down shirts and chinos to school, enduring the taunts of the "Super-Fly" crowd with a cool indifference.

Both children took immense abuse for their accents. Elizabeth, anxious that her children succeed, had carefully guarded their tongues from any acquaintance with black English. In fact, both children spoke with a slight East-Coast accent.

Every time they tried to recite in class, their classmates would jeer them down, calling them "oreos," "Uncle Toms," "honkies," or simply and more commonly "you white motherfuckers."

The teachers protested feebly but were frightened and could not control their students. They stood aside as the screams and taunts of their students fell on the children's heads. One boy even came up in his history class and pushed Ted out of his chair. Ted sat on the floor, stunned. The rest of the boys were poised to beat him senseless when the teacher had the sense to grab Ted by the arm and send him to the principal's office for protection.

He sat there for the afternoon, doing his algebra homework. The principal transferred him to a new history class.

"Black Heritage Month" in February brought the taunts of schoolmates to new heights. The school scheduled several assemblies for the students, who filed into the school gym and saw two soft-focused, emotional films on the life of Martin Luther King.

The core of 200 white students huddled together in sullen silence in a corner of the gymnasium bleachers.

The blacks, on the other hand, wept, howled, and talked back to the movie as they watched Alabama rednecks pelt King with rocks and a fat, jowl-faced Mayor Daley swear that he would never let "that man" march in the streets of Chicago.

Several boys threw books at the screen. One threw a knife, which cluttered harmlessly to the gym floor.

Ted and Pamela sat in stony silence amidst their respective howling classmates. Their father had often spoken of King and had given several emotional testimonials over dinner as to how important his work was to the "progress of the race," as he had termed it. Ted and Pamela had listened; such outpourings were the only times Mike had shown any deep emotion.

His performances had embarrassed his children. None of their white friends' parents in Naperville had cried over King, or anyone else for that matter, acting like they'd just been delivered into the Promised Land. They sold insurance or went downtown to their offices to work. On weekends, they went to their sons' football games.

Some of the kids at Naperville-West High School had given Ted and Elizabeth a hard time about being black. Ted had even gotten into a fight with a pimply-faced white kid his freshman year.

But for the most part, the whites there had ignored them. Ted and Pamela had blended into the school, made friends among the whites, and joined teams and club. They started wondering what they wanted to be when they grew up.

Ted even started dating a white girl from a particularly progressive family, much to Elizabeth's dismay. She believed in fitting into the mainstream but cross-racial dating was going too far. Of course, Ted had no choice. There were only 24 black children in the high school and he didn't like any of the girls.

The whole situation was a far cry from where he found himself now, among his crying and moaning classmates carried along on the emotion of the film on King. He felt like a European explorer who had stumbled upon a wild tribe of black Africans in the midst of some sacrificial rite.

The showing of the King films was a particularly stupid blunder on the part of the Horton-Gary High School administration. The day after the first film was shown, a gang of black boys beat up Ted in the parking lot after school, a stream of "you white motherfucker's" and "you dirty honky" falling on his head.

He went home with a broken rib and a knife slash on his cheek.

He was lucky they hadn't killed him.

* * *

When she came home from work that night and saw Ted, Millie was horrified.

"Who did that to you?" she demanded, throwing her car keys and a bag of groceries on the kitchen counter.

Ted shrugged, his face puffy with black and blue marks, the slash on his cheek encrusted with dried blood. "Some kids," he said softly. "Just some kids at school."

"Who? I want names!" Millie yelled.

He looked away. "I don't know," he said. "Some kids." Of course he knew. He just didn't want to get killed by squealing on them.

"Now you look at me, Edward Davis," Millie said, grabbing his arm and yanking him toward her. "I want to know who these criminals are and I'm going to press charges against them. These are animals."

"Aunt Millie," Ted said, his face expressionless. "I'm alright. Really. No harm done." He smiled weakly and tried to pull away from her, but his broken rib moved. He collapsed in pain on a kitchen chair.

That did it. Millie grabbed him under one armpit, marched him to the car, and took him to the emergency room at the West Gary Community Hospital. A young intern from Pakistan wrapped his ribcage in a big white bandage then cleaned and laid a white gauze dressing over his knife wound.

Millie and Ted drove home in silence.

When Harry came home from work, Millie jumped up and dragged him into the kitchen where Ted was sitting stiffly on a kitchen chair.

"What the hell happened to you?" Harry said, his eyes wide with shock at Ted's battered and bandaged face.

"School. Some damn niggers at school beat the hell out of him," Millie said.

"What did you do?" Harry said. "Spit on their cars?"

"He didn't do a thing," Millie said excitedly, walking behind Ted's chair and waving her hands. "Didn't do a thing and those niggers jumped him."

Ted looked at her in surprise. He hadn't told her a thing about the ambush. Both his aunt and uncle glared at him, Millie's eyes firey with the desire for revenge and his uncle's filled with suspicion.

"Look, Uncle Harry," Ted started. "I know you and Aunt Millie want to do something about this." He pointed to his puffy face, the white gauze glued to one cheek.

"He cracked a rib, too," Millie said, pulling the boy's broadcloth shirt up to show the white bandage. "Do you believe what those. . . "

". . . but I really don't think we can do much about it," Ted said loudly, drowning out his aunt. "If I tell on those kids they'll beat the shit out of me and I may not come home from school at all."

He ran the last words together and started crying. His thin shoulders shook with sobs.

Millie leaned over, put her arms around his shoulders, and clucked softly in his ear.

"I can't take it," he sobbed into her arms. He lifted his tear-stained face. "I'm scared. I think they're going to kill me."

Harry looked at the floor and coughed into his hand.

The situation confused him. He knew Horton-Gary was a tough school, but Franklin and Lavonne Rae had had no problems and pulled B averages.

He looked at his nephew, coughed into his hand again, and let his mind drift. Franklin was doing badly at Purdue. Six months into the engineering program and he was pulling D's. His campus advisor hinted strongly that the boy drop engineering. Franklin didn't know enough math, he said.

"You need calculus," Franklin had told his father last week. "I never even had trigonometry."

Harry had sighed and shuffled one foot. He felt betrayed. Franklin would never be an engineer. And now his nephew wouldn't even get a chance to get a *bad* education: the other students would kill him before his junior year.

He looked up at Ted.

"Isn't there some way you can get along with these guys?" Harry said limply. "You know, play along, try to blend in. Make friends with them?" He warmed to his subject. "I work with lots of guys I don't particularly like. We all get along . . . more or less." His voice trailed off.

Ted stared at him then stood up slowly, Millie holding him up under his arms. He swayed slightly from side to side, his mouth twisted in pain.

"I'm going to lie down," he said. And he tottered down the hall toward the bedroom he shared with Franklin.

Millie sighed, walked over to the kitchen counter, and started unpacking groceries for dinner.

Harry stared at his feet. What was he supposed to do? Send the kid to a private school? He wasn't a millionaire. He needed a new car, the house needed a new roof, and he was only steps ahead of the tuition bills for Franklin and Lavonne Rae. Private school was out of the question.

He was supposed to do more for his nephew than he had done for his own son?

"I think we should find out who beat him up and press charges," Millie said, clunking down cans on the kitchen counter. "We can't let this kind of thing go on. We have to take a stand." She pulled out a frying pan from under the stove. "I really think . . . "

"Millie," Harry said, sighing. "The kid has to go to school there."

"But don't you think. . ." she started.

"No," he said softly. "I don't."

And he shuffled into the living room to read the evening paper, his heart heavy and sad.

* * *

After he was beaten up, Ted started doing poorly in school. His button-down shirts wore out and he replaced them with teeshirts decorated with pictures of rock stars and gaudy drawings of motorcycles. He became even more quiet and sullen. He and

Franklin started smoking dope in their room, the window cracked to exhaust the smoke.

Ted's Bostonian accent, so carefully cultivated by his mother, became interlaced with ghetto slang and swear words. He stopped talking about becoming a doctor.

Franklin liked him more and more. From complaining that Ted took up room and was bothersome to be with, he started telling his father what a great guy his cousin was.

Harry and Millie were pleased that they got along better. Ted's sliding grades distressed them, but at least he wasn't getting attacked. He wasn't getting an education either, but he would survive until graduation.

Pamela's grades also deteriorated, but, unlike her brother her personality brightened — or rather it became louder and more vulgar. She seemed to conduct her entire life at high volume, screeching into the phone and shrieking at Lavonne Rae, conversations with whom were filled with constant repetition of the words, "girl," "you dumb nigger," and "you bitch."

Lavonne Rae complained constantly to her mother about Pamela: she was a pig, she left her clothes on the floor, she played the radio too loud, she wore Lavonne Rae's clothes without asking. Pamela was gaining weight. More and more she found Lavonne Rae's wide-cut jeans and huge sweaters fit just right.

She also smoked all of her cousin's dope and took any pills loose in her purse.

Lavonne Rae couldn't very well tell her mother *about that.*

So she took to hiding her drugs in ever-changing locations that Pamela inevitably found.

Millie had always worried about her daughter's foul mouth and thought she had won the war against it. Now that her niece took up swearing, she became doubly fretful, scolding both girls when she heard them. They just stopped talking in front of her which pleased her just fine. Pamela's weight gain worried her but she rationalized it as a combination of puberty and stress and lectured the girl about eating too many barbeque potato chips, her favorite snack food.

She bought oranges and apples for after-school snacks, but they rotted in the refrigerator.

* * *

On Sundays, Harry dragged all four children and his wife to
church. Harry was the most enthusiastic deacon in the Mt. Olivet
Missionary Baptist Church of Horton Beach. He was also the
loudest baritone in the continuous singing and chanting that made
up the Sunday service. Millie clucked along in a cracked alto; she
would have rather been home cooking and reading the Sunday
paper than spending all morning in church.

Harry forced Ted and Pamela to come and told Franklin and
Lavonne Rae that they could not continue to live at home unless
"they worshipped the Lord in his holy temple" every Sunday. So they
came, yawning and heavy-lidded, every Sunday morning at 9, trailing
their father as he shook hands with every member of the
congregation with a joyous "Praise the Lord, Brother. The Lord's
blessing on you."

Ted and Pamela had been raised Episcopalian. The nearly
manic enthusiasm of their uncle for his religion at first amused then
embarrassed them. When they found they were expected to spend
three hours of every Sunday in a decrepit frame church, swaying to
and fro with the sweating bodies of the brethern, they became
alarmed.

"I'm really an Episcopalian, Uncle Harry," Ted had said after
they'd attended several services. "Isn't there an Episcopal Church
we can go to?"

Harry considered Episcopalians only steps removed from the
Catholics, who were practically idolaters in his mind.

Plus, Episcopalians were white.

"No," he said abruptly. "You come with us. You're a child of
God."

Besides, Harry had been praised by the church elders for
bringing in his niece and nephew to the true fold. He hoped they'd
be reborn and baptized soon, just as his two children and Millie had
been.

Pamela and Ted responded by attending church but sleeping on
their arms or just slumping in their seats, their chins resting on their
chests. But it was hard to sleep with the continuous ruckus of
"amens" and "praise the Lords" filling the air and the minister's wife

pounding out hymns on a battered upright piano in the front of the room.

* * *

Then, one Sunday after his beating at school, Ted had a calling from God.

Just after Reverand McDougal's first homily, Ted shook himself awake. The choir broke into a chorus of "Sweet Jesus, My Blessed Savior, Pour your Holy Love Down on Me."

To the pleased surprise of his uncle and the total disgust of his cousins and sister, Ted began singing, not a timid mumbling but a full-throated tenor that blended well with his uncle's deep voice. Then he sat up straight and listened attentively to Reverand McDougal's second homily, answering "amen, brother" and "that's right," and "tell it like it is" as the minister exhorted his flock.

After the service, Ted smiled and pumped hands with half the congregation. Harry was so pleased, he took the Reverand McDougal aside and started planning Ted's baptism.

Franklin approached his cousin outside the church.

"What's got into you, man?" he said, grabbing Ted by the arm. "You becomin' some sort of Bible-thumper or what?"

Ted looked at him coolly. "I'm returning to the house of my Lord," he said. He glared at Franklin. "I'd advise you to repent and return to Jesus."

Franklin looked at him in disgust and went to the car.

That afternoon at dinner Ted and Harry dominated the conversation with a discussion of some obscure passage of the Bible involving walking through "the valley of sin and destruction on the path to the temple of the Almighty."

Franklin stopped talking to Ted and started complaining that Ted was a jerk-off.

Ted continued to attend church with enthusiasm and even signed up for a Bible-study group on Wednesday nights. His grades at school improved, although that merely meant he had progressed from not studying at all to minimal effort. He stopped smoking dope with Franklin, who, by this time, had dropped his engineering courses at Purdue and was now studying heating and air-conditioning contracting at Hammond Junior College.

Two weeks after Ted graduated from Horton-Gary High School, Ted was "reborn" and baptized at the church. He started singing in the choir.

Three weeks later, he brought Leila home and introduced her to his aunt and uncle as his fiancee.

Chapter Three

Under other circumstances, Harry and Millie would have liked Leila. But two facts militated against it.

First, they felt that at 18 years of age Ted was too young to marry. Second, Leila was white.

A plump young woman of Slavic descent, Leila Pritchett was more than white. She was practically an albino. She had white-blonde hair; pale, red-blotched skin; and nearly colorless blue eyes. Against Ted's rich black skin, she looked like some ghost returned from the dead.

She was a secretary at the Farnsworth Paint Company in Hammond, where Ted had gotten a part-time job as an outdoor maintenance man at the beginning of his senior year. Now that he had graduated high school, he was working there full-time.

He spent his days painting the twisting, climbing miles of pipe connecting the cauldrons and holding tanks that made up the plant. He'd met Leila in the employee coffee room.

Harry and Millie had no idea the girl was white until she appeared for dinner that hot night in late August, a fringed white shawl topping her cheap polyester dress with its tiny rosebud print.

Millie immediately stared at the girl's stomach to see if she was pregnant: she couldn't tell. She fished for information all through that first awkward dinner, finally blurting out the question over dessert.

"By any chance, you're not pregnant are you, my dear?" she said, cutting the girl a big slice of apple pie.

Leila blushed and stared at her plate. "As a matter of fact," she said, looking up into the spellbound faces of her future in-laws, "I am."

Millie inhaled sharply, Harry glared at Ted, and Ted's cousins and sister looked at him with new respect. Franklin was especially impressed. Twenty-two-years-old, Franklin had never been able to even date a white woman. His Bible-thumping, 18-year-old cousin had already knocked one up.

Dinner lumbered on. Leila wasn't a good conversationalist and Millie and Harry were so horrified by the situation that they were struck dumb. So Ted and Pamela and Franklin and Lavonne Rae discussed the latest music they had heard on the radio and talked about taking a trip to the Great America Amusement Park just north of Chicago some time in September.

Dinner fizzled to an end at 7. Ted took Leila home; she lived with her mother and two younger brothers in Whiting. When he returned around 8:30, his uncle was waiting for him.

"Just what is going on?" he demanded as Ted walked into the living room.

"I'm marrying the woman I dishonored and asking God to forgive me my sin," Ted said.

Harry couldn't very well argue with such upstanding Christian virtue; he tried a new tack.

"She's not one of us," he said.

"What's 'us'?" Ted said, feigning ignorance.

"Black folk, of course."

"She's an upstanding Christian woman," Ted said. "God knows no colors. Would you want me to murder the child He has seen fit to bless us with?"

At this allusion to abortion, Harry shuddered. Even to think of it was a sin. But he cringed to think of Ted and Leila at church, the whitest, palest blonde he'd ever seen bouncing a cafe-au-lait baby on her knee in front of the entire congregation. His reputation would be ruined.

Briefly, he hoped Leila would fall down the stairs and miscarry.

"How will you support her?" he asked.

Ted looked at him sternly. "God will provide." He stood up. "Good night, Uncle Harry," he said formally.

And he went to bed.

* * *

Leila and Ted were married a month later on a Thursday afternoon in a civil ceremony in the Whiting City Hall. Leila had cried the whole week before. Raised Roman Catholic, she had always wanted a big, formal wedding in St. Clothilde's, complete with incense, bridesmaids, and all her high-school girlfriends standing jealously in the pews as she swept by in an expensive bridal gown.

Instead, she was standing next to a black man in a badly cut summer suit, wearing the pink summer dress she always wore to Sunday mass, and clutching a bouquet of daisies. Her mother, a dough-faced woman in a blue dress, stood behind them on one side, weeping silently into an old lace handkerchief.

Harry and Millie stood on the other side. With their rigid faces and dark clothes they looked like they were attending a funeral.

The magistrate looked at Ted and Leila with indifference. He'd married stranger pairs than this. He clipped through the ceremony at a healthy pace, watched them exchange their cheap wedding rings, and pronounced them man and wife. Embarrassed, the young couple kissed, then turned to face the fallen faces of their families.

Leila's mother kissed her woodenly on the cheek, glared at her new black son-in-law, and turned and left without saying a word. A devout Catholic, Sophie Pritchett had raised Leila to love God, go to mass, and obey the dictates of the Church. The injunction against abortion was now proving a devastating rule to live by. And Sophie could not bear to think of her daughter as an unwed mother.

But marriage to a black man was an unbelievable turn of events, especially to one with a three-inch knife scar down his cheek, Ted's legacy from his beating at Horton-Gary High.

Sophie had come to the wedding, but that was it. She planned to cut Leila out of her life.

Millie and Harry were left standing in the chancery office with the newlyweds, the young bride crying on the shoulder of her new husband.

"There, there, my dear," Millie mumbled, absent-mindedly stroking her daughter-in-law's hand. "Your mother will get over it. It's just such a . . ." she searched for the right word, "shock to her. She'll be back.

"Mothers always come back," she said without conviction.

Leila gave her a weak smile, but the tears kept dripping down her cheeks. Ted stared straight ahead, his jaw tight with anger.

"Why don't we go eat?" Millie said, trying to smile. The newlyweds looked at her like two children abandoned on a street corner.

The four of them drove to a seafood house in Hammond. The wedding supper was a grim affair, Millie trying to make polite conversation while Leila dabbed at her eyes with her handkerchief.

Harry played with his silverware and stared out into space. He was totally opposed to the marriage. Imagine Ted marrying a white girl, and a Catholic at that. He could see Mike looking down from heaven and shaking his head in disgust at his brother's efforts to take care of his son. He had failed Mike, he knew it, and he felt guilty.

They all toasted the marriage with champagne then quickly finished eating. Harry picked up the bill and they left, bidding each other stilted good-byes in the parking lot. Harry drove his old Chevrolet toward Horton Beach; Leila and Ted got into Leila's 10-year-old Horizon. They headed for Whiting and their new life together.

* * *

The young couple had rented a small, three-room apartment only five blocks down from the McClosky Steel Company's Whiting Works. The top floor of an old frame three-flat, the apartment was a true garret with sloping walls, ancient plumbing, and old windows that rattled in their frames. Heat was provided by a gas space heater at one end of the living room.

The windows provided an excellent view of McClosky's bleeder smokestack, which spewed fire and heat as it burned off the gases coming from the blast furnaces below. The air was heavy with the smell of coking coal; Ted could see the brown stains from the air on the old roofs of the neighboring buildings.

The neighborhood was made up mostly of poor white people, but there was a heavy Mexican element and a smattering of blacks. Their landlady was Mexican. Mrs. Blanco, her steelworker husband, and their three children lived on the first floor in a six-room apartment that looked like a street fair in Guadalajara.

Every room was painted a different bright color, which clashed with the intensely colored throws on the furniture. Pictures of the Virgin Mary or Jesus and His bleeding heart hung on one wall of every room.

The second floor housed two aged Irish bachelors, their even-more-aged spinster sister, and their innumberable cats.

Mrs. Blanco had liked Leila, but she gave Ted, his black skin, and his scar a doubtful eye. He was polite and insistent, showing her his paycheck stubs from the Farnsworth Paint Company. She had finally relented and rented to them.

Ted couldn't believe he'd had to practically beg Mrs. Blanco for the privilege of paying her $250 a month plus heat for an apartment that was hardly bigger than the closet space in his old house in Naperville.

Naperville. He sat on the old mattress on the floor that he and Leila had acquired for a bed and stared at a crack in the wall. It was hard to believe that he had once lived in a beautiful house with an adoring mother and a well-dressed father who wore expensive suits and took the train into the city to his office everyday.

It was hard to believe that he had once wanted to be a doctor.

Now he was married to a not-too-bright woman of the wrong color, expecting his first child, and making his living painting tubing at a paint plant for $7.00 an hour. He was still a member of the Mt. Olivet Baptist Church, despite the Reverand McDougal's refusal to marry him and Leila in the church. She was a Catholic, he'd said. He suspected his uncle had put McDougal up to it.

He turned and watched his wife. She walked disconsolately around the apartment, unpacking a dish here, a box of clothes there, and shoving them into the tiny cupboard behind the kitchen or the tinier closet in the bedroom. She kept crying and blowing her nose, her pale face red and swollen.

"Leila, honey," he called to her. "Why don't you come here and sit down."

She set down a plate on the kitchen sink, walked into the bedroom, and sat down heavily on the mattress. He pulled her close to him and nuzzled her ear. She was not pretty, but she was warm and soft. He felt less lonely holding her.

"I love you," he whispered in her ear and she smiled back weakly.

It was a lie, of course. His marriage to Leila had been a complete mistake. He'd met her in the days when he was still hanging around with Franklin, drinking and drugging, the days before he'd turned to God.

He had talked tough then and slept with all the sluts at Horton-Gary High. He was popular with them. He would turn on his Boston accent for them; they would laugh and let him come inside them again.

He was cocky when he got the part-time job at the Farnsworth Paint Co. He was one of the few kids at school to have a real part-time job; he didn't want to make his money dealing drugs or stealing from the local merchants. It sounded too dangerous, although Franklin was keeping himself in spending money selling crack and pot to grammar-school kids.

Ted had chosen the paint factory. He had met Leila in the coffee room one day, sitting with two girlfriends drinking coffee in the corner. The night before, Ted had just laid Tamara Jones, one of the prestige sluts at Horton-Gary. He was feeling daring.

Besides, one of Leila's companions was black. That gave him courage. Since he'd left Naperville, he'd become more reticent about approaching white people.

"Hey, ladies," he said, walking up to them with his best swagger. "Can I join you lovely ladies for some coffee?" The black girl sneered at him, but the two white women were embarrassed and flustered. They weren't used to talking to black men and they didn't want to appear rude.

"Sure, sit down," Leila's white companion said. Her name was Susan; she looked about 25 and had dark hair and the bushiest, darkest set of eyebrows Ted had ever seen on a woman.

"So how long you been working in this place?" he said, looking around at the dingy coffee room.

"Five years," Susan said.

The black woman didn't answer.

"Six months," Leila said softly.

"You just started, hey?" Ted said.

"I just graduated last year," Leila said.

"Oh yeah, from where?"

"Holy Constance." Our Mother of Holy Constance was a Catholic girls' high school on the west side of Gary.

Ted had never heard of it.

"So my name's Ted," he said, giving his best smile. The women introduced themselves. The black woman was Francesca.

"So what do you ladies do for fun around here?" he said, leaning on the table and trying to look nonchalant. Francesca rolled her eyes to the ceiling, but Susan and Leila blushed.

"Oh, nothing, not much," Susan mumbled.

"Well, lovely ladies like you, you have to get out and party more," Ted said. "Show yourself around. Don't keep your lights under bushels, and all that."

They giggled.

Not quite sure what to say next, he decided on a dramatic exit. He stood up. "Well, ladies," he said. "Nice chatting with you, but I've got to get back to work. See you round." He loped off in his best Super-Fly shuffle.

He was very proud of his performance.

Two days later, he walked into the coffee room again. Leila was sitting by herself in the corner. "Hi, there, gorgeous," he said, walking up to her.

"Hi," she said shyly.

They made small talk about the latest accident at the plant. Eight workers had been scalded by hot paint; the incident had made the 10:00 news the night before.

Ted decided to make a bid for white pussy: he asked her out.

She looked flustered but agreed. In reality, she had no desire to date a black man, but she did not know how to say no. Besides, the sisters at Holy Constance had always taught the girls to be open-minded. We were all the same under our different colored skins. Going out with Ted would be Leila's contribution to civil rights.

They set up a date for a movie Saturday night.

She suggested they meet at a drugstore in Whiting.

Civil rights or not, she didn't want her mother to know she was going out with a black boy.

Chapter Four

Ted met her at the drugstore that Saturday night. He had borrowed his Uncle Harry's Chevrolet; they drove to see a horror film in Vondola, a prosperous white suburb 15 miles south of Gary. Leila sat through the movie gripping a box of popcorn with one hand, and daintily dipping into it with the other, withdrawing one kernal at a time to eat.

Ted kept trying to put his arm around her, but she would shift uncomfortably and pull her coat around her. "I'm cold," she would mumble.

Ted got the idea and put his hand in his lap.

White pussy wasn't so easy to get after all.

After the movie, he wanted to go to an all-black bar in a rough section of Gary. What good was it going out with a white chick, no matter how ugly, if you couldn't show her off?

But Leila refused. Instead, they had coffee in a restaurant near the movie theatre. The patrons were mostly white and kept sneaking glances at Ted. Used to being black in an all-black neighborhood, he shifted in his seat uncomfortably.

He was determined to get Leila into bed. He turned on his Boston accent.

She found it funny. He told her he didn't use it because other blacks didn't like it, which was true.

Her eyes lit up in sympathy. Then he told her about his life in Naperville and the fancy white high school he had once attended.

Actually, he said, he was just staying with his aunt and uncle until his father and mother came back from Africa.

"They're important members of the South African freedom-fighters," he said in his Boston accent. "They donate all their time and money to freeing the black peoples of South Africa from the chains of apartheid. My father is a personal friend of Bishop Tutu."

At the mention of the prelate's name, Leila leaned toward Ted intently. The nuns of Holy Constance had kept their girls up-to-date on the evils of apartheid and the noble efforts of Bishop Tutu. The bishop was so saintly he was almost a Catholic.

Leila found it all so romantic. She had marched in a big, anti-South-African parade in Chicago the year before. The nuns had sent a bus.

She'd heard some South African black political leaders address the crowd. They'd looked distinguished and exotic in their business suits with tribal robes or animal skins draped over one shoulder. They spoke English with an English accent. Several were handsome.

". . . And my dad knows Nelson Mandela," Ted was going on.

Leila was glowing now.

"Have you ever been there?" she said, her eyes bright.

"Oh yes," Ted said in his best Boston English. "It is a wonderful place. The black people there are so kind."

"Really?"

"Oh yes." He had no idea what he was talking about, but he knew instinctively that he was on the right track. "They sing while they work. The women are especially beautiful. The whites keep them poor, but they weave their own clothing. They are very elegant."

He smiled winningly at Leila.

For the first time that evening, she smiled back with real warmth.

Inspired, he launched into a description of the glories of the South African countryside, based entirely on an article he'd read in the *National Geographic* the previous week.

He was moving in for the kill.

After a particularly heartrending discourse on the horrors of South African prisons, he reached out and took her hand.

She withdrew it quickly. "Not here," she said, looking around at the white suburban clientele drinking coffee and feeding their children ice cream. She dropped her voice. "They wouldn't understand," she whispered.

Ted couldn't let this moment drop. He waved frantically for the waitress. He paid the bill and hurried Leila to the car.

He moved to put his hand on her hair, but she pushed it away. "Not here," she said impatiently.

"OK," he said, smiling. "I know a place."

He drove quickly to the local make-out spot, a rutted dirt road that circled the Gary Municipal Dump. A series of cars was already there, their engines running and the exhaust rising up in clouds. In the feeble light of the only unbroken streetlight in the area, he thought he recognized two of his friends, dealing dope.

Leila was frightened.

"Where are we?" she said.

"In the heart of the ghetto," Ted said, dousing the headlights. In the dark he could barely make out Leila's pale skin. "Don't worry," he said in his best Bostonese. "You're with me. No one will hurt you."

Then he leaned over and pulled her toward him, the sound of the car engine humming in the background like distant tribal drums.

Her lips were cold and dry, but her breasts were warm and soft. She shuddered when he touched them and moaned.

He tried to climb in with her in the passenger seat, but there wasn't enough room. He fumbled for the lever on the seat and it flipped back suddenly. He fell on top of her.

She giggled.

He cursed under his breath and crawled into the backseat. Then he dragged her after him. It wasn't easy: she was a big girl and had decided to play passive.

He finally wrestled her onto her back and got on top of her.

To his surprise, she wasn't a virgin. In fact, she knew what she was doing. She dug her fingers into his buttocks and pushed him inside of her.

She felt as good as Tamara Jones.

She felt better than Tamara Jones. And, in the dark, he couldn't tell what color she was except for the occasional glimmer of light on her white-blonde hair.

* * *

Ted told no one about Leila. She wasn't pretty and if Franklin found out about her, he would put the moves on her. Franklin was like that. Your pussy was his pussy. He was very ecumenical. Ted didn't mind sharing the black sluts from the high school. There were lots of those.

But Leila was different. She was white pussy. That was rare, and he didn't want his 22-year-old cousin sweeping in and carrying her off.

Not that he would have had much chance. Franklin didn't even know Leila, the girl didn't like blacks except for Ted, and he'd never run into her on the street.

But Ted was taking no chances.

When he came home, he told Franklin he'd gone out with Tamara.

"Was she a good lay?" Franklin asked, laying on the bottom bunk bed and holding open *Schematics of Basic Heating Systems* on his chest. He was cramming that weekend for a final on Monday, hoping that two days of study could make up for a semester of indolence.

"Great. Just great," Ted said, stripping down to his underwear and jumping into the top bunk. "That girl can really put out." He lay down and his feet hung over the end of the bed. It was ludicrous to be 18 and still be sleeping in a bunk bed.

"Say, I need some help tomorrow night," came Franklin's voice.

"Yeah?"

"Callen is dropping off some shit tomorrow night and I need someone to watch for cops."

"I gotta' work tomorrow night."

"No you don't." In addition to keeping track of Ted's women, Franklin kept track of his work schedule.

"Franklin, I'm not your gopher. I'm not going to sit around and get in trouble so you can make a fortune off me."

"I'll give you $20."

That was almost three hours worth of tube painting at Farnsworth Paint Co., before taxes. He'd spent a lot of money on Leila that night. Usually he didn't take girls to the movies: they just went out and fucked. He needed money to keep Leila in his bed.

"Alright," he said.

"I knew you were no fool," came the reply from the lower bunk.

Ted rolled over and pulled the pillow over his head to block out the light from the overhead light. Several minutes later Franklin gave up on his studying and turned off the light.

The noise of his snoring rose to Ted's ears, a counterpoint to his dreams of feeling Leila's soft, full breasts under his hands.

* * *

The next day Ted went to the mall and spent his entire paycheck
on clothes. He bought a little round black leather hat that sat on top
of his head, a leopard-print shirt, and some gold-colored snaggle
teeth on a chain. It was his idea of what South African blacks wore.

It was pussy insurance. If he was telling Leila he was big friends
with the anti-apartheid crowd, he should look the part. Otherwise,
she might never put out for him again.

He was modeling his new purchases in the mirror of his bureau
that evening when Franklin suddenly walked in.

"What the hell kind of outfit is that?" he said, staring at Ted's
leopard-print shirt. "You some sort of back-to-Africa nigger or
what?" Franklin wore slinky polyester shirts, shiny sharkskin pants,
and pointy alligator shoes. He looked like a black Vic Damon.

"I'm recovering my roots, man," Ted stuttered, looking at himself
in the mirror. He felt like he was dressed for Halloween.

"Put on some decent clothes and let's get out of here. Callen's
coming at 9:30."

Ted took off the leopard shirt and pulled on a plain teeshirt and
a jacket. They took Franklin's car, an old blue Ford Escort Harry
had picked up for Franklin to drive to school.

They were meeting Callen behind the dumpster in the parking lot
of some all-night rib joint in west Gary.

Callen was right on time. A well-muscled black man of about 22
in a black leather jacket, he shuffled up on foot to Franklin and Ted,
who were standing behind the dumpster watching a particularly
large rat scurry into the overgrown, vacant lot behind the parking
lot.

They talked briefly. Callen gave Franklin several pounds of pot in
plastic bags and a tiny chunk of crack. Franklin would repackage it
and sell it to the junior high kids at the Martin Luther King Jr.
Elementary School down the street from the Davis house.

In the world of Horton Beach drugs, Franklin was a small player.
Callen just dealt him in at all because he and Franklin had played
basketball together at Horton-Gary High School.

Ted shuffled his feet and stared at the garbage spilling over one
edge of the dumpster. Franklin was so melodramatic about his
drug-dealing. He didn't need someone to watch for the cops. They

were over busting heroin dealers on west 8th. Corruptors of the young like Franklin were small change.

"Let's go," Franklin said finally. They were just heading for their car in the back corner of the lot when they heard what sounded like a yelp.

They turned around to see four men grab Callen under the arms and drag him off into the bushes of the vacant lot. Ted could see the glint of a knife and hear Callen's screams.

Ted and Franklin ran for their car and quickly drove home, their hearts pounding in their mouths. The next morning, they went through the newspaper carefully.

There it was, on page five in the bottom corner:

> An unidentified young man in his
> early twenties was found stabbed
> to death late last night next to
> Fontaine's Barbeque Rib Palace on
> East Moline Street. Police say
> the victim died of multiple stab
> wounds to the head and chest . . .

Ted closed the paper quickly and poured himself another cup of coffee. His hand shook as he lifted the cup to his mouth. Franklin was more controlled; he mumbled something about "poor Callen," skipped breakfast, and went to school.

Ted, on the other hand, had decided to return to God.

* * *

What was God going to do about Callen's death? What was God going to think about him coming back to prayer and right-thinking after months of sinning and drugging?

What was God going to think about him and Leila?

Ted stopped doing drugs and started praying for forgiveness at night. Franklin thought he'd lost his grip.

"Hey man," he'd say when he came into their tiny bedroom and saw Ted reading the Bible at the tiny desk in one corner. "I had me some great pussy tonight, great pussy. Don't you think you'd want a little?"

Ted would look at him firmly. "No," he would say. "But let me read to you from the *Book of Psalms*."

"No thanks, brother," Franklin would say, leaving the room quickly. "I ain't wiggin' out, too."

Ted felt the best he had since his parents had died two years before. He felt anchored. He belonged somewhere and his life had structure and a goal: he would try to save his soul. The Mt. Olivet congregation was friendly. His uncle was proud of him. The Reverand McDougal thought he could be a deacon soon if he kept up the good work.

He started memorizing Bible passages at the coffee room at work. Leila thought he'd gone mad.

"Aren't you going a little overboard?" she'd said after he'd spent an entire week of coffee breaks studying *Deuteronomy* at a tiny formica table near the coffee machines.

"Not at all," he said pleasantly. "I'm getting closer to my Lord."

"Oh," she said, laying back in her chair.

Since Ted's return to God, he'd stopped dating Leila. The only thing he had wanted was her body. Now that he was giving up sex outside the sanctity of marriage, they had nothing in common.

Besides, God did not want the races to intermingle. It was sinful to want a white woman. Every time he thought of what he and Leila had done in the backseat of his uncle's car, he cringed.

Then he thought of the pleasure and prayed even harder.

He had to cut her out of his life.

Leila was disappointed. After his return to God, they didn't talk to each other or go out for several weeks. Then, one day, she stopped by his formica table in the coffee room.

He looked up impatiently. "Yes?" he said, with forced politeness. He'd started thinking of her as the she-devil who had tempted him to sin.

Even she-devils had souls, he reminded himself.

"Can I sit down?" she said nervously.

He sighed to indicate that he was deep in his religious studies. "Sure," he said, moving some books off a chair.

"I have something to tell you," she said, twisting her hands on her lap.

He nodded sagely.

"I'm pregnant," she said.

He stared at her.

"I'm going to have a baby," she said.

The white she-devil with the white-blonde hair was carrying his child. That was impossible.

He leaned down close to the table and whispered, "You're sure it's mine?"

"What?"

"Maybe it's one of your other boyfriends?"

"What other boyfriends? My last boyfriend was a college boy from Notre Dame and that was two years ago. You're the only one I've had since."

"You're sure?" he asked idiotically.

"Of course I'm sure."

"We just did it once."

She just shrugged.

He looked at her, frightened. "What are we going to do?" he whispered.

"I don't know." Her eyes started filling with tears. "I just found out yesterday. I haven't even told my mother. It would just kill her."

Ted thought of an abortion, but put the thought immediately out of his mind. God would never stand for it. What would He do, a voice in the back of Ted's head said. Strike you down dead on the expressway? But Ted knew it was the devil speaking to him.

He had to do his duty. Then it hit him: this was the ultimate test from God to see if he was worthy to be a Christian. It was the trial of his life.

He saw himself on a mountain, a latter-day black Moses, his robes pulled tightly around him in a driving wind, standing up in the face of overwhelming odds. He had to triumph.

He looked down at the table and saw only Leila, one hand over her face, crying.

"Don't worry," he said, in his best adult voice. "I'll marry you."

She looked up, her face streaked with tears. "What?" she said.

"I'll marry you," he said again, his nerve going already.

She stared at him. He could see in her hard little eyes that she was calculating her options. As a Catholic she had two choices: it was him and disgrace or unwed motherhood and disgrace.

"OK," she said.

Ted wondered if that meant they could have more sex before they were married.

But that was just the devil talking to him.

Chapter Five

The parents had all responded as expected. Leila's mother had screamed at her and thrown her out of the house. The Davis's had acted like Ted and Leila were entering the Valley of Death.

And here he was now, sitting on a lumpy mattress in a rundown apartment in an even more rundown neighborhood. He was renting from Mexicans; that was the lowest.

Leila sat next to him. She smelled of cheap perfume and looked fat, although it was just her pregnancy starting to show.

Well, he thought, the best part of the whole mess was that he could have white pussy anytime he wanted it. He leaned over toward Leila and grabbed one of her breasts. Then he nuzzled her neck.

"What are you doing?" she said impatiently, pushing his hands away from her.

"This is our wedding day, baby," he said, leaning into her even more.

"Go away," she said. "I'm pregnant." She stood up quickly and walked toward the kitchen.

"What does that mean?" he yelled after her. "Pregnant women can still screw."

"How do you know?"

"They do it all the time."

"I've got work to do."

"What work?" He got up and followed her into their cramped little kitchen. She stood in the midst of brown cardboard boxes covering the entire floor.

"I got to put all this stuff away. Then we got to go to work tomorrow. I'm tired." And she started pulling dishes out of a box and setting them on the cupboard shelves.

Ted took her arm and tried again. "Come on, Leila," he said. "It's our wedding day."

"There would never have been a wedding day if you hadn't tricked me into getting pregnant," she hissed. "You think I would have married a nigger loser like you otherwise?"

Ted was stunned. Up to this point, Leila had said little about their marriage. Apparently she was glad to get out of the situation with some kind of honor. Now she was letting him know how she really felt.

"You should have used a rubber or something," she said, grabbing a platter and shoving it angrily on a shelf. "But no-o-o-o, Mr. Macho has to go bareback and get me pregnant." She picked up another plate and glared at him over its edge. "Now look at the mess we're in. Black and white, we are. My own mother won't even come to visit me and your parents act like I'm some sort of disease.

"I should have never agreed to go out with you," she said. "You lured me into this." She glared at him. "You lied about Nelson Mandela!" she yelled. "This whole thing is your fault and I'm never going to let you forget it!" She took a pile of plates and dropped them with a clatter on a lower shelf. "I hate you."

Ted stood there with his mouth open. All he had wanted was a little white pussy and to do right for her by God. Now he was accused of ruining her life.

"Why didn't you use a diaphragm or something?" he said angrily. "Why weren't you on the pill? You trapped me. If you didn't want to get pregnant you would have been on the pill. We wouldn't have had to worry about nuthin."

He warmed to his topic. "Don't give me this shit about it's all my fault. It's not my fault. I didn't make you spread your legs and drag me inside. I didn't rape you. You wanted it. You wanted it bad.

"Now you got it, and you got a little something in the oven to boot and you make it out like it's my fault. No way.

"I did you a big favor marrying you, baby," he said, pointing his finger at her. "A *big* favor. I could have left you on your mama's doorstep without a pot to pee in. And here I am, giving you all my worldly possessions to support you because it's the right thing to do, because Jesus, my personal savior, told me it was the right thing to do." He dropped his voice.

"You should be grateful, bitch, you should be real grateful."

She looked at him, her eyes filled with hate, and went back to unpacking her dishes. Ted walked unsteadily into the other room and lay down on the mattress.

Did God really want him to marry this woman? He went over all the passages from the Bible he could remember about marriage. None of the Biblical wives he could remember hated their husbands. They were patient and kind and quiet and good with the children. They were docile and subservient to all their husband's wishes. And he was certain they put out for their men whenever they wanted it.

What was Leila's problem?

She'd been raised wrong. She'd been raised Catholic. If he could only get her into the hands of the good women of Mt. Olivet. They would set her straight.

There was even a young woman he'd had his eye on before this whole thing with Leila came about. Melinda Mayberry was dark black with big breasts, big hips, and soft brown eyes with thick lashes.

She was a good Christian. She'd been born again. He had met her in his Bible-study class Wednesday nights. He didn't even know if she had a voice, much less a brain, because she never said anything unless Reverand McDougal asked her to recite. But she knew her Bible; she could recite whole passages from memory in a fast, quiet hustle, like she was chanting.

She'd been making eyes at him for the last six weeks. He bet she'd be a good lay.

His reverie was broken by the sound of breaking glass, followed by a stream of four-letter words: Leila had dropped some glasses in the other room.

Ted closed his eyes and banned all thoughts of Leila from his brain. This marriage was a punishment. God was punishing him for wanting white pussy. Did God have to go so far as to make him marry it?

Why did God hate him so much? It had been an innocent mistake.

It must have been a bigger sin than he thought. He got up from the mattress, Leila's cursing still coming from the other room, and went out to the corner bar. It was filled with Mexicans, who stared at him when he walked in and ordered a beer. He gulped it down quickly and went home.

When he got home, Leila was getting ready for bed. She wore a heavy nightgown that covered her completely. They climbed into bed together, Leila clinging to one side, he to the other as if a wall ran down the middle separating them.

He wondered if he would survive being married to Leila and prayed hard to God for help.

But God didn't make her want to have sex. Instead, she rolled over on her side and started snoring lightly.

* * *

Their hatred for each other dulled to an aching pain, but they could not get used to being married. In addition to their differences in skin color, they differed in everything else.

Leila was a Catholic; Ted was a Baptist. Leila wanted her baby; Ted couldn't care less. Leila thought they should save more money; Ted complained they didn't have enough to spend as it was.

They even fought over food. Ted thought Leila's meatloafs and cabbage rolls heavy and starchy. She complained that he liked everything deepfried and would eat strange parts of animals, like strips of fried pig intestine. It made her nauseous to think about it.

But their biggest problem was with their friends. Blacks or whites, they belonged to neither group.

Leila had definitely fallen to new lows in her friends' eyes. They thought Ted was some subspecies of ape. One of her friends had even asked her if Ted was hairier down below—you know—than white men and if his penis was bigger.

Leila had never seen his penis. She had been impregnated in the dark and had shown no desire to see it ever since.

But she had to save face. "Oh yes," she told her friend. "He's marvelously well-hung."

It wasn't that her friends still didn't ask her out, but that they would sneak glances at Ted and be especially polite to him, as if he weren't really one of them, but some Martian that one had to be especially nice to so that he would go back to Mars with a good opinion of the human race.

Ted's friends, on the other hand, were just rude. They would ignore Leila and just talk to Ted, leaving her to sit, bored, staring at her drink or playing with the key ring from her purse.

Besides, it was dangerous for a white woman to go to some of the bars Ted took her. Sometimes when she went to the bathroom black women would curse her under their breath or a black man would mumble some incoherent obscenity on her way back to the table.

So, a lot of nights, they just stayed home, watching TV and eating ice cream, not talking. They could have been two people living two separate lives in two separate apartments with the only reason they had to talk at all their joint ownership of a TV.

The TV offered respite from their problems: they liked the same TV shows. They watched "Dallas," and "Dynasty," and "Miami Vice." Every Friday night they got a movie for the VCR; every Saturday, they watched "The Saturday Night Movie."

They could have gone on like this indefinitely, but Ted's hormones got the best of him.

"Leila," he said one night when she was eight-months pregnant and they were watching David Letterman in bed. "Leila, honey, I can't take this anymore."

She stared at him with her colorless eyes.

"I need a wife. We haven't screwed for four months. I've got physical needs, you know."

She looked at him and pursed her lips. He'd won points in her eyes by giving her his paycheck every week and taking on a second job as a part-time janitor at a local school. He was talking about going into the heating and air-conditioning business just like his cousin Franklin. Maybe he'd take some courses in it next year at the community college.

She figured she'd better reward him for his efforts. He might run off with one of those big-busted black mommas she saw staring at him when they went out with his black friends. There was probably a whole nest of them at that Bible-thumping church he went to, too. He could run off with one of them.

Then where would she be?

But she was eight-months' pregnant and an additional 35 pounds overweight. She could hardly move, much less go through the gyrations of sex.

"I can't move," she said, but her eyes gave him hope.

"How about just sucking me off, then," he said. "Seminal pressure is just killing me."

Leila had never heard of "seminal pressure" and was revolted by the thought of her husband's penis in her mouth, but she was scared. He could skip out and leave her cold, his strong belief in "Jesus, his personal savior" relenting in the face of physical need.

She made a face. "OK," she said.

He smiled happily and turned around, his powerful black legs sticking through the covers. She was face to face with his penis.

My God if it wasn't bigger than Tommy Shannon's, her only other lay. He'd been a nice college boy from Notre Dame who actually took an interest in her until he'd gotten some better-looking girl from Purdue to put out for him.

She closed her eyes and did her work, pulling her mouth away just in time to have her husband's semen spill in a sticky puddle on the bed.

Ted's whole body relaxed: Leila's mouth was better than his hand, but not by much. He thought she was going to chew off the end of his dick.

But it was better than nothing. And the Bible said it was her wifely duty to service her husband's needs. It said that somewhere.

He was holding up his end of the marriage; she could damn well hold up hers. He started having her suck him off at least three times a week. He never touched her otherwise; her immense pregnancy revolted him.

Three weeks later, her water broke one morning while she was typing a letter at work. It drenched her skirt and chair and dampened the carpet; she broke into hysterical tears. The entire secretarial staff in the executive offices of Farnsworth Paint Company stopped work. Someone found her an extra skirt, another called a cab, and a third, whose boss was out of town, went to the hospital with her, filling in the forms at the admissions desk while Leila sat in a wheelchair and moaned out answers.

The girls back at the office tried to reach Ted, but he was in transit between his job at Farnsworth and his janitorial job at the school. Someone left word at the school, but he never got the message.

He finally realized what was happening when he went home and Leila hadn't shown up by midnight. He called the hospital to find that she had been admitted and got there to find her lying in the recovery room.

She'd had an easy delivery: Leila was born to reproduce. After four hours of labor she had produced Rachel Jean Davis – 8 pounds, 2 ounces of skin the color of cocoa powder and thin curly hair to match. Except for her dark brown eyes, she looked as if someone had dipped her completely in light chocolate.

Ted stared at his daughter in the newborn nursery and wondered who the hell she was. He mouthed a prayer to Jesus, thanking him for his new daughter, but he felt no thanks in his heart.

This was Rachel, named after a long fight with Leila about giving the girl such an obviously Biblical name. Leila had wanted to name her Stephanie. They had compromised by giving her the middle name of Jean, after Leila's Grandma Pritchett.

What was this child to him, he thought. What was he supposed to do now? Was he supposed to be overcome with love and devotion, claiming he would defend her from evil and protect her with his life?

He didn't feel that. He felt like she was some unknown variety of mewling little animal, the hand-lettered sign with his name, "Davis," hanging over the end of her crib. He felt like he was at the zoo and she was a baby chimpanzee.

This little creature was the one who had ruined his life, he thought, the one who had tied him forever to Leila. He looked at Rachel and hated her. Embarrassed, he lectured himself about the evil of hating a small defenseless child, a gift of God. He asked God to forgive him.

Then he turned and went looking for Leila.

But he wished God would keep His little gifts to Himself.

* * *

Two days after Leila came home from the hospital Ted came home from work to find his mother-in-law cleaning cloth diapers in his bathroom sink. He went in to take a whizz and there she was, her squat figure clad in a red wool jumper and apron, her hands in sudsy water.

"Hello?" he said, surprised to see Sophie.

She gave him a thin smile, wrung out the diaper from the sink, and pushed by him.

"Hi," she said brusquely.

He followed her into the kitchen, where she used the diaper to wipe off crumbs from the kitchen table. She carried a plate sticky with grape jelly to the kitchen sink where it joined a collection of dirty lunch dishes.

"Where's Leila?" Ted said.

"She took a walk," Sophie said, running water over the plates in the sink. "She needs her exercise," she added. "Young mothers need to get outside." She began filling up the sink with soapy water.

"What are you doing here?" he said pointblank.

She turned, leaned her ample hips against the sink, and wiped her hands on her apron. "I'm helping," she said simply.

"Leila doesn't need help," he blurted.

"How the hell would you know?" she said.

He just stared at her, confused.

She shook her head in disgust, mumbled something under her breath, and went back to her dishes.

He walked quickly to the bedroom he shared with Leila and went to the crib in the corner. Rachel Jean slept quietly under a cheap pink-nylon baby blanket that he didn't recognize.

He went back to the kitchen. "Where'd that blanket come from?" he said.

"I brought it, of course," Sophie said. "You want something to eat?"

"Sure," he said, taken aback. Leila never asked him if he wanted anything to eat. Since he hated her food he'd either buy sandwiches at the local delicatessan or his Aunt Millie would make up a batch of fried chicken and okra and send it over via his sister Pamela, who would duly return and report to her aunt on the ongoing squalor of Ted's life.

Sophie opened the refrigerator door. The refrigerator was filled with food. She pulled out slices of corned beef wrapped in butcher paper and a jar of mustard, then fished out a loaf of rye bread from a paper bag on the counter.

She made him a wonderful corned-beef sandwich, complete with dill pickle and a small cluster of potato chips on the side.

Then she finished the dishes, dried her hands on her apron, and hung it on a hook on the wall. The next thing he knew she was standing in front of him, pulling her ancient green winter coat up over her shoulders.

"Tell Leila I'll be back tomorrow at 7," she said. "Good-night."

And he heard the door slam after her before he could swallow the last bite of his sandwich and say good-bye.

Chapter Six

For the next two weeks, Sophie Prichett came every morning at 7 and left every evening at 6 after cooking dinner for Ted and Leila. She was a much better cook than her daughter. Ted ate better than he had in the five months since he'd been married to Leila.

Leila enjoyed Rachel Jean. She cooed to her, nursed her, and didn't seem to mind that the child was at least five shades darker in skin tone than she herself.

"You could almost take her for an Italian," Ted heard her tell her mother one morning as he got ready for work. He laughed to himself. Rachel Jean had a wide negroid nose and full lips. Aunt Millie had assured him she looked just like him when she'd made the pilgrimage to see her first grandniece, one Sunday after church.

White people could be such idiots.

He went to work that morning hoping his mother-in-law would make the stuffed pork chops she'd made two nights ago for dinner.

When he came back, Sophie, Leila, and Rachel were gone as were the baby's crib, most of the furniture, and all of Leila's clothes.

He picked up the phone and punched Sophie's phone number into it from a number penciled in on the kitchen wall.

Sophie answered.

"Sophie, what's going on?" he yelled into the phone. "I come home and this place looks like I was cleaned out by a bunch of nigger cat burglars."

"Leila, it's your husband," Sophie said flatly, turning away from the phone. He could hear Rachel fussing in the background. The phone changed hands.

"Hello?" It was Leila.

"Leila, what are you doing there?" he said more calmly.

"I'm leaving you," she said, her voice flat like her mother's. Rachel started crying. He could hear Leila hand her over to Sophie. "I want a divorce," she continued, like she was reading a script. "I'm going to live with my mother. You can pay me alimony and child support for the baby. I never want to see you again."

"But divorce is against the law of God. . ." he started.

"My uncle is a priest," she said. "He says the pope can have it annulled, like we were never married at all."

"But we have a child."

Didn't this woman realize all he had done for her out of love for God? Now she was throwing it back in his face. How would he explain a divorce to Reverand McDougal and his Bible group at Mt. Olivet? "You'll go to hell for this," he told her.

"Don't be crazy," she said. "It's miscegenation." Her tongue twisted itself in the middle of the word.

"What's that?"

"Black and white together," she said. "It's against the laws of God for the races to marry."

"So was having a child out of wedlock," he said. "John 24: verse 36. . ."

"Father Kaneverts says miscegenation is a sin," she said, cutting Ted off in full quote.

What wasn't a sin? Ted thought. What sin was he supposed to choose? The sin of having a child out of wedlock or the sin of sexual mixing of the races? Reverand McDougal and most of Mt. Olivet had apparently chosen the latter. They had been treating him like an unrepentant sinner since he'd married the white she-devil.

Fuck it.

"Fine, Leila," he said. "You get yourself a divorce. That's just fine with me."

And he hung up without another word and stared at the cracked plaster wall where the phone hung. Then he smiled to himself and went to the refrigerator.

A few slices of corned beef still lay in the butcher paper. He stuffed them into his mouth and gulped Coke from a big, half-filled bottle left on the top shelf.

"Free at last," he mumbled to himself, feeling the fizz of the Coke bubble up his throat. "Lord God Almighty, free at last."

He wondered what Aunt Millie was making for dinner that night.

* * *

She was reheating Sunday's big beef roast with baked potatoes along with pots of black-eyed peas, collard greens, and three packages of Gloriosa-brand creamed string beans with almonds on the side. The local supermarket had had a sale on them; Millie was a big one on making sure everyone ate enough vegetables.

When Ted called and said that Leila had left him, her first response was: "Come home for dinner."

And he did.

"I never liked that girl, boy. I just never did," Millie said as she shuffled around her kitchen stirring pots. "You can have your old room," she said, handing him plates. "She robbed you of your childhood."

Ted was nearly 19 and had a thick beard, but he grinned. That's right, he thought, she robbed me of my childhood. He felt giddy with relief.

Despite their differing schedules, Millie insisted that the entire family eat dinner together in the evenings. She was a good cook, the food was free, so unless someone was tied up in traffic or stuck in a late-night class at school, everyone made it home for dinner at 6:30.

They were mildly surprised to see Ted.

They were completely surprised when he said Leila was gone.

"She just picked up the kid and went to her mother's and that was it," Ted said, spearing a big chunk of baked potato and stuffing it in his mouth. "I never even knew anything was wrong," he said virtuously, as if the whole situation hadn't been completely wrong from day one.

"You're good to be done with her," Franklin said. "She was bad news, real white trash."

"Franklin," Harry said, "that's not a Christian comment."

Franklin rolled his eyes at Ted.

"So what happens to Rachel Jean, that trusting little soul God gave you?" Harry said quietly, cutting the meat on his plate and staring at Ted. "Does she just slip away into the web of Catholic conspiracy or has an appropriate vehicle been found to preserve her blessed soul in Christ?"

Harry was trying to become head trustee at the Mt. Olivet church council and had started trying to sound more profound.

Ted stared at his uncle. "Excuse me?" he said.

"What happens to the baby?" Harry said, exasperated.

"She's staying with her mother," Ted said.

"But what about her immortal soul?"

"That stays with her mother, too."

Lavonne Rae and Pamela snickered, but Harry quieted them with a glare.

"Another soul you're commending to the papist conspiracy? You're going to let another child of God fall into sin? The shame of it." And he went back to slowly and virtuously eating his black-eyed peas.

"What do you want me to do, kidnap her?" Ted said.

"You have to do what's best for her soul."

"And what's that?"

"Bring her back here for me and your Aunt Millie to raise in the shadow of God's love."

"Harry!" Millie said, looking up from her plate. "Are you crazy?"

"Of course not," he said. "I'm trying in my own small way to be a good Christian."

Actually, he had weighed his choices and found this one the least horrible. First, his nephew marries a white woman. Then he divorces her. Then he lets her carry off the baby. The Mt. Olivet congregation would never stand for it.

Raising the damn kid himself was his only way out.

He *really* wanted to be Mt. Olivet's head trustee.

"I don't want to hear another word about it," Millie said. "Not one word. It's totally ridiculous." She spooned out another serving of peas on Ted's plate.

Harry drew his mouth into a thin line and stared straight ahead, silenced.

"The idea," Millie mumbled, shoveling more peas on her own plate.

Then Lavonne Rae asked her mother if she could borrow her car while her own was in the shop on Wednesday, and Pamela said she needed a new pair of shorts for gym class, and Franklin asked his dad for more money for schoolbooks.

"What? I just gave you $150," Harry said.

"I need a lab manual that costs $34.95 . . ." he began.

"What's it made out of — gold?"

And no one said another word about Ted, Leila, or their baby.

Ted stuck his fork in a thick clump of collard greens and shoveled them happily into his mouth. It was as if nothing had ever happened. The marriage to Leila had all been a bad dream.

He was free to start over again, no strings attached.

* * *

The next day he went back to the apartment, cleaned out his clothes, and told Mrs. Blanco he was leaving.

Two days later Franklin came and helped him move what was left of the furniture: the mattress, a kitchen table with a broken leg, and an armchair with one ripped arm. They moved it to the Davis's basement.

Ted moved back into the cramped bedroom with Franklin and climbed into the top bunk with a sigh, his feet hanging over the end and Franklin complaining that they should have moved *out* of the bedroom and *into* the apartment, not the other way around.

It was good to be home.

* * *

Two weeks later, Ted received an official-looking letter from a lawyer in Whiting — Leila's lawyer.

He scanned the three-page, single-spaced copy. She was filing for divorce, wanted the baby, wanted alimony, wanted child support, would give him visiting privileges on alternate weekends, there would be a meeting, blah, blah, blah.

Fuck her, he thought. She could have everything — such as it was. And he stuck her letter in the top drawer of his bureau.

Three days later she called.

"Are you coming to the meeting?" she said.

"What meeting?" he said.

"About the divorce."

"Yeah, I guess so."

She gave him an address, a time, and he swore he would come.

He did make it, coming on his lunch hour from Farnsworth. He told no one. All he needed were Millie and Harry second-guessing

him, telling him what to do. He was going to be free of the white
she-devil and their devil child. Wasn't that enough?

The lawyer's office was in a crumbling brick building with a heavy
red door. The lawyer was a fat white man with a thick Slavic accent
and a cheap suit. He mumbled gibberish about "rights" and "child
support" and whatnot. Leila sat on a dirty plaid couch with Sophie,
a less-decayed version of her mother.

Ted didn't even take off his coat. He played with one of his
gloves and listened to the lawyer. When the lawyer finished talking,
everyone looked at Ted expectantly.

"Fine, fine," he mumbled. "Let me sign."

And he did, an entire sheaf of papers.

The lawyer gathered them up, smiling, and everyone got up to
leave.

Ted and Leila had barely spoken three words to each other.

"I thought we were getting an annulment," he said.

"We are," she said. "But I didn't want to take any chances."

And she and her mother walked out. It was Wednesday and that
night he went straight to his Bible class from work. At coffee break,
he walked up to Melinda Mayberry, now the assistant group leader
of the Bible study group, and asked her out after class.

"I thought you was a married man, Mr. Davis," she said, both
hands of delicate pink and black fingers wrapped tightly around a
big styrofoam cup of coffee. About 18-years-old, she was dressed in
a neat skirt and sweater that emphasized her voluptuous figure.

"No more, no more, Miss Mayberry," he said. "To my great
sadness, my wife has decided to go, with our child, and leave me
alone in this world." He sipped his small cup of coffee, his big eyes
looking over the edge of the cup at her.

She eyed him suspiciously. "You ain't wastin' any time getting
back into circulation are you, Mr. Davis," she said.

He smiled with affected shyness and put on his fake Boston
accent. "At a time like this it's better for a man to make the
acquaintance of, and cherish the company of, good Christian women
then to be left alone to his own devices, Miss Mayberry," he said.

Melinda looked at him with her immense brown eyes and
thought about that for a moment.

"I suppose so," she said.

"So how about it?" he said eagerly.

"Let me talk to my spiritual advisor," she said.

He looked at her, puzzled.

"I want to ask the Reverand if it's alright for me to see you," she said. "I'll tell you at the adulation." The "adulation" was a weepy prayer service held every Sunday night at Mt. Olivet, and accompanied with much chanting and singing. Ted found it tasteless and couldn't imagine that the Lord really wanted to hear all that racket.

"Meet me at the adulation, and I'll tell you," she said.

"Of course, Miss Mayberry," he said.

And they went back to their discussion of the *Book of Job*.

* * *

Harry was delighted that Ted wanted to attend the adulation. It was Harry's personal favorite of the Mt. Olivet repertoire of religious services. He also thought it would look good to the congregation to see his nephew repentent after his terrible sins of defying the Lord by marrying the white she-devil.

Franklin knew better.

"You got some black pussy lined up, I just know it, I can smell it," he told his cousin as Ted finished knotting his tie that Sunday evening.

Ted looked at him. He was interested in Melinda's soul, not her body. She was a pure, holy spirit, studying to be a licensed practical nurse at East Chicago Junior College and living with her God-fearing family.

"Franklin, you live in a toilet all the time," he said, finishing his tie knot with a yank. "Watch out you don't end up smelling like shit."

Franklin groaned.

"I'll pray for your soul, brother," Ted said, walking out of the room.

"Pray for your own, you dumb nigger," Franklin called after him. "You're the one who can't keep his dick in his pants."

Chapter Seven

The Mt. Olivet Missionary Baptist Church was hopping when Ted arrived. Every light was on; cars pulled up front and dropped off load after load of people. The adulation worshipers were a formal lot. The women wore big picture hats with wild collections of fake flowers and feathers stuck in them and bright-colored dresses, many of blue or pink chiffon.

The women laughed and talked while they streamed into the church; the men wore more solemn expressions and looked uncomfortable in their cheap suits in off shades of gray, blue, and brown.

A big old white frame building, badly in need of paint, Mt. Olivet had formerly been a Methodist Church when Horton Beach was a white neighborhood. But the Methodists and their religion had left for the suburbs, leaving their large, simply designed church to the black hordes that followed. The church still had beautiful clean lines and simple pillars, but the poverty of the present congregation prevented any but the most minimal maintenance.

The varnish had worn from the wood floors, the pews displayed the ground-in dirt of years of sweaty hands and bodies, and paint peeled in large scabs from the ceiling.

Ted thought of the neat and prosperous Church of St. Peter, the Episcopal Church he had attended with his parents in LaGrange. He wondered if he had only attended its measured and well-mannered services in another life.

Besides, Episcopalians were one step removed from Catholics, which, of course, were one step removed from the devil and part of the international papist conspiracy.

Or so Uncle Harry always said.

The church was already hot and crowded with bodies when Ted walked in 10 minutes before the service. He had come with Harry, who talked with every worshipper that came in and shook hands enthusiastically. Standing at the door, Harry looked like the official greeter.

Ted scanned the crowd looking for Melinda. He found her immediately, sitting in the third row, sandwiched between a huge, hulking man and an entire row of children in their best clothes, like a line of little blackbirds sitting on a telephone wire. At the aisle end was a big woman in an enormous hat with at least six inches of fake vegetation springing from its crown.

He was about to approach Melinda, but the choir started up, a loud rendition of "Take Me to the Water; Let Me Drink at that Holy Spring." Reverand McDougal's wife hit every note on her ruin of a piano with terrific force.

Ted squeezed himself into an aisle seat several rows behind the Mayberrys. The congregation began singing; most knew the words by heart.

After five minutes of song, Reverand McDougal came out and started preaching. He talked about sin, hell, damnation, the "blessed light of sweet Jesus our savior," and the general presence of evil in the world. Then he quoted four or five long passages from the Bible, none of which Ted recalled, though he could see Melinda bobbing her head in recognition.

Then the choir threw itself into another rousing hymn and the circus was on. The entire church stood up as one. Jammed against the aisle seat, Ted could feel himself practically sucked up on to his feet.

They all began to sing. They sang of crossing deep rivers and dark valleys to find their sweet Jesus, of laboring in the vineyards of the Lamb, of going home to their blessed Lord. They sang, they swayed. Someone in the choir started beating a tambourine. The tempo of the music picked up. "Jesus, Jesus, Jesus," they sang, "save me from that wicked road to hell. I'm coming home, my blessed savior. I'm coming home to Your saving grace." Someone in the choir took off on a high-pitched counterpoint.

Then the congregation started talking back to the music. "That's right," someone called from a back row. "That's right, brother. I mean it." The old lady next to Ted started moaning and putting her hands over her face.

He watched Melinda from the rear. Her broad rump swayed. She grabbed herself with her arms then threw back her head and sang loudly.

She looked like an African princess in the throes of some ritual dance of puberty. Ted imagined the row of her swaying brothers and sisters as her attendants. He saw Melinda in his mind's eye, her powerful hips wrapped in a colorful cloth, her big, full breasts swaying unfettered by clothing while her arms of jewelry clattered and jangled. He could hear drums in the background, the howl of the village warriors as they encircled the princess to celebrate her crossing into womanhood.

He broke into a sweat of excitement. He would be the prince. He would wear a lion skin, and his body would be painted with sacred symbols. He would come with his band of warriors from a neighboring village to claim the princess as his own. Their hands joined together by the chief, her father, they would retire to a decorated hut lined with sweet grass for a night of indescribably beautiful lovemaking.

He trembled at the thought. Ahead of him, Melinda rolled her hips wildly and clapped and howled to the music. She shook her head and her hat fell on the seat of the pew behind her; her dark curls shone in the overhead light. Her shoulders swayed and her huge breasts quivered and shook in the overstressed bra under her filmy blouse.

He couldn't take his eyes off her. "Come here, my beauty," he muttered. He felt like crawling over the pews, grabbing her, and taking her in the aisle.

No one would probably notice. People were hopping, jumping, singing, clapping, and a few already danced in the aisles. The walls shook with their voices. Certainly, the Methodists never worshipped with the fervor of the Mt. Olivet Baptists.

"Let me plow your fertile fields, let me rest my weary load," the old lady next to him sang, loudly and off-key, in his ear.

The service continued for 45 minutes. It ended on a high note of clapping and singing, the choir continuing to softly croon as people bent, smiling and dazed, to pick up their hats and coats or rearrange their clothing.

Ted pushed out of his pew and ran up to Melinda. She glistened with sweat; her blouse was soaked with it. He could see her nipples protruding hard and big under her blouse. She gave him a big smile, and he half-expected her to fall into his arms.

Instead, she turned to the hulking man next to her.

"Daddy, this is Ted Davis," she said.

"Pleased to meet you, sir," Ted said, off-balance, shaking the giant man's giant hand.

Mr. Mayberry acknowledged the introduction with some polite mutterings, then excused himself to find the Reverand McDougal.

Ted helped Melinda on with her coat.

"Well," he said, getting directly to the point, "did you talk to your spiritual advisor about going out with me?"

"My spiritual advisor?" she said, looking at him with her big eyes. "Oh yes, yes," she said, remembering. "I did."

"And?"

"He said you were still in the process of spiritual growth and advised me to seek out young men of more appropriate spiritual discipline." Her eyes opened in wide innocence, she buttoned her prim plaid coat over her amazing bosom.

"In other words," she said, her voice low and full of naivete, "the Reverand McDougal considers you too worldly for a young girl like me." Her eyes opened even wider. "You've already been married, once," she said, as if that put him in a different race of creatures. "My daddy doesn't like that either."

Ted bit his lip. "I see," he said.

"I am sorry," she said, smiling and friendly, as if she had just spilled coffee on his tablecloth instead of shutting down his last available option for love. "I'll see you Wednesday night." Then she took her amazing black-princess body swaddled in its tight coat and walked primly down the aisle and out the church door, holding two of her little brothers, one by each hand.

Ted sat down in a pew, picked up a worn hymnal, and began tearing out one page at a time, slowly and carefully. He crumpled them into balls and threw them on the floor.

Then he went home and crawled into bed without saying a word.

* * *

The next evening at dinner, Millie announced in a shaky voice that Pamela was pregnant. The girl sat there, round and contented, while her aunt gave the family the news.

Lavonne Rae muttered under her breath and kept eating, Franklin smiled, and Ted and Harry looked at the girl like she had gone mad.

No one said a word until Harry carefully put down his fork and turned to her. "You'll have to marry the father," he said.

"But I don't know which one it is," she said happily. "It could be Tyrone, Powell, or Jackson. They're all my boyfriends." Then she sat back in her seat and continued to smile happily, a young woman well-loved by young men.

Now she would be a mother, just like many of the other 16-year-old girls at school. She would be free from the school's drafty classrooms and her battles with the mysteries of algebra.

She could stay home, watch TV, and play with her baby while accepting the adulation of her visiting girlfriends. Her baby would be the most beautiful of all; she had only slept with good-looking boys.

She hadn't been this happy since before her parents had died.

"You're in big trouble, young lady," Harry said, his voice deepening.

"Yes, Uncle Harry," she said brightly. Why did adults carry on about it like this?

"You'll have to marry one of them," he said. "Pick the most likely father."

She stared at him. "But I really don't know which one it is."

"So make a guess."

"Uncle Harry!"

"Don't you Uncle Harry me!" he suddenly yelled, pounding his fist on the table. The dishes clattered and everyone jumped. "You pick one of those boys and you marry him. No niece of mine is going to end up wandering the streets, an unwed mother, disgracing our family name."

Harry slammed his fist down on the table again. "Damn it, girl!" he yelled. "Just what kind of morals did my useless brother teach you?" He cast a sidelong glance at Ted to include him in the condemnation. "How can you bring this sin and disgrace into my house? How can you humiliate the family that took you in when you were wretched orphans on the street? How can you drag us through the dirt like this?"

Pamela stared at her hands; she'd thought motherhood was a good idea. She had more friends than ever at school. For the first time since her arrival at Horton Beach, she was actually popular.

"Pick one and marry him!" he bellowed again.

She shrugged her shoulders and put her finger to her lips in thought. Powell was well-built but had a harelip, and Tyrone's car was an embarrassment to ride in, but Jackson McCahey was a strong candidate. He wore nice clothes, had popular friends, and drove a 1978 T-bird with gangster white-walls and fuzzy pink dice hanging from the rearview mirror.

"It was Jackson," she said. "I know it was him." She wouldn't mind playing house with Jackson for awhile to humor her uncle. Jackson would eventually leave her and she could move back in with Millie and Harry. She saw herself spoonfeeding her baby rice pudding from a jar and watching "All My Children" on TV.

She'd name the baby "Prince," after the rock star, and "Luigi," after the name of a character in a commercial for spaghetti sauce that she had liked on TV. The actor had a wonderful black moustache and a deep brown Mediterranean coloring. He could have been a high-yellow black.

Prince Luigi McCahey.

What a wonderful name.

"Pamela!" It was Uncle Harry.

She gave him another dazed, happy look.

"So give me this boy's telephone number," he said. "We should take action immediately."

Pamela didn't know his phone number but Harry found it in the phone book and called the McCahey house that night. No one answered the phone. So the next day at school Pamela cornered Jackson in the hall after third period.

"You're the father of my baby," she told him. "My uncle says you'd better marry me."

Jackson looked at her, a wide-beamed 16-year-old in overtight jeans, and started to laugh. He threw his head back and laughed so hard his shoulders shook.

He was 18-years-old, good-looking, and could bang any girl in the school. He was universally held to be Horton-Gary High School's most attractive male. Why would he want to marry *anyone*, much less some pathetic, fat-assed junior who he'd screwed when he'd been high one night and whose name he couldn't even remember?

He kept laughing as he turned and walked down the hall.

Pamela shrugged and turned the other way. She knew it would turn out this way. Why wouldn't they just let her have her baby and stay home?

That night at dinner, she told Harry that Jackson had turned her down. Lavonne Rae snickered.

Harry got up from the table, went to the phone, and called Jackson's house again. No one answered. He came back and sat down.

"Try one of the other boys," he said.

Pamela pursed her lips. She didn't like Tyrone much, but Powell would do. She told her uncle that she would ask him the next day at school.

When she did, the boy looked at her like she was crazy.

"You outta' yo mind, girl?" he said. Then he turned and walked away.

She didn't even bother asking Tyrone.

"No one wants to marry me," she told her uncle at dinner that night. She hoped he would give up the idea and let her have her baby in peace.

But no, Harry got the boys' phone numbers, called their houses, and asked for their mothers.

Jackson's mother was out, but Tyrone's was home. She said Pamela was a slut; her boy wouldn't do something like that. Powell's mother was drunk and incoherent on the phone.

The next night Harry called again and asked for the boys' fathers. The small child that answered the phone at Jackson's said they didn't have a father, the teen-ager that answered Tyrone's phone said his father was at work, and Powell's father said he would talk to his son and call back.

He did, five minutes later. "He says he's not the father," was the unsurprising response.

"Well he is," Harry said.

"He oughta' know where his dick has been," the man said. "He says he never set eyes on your daughter in his life."

"My niece," Harry said pointedly, "insists that he's the father."

"Maybe you just better ask her if she can tell the difference between one dick and another in the dark 'cause my boy says he's never even talked to her much less knocked her up. I'd try knocking at some other door," he said, hanging up the phone.

Harry looked at the phone in his hand and set it down in the receiver. Turning around, he saw Pamela in front of the big console TV in the living room. She was laying on her stomach and watching some sit-com, her eyes screwed up over her English homework, which she penciled in with a big pencil, chewed-on and worn down to a stubby nub.

"Pamela," he called.

She turned and looked at him.

"Come here," he said.

She got up heavily and came over to him, glancing back over her shoulder at the TV.

He slapped her, hard, across the face. "You're a slut, a disgrace to the family," he said. She put her hand to her face and tears came to her eyes. Lavonne Rae and Millie, who had been watching TV with her, looked up in surprise. Millie even let a soft "Harry" escape from her lips.

"Go to your room!" he barked.

Pamela slunk down the hall to the bedroom she shared with Lavonne Rae and slammed the door.

Harry went into the kitchen, pulled a beer from the refrigerator, and put his head in his hands. He'd never make lead trustee after this. He wished he believed in abortion.

In her room, Pamela turned on the radio and lay down on the frilly blue bedspread over her bed. She hugged her favorite stuffed animal, a foot-long plush tiger with a worn spot over the snout.

She was going to be a mother. She closed her eyes and dreamed of her friends coming to visit her. Her friend Fantasia Marie was having her baby the same time as she.

But she was sure Prince Luigi Davis would be handsomer.

* * *

Several weeks later, Ted came home from work to a pile of official-looking letters on the table. Leila, Leila's attorney, and the "Center for the Preservation of Family Life—Northwestern Indiana Chapter" were all writing him for money. He and Leila had been divorced six weeks and he hadn't paid her any child support yet.

In fact, he had no intention of *ever* paying her *any* money. Her useless mother could support her. He had signed the papers and gotten them out of his life. Let Sophie pay the bills.

Millie was curious about his formal-looking mail.

"I'm still arguing with Leila over the divorce," he told her, then walked back to his bedroom before Millie could offer advice. His aunt and uncle still thought he and Leila were just separated.

The letter from the Center for Preservation of Family Life was a heartrending form letter on blue paper, pleading with him to consider the fate of his wife and unsupported daughter.

"We are writing you on behalf of your ex-wife, Leila Pritchett Davis," the letter read. Leila's name had been typed in crookedly on an empty line. "Caught in a dead-end job, or no job at all," the letter continued, "she has nothing to support herself or your precious child."

It read like that for several pages. Ted wadded it up and threw it in the wastebasket by the tiny desk he shared with Franklin.

The attorney's letter was more to the point. "Please pay the amount due immediately or we will be forced to take legal action."

The amount due was $560.

Ted's jaw dropped. That was half his monthly pay—before taxes.

He opened Leila's letter. "How can you let me and my child starve?" it began.

She wasn't starving. She was living with her mother. The thought of Sophie's special stuffed pork chops made his mouth start to water.

"Stephanie needs everything."

Stephanie? His daughter was named Rachel. Leila had renamed the kid without even asking him.

The letter went on about the high cost of disposable diapers, baby-sitters, and baby clothes. Stephanie, a.k.a. Rachel, needed a snowsuit and a stroller; Sophie's rheumatism was bothering her. She would probably have to quit work for a few weeks. Starvation would be at her door.

He thought of his obese ex-wife; starvation would be good for her.

He was supposed to be supporting this whole show while he made $7.00 an hour on the maintenance crew at a paint factory?

Why had he ever married her in the first place?

His religion. It was what God had wanted.

Well then, God could just come up with the money to support her. It was His stupid idea to begin with.

He cursed himself. How could he talk about God that way?

So he should borrow money from his uncle to send to Leila, or send her half of his already pitiful paycheck, just because he'd been stupid enough to stick his dick in her for two minutes of "love?"

She had to be ought of her mind.

He looked heavenward. And so was He.

He wadded Leila's letter into a ball, then shredded the letter from her attorney into neat strips of paper on his desk. He cleared the whole desk with one side of his arm, sweeping everything onto the floor.

They could all go fuck themselves: Leila, her mother, and God.

He wasn't paying *anyone anything*.

And he threw on his coat and walked down to the corner bar where his cousin Franklin often hung out before dinner. Maybe they could shoot a little pool, then come home for a little of Aunt Millie's homecooking.

Chapter Eight

Three Sundays later Ted announced that he wasn't going to church.

His horrified uncle came into Ted's bedroom just before it was time to go. He glared down at his nephew, stretched out on the lower bunk in his pajamas, reading a comic book.

"You're going to make us all late for services," Harry said, his voice ominous.

"I'm not going," Ted said, flipping to the next page of comics and looking up at his uncle. "I don't feel good."

"You look fine to me," Harry said.

"OK," Ted said, going back to his comics. "I just don't want to go."

"Get up," Harry said. "Put on your clothes." He grabbed his nephew by the arm and tried to pull him up, but Ted went limp.

"Get up!" Harry yelled.

"Fuck you, man!" Ted yelled back, trying to pull his arm away. "I'm not going anywhere."

"God will punish you for this!" Harry yelled, tightening his grip.

"Fuck God! He hasn't done anything so great for me lately!"

Harry was so shocked he dropped Ted's arm and stepped back a step. "How dare you talk about your lord and savior Jesus Christ like that!" he yelled. His face started turning red. "It's blasphemy! It's a sin against God and nature!"

"Fuck, fuck, fuck, God, God, God," Ted chanted.

By this time, the entire family had gathered by the door to the bedroom.

"You're out of here, kid," Harry said, his voice dark and controlled. "You're gone. You're leaving my house immediately.

"When I come back from worshipping my lord and savior Jesus Christ and begging Him on my hands and knees to forgive your vile and blasphemous mouth, I want you out of my house. I don't want to see you or talk to you or have anything to do with you."

Ted could hear Millie gasp in the hallway. "Harry . . ." she started.

"Hold your tongue, woman," he hissed.

Ted rolled over on his side and turned his back to his uncle.

"I gave you everything," Harry said. "I took you in when that miserable brother of mine got himself killed and left you on my doorstep, a penniless orphan. I educated you, I fed you, I brought you to the altar of our Lord as a penitent sinner.

"And this is how you pay me back!" He was yelling again; he suddenly dropped his voice. "You are scum. I never want to see or hear from you again."

Then he turned on his heel and walked out the door, followed by Millie, who was mumbling to him about "not being so hard on the boy."

Franklin leaned against the jamb in the doorway.

"Man, you are the biggest fuckup I've ever seen," he said. "What the fuck are you trying to do?"

Ted turned over again and propped himself up in the bed. "Got me," he said, shrugging his shoulders.

"I mean the old man doesn't get this pissed-off unless you throw pictures of 'his lord and savior' on the ground and take a leak on 'em," Franklin said.

Ted shrugged his shoulders again. "I guess I should get out of here," he said.

"I guess you better, man. The old man will come back and have your balls for Sunday dinner if you don't." Franklin started to turn away, then stopped. "You have someplace to go, let this thing blow over?"

Ted shook his head no.

"Go stay with the Gopher. Tell him I sent you." The Gopher was Franklin's main drug contact since Callen's murder. A skinny black man with a pockmarked yellowish face, the Gopher played the grand man of the neighborhood. His run-down shack of a house two blocks over was the drop-in center for every homeless drug addict and bum within miles.

"Tell him 'the Con' sent you," Franklin said. "The Con" was the name Franklin affected on the street.

"Right," Ted said.

Franklin smiled. "See you later," he said. And he disappeared from the doorway and went to church.

Ted sat up and put his feet on the floor. He held his head in his hands and ran his fingers through his matted hair.

What had happened to his life?

Where the fuck was he going?

He had $7.50 in his checking account, $353 in cash, no car, a daughter to support, and a job at slave-labor wages for a decaying paint factory where you could hardly breathe the air without gagging.

He thought of his dead parents. His father was a hazy figure dressed in a suit, but his mother appeared before him clearly. Plump and wrapped in a fur coat, she was correcting his diction and tying a ridiculous little hat with a brim on his head. He must have been seven or eight.

He looked at his grimy fingers and jagged nails. She'd roll over in her grave if she could see him now.

He got up, walked to the bureau, and gazed at himself in the tiny mirror hanging over it. He saw a young man with a matte of kinky hair and tired lines around a pair of sad, brown eyes.

He didn't want to go to the Gopher's; somebody was liable to knife you while you slept. But he had no other real friends. A hotel was out of the question.

And he was hungry. Very hungry.

So he went to the phone book, looked up Sophie Pritchett, and invited himself to Sunday dinner.

Sophie was surprised to hear his voice when she picked up the phone. He told her he wanted to bring child-support money for Leila.

"I'll come over around 1," he said.

"We're eating then," she began.

"That's alright. You can lay another plate for me."

"But. . ."

And he cut her off by hanging up.

* * *

Ted packed a small suitcase with his clothes, filched the bus schedule to Chicago from a kitchen drawer, and walked to downtown Horton Beach, about a mile from the house. He had coffee and pie at a small, overheated restaurant that smelled of congealed grease.

Then he hitchhiked to Whiting. It was late July and muggy. He stood for a long time waiting for a ride, the hot sun draining him of energy.

A bunch of joy-riding black high-school kids, high on something, picked him up and dropped him at Sophie's door.

She was alarmed to see him carrying a suitcase.

"Uncle Harry is sending me on a short vacation to see my cousin Dennis in Chicago," he lied. "I'll be back soon."

Then he had opened his checkbook and wrote Leila a check for $756.

"For child support," he said, handing the check to Sophie. In reality, he had $7.50 in his checking account.

Sophie smiled broadly. She almost looked friendly. She dished him up generous servings of food at dinner.

Dinner was good—big plates of cabbage rolls and dumplings and apple pie for dessert. But it was awkward. Leila sat sullenly at one end of the table and kept getting up to attend to Rachel, now named Stephanie, who cried on and off in another bedroom.

Leila looked worse than he remembered. Not only was she fat, but she looked tired. She got up slowly each time the baby cried and lumbered off. Her two younger brothers talked only with each other and played with their food.

Ted ate quietly and quickly. It was certainly the best meal he'd ever had for $7.50.

After dinner, Sophie gave him a ride to the Whiting bus station and wished him a good trip. He smiled broadly, knowing that he would never see her, Leila, and whatever his daughter was named, again.

He arrived in Chicago in late afternoon. It was very hot; the downtown stores were closed. He asked a cop where a poor man with no money could stay the night and he directed him to the Heavenly Host Garden of Refuge on the south end of downtown.

He was lucky; he got one of the last places for the night, right in line of the air stream from a big fan.

That night he slept badly on an old cot in the refuge's big dormitory, the sounds of men coughing and mumbling in their sleep all around him.

The next day he enlisted in the air force.

He debated: navy, army, air force. In the end he took the air force; he liked their uniforms best.

He filled in the forms carefully. Under "marital status" he checked "single, never married." Under "nearest living relative" he wrote nothing.

"You have no family at all?" the recruiter said.

Ted smiled. "None," he said. "I'm an orphan."

Then he went out and got drunk at a bar around the corner from the mission. But he was careful to be back in line for a place at the mission by 3 that afternoon.

He had two weeks to kill before the air force took over his life and he didn't want to sleep on the streets. He spent the time playing pool, moving from bar to bar, and playing cards with some of the regulars at the mission who didn't smell too bad. One of his favorite card partners was an old white bum with a daughter in Florida. Every week, she sent him a check for $50 which he gambled away.

"She thinks I'm living in one of those old people's retirement homes and spending my money on church offerings," the man said. His name was James. "But she don't have no spirit. She don't know how to live." And he dealt out the cards in another of the endless rounds of poker he played during the day.

James was good. He won most of Ted's money and his camera. He also won most of the newcomers' money. Ted knew he was cheating, but he couldn't figure out how.

He never did find out. After Ted had no more money or cameras to bet, James stopped playing cards with him. He turned a deaf ear to Ted's pleas for credit and a chance to earn his money back. The guy must have had a fortune in the bank.

The mission's social workers didn't like the card-playing but found it hard to stop. They would constantly break up the games in the day room, but the players would move outside, or to another room, or even to the bathrooms. The social workers were a starchy lot and very Christian. They required all mission "guests," as the bums who stayed there were called, to attend religious services every evening before they ate supper.

Most sat listlessly through the 45-minute, halting sermons of the service, usually given by beardless young men from the mission's training program who were learning to "bring the gospel to the homeless." Most were Ted's age, very white, and very nervous. They tripped and blundered through their pointless sermons, trying to remember all the points they'd learned in their class on homiletics on how to effectively convey the word of God to the downtrodden.

They spoke simply, they "used simple symbols the underprivileged could understand," they waved their hands, and they smiled constantly. Constantly. Big, white, toothy smiles.

Sitting through the 10th sermon of his stay, Ted understood why the mission's population turned over regularly. They simply couldn't stand it anymore.

Having no money, he had no options. So he slouched in his chair, folded his arms, and tried to think of other things, mostly pussy. Sometimes he tried to nap, but one of the "brothers," as the social workers were called, would come by and gently nudge him awake — with a big smile, of course.

It felt like Chinese water torture.

He was glad when his day of induction came.

* * *

The induction center was a windowless, red-brick building just west of downtown. It covered a full city block. A passerby could mistake it for a big telephone or electric company substation if it wasn't for the tiny lettering on the front: Induction Center: U.S. Armed Forces.

Inside it was a clean-painted warren of rooms and amazingly shiny green linoleum floors. The place smelled of wax and industrial cleaners and was full of crisp young men in crisp uniforms directing the recruits as they came in. They reminded Ted of cattle handlers.

Within one hour of entering the place, he was standing in his underwear, holding his urine sample in one hand, and going from room to room in the warren. White-coated doctors looked up his nose, shone lights in his eyes, and asked him to bend over and spread his cheeks.

Half the inductees were black, a good third Hispanic, and the rest were whites, many with southern accents.

Despite their fresh young faces, the whites looked sickly and unhealthy with fleshy hips, protruding bellies, and washboards of ribs sticking through their skinny chests, their spines curving back in gentle "S's."

This was the "master race?"

At least black skin looked better under the miles of fluorescent lights strung through the puzzle of rooms and halls.

By 10 that morning he had been probed and palpated, signed a wide variety of papers, and been stuck on a bus for Camp Forsythe, an air force recruit training camp on the Gulf coast of Texas. It was another hot day. The bus's air conditioning lurched and gurgled. He turned around and pressed his face against the window to watch the familiar skyline of Chicago ever so slowly fade behind him.

Eventually, he got a crick in his neck and turned forward. He was sitting next to a bug-eyed black man cracking and eating pistachio nuts. The pink ends of the man's fingers were deep red from the dye on the nuts' shells.

The man was named Rutherford; he was from Milwaukee. He offered Ted some nuts then slipped on a set of Walkman headphones, turned up the volume, and went to sleep.

Ted turned toward the window. The bus rolled by the familiar exits for Naperville, ramps he'd ridden many times with his family as they headed to southern Indiana to see his mother's mother, an ancient woman who lived in virtual seclusion with an old maiden aunt watching over her.

He leaned his head against the window and started to cry. He cried for his dear dead mother, his proud dead father, for his destroyed sister Pamela, and for himself — adrift and alone with a bunch of honkies in uniforms on his way to the deep South.

He was black; he was supposed to be going the *other* way.

He had a strong urge to get up and get off the bus, to hitchhike to his old house, beg the present inhabitants to let him in, and throw himself weeping on the floor of his old bedroom.

How life had cheated him. This was God's love in action?

How could God be so mean and vindictive? He thought of God as a giant walking through a field and kicking over anthills. As the panicked ants fled, he smashed them with his hobnailed boot, just for amusement.

He was an ant; God was a mean-spirited bastard.

He sighed deeply and wiped his eyes with the end of his sleeve. He looked over at Rutherford, his bug eyes closed like two big capsules on his face, sleeping peacefully with the Walkman playing in his ears. A sharp-faced young officer walked down the aisle of the bus to the bathroom in the rear.

Ted thought of him as his jailer.

He'd made a big mistake joining the air force, he told himself.

He should have stayed home and gone into heating and air conditioning.

The bus sped on. No one talked; they were all in their private reveries. Besides, the uniformed men with the severe haircuts didn't look like they would tolerate much conversation.

The bus stopped for lunch at a McDonald's. For dinner, they ate at a Burger King. Back on the bus they curled up, each in his own cramped seat, and tried to sleep.

They woke up the next morning to mountains, which faded away to hills, then plains of scrubby pine and blasted trees interspersing fields of the reddest dirt Ted had ever seen. His stomach growled with hunger, but the bus didn't stop.

Then, just before noon, the bus pulled into Camp Forsythe, miles of chain-link fence topped with barbed wire encircling row upon row of long, squat buildings. They were all painted beige. Only the doors were different colors.

The bus dropped them at the central parade grounds, a gravel-covered square with a perfectly tended plot of red, white, and blue petunias in the center. A shiny silver flagpole sprouted from their midst, a crisp new flag beating against it in the breeze.

The heat was unbelievable. Within 10 minutes of leaving the bus, the entire group was drooping and bedraggled.

Bands of men with close-cropped hair and green fatigues marched by. One group trotted, double-time, across a green expanse of grass toward of clump of red-doored buildings.

Ted hoped he'd be fed, but instead, the uniformed men on the bus hurried them off and into a ragged line on the parade grounds.

A thin white man in a perfectly pressed uniform and a green-brown, Smokey-the-Bear hat started yelling at them to get in line, stand up straight, stop shuffling, look like men, suck in their guts, etc.

The man's list of complaints was endless. He started swearing at them. They were sons of bitches, fatheads, fuckups, dirtbags, sons of whores. The men shifted uneasily in their places and stared at their feet. The man kept yelling at them.

After two minutes of continuous cursing, he fell silent. Then he introduced himself: Master Sargeant James Madison Johnson, United States Air Force.

They stared at him, dull-eyed.

Then he barked at them to march on. They all tried to stand up straight and look military. He yelled at them more: they were shitheads, dumb cunts, SOBs, jackasses. Johnson had an endless list of abusive names on immediate recall.

The uniformed men herded them off to a collection of yellow-doored boxy buildings near the entry to the camp: complex 14, buildings D, E, and F. The buildings were filled with a long row of bunk beds covered with pea-soup-green blankets. It was cooler inside, but not by much.

Just like home, Ted thought, thinking of the bunk beds he had shared with Franklin. He threw his suitcase on a top bunk of a set halfway down the room. The only thing missing was Franklin tossing on the bottom and pulling on his dick half the night.

Chapter Nine

The rest of the day was a blur. They were issued uniforms, consisting of baggy green fatigues, a pair of black boots with dozens of eyelets for laces, and thick green socks. They had their hair shorn down to a stubble and were given more blankets, three thin towels, a mess kit, and a whole trunk of assorted junk including soap, toiletries, gym shorts, more socks, boot polish, and even underwear. The air force thought of everything.

Around 3 they were finally fed lunch: a soupy stew of stringy beef and canned vegetables, mounds of soured coleslaw, and spongy white bread, all washed down with weak, hot coffee.

Lunch took all of 20 minutes, then Master Sargeant Johnson was yelling at them again. They were hurried back to barracks where they changed into their new fatigues. By 4 that afternoon they were doing repeat sets of pushups and jogging around the web of gravel roads among the camp's buildings.

Ted was constantly out of breath; his head felt naked with his hair cropped to one-half inch. His knees ached from squats. The heavy hot air made it hard to breathe, much less run.

They were herded to dinner at 6, fed hamburger steak and french fries for dinner, and went to see a patriotic movie at 7: "The Air Force: The Legend Lives On!"

It exhorted them to strive for excellence, push through boot camp, prove themselves "on the field and in camp," and finished with some surprisingly young-faced white guy being made a general with fighter jets crisscrossing the sky behind him.

Then they were herded to showers and bed. Lights were out at 9:30. They were getting up at 5 for a three-mile run, Sargeant Johnson said.

Ted felt like his life had been taken over by alien life forms. The uniformed men could have been Martians; Sargeant Johnson was their evil commander.

He stretched his aching body out on his bed. Just like home, his feet hung over the end. He wished he'd stayed home. The food was a lot better and he could sleep late.

***

Ted survived the three-mile run the next morning, but just barely. His left knee inflated to the size of a small softball and he barely managed to limp over to the plot of grass where Sergeant Johnson had let them all collapse in the dew.

His colleagues lay around him, panting and swearing, a good number of them complaining of aching knees, blisters, and shin splints. One nearby moaned that he'd twisted his ankle.

He was a big black man with a huge frame and dark, dark skin. No honky had polluted his bloodlines.

The name stenciled over his pocket identified him as "Kirkson."

Ted rolled over on his side and decided to make friends.

"Say man, this runnin'-around shit sure is doin' nobody no good," he said, looking at the man's ankle sympathetically.

Kirkson looked at him, his face twisted in pain. "Man, I got flat feet. I run like this mother wants you to run and my ankles pop right out." He moaned again. "I weren't built for no runnin' like this."

"Where you from?" Ted asked.

"Peoria."

"I'm from Naperville," Ted said, without thinking. His sojourn with his aunt and uncle had sailed right through his subconscious.

Kirkson grunted, turned his ankle slowly, and grimaced in pain. "I twisted this sucker alright," he complained through gritted teeth.

One of the uniformed flunkies came strolling through the bodies sprawled on the lawn. "Up and at 'em, men," he called. "Time to hit the exercise field." Men staggered to their feet all around them. Kirkson tried to get up, but fell down in pain.

The uniformed man was over them in a minute.

"What's the problem here, airmen?" he said. He was a white man with sandy hair, not more than a year older than them.

"I twisted my ankle, sir," Kirkson said.

The uniformed man, identified on his shirt pocket as Staff Sergeant Dowling, stared at Kirkson, as if by staring at him long enough he would be able to tell if Kirkson was lying or not.

After 15 seconds of silence, he decided on the conservative route.

"You," he said, pointing to Ted, "help this man to the infirmary."

"Yes, sir," Ted said. He painfully got up on his own swollen knee, then leaned down to help Kirkson up. The man's 250-pound frame nearly pulled him down. Somehow they both got to their feet and hobbled off in the direction indicated by another uniformed man.

Ted fantasized that they were two battle-scarred veterans staggering off the field of combat, instead of two disgracefully out-of-shape young men tottering off after a run that a reasonably athletic housewife could pull off before waking her husband to go to work.

Kirkson had indeed twisted his ankle. The nurse at the infirmary, a small white man with a dark mole over one lip, wrapped the ankle tightly with an Ace bandage and gave Kirkson a white plastic bag filled with ice.

"Ice it 15 minutes every hour until the swelling goes down," he said, filling in some eight-part form with his diagnosis.

Kirkson looked at him, mystified.

"You get refills on the ice at the dispensary," the man said, nodding down a hallway of green concrete block and dark green linoleum floors. He looked up from his forms, drew a few big circles with his ballpoint pen on the bottom, and ripped off a canary-yellow copy which he handed to Kirkson.

"Back to barracks, airman," he said. "You're off your feet for a week."

Kirkson grinned from ear to ear.

Ted decided to take a stab at it. "My knee's swollen up like a football," he said in his best Boston accent, trying to concentrate a look of pain into his eyes. He pulled up his pants and the nurse leaned over the counter to look at the knee. The nurse screwed up his mouth and his mole twitched.

"Just looks a little swollen to me," he said, finally.

"Swollen! I'm in agony," Ted said, forcing a big moan and carefully moving his knee.

"I don't think it's all that bad, airman," the nurse said. "Exercise is good for your knees." Then he stood back up, turned around, and went back through two metal doors leading to the rest of the infirmary.

"Shit!" Ted said under his breath. "Now I gotta' go run around on this crapped-up knee like some honky jogger." He turned to

Kirkson, who was happily fingering his ice pack and watching a company of men marching between two barracks.

"Let's get the fuck outta' here," he hissed at Kirkson. He leaned his shoulder into the pit of Kirkson's arm; the two of them hobbled off to barracks. Ted helped Kirkson into his bunk, a lower one by luck. Ted got up to leave, but Kirkson stopped him.

"Wait," he said. "I got somethin' for you." He motioned to the trunk at the foot of his bunk. "On the bottom," he said. "A little something to ease the pain."

On the bottom of the trunk was a nearly full, half-gallon bottle of Wild Turkey. Ted and Kirkson grinned at each other. Ted sat down on the bunk, unscrewed the bottle, and passed it to Kirkson, who took a big swig and passed it back.

"How'd you ever get here?" Ted said, wiping his mouth with the back of his hand.

"No one goes nowhere in Peoria. I couldn't get a job. So, I thought I'd sign up and see the world," Kirkson said, adjusting the ice pack on his ankle.

"Gary's nothin' special either," said Ted.

"I thought you said you was from Hooterville or somethin' like that," said Kirkson.

"Naperville. I grew up there, but then I went to live with my uncle in Gary."

Kirkson took another long swig and concentrated his stare at an air-intake grill on the far wall. A few moments later he uttered a deep sigh. "Ain't no place for black men in this white-man's country," he said mournfully.

Ted nodded in agreement. "You got that right, brother," he said. He took another long drink from the bottle.

"You're just a third-class citizen."

"That's right."

"They don't want you to go nowhere. You gotta' be a slave your whole life."

"You got it."

"We should all get up one day and murder those white motherfuckers."

"Ain't that the truth." Ted felt a warm glow come up through his back. One-third of the bottle was already gone.

They drank quietly for several minutes.

"Those black Muslims ain't all wrong," Kirkson finally said. His face glistened with sweat, bringing out the red of his eyeballs.

"Back in Africa," Ted said. "That's where we belong."

"Tell it like it is."

"Darkies on the plantation, picking around among the white-man's garbage, living off the shit he leaves behind. What kind of life is that?" Ted said.

He puffed his chest out and sat up straighter. He felt like a real freedom-fighter, a lord of the jungle. Maybe, instead of joining the air force, he should have jumped a ship for South Africa to help his black brothers fight the crazy honkies there.

He thought of the round leather cap and leopard-print shirt he'd bought to impress Leila. He blushed with embarrassment.

"Give me that bottle," he said, grabbing it from Kirkson's hands.

Kirkson let go and Ted drank more. He felt dizzy. He stood up to prove he wasn't dizzy, then promptly sat down.

He took another drink.

Kirkson started talking about his family. His father was a bartender, his mother had eight kids, and they had lived in a two-bedroom house at the end of a potholed road. A well-used freight line to Chicago bordered the backyard. The entire house shook when the freights went by, usually three a night and four during the day.

One had even derailed once, just two blocks from his house.

"Squished these two little kids like bugs," Kirkson said, putting together his two fingers and making a squishing motion. "Never knew what hit 'em. They was just watchin' that train and suddenly—whamo!—it was all over.

"Just squished 'em like little doodle bugs," he mumbled in a low voice, then took another swig from the bottle.

He lifted his eyes and looked steadily at Ted. The whites were now completely red.

"It was a real sorry day in Hatchett," he said.

"Hatchett?"

"That was the name of our neighborhood."

"Oh."

Ted stared at his feet. Kirkson's eyes started filling with tears. "Those poor, cute little kids," he said, shaking his head. "Just like bugs . . ."

Fifteen minutes later, Staff Sargeant Dowling came into the barracks looking for his lost sheep. Kirkson lay back in his bed, his eyes wet with tears, his arms around the empty bottle, half-asleep.

Ted sat at his feet and leaned against a support for the top bunk, his eyes half-closed. He burped up Wild Turkey fumes. He was dreaming of pussy, of indiscriminate color.

When he saw Dowling coming toward him, he stood up in a panic, hitting his head on the bottom support of the bunk.

"What the hell is going on here?" Dowling started yelling halfway down the barracks.

"I can explain," Ted said, swaying as he stood and rubbing the back of his head. Pot, hash, cocaine, pills, he could handle those. But booze always put him right under.

"Sir," Dowling snapped.

"Sir, Dowling, sir," Ted mumbled. He burped again. "You see Kirkson here sprained his ankle and we was, were, having a little medicine to ease the pain."

Dowling glared at Kirkson and glared at Ted. His pale white face turned red to the roots of his sandy hair; his blue eyes became bullets.

He blew up.

He called them worthless assholes, sons of bitches, and a long string of epitaphs that Ted only heard vaguely through the boozy fumes in his head.

What it all amounted to was that Ted was going to be punished. Dowling marched to the end of the barracks and called to another noncommissioned officer. In less than a minute, two men in military-police uniforms, carrying clubs, were standing next to Ted. They grabbed him, one under each arm, and took him to a square beige building with a black door.

They locked him up in a cell with a toilet, a washbowl, and the universal set of bunk beds. The barred door shut with a clang.

Ted tottered a moment on his feet then crumpled in a heap onto the bottom bunk. He heard the drunken moans of men from neighboring cells.

Then he fell asleep. The next morning, he awoke with a terrible hangover. At 6 am, they fed him some watery cereal for breakfast. Then Dowling came to retrieve him and gave him a 15-minute dressing-down for drunkenness.

Dowling swore he would be on the next bus for Chicago if he didn't shape up.

The thought of returning to the Heavenly Host Garden of Refuge, his child-support payments, and his righteously angry uncle cleared Ted's head. He groaned and moaned his way through the 100 pushups Dowling exacted for punishment, then rejoined his company.

* * *

That day the company fought the battle of the paperwork. They spent the entire morning in a long beige building with a blue door where they filled out forms and took aptitude and intelligence tests.

That afternoon they were measured for their dress uniforms.

If he played his cards right, the air force would take care of him. He could be part of the air force family. They would tell him what to do, when to do it, and make something of him. That was more than he could do for himself.

He resolved never to touch Wild Turkey again.

* * *

Boot camp was awful. Every morning they rose at 5 for a three-mile run that by the third week of camp had lengthened itself into a five-mile jaunt around the camp's perimeter. Following that was a delicious breakfast of instant eggs, charred bacon, and piles of burnt white toast.

Then it was time for class. Ted was going to be in radar, or "electronic-detection science," as it was now known. He knew it had something to do with radio waves slithering through the air and bouncing off unsuspecting objects. He would learn to read their secret patterns.

It sounded exotic.

After lunch, the company worked out more, then marched and drilled on the parade grounds until he had memorized the location of every window and window pane on the green-doored beige building closest to the drill area.

He lost weight. His chest and arm muscles filled out. He could do 75 pushups and chin himself easily on the wooden bars in the training field at the far corner of the camp.

He looked good and avoided Kirkson, who was still hobbling on his gamy ankle nine weeks into boot camp. Kirkson was still fleshy and huge, his hulking gorilla frame always the last to finish an exercise or make it over the wooden wall in the obstacle-course drill.

Boot camp finished in 12 weeks. Ted was transferred to another barracks on the other end of camp and started in on his special training: 12 weeks of radar training mixed with general classes on air-force history and aeronautics. He didn't care for the history and aeronautics courses, but he liked radar.

He could spend hours looking at the screen watching the tiny blips and dots weave their hesitant paths across its surface. He felt like the master of the universe sitting on his throne and monitoring the comings and goings of his inconsequential subjects.

He had his fingers on the pulse of life.

Then, suddenly, his training was over. He precision-marched his way through the ending ceremony, actually shook hands with Master Sargeant Johnson, and received his billet: "electronic surveillance staff" at Foster Air Force Base in Michigan's upper peninsula.

He'd been hoping to go to southern California.

"Bad luck," said Remy, the occupant of the bunk below him and a creamy-brown Creole from a fishing town west of New Orleans. Remy was a fuel-engineering technician: that is, he filled jets with their high-octane fuel from a sporty little truck. His training consisted of learning how to hold a hose straight and pull it out when the automatic shutoff clicked on. "Michigan is so cold, man," he said in his heavy patois. "Your balls are going to freeze off and roll around on the ground like cat's-eye marbles."

Remy was going to southern New Mexico.

"Lots of pussy and drugs," he told Ted. "Those Indian femmes put out and the Mexicans sell you dope wholesale."

Ted had never liked Remy; the man was a braggart. He was also going someplace warm. And so was nearly everyone else in his company — except he and Kirkson. They were both going to Foster.

They had two-weeks liberty before their assignment. Kirkson went home to Peoria. Ted went to Amarillo where he spent most of the two weeks drunk, chasing Mexican whores, and soaking up the desert heat.

They reassembled back at Forsythe for their assignments. Ted and Kirkson flew up to Foster together on a crowded commercial flight out of Houston.

Kirkson complained the entire way. He was in computers, part of the "computer-engineering support and maintenance staff." That meant he knew how to dust computers without setting off static charges. He could also rearrange the computer manuals in the computer's reference room into neat piles.

He hated it. "Hey man, I was built to be more than some dumb cleaning lady," he said. "Them tests I took was wrong. Somebody made a big mistake."

Then he told Ted about how he was filing with this appeal group and that board to get himself into a higher position.

Kirkson thought he should be in combat-system design, programming computers. He showed Ted the letters he was writing to the authorities, pleading his case. They were carefully hand-printed on wide-ruled paper ripped from a torn spiral notebook.

Ted read one. It was excessively polite and referred to "the great wrong done to me, a *black* airman, by the machineations (sic) of the air force's bureaucratic doings."

Finally, Kirkson calmed down. He started working on his "correspondance," as he called it, his stubby pencil chewed down and wet from sucking it in his mouth.

They flew up to Foster on a clear day in late January. From the airplane's window, Ted watched the brown-green of Texas fade into the snow-dappled brown of the midwest. Over the middle of Michigan they hit a snowstorm.

When they landed in Marquette, the plane bounced and nearly skidded on the snow-covered runway. Snow swirled around the windows of the terminal.

He had entered the land of eternal winter.

Chapter Ten

It was 15 below zero on the ground. A corporal in a green minivan met them at the airport and drove them to the base through more snow than Ted had seen in his entire life. It was piled up 10 feet high on the sides of the road and still covered the road surface. It fell in clumps from the boughes of the pine trees lining their way.

No one seemed to live here. The road was lined with miles of snow-covered pine forests, broken occassionally by the light of a small house or a cluster of bars and a grocery store masquerading as a town.

Foster Air Force Base itself reminded Ted of scenes he'd seen of government camps in Antarctica. Everywhere were huge piles of snow surrounding squat dingy buildings that could have been a duplicate of Camp Forsythe – except they weren't all painted beige. Some were green or even brown.

The insides of the barracks were the same: long buildings filled with beds, except here the men got more blankets. He could hear the heat hissing up through the old steam radiators lining the walls. The small windows were etched with ice.

He and Kirkson were bunking together. Ted dutifully piled his duffle on the top bunk then unzipped his suitcase and pulled out a thick green air-force sweater. The hooded winter jacket they had issued him at Camp Forsythe was not going to be enough in this climate. He would spend every dime of his first paycheck on warm clothing.

Then he and Kirkson reported to their new masters.

* * *

Staff Sergeant Marcus Flint ran the barracks. A black man of medium build, his military haircut made his head look like a peeled grape with his large protruding lips and big bulging eyes as accents.

He spoke with an urban black accent and was surprisingly polite, which Ted guessed must be due to the weather. When you're locked up with several hundred other men for weeks at a time in nearly arctic conditions, you don't want to pick fights with anyone.

Staff Sargeant Flint sent Kirkson on his way to the computer rooms, in tow to some baby-faced, white airman first-class. Then he turned back to Ted and handed him a sheaf of letters.

"These came for you last week," he said, smiling. Before Ted could open them, Sargeant Flint called up another airman first-class and told him to take Ted to "the electronic-surveillance service unit office." It turned out to be a small green building with two giant snow piles flanking its heavy metal door.

Inside was dirty-white linoleum puddled with snow and an entire wall of screens blinking with lights or glowing with flourescent intensity. Five men wearing headphones sat staring at the screens. A long green counter separated them from the entranceway.

The guide-dog airman turned Ted over at the counter to another airman who led him back between two desks to a small office on the left.

It was a messy office. Second Lieutenant John Cramksi, a fat Bohemian from Seattle, Washington, sat squeezed in his government-issue chair shuffling through a pile of computer printouts.

"Airman Edward Davis, sir," Ted said, giving his best salute and staring straight ahead.

"At ease, airman," Cramski said, trying to extricate himself from his chair. It came up off the ground several inches before finally disconnecting from his body. He came around the desk and shook hands with Ted. He was the friendliest officer Ted had ever met.

"Welcome to Foster AFB," said Cramski, pumping his hand.

"Thank you, sir," Ted said.

Cramski went back behind his desk, squeezed himself back into his chair, and told Ted to sit down.

Ted then handed him his assignment papers, which Cramski skimmed through and stuffed haphazardly in an overstuffed drawer on the left of his desk.

"We're on the cutting edge of defense of the free world here at Foster," Cramski said, his voice serious and heavy. The words were funny coming from such a plump-faced guy in his early 20s. "Our friends in Canada watch for some of the birds, but we're the northern outpost here in the midwest," he said.

"Birds?" Ted said shyly.

"Rockets, missles, airplanes, anything the enemy could send over our airspace. It's our job to track them, as well as to keep the flyboys from crashing into each other with their fancy dancing."

Ted looked bewildered.

"We don't want the pilots crashing their high-performance jets into each other," Cramski translated patiently. "We work with the air-traffic controllers here."

Ted nodded.

"I'll have Hadleigh start you on the big screen at 1500 hours," Cramski said. He looked at the clock. It was 11 am. "Why don't you head out to barracks and settle in?" he said. "I'll send Keeshin with you."

He walked to the door and motioned to the airman first-class who had led Ted to the door originally. "Take this man to barracks, airman," he said.

Ted gave his snappy salute, then walked out after Airman Keeshin into the bitter cold. Their breath billowed around their heads in clouds of steam. The cold stung their faces. Keeshin picked up his gait to a run; Ted followed. His barracks was a two-minute jog from the radar hut.

Everyone on the base moved at a quick jog, Ted noticed. At 15 below zero, noses and lips could freeze in minutes. Ted's eyelashes were frozen by the time he pushed through the barracks's two entryway chambers and burst into its damp warmth.

It felt so good. No one was there. He went to his bunk and noticed that Kirkson had left all his gear on the bottom bunk, unlocked. The guy was such a slob.

Ted arranged his gear in his chest at the foot of the bunk beds. As he leaned over, the letters Staff Sargeant Flint had given him fell on the floor. For the first time, he really looked at them. One was an official dispatch from the air-force's personnel department. Another was from his bank back home. The remaining two were in women's handwriting.

His heart was in his mouth: one of the handwritten ones could only be from Leila.

And it was.

The letter started out: "Dear Shithead, You thought you could dump me and Stephanie but the long arm of the law has found you."

Then it explained how as part of a routine check by the air force's personnel department, the service had discovered the existence of Leila and his daughter and his "cowardly attempt" to leave them both to starve.

"Thank God for justice and the U.S. Air Force," Leila wrote. "Without them I would be an indigent mother."

That really scared him. He tore open the air-force letter to discover that the service was forwarding 80 percent of his monthly pay to Leila to fulfill his child-support agreement with her.

He would get $100 a month to live on.

His eyes bugged out, he started breathing heavily. He was trapped. He had taken the six-year enlistment; he was stuck supporting Leila and her kid for six years. He felt sick to his stomach.

He needed a drink. He fumbled through Kirkson's belongings on the bottom bunk, finding his ever-present bottle of Wild Turkey in the middle of his duffle. He pulled it out and took a long, desperate drink.

Then he opened the other two letters. One was from his Aunt Millie, bawling him out for joining the air force and not telling them. If Leila hadn't called and told them, she wrote, they still wouldn't know where he was.

She would send him some warm clothing; she understood it was cold where he was. The letter had a curt, annoyed tone to it, as if he had abandoned the family instead of being kicked out by his uncle.

He took another long draught of Wild Turkey.

The final letter was a well-forwarded one from his bank back home. They wanted to know when they were going to get their $748.50 plus $15 service charge to cover the overdraft. Apparently Leila had cashed the check for cash and then disappeared. The bank had been unable to find her much less get her to return the money.

They threatened legal action unless a cashier's check or money order for $763.50 was sent immediately. The letter was dated August 15. This was January 27.

He wadded it up and stuffed it in his duffle bag then took another long drink from Kirkson's bottle.

The long hand of destiny had sure found him. He skipped lunch and kept drinking. At 2:30, he found the PX and bought a box of breath mints, which he ate in handfuls on his way to the radar hut.

He didn't feel cold at all.

* * *

He could hardly stand. Lieutenant Cramski looked at him, sighed deeply, and sent him back to barracks with orders to sleep it off and come back tomorrow at 0700 hours.

He was surprised. He thought for sure Cramski would have put him in the drunk tank. He staggered back to his bunk, crawled into the top bed, and dreamed that he was being eaten by fire ants. He alternately woke and slept through the day, awakening at 10:30 that night, hungover, to find the barracks filled with sleeping men.

He could hear Kirkson already snoring below.

He felt trapped. Trapped by his ex-wife, trapped by the air force, and now trapped in these damn barracks. Where could he go? He could hear the wind outside whistling around the corners of the building. It was probably 20 below out there, pitch black, and he wouldn't be surprised if polar bears lurked in the camp's perimeters looking for stragglers.

He pulled the covers over his head, scrunched down in the warmth of his bed, and wished he could start his life over.

* * *

0600 hours came sooner than he thought. Staff Sargeant Field marched down the center of the barracks banging on the ends of the beds and yelling at the men to get up.

The barracks floor was freezing. Ted scuffed into his shoes and shuffled into the communal bathroom, Kirkson tagging along behind him like an overstuffed teddy bear with foul breath.

Ted put on long underwear, his uniform, a sweater, two pairs of socks, and pulled on his winter jacket along with a heavy stocking cap and thick gloves. He wrapped his face in a muffler.

Outside, it was black night and 25 below. It was a 250-yard run to the mess hall; the snow squeaked as he ran. He felt frozen by the time he reached the mess's big gray metal doors.

The mess was filled with steam, cigarette smoke, and 146 men. It smelled of burnt grease. Ted ate two baking-powder biscuits, an order of watery grits, and two big cups of coffee. He felt nauseous, but fought it back. He hunched over his coffee cup. The steam from the coffee cleared out his sinuses and warmed him.

He saw Kirkson in a far corner, talking with some skinny black airman.

Ted looked around him and had no desire to talk to anyone. At 0650 he drew on his coat and headed for the radar shack.

* * *

All the friendliness Lieutenant Cramski had shown him the day before was gone this morning. The first thing he did was stick his nose in Ted's mouth and smell his breath.

"We're a little more ready to deal with the defense of the country today, are we, airman?" he said, glaring at Ted. "Hadleigh, set Airman Davis the Drunk here up on Miss December, will you?" "Certainly, sir," came the soft nasal voice of a small white man standing behind Ted. Cramski then walked into his office and slammed the door.

"You made a big hit with the man-in-charge," Hadleigh said in his nasal tones. "Not too many guys report shitfaced on their first day of duty."

Ted opened his mouth to say something but then closed it without a word.

Hadleigh led him to a console in front of a bank of small screens. A pinup of a white woman with huge melon breasts, tiny hips, and incredibly long legs was stuck to a narrow piece of gray metal between the screens. She wore nothing but a Santa Claus hat; pine boughs were piled at her feet. It was Miss December.

Ted stared at the amazing detail of her crotch, which was right at his eye level. She was the ultimate in white pussy, right there, right in front of him, her private parts staring him right in the eyes.

And this was what he wasn't ever going to get for the rest of his life. Why did he have to look at it? He almost stood up and ripped the photo down but caught himself. Hadleigh was already halfway through his explanation of the equipment.

"Here's the ace-out, the vertical-down and fly-in detail, the zoom, and the back-up," he droned through his nose, his fingers dancing over the console keyboard.

He reached over his head to a small door next to one of the screens and flipped it open to a panel of switches. "Over to the right here are the interconnect and master tie-in switches." He danced his fingers over five switches covered in yellow plastic and another three tinged in red.

He then turned around and pointed down the row of consoles toward Cramski's office. "The mother screen is down there," he said, pointing to a pimply young white man sitting in front of a large blue screen. "You let him know when you see something real. He turns the big stuff on."

He nodded toward three men with telephone headsets sitting in a far corner, staring in boredom at some blank screens. "Those guys work air-traffic control," he said. "They'll get busy once the prima donnas who fly those things get their asses out of bed."

Then he turned to Ted and smiled.

"And that's basically it," he said. "We're just an outpost in the middle of nowhere, monitoring a lot of useless crap. It's a cushy job."

Then he motioned for Ted to take a seat in front of the screen and sat down next to him. The equipment looked familiar to Ted; he'd been drilled to death on it at electronic-surveillance school.

He stared at his collection of screens. They were all blank.

Suddenly, a tiny V-shaped collection of objects moved along the lower left-hand corner of his top right screen. He looked expectantly at Hadleigh, who was cleaning his nails with a plastic coffee stirrer.

Hadleigh glanced at the screen. "Canadian geese," he said. "You see a lot of them. There's a bubbler and open water over at the waterfowl refuge up the road. The rangers feed them. So the geese hang around all year."

He went back to his nails.

Ted sat there for four hours that morning. He saw six flocks of Canadian geese, a flock of mergansers, and what were probably a collection of arctic terns. "You can tell by their flight formation," Hadleigh said. "The mergansers fly low. The terns have this sort of loopy, up-and-down flight."

He moved his hands in an up-and-down motion like a roller coaster. Then he leaned down and pulled a well-worn copy of Peterson's *A Field Guide to the Birds* from under the desk.

"Office copy," he said solemnly to Ted. "Don't ever let it leave here."

Ted nodded.

Hadleigh thumbed through the book's pages. He reached the section with seagulls and terns and showed Ted one of a tern with a black head. The arctic tern.

"Lovely, aren't they?" he said.

Ted smiled.

"Sometimes we get glaucous gulls, too," Hadleigh said, getting excited. He closed the book with a contented plop. "You see more birdlife in the autumn and spring," he said. "They're migrating then."

Ted nodded.

"Well, why don't you carry on here," Hadleigh said. "I've got to backup some screen checks." Then he got up and left, leaving Ted to a screen filled with dipping and soaring birdlife.

Ted wondered if the base organized birdwatching trips in good weather.

* * *

Lunch was a watery bowl of tomato soup and a grilled cheese sandwich with the ever-present side cluster of potato chips. Against his better judgment, Ted sat next to Kirkson, who told him how bored he was in the computer room.

"They won't even let me get near the computers," he said. "I'll be stuck piling up computer manuals for six years. What kind of job skill is that?" And he sunk his huge gorilla head on his fleshy pink hand and pouted. "The air force done fed me a line of horseshit.

"Where the fuck are we, anyway?" he said, looking around the room at the clusters of young men, dressed in layers of ugly green clothing. "I mean I didn't sign up for no dog-sled corps. I signed up to make myself a ca-reer," he said, overemphasizing the last syllable of career.

"But this ain't no ca-reer," he said. "This is horseshit. This is real horseshit."

Somehow, with a seventh-grade reading level and a barely passing average from one of Peoria's worst high schools, coupled with 13 weeks of technical training, Kirkson thought he was ready to run IBM.

"Those honkies are just keeping us down," he hissed in Ted's ear, glaring at the rosy-cheeked young white men who had just come in to eat. "They want us to be slaves."

He waited expectantly for Ted's emphatic response, but Ted said nothing.

"I mean look at those honky bozos," Kirkson said.

Ted got up suddenly. "See you later, Kirkson," he said.

"What's your problem?" Kirkson yelled after him as Ted walked his tray back to the kitchen.

Ted said nothing and walked out the door into the frozen white. After birdwatching all morning with Hadleigh, he didn't consider the whites here any better off than he.

Chapter Eleven

Ted's life took on its own rhythm. He sat at Miss December all
morning, ate lunch, then moved over to Miss May all afternoon. She
had five screens instead of four; another screen to be filled with
birds. At five he'd have dinner, then head back to barracks for a
couple of stiff drinks from his private supply. He'd watch TV in the
enlisted-men's TV room until lights off at 10:00, sometimes playing
cards, sometimes just oogling the perfect bodies of the TV starlets.

Four times a week Staff Sargeant Flint would run them around
the base's tiny gym and through a set of calisthentics. Once every
two weeks Ted would get liberty and hitch a ride to Squamo, the
nearest town. There he'd get drunk and watch TV in a bar instead
of the enlisted-men's TV room.

Every two weeks, he'd get paid – a $50 check for him with a
computer voucher showing that $256.34 had gone to Ms. Leila
Pritchett per his "automatic-withdrawal" program.

He'd tremble with helpless rage. He could not afford a pair of
warm socks. Meanwhile, Leila was living at her mother's house in
the lap of luxury.

He always imagined Leila leaning over the bathtub, her heavy
stomach stuck out in front of her, painting her toenails with
expensive nail polish in a bright shade of purple.

And that was the pattern of Ted's life. Sometimes he varied it by
going to Marquette to get drunk.

He kept up his constant drinking, but he found he could regulate
it, like a conductor adjusting the intensity of his string or brass
section. Evenings, he would get quietly shit-faced, his face earnest,
his eyes expressionless.

Afternoons, he would only drink enough for a little buzz, enough
to make it through his shift of electronic birdwatching without going
too off from boredom. He never came in totally drunk, as he had
done the first time with Cramski.

He was good at radar and was liked well enough by his
colleagues. At least no one picked fights with him. And he was the
one who saw the first collection of glaucous gulls that spring.

He also was the only one to see the Cessna, wobbling along 200 feet off the ground, its businessman pilot lost and in trouble over Lake Superior. Ted's locations helped the coast guard find the wreckage and the body that evening.

But, for the most part, Ted was bored out of his mind.

Sometimes he'd go out on the airfield and watch the pilots posture. Mostly white and arrogant, they thought they were hot stuff. They climbed in and out of their $20-million jets with athletic leaps and bounces and hung around in cliques like groups of gossipy high-school girls. Some of them even had white silk scarves they knotted around their necks like ascots, a loose fringed edge hanging rakishly over one edge.

The pilots thought they were macho. The enlisted men thought they were fairies and called them "tinkerbelles" behind their backs. Every year at least one of them would crash into the forest or the lake. One had even crashed just yards from the house of Colonel Harwick, who ran the base.

The base's flags would be dipped to half-mast, they'd have a small, dignified ceremony honoring the dead, and the air force would send out an investigating team from Washington.

The enlisted men enjoyed it greatly. Another flying fairy had bitten the dust.

* * *

Aunt Millie was the only one in Ted's family who bothered to write. She wrote chatty little letters on a feminine paper bordered with pink flowers.

Pamela had had her baby, a little girl, whom she had named Zondervan. Franklin was apprenticed to a heating and air-conditioning contractor in Gary. Lavonne Rae was a nursery-school student teacher in East Chicago Heights. Uncle Harry had made head deacon at the church.

And everyone still lived at home. Pamela was probably washing and hanging baby diapers all over the bathroom.

Ted wrote back and asked for warm socks.

Two months later, she sent an old pair of Harry's wool socks, darned at the heels and too late to do Ted any good. He stopped writing back. Over the next six months, her letters reached a crescendo of angry "why don't you write's?" then stopped coming.

Six months after that he was promoted to airman; another six months and he received a new posting—the Catalban missle silos near Filton, South Dakota.

* * *

Filton, South Dakota was a small town in the middle of flat nothingness. It contained four grain silos, a feed store, a gas station, and seven bars—the latter a tribute to the drinking appetites of the airmen who staffed the Catalban missle silos 26 miles to the north.

The Catalban base was nothing to see from the air. From there it looked like a collection of three, giant garbage-can lids faintly outlined in the dusty, brown ground.

At ground level, the base could have been a relay-pumping station for the gas company. Two big pipes surged up out of the ground, then plunged back below, like the intestines of a giant popping out in a huge hernia. The garbage-can lids turned out to be three huge circles drawn in the dust with a foot-wide band of concrete. They resembled municipal skating rinks, filled in with dusty soil and retired for the summer.

On one side of the base were a few small outbuildings, a radar dish, and a radio antenna. On the other were two barracks buildings, a mess hall, and a warehouse. A few tumbleweeds stuck in the chain-link fence topped with barbed wire that circled the mile perimeter of the site and ended in a guardhouse at the camp entrance.

And that was it—above ground.

For the life of Catalban was all underground.

A visitor would enter one of two small, grayish outbuildings. But instead of a few closets of pipes or a rusted old truck, the building housed a bright aluminum elevator door. The elevator to nowhere.

The elevator didn't go up. It went down. Down, down, down, hundreds of feet below ground, as if Alice could take an elevator instead of falling down the rabbit hole to Wonderland.

That's, at least, how Ted experienced it the first time he came to the base, a scorching hot day in mid-July. The Great Plains were baking; 110-degree heat shimmered over the wheat fields and rangy pastureland.

After reporting to his commanding officer, a runny-eyed, black-haired southerner with a pronounced drawl named Macon, "as in Georgia," Ted was escorted to his first assignment by a small airman, Bradley.

Bradley led him to one of the outbuildings and its elevator. He pushed the call button. Thirty seconds later the bright aluminum doors opened to a big, gray metal cab. A green panel of buttons filled with coded numbers covered an entire square foot by the door. Bradley stuck a magnetic card into a small slot by the square, then pushed a button labeled "A364."

And it was down the rabbit hole.

The cab rattled and banged its way down the shaft, wind whooshing up along its sides. They passed pipes and valves that hissed and banged, then faded off as the elevator sped by.

It was a long ride down, a good two minutes. The elevator slowed, then stopped with a sudden, bouncing lurch, as if it had landed on giant springs. The doors opened onto a long corridor. With its cement-block walls, green linoleum floors, and fluourescent lights, it looked like a hospital. Ted half-expected two orderlies, a patient on a dolly, and a clump of nurses to come around the corner.

Instead, the corridor was empty.

Bradley marched out and headed down the hallway. A few doors with numbers on them broke up the expanse of wall, but they soon disappeared. Bradley and Ted just kept walking.

They passed three checkpoints. Guards with machineguns and lists checked the authorization papers that Bradley gave them. Finally, after 10 minutes of walking and getting cleared, they reached the radar room.

* * *

It was a misnomer. It looked more like the control room for NASA.

It was a darkened room with a 25-foot ceiling, lined from top to bottom with glowing screens. They glowed green, red, and the most lovely shade of irridescent, aqua blue.

Some screens were huge: five feet across with complicated gridwork overlays. Tiny black dots drifted leisurely among the black lines. Other screens were tiny and intense with blips and waves surging across.

The room had its own system of highways: catwalks and ironwork stairways laced the air and roamed by the giant screens on the upper reaches of far walls.

A bank of tiny screens, monitors, and control panels stood on an elevated platform in the center of the room where four men rolled around on wheeled chairs, headsets over their ears, scanning the panels and talking into their tiny microphones.

A fifth man leaned back in his chair, his feet up on the console, fast asleep.

The screens and consoles blipped and crackled, but the men's voices were dull and flat. Bradley and Ted came closer. Ted could make out part of the most animated conversation going on in one corner of the platform. The man appeared to be arguing about baseball batting averages with whomever was on the other end of the line. Occasionally, he'd lean forward, flip a switch, stare at a dancing screen for a minute, then go back to his conversation.

This was First Lieutenant Harold Majors, officer in charge of the radar swing shift. Ted and Bradley stood respectfully by while Majors finished arguing with his mystery correspondant over National-League batting averages in 1978. Then he turned to Ted.

Majors was black, hot, and not happy to see them.

"Who's this?" he said brusquely, leaning forward and flipping a handful of switches. His long, pink-ended fingers moved like those of a concert pianist. "I hope you're here to fix the air conditioning," he said, flicking a set of black-tipped switches near a blue screen. "We've been frying our asses down here since 1600 hours."

"Airman Edward Davis, sir," Ted said, snapping a salute and handing him his papers.

"Christ, not another one," Majors said. He pulled a large wrinkled handkerchief from a back pocket and drew it across his forehead, which was beaded with sweat. Then he took Ted's papers, glanced at them, and looked at Ted. Majors was a powerfully built man; his shirt and pants pulled tight across his body. Two arms of well-muscled black flesh stuck out from the ends of his short-sleeved shirt.

"I don't suppose you can fix the air conditioning?" he mumbled.

"No, sir," Ted said, still stiff at attention.

"Well, welcome to life as an underground animal, Davis," Majors said. He turned to Bradley. "Get him outta' here and send him to Klinga," he said.

Then he turned around and banged some buttons on another console.

"This is Lieutenant Majors — again," he yelled into his headset. "You don't get some air conditioning down here I'm gonna' write you up from here to Timbuktu. You'll be putting in heating systems in Point Barrow, Alaska, you fucking slum bucket!"

Bradley led Ted down from the platform then up through a maze of catwalks to a small, windowed room halfway up one wall. Ted could see a room filled with blinking, multi-color screens.

Bradley knocked on the door. A faint voice told him to enter.

In one corner of the room Second Lieutenant William Klinga was on the floor, under a console, with a screwdriver in hand. A clump of pink wires hung down over his head, like the hanging nest of some exotic bird in the jungle.

Ted clicked his heels and did his snappy salute.

Klinga told him to relax and got to his feet with considerable effort. Klinga was a small, stooped man with poor posture, thinning brown hair, and a bereft look. About 30-years-old, he managed to move and act like a man dying of cancer at the age of 50.

Every movement of his small, birdlike hands appeared to be an effort. He set his screwdriver down on a small desk and collapsed into a swivel chair.

"So, Bernie, you bring me another one," he said, giving Bradley a fishy little smile and taking Ted's papers. His voice was soft and toneless.

He pulled out a pair of thick glasses from one pocket and began reading, moving his lips as he read. He read every line of Ted's papers, even turning the page to see if there was anything on the other side.

"So, Davis," he said deliberately, "you have no experience with the XF4300-series equipment, the 4Q-Clark monitors, nor Gazzball-intro scanners for high-rez-mode recon?"

Ted shook his head no in bewilderment.

"Good," Klinga said with his dead-mouse smile. "Then you won't have to unlearn any bad habits. 0700 hours tomorrow with the rest of the baby ray men. See you then."

He got up from the chair as if his bones would creak, crawled back under the console, and attacked the pink wire nest.

"Don't worry about Klinga," Bradley said, leading Ted down a maze of catwalks toward an exit sign. "He really is an OK guy." He said it in such a way that indicated Klinga was really very strange.

Bradley led Ted back out into the main corridor and through the turns, twists, and checkpoints back to the elevator. The corridor was filled with men now, walking with purpose, on their way to somewhere.

A crowd of 20 men stood at the elevator, waiting for the next ride. Ted and Bradley jammed in with them and were sucked back up to the surface, the men talking quietly among themselves as the car banged its way to the top of the shaft.

When the doors opened on the surface, the men surged out, talking and laughing. They pushed their way through the double doors of the small outbuilding into the desert-hot air like ants leaving an anthill.

Bradley led Ted back to Macon's office where another airman, this one a medium-sized black man, led him to his barracks.

It looked just like the one he had slept in at Foster.   The only additions were some random ceiling fans which were useless: it must have been over 100 degrees in the barracks. The place was deserted.

His escort led him to a group of bunks in the center of the room. With no windows and no fans, it was a good five degrees hotter there.

"Sorry," the airman said, "all we got left."

Ted chose a lower bunk and unpacked his duffle. The sweat dripped down his face and onto the bed as he stowed his clothes in the footlocker.

He pulled a pint bottle of Wild Turkey from its packing in his nest of socks, took a long drink, and sat on his bunk. All he needed to complete the picture was Kirkson leaning back against the bunk support, grabbing for the bottle.

But Kirkson had been transferred to South Carolina. His complaints had paid off; the air force was sending him to computer school.

Ted took another swig from his bottle. He walked to one window and looked out. All he could see was dust, brown dirt, and an occasional wheat field, all under a cloudless scorching sky.

Didn't the air force operate any bases in *nice* climates near lots of friendly people?

There probably wasn't any non-dehydrated pussy within 300 miles of here.

He was so depressed he finished half the bottle. Then he pulled out a roll of breath mints from the bottom of his duffle, popped one in his mouth, and went to the mess hall to catch the last round of dinner.

Chapter Twelve

At 7 the next morning he stood with four other airmen before Klinga in his windowed room full of screens. Of the five airmen, three were black, one Hispanic, and the fifth Chinese.

Klinga looked at them with his fishy dead look, mumbled something about "teaching the mongrel races," and leaned against his desk.

"We're going to be studying new radar systems in use only at this base," he said in his feeble voice. Everyone leaned forward to listen.

"I will teach you the basics. For you to go up the ladder here, you will need to learn more. That will require higher security clearances and will be a decision made by me and your commanding officer based on the talent you show for electronic- and radar-device manipulation."

It was a canned speech. Ted could see him giving it week after week to the stream of new radar men coming through this cluttered office.

Klinga went on about how radar played an important role in the defense of the country, about how important Catalban was in the "circle of nuclear protection shielding the United States from enemy forces," and about how he was going to teach them everything, but it would take practice.

"Drill, drill, drill," he said, his voice picking up volume. "We're going to drill until our butts get sore, our eyes can't see, and you can do everything I teach you in your sleep."

The men looked pained.

He led them through a small door to the next room. Windowless, it was lined with more screens, these a plain blue with white lines on them. Seven consoles stood along the walls while a master console sat in the center of the room.

This was the training room.

The men sat at the consoles and Klinga harangued them from the central controls, sending them tiny blips and bumps on their screens, shifting their gridwork when they didn't expect it, and delivering a running commentary on their inability to distinguish one blob of electronic interference from another.

It reminded Ted of playing video games with some jerk behind you yelling at your mistakes. But instead of one or two levers to jiggle, a sea of switches, buttons, and dials stood at his command.

It was the ultimate video game.

The four other men in his training group grumbled and jabbed anxiously at their controls, but Ted was a natural. His eyes saw; his fingers moved. He lined up blips, bumps, and grids and pushed buttons with grace.

Klinga was impressed. While he yelled at Ted's compatriots, he praised Ted. Ted glowed. He couldn't believe the others found something that was so easy so difficult.

Of course, Klinga wasn't making it easy. He delivered his incomprehensible explanations in an inaudible mumble. Ted couldn't understand him. But while his colleagues froze in front of their machinery, Ted plunged in.

He punched and tickled his console. The screen lit up; the gridwork expanded into three wide black lines with wide expanses of space between them. Then it shrunk into a tiny blot of black. He nearly laughed with delight.

Catalban's radar systems made Foster's look like black-and-white TV. To think he had spent so much time watching arctic terns when he could have been playing with this stuff.

When they broke for lunch, he could hardly wait to get back and play some more.

* * *

Unfortunately, what had started out as a game soon turned boring.

Klinga taught them only so much about the system, the CZ4920 Frontiersman scope series, then started drilling them.

What did they do when this buzzer sounded? What did they do when the control icon hit the lower-right quadrant of the active-module window screen?

How did they relieve the officer on duty? What was the first thing they did? The second?

Ted understood it all within the third review, but Klinga kept making them do it — over and over and over again. Turn this key, push that button, clear this screen. He did it until he could do it in his sleep.

He *did* do it in his sleep, stuck one night in a nightmare in which he was chained to a swivel chair and just kept pushing the same buttons over and over again while the piano ditty "Chopsticks" repeated itself in his brain.

He woke up shaken and padded to the bathroom. He leaned against the wall by the urinal and sighed. Four more years he had of this bullshit. Four more years of having all his money sent to Leila and being a human automaton.

He went back to his bunk but could not go back to sleep. He kept hearing "Chopsticks" in his brain. He was so tired the next morning that he snuck his bottle of Wild Turkey into a bathroom stall and took a big strong gulp—just to get himself going.

Two hours later he was drilling in front of his screen again, the blank faces of the other airmen around him, Klinga yelling from his central console—and the tapping of "Chopsticks" in the back of his brain.

* * *

He was trapped in Klinga's torture chamber for six weeks before being assigned to the midnight to 6am shift of low-lying radar surveillance for the south-southwestern quadrant of Saskatchawan. That meant he sat in the far corner of the main radar room staring at the flat, grainy-white surface of a little screen all night.

Nothing ever happened in south-southwest Saskatchawan.

At shift change, he would do his little drill with his replacement, a ceremonial dance and exchange-of-duties ritual. The rest of the time, he would stare at his screen, pare his nails, and listen to the officers on the central deck bullshit each other.

He was bored out of his mind.

And he had no reason to expect any more. The radar room was filled with officers with engineering training, happily hopping from one screen to the next. If excitement existed in radar, they had it.

With his few months of radar training and a high-school degree, Ted was going nowhere. If he was lucky, they might add north-southwest Saskatchawan to his list of assignments.

For three months, he watched his grainy-white screen, did his drill dance twice a day, and drank increasing amounts of Wild Turkey. Then, around Christmas, a miracle occurred. The air force did a quick security check on him and transferred him to the 2am to 6am shift at Central Control.

* * *

Central Control was another big room in another corner of the rabbit warren of corridors and rooms that made up Catalban. It was twice as large as the radar room and had its own subset of small rooms and corridors off on either side.

Central Control was the brains of the base. Here was where they could make the decision to start World War III by launching the Fantode-DX nuclear missles dug into the South Dakota dirt. Rumor had it that all 13 missles were aimed at Moscow.

One of the low-level radar men assigned to Central had gotten appendicitis; Klinga called on Ted to take his place. Ted was excited by the change, but the job turned out to be easy. He sat in front of another grainy screen, this one blue with black gridwork, and waited for little blips to float by. The only way they ever would would be if the Chinese army crossed the border between North and South Dakota.

And, of course, he drilled. He saluted and passed keys and checked empty gridwork and filled in detailed reports. His mind was always playing "Chopsticks" now.

He was promoted to airman first-class and got a small raise. Leila wrote the air force and said she needed more money to live on; Ted's air force pay was still not enough to meet the child-support agreement he had signed.

The air force sent her all of his raise.

He started drinking more. He made friends with a boozy second lieutenant from Burbank, California who had an endless supply of liquor and a big heart. Ted was never without a flask of Wild Turkey now.

He started taking it to Central Control and pouring it in his coffee. It helped to make time pass at 2 in the morning. It also made the harsh light of the screens easier to bear.

Central Control was a big room but it was run by only a skeleton staff of four, including Ted. He sat in a far corner with his radar screen. The other three men sat in an alcove on the other side of the room. The alcove was almost a closet, with three walls lined to a height of eight feet with electronic equipment. The fourth wall was a waist-high partition open to the rest of the room. It housed a collection of control panels. From where he sat, Ted could wave at the man sitting at the panels.

Central Control was even more boring than radar. Nothing ever happened. Nothing was supposed to happen. If something did happen, it would be the end of the world. Until then, there was nothing to do.

The men watched their blank screens and monitors, the continuous humming of the machinery making them sleepy and unfocused, like well-fed boa constrictors. They perked up every four hours when a new crew came on. They saluted, passed official papers and keys, and reported on the long list of unchanging vital signs they were supposed to be tracking.

Then the next group would come in and spend four hours waiting for nothing to happen.

* * *

To alleviate his boredom, during his shift Ted would sometimes come over and talk to the men in the alcove. A friendly lot, they would chat about sports or the wretched South Dakota winters.

It was now January. Above ground, it seemed to nearly always be 23 below with a blizzard in progress. Ted was now glad his bunk was in the center of the barracks; it was the warmest spot in the house.

He started bringing over his flask of Wild Turkey to his new friends in the alcove. Everyone's eyes lit up. They all held out their styrofoam coffee cups for "an extra hit of cream" as Ted called his addition.

They stood around talking, leaning against the master control panel and watching their monitors out of the corner of one eye. Space was tight; occasionally someone would jostle someone else by accident.

Once, before Ted had arrived, someone had accidentally pushed against the man at the console. He had spilled his coffee on the master control panel.

Horrified, the men in the alcove had stared at the console. But nothing had happened. The console was "coffee-proof." They all breathed sighes of relief; the first lieutenant in charge ordered no coffee drinking while on duty.

But he had been transferred to a new unit three months ago. The new man in charge, a blonde with a bad complexion, hated his 2am shift, needed the caffeine to stay awake, and was damned if he would give up his coffee just because some airmen were klutzes. Everyone would just have to be more careful.

The beat-up coffee pot on a small hot plate was retrieved from a drawer in a back room and brought back into service. And Ted's Wild Turkey "cream" was an exciting new addition. It made the time pass more quickly.

One night Ted was standing by the console, holding court and pouring large dollops of Wild Turkey into waiting coffee cups held out in front of him. Leila had just written him and said she was filing for larger child-support payments. She and Stephanie couldn't make it on the money he was sending.

"Mother is sick," she wrote. "They think it's cancer of the stomach. She can't work. All she does is throw up. I don't know what to do."

What else could Leila take? His underwear? He only got $100 a month from his pay as it was. If it wasn't for the friendly first lieutenant back in radar, he couldn't drink at all.

He stared at the dregs of his nearly empty coffee cup. He needed a friend. He filled his cup three-quarters full of Wild Turkey.

"Hey Davis, there's something on your screen," one of the men said, pointing at an orange blip happily weaving its way across the blue expanse of his radar screen.

"Damn it," he mumbled. He set his cup down on the edge of the master console and hurried to his screen. The blip was nothing; he had forgotten to remove the subordinate filter-check program and the backup top-ranked radar computer was now reminding him of his error.

He hit a few keys, the screen turned a complacent and clear blue, and he started walking back to the alcove.

In the alcove, Jason Kiertacq, a pale, red-haired airman, was standing by the master console when the first lieutenant in charge hurried by on his way to a file cabinet to get a new shift-relief clearance-approval form. The lieutenant accidentally pushed Kiertacq, who stumbled against the console and spilled Ted's cup of Wild Turkey all over the lower half of the control panel.

"Shit!" Kiertacq yelled. "We're in deep shit now!"

The alcove crew ran to the console. The first lieutenant came running out of the back room and Ted ran up behind him.

They all stared in terror at the console.

But nothing happened. No lights, no sirens, no blinking warnings, nothing. The console sat there, a happy Bhudda of two blue little monitor lights for eyes, a string of yellow lights for a smile, and a small red computer screen with nothing appearing on it but "System/cvx.435 approve rest."

That meant the system was just sitting there.

"Clean that mess up," the first lieutenant barked, breaking the silence. "It smells like a fucking distillery here.

"Whose cup was that?" he added, looking around. Everyone's eyes settled on Ted.

"Davis, clean that mess up," the lieutenant sighed. "I want to smell nothing but kitchen cleanser by the time you're done."

"Yes, sir," Ted said.

He went into the side room where they kept the coffee pot and found a rag and some dish detergent. He wet the rag at the water cooler at the far end of the room, then came back into the alcove and started wiping down the console.

It gave him its happy Bhudda smile.

* * *

Unfortunately, its smile masked what was going on in its circuitry.

Hewiton-Follard Corporation, defense contractors to the Pentagon, had designed the Fantode Master Control and Missile

Launch-Panel Module to withstand spills of coffee, soft drinks, water, and tea.

But retired Colonel Howard Taskerson, executive vice president of design at Hewiton-Follard and the man behind the Fantode system, was a good Baptist and patriot. He had never suspected America's fighting men would be standing over the console controlling the destiny of the world with a cup of bad whiskey in one hand.

Nor did he in his wildest dreams ever suspect they would be stupid enough to spill it.

But they did.

At the very moment Ted was brooding about Leila and wiping the master control panel with a paper towel scented with Springtime Pink Sudsy Dish Detergent, Wild Turkey was eating holes in the delicate circuitry underneath his fingers.

In five minutes, it had short-circuited the entire warning-alert system. In another three it had triggered the missile-activation program, disarmed all manual controls, and was retracting the giant garbage-can covers that covered the three silos, dislodging an entire family of sharp-tailed grouse that had nested in the weeds along one silo's concrete lip.

No one even suspected what was happening. The men on duty in other corners of the silos' bowels hunched over their monitors, but saw nothing unusual.

Why should they? Wild Turkey had severed all communication with the master control system.

They did hear a deep-seated rumbling. It was the missiles' powerful engines getting ready for liftoff. But it could have been the elevators. That week, five of the base's 10 internal elevators were having serious problems, banging and knocking against their shafts with such intensity that the noise had reverberated throughout the underground community. More than one airman had had to stop talking because he couldn't hear himself speak as they rumbled by.

And so, no one paid any attention to the rumblings all around them. The first set of missiles lifted out of the ground in the fierce dark cold of an early winter morning in South Dakota, the only witnesses the clump of sentries at the base gate, hunkered down in awe behind the walls of their gatehouse.

The grouse were fried to a crisp.

All 13 missiles were airborne and halfway to Moscow, Minsk, Novosibersk, and a Soviet missile base in the Urals before the hysterical voices from monitoring stations in Alaska started chattering over the airwaves to Catalban's base commander.

Frantic phone calls were made. When the missiles were 10 minutes outside of Moscow, the President reached the Chairman. The President garbled and gagged and tried to explain what had happened. The Chairman's translator was half asleep and could barely make out what the President was saying.

When he did figure it out, the Chairman started screaming over the phone in Russian.

The President told him he was sorry.

Sorry? The Chairman hung up, speechless with rage, two minutes before the missiles were scheduled to land in the outskirts of the city.

Sorry? Sorry? He'd show them "sorry." If this was the end of Russian civilization, he was damned if the Americans were going to survive to sing its funeral dirge.

He called up a major nuclear strike against the United States, poured himself a glass of vodka from a crystal decanter on a small side table, and sat back in the red plush chair dating from the reign of Peter the Great that sat in the small office adjacent to his bedroom.

He didn't even have time to call his wife before he was incinerated in a blinding flash of light.

Meanwhile, in South Dakota, Ted stood at his newly cleaned console, admiring his handiwork, and bemoaning the loss of so much Wild Turkey down the gullet of this worthless piece of machinery. He had another drink in his hand.

Suddenly, the door to the Master Control Room was flung open. Sixteen military policemen marched in, grabbed the five men in the alcove, and marched them off. A squadron of men ran into the room. Technicians crawled over the control console, which still showed its Bhudda smile. They unscrewed panels, pulled at multi-colored wires, and jabbed at the boards of microchips with screwdrivers. Once the panels were off, the strong odor of Wild

Turkey came up from the console's guts. Five microchip boards were sticky with it.

Suddenly, Ted's radar screen lit up with little blips flying in formation. The southern corner of southwestern Saskatchawan had never seen such action.

"Holy shit!" screamed the little airman who had run in to take his place. "We've got birds all over the place!"

Five minutes later, Catalban Missile Base was a desolate crater in the ground.

A mushroom cloud rose above it over the prairie, its brilliant glow creating daylight for 100 miles in each direction.

In a farm outside of Sioux Falls, a red-plumed rooster stretched his legs, felt confused, and greeted the unexpectedly early dawn with a vigorous cry.

The End

Divorced

Chapter One

Marianne Glenn Trabert divorced Danny Trabert when she was 34-years-old.

After 10 years of marriage and seven years of fighting, she'd had enough. She and her two boys, Tommy and Sean, moved in with her mother after Danny locked them out of the house the night she filed for divorce.

"I pay the bills, I make the choices," he'd told her. "And my choice is you move out — now."

She swore she'd get another $50 a month child support out of him for that crack.

Marianne's mother had been as happy to see her as farmers are to see an infestation of grasshoppers. Wanda Glenn lived with Marianne's spinster sister, Katie, in a small, incredibly neat, two-bedroom bungalow in a run-down suburb just south of Chicago.

Gilbert Heights was nearly 80 percent black and 100 percent around Wanda's house. Wanda had the only green grass, weeded flowerbeds, and painted porch on the block. Unemployed young black men roamed the streets, drinking from bottles in paper bags. Wanda often found the empties in her rosebeds. Occasionally she heard gunshots at night.

Wanda and Katie didn't talk about the neighborhood, except for a few remarks about the "damn niggers" whenever they fished broken glass out of the roses. They couldn't afford to move. Why complain and make themselves miserable?

But Marianne could barely stand the place.

Every morning she got up at dawn to drive the boys to school in Lombard, the western suburb where she and Danny had lived. Then she drove back south to Burr Ridge and the bright-walled warehouse and assembly plant in an old industrial park where she worked.

She was the secretary to the vice president of manufacturing of Doyen Tool and Power Bearings Company. After 10 years of working there, all she knew about the business was that they made parts for forklifts, Mack Trucks, and a variety of machines the names of which she never remembered.

Every morning, she breathed a sigh of relief when she left her mother's dangerous neighborhood. When she returned every evening she inhaled sharply again, the boys in the backseat, hungry and cranky from their four-hour stay at the after-school daycare center.

Wanda tried to make her feel guilty about staying with her. "I'm not a rich woman," she said one night as she dished out the mashed potatoes for dinner. "You really can't stay here too long."

"Yes, Mother," Marianne said politely.

"I'm just living on social security you know." Wanda dropped her voice to a hushed tone. "God bless President Roosevelt for bringing such a salvation to the old."

Marianne rolled her eyes to the ceiling then concentrated on the chunk of pot roast on her plate.

"So when will you be moving out?" Wanda said, sitting her ample rump down on a kitchen chair. Marianne remembered the chairs from her childhood — neat plastic-covered chairs in a print that matched the formica of the old kitchen table.

"Mother, I've only been here three weeks."

"I'm not trying to hurry you, but you should be out on your own," Wanda said, waving her hand distractedly and cutting the meat on her plate. "I mean it's just me and Katie here and we like our peace and quiet, don't we Katie girl?"

Katie smiled. A dough-faced, plump women of 28, Katie was unmarried and rarely spoke although she was the receptionist at the executive offices of the Boldheimer Steel Company, just due east of the house. Maybe she was tired of being cheery and helpful all day, Marianne thought. She was sure Katie wasn't listening now.

"So why don't you get a nice apartment for you and the boys?" Wanda continued. "Now that that deadbeat husband of yours is out of the picture, it's time for you to get up and running on your own."

Marianne set down her fork and sat back in her chair. Tommy and Sean, ages 9 and 6, motored through their food like they hadn't been fed in weeks. Marianne wished they didn't eat so much. Wanda watched everything they put in their mouths as if it were food out of her own.

"Mother," she said, exasperated, "I'm doing the best I can. I just filed for divorce three weeks ago. I don't know what Danny's going to do, if I'm going to get the house, what kind of child support I can finagle. Everything's up in the air. I'm paying you room and board for me and the kids.

"So why don't you just give me a little breathing room? I'm not real happy at the moment."

She pursed her lips to keep from crying and stared at her mother and sister. Her mother looked back with a rigid smile on her face.

"I just want to make sure that you're thinking of the future, dear," Wanda said. "There is life beyond Danny Trabert." She went back to methodically cutting up her pot roast into little cubes.

Katie gave Marianne a drifty smile and served herself another huge chunk of pot roast. Katie ate more than Marianne and her two boys combined.

"So any more news about the big jerk?" Wanda said, popping a tiny cube of meat into her mouth.

"Mo-ther," Marianne said, eyeing her two sons. "Don't talk about Danny like that in front of the boys."

Tommy and Sean looked up, all ears, then went back to their meal. They'd heard their mother call their father a lot more horrible things than that over their lifetimes.

"I mean he is their father," Marianne said virtuously. "We just had some differences of opinion on how to conduct our lives. We just grew apart."

"Differences of opinion don't tear marriages apart," Wanda said. "And he is a big jerk. I told you you should have never married him. From day one I didn't like that man. A big lout, with 'I'm going nowhere' written across the top of his forehead."

"Mother, he's a foreman now."

"I don't care if he's president of the United States. The guy's a loser." She stabbed at her canned green beans almondine with her fork. "He had a snotty way about him, like he didn't care about anybody or anything. I'm surprised you two lasted as long as you did."

"It wasn't that bad."

"What are you defending him for? You're the one who's divorcing him."

Marianne slumped in her seat.

What was she defending him for? She'd been swearing she would divorce him for years. Three years into the marriage, just after Sean was born, she knew she'd made a mistake.

Now she was acting like he was an angel and she was leaving a bed of roses. She pursed her lips and stared at her plate. Wanda went back to the stove to dish out more pot roast on the platter.

What had been the matter with Danny Trabert?

Marianne stirred her food around on her plate and squished her green beans into her potatoes.

Danny was a nice guy, not too bright, not too dumb. He liked beer and bars, bowling on a league with his friends from work, barbeques, and Sunday-afternoon football. He watched Johnny Carson at night with Marianne, the two of them lying in their kingsize water bed, staring at the aging talk-show host over the tops of their toes.

He'd make love to her twice a week, Tuesday and Thursday nights, a nice little rythmic dance where she'd have one thin orgasm while he came into her with great drama and moaning then rolled over and fell asleep.

A big sloppy man, Danny had the eyes of a springer spaniel—sad, droopy brown eyes that made Marianne feel guilty when she yelled at him, which was a lot.

Except for his marriage to Marianne, he was a happy man.

And that was a big exception.

They'd married after four months of dating. He'd thought she was cute, well-dressed, and as good as any woman who would ever be interested in him. She was your basic, class-A, generic wife. He wasn't picky.

She'd married him because she was 24, flighty, and afraid of being a spinster. A graduate of the Cressida School of Commerce, she had studied executive secretarial skills. She had already been working five years. She had smart clothes and rode the commuter train into the Loop every day from her mother's house in Gilbert Heights.

Danny was friendly, easy to be with, and relatively good-looking. He liked her friends. And he had a good job working in the freezers at a big meat-packing plant on the south side of the city.

They had a big wedding. On their honeymoon, she put in her new diaphragm sideways and got pregnant with Tommy.

In one year she went from Marianne Glenn, carefree career girl, to Mrs. Danny Trabert, a tired, overworked woman with a colicky infant, an eternal backlog of housework, and a husband to cook for every night of the week once she dragged herself off the commuter train to their cramped house in Lombard.

She complained to Danny. He looked at her with his droopy spaniel eyes, nodded sympathetically, and pledged to help with the housework. He started turning his socks right-side-out before he put them in the hamper, stopped dropping his dirty underwear on the floor, and started cooking hot dogs and beans for dinner one night a week.

It was always hot dogs and beans: Danny hated to cook. He hated housework.

Danny was not stupid.

Marianne smiled painfully, squawked a little about his lack of cooperation, then gave up. Her pleas were met with sympathetic agreement, backrubs, and no assistance. Danny was always "busy."

It was three years into the marriage and just after Sean was born that she began to hate her husband. She stared at him one night over the dinner table. Tommy was sitting on a stack of phone books in a chair and throwing his cooked peas on the floor. Sean was sleeping in the impromptu crib she had set up in the dining room.

Danny was eating his meatloaf in careful, delicate bits that belied his size, much like a huge boar nibbling on an apple.

"How was work, honey?" Marianne said, wiping Tommy's mouth. She was home for her three weeks of unpaid maternity leave.

"Fine," he said, not looking up. "I start swing shift again next week."

"Oh no," she said. She never saw him when he worked swing shift. He left for the plant at 3 in the afternoon while she was still at work. When he came home at 1 in the morning, she was asleep. And when she got up at 6 in the morning, he was in deep sleep, a chorus of snores and gurgles accompanying the gentle heaving of his chest.

"It'll only be for two or three months," Danny said. "It won't be too bad." He looked up, smiled, and went back to his meatloaf, the subject closed.

Tommy howled and spilled juice on himself.

"Damn it, Tommy," she mumbled. Her husband didn't look up. She dabbed at Tommy's chin with the end of his bib.

Danny's new hours would screw up everything. She would have to stay home evenings. He wouldn't be there to baby-sit the boys and they couldn't afford to hire any more baby-sitters.

She smashed her fork in Tommy's mashed potatoes and stared again at Danny.

Who the hell was this guy? Why was he here?

Her boys she could understand. They were her own flesh and blood. But who was this lumpy creature sitting across from her, a creature who only did things that messed up her overburdened schedules, inconvenienced her, or generated laundry or dirty dishes?

She set her fork down and stared at him harder. He had cut himself shaving that morning; a patch of red glared at her over the collar of his shirt.

He was her destiny. She was supposed to spend the rest of her life with this man.

He looked up. "Pass the rolls, would you honey?" he said. She passed him the roll basket. He smiled his lazy, sleepy smile and selected a plump white roll.

She felt the urge to flee.

If this was love and domestic tranquillity, it was greatly overrated, she thought. More likely, it was boredom and aggravation.

Boredom and aggravation.

She was bored, aggravated, tired, and definitely not in love.

Love. What was love? Certainly not two people rubbing their genitals together in the dark. She and Danny did enough of that for her taste.

Love. Love. Love.

Love and passion. Three years ago she had wanted to get married more than she had wanted love. Danny had conveniently appeared. She had liked him well enough.

Now she wanted love.

Anyone could get married and have kids. But being loved was something else. She twirled her fork in her fingers and stared at Tommy's plate.

She wanted to be loved.

Maybe there was hope for them?

She looked at the unsuspecting Danny, now steadily working his way through his mashed potatoes.

No. He was not made for love. It had all been a big mistake. Except for her children, this wasn't what she had wanted at all.

Her mother had made the same mistake. She had divorced her father just after Katie was born for reasons she had never explained. He had disappeared from their lives.

Danny looked up and was startled by the intensity of his wife's gaze. "Is there something the matter, honey?" he said.

"No, no," she said hurriedly. "I was just daydreaming." She smiled nervously and absentmindedly shoveled a huge spoonful of cooked peas into Tommy's mouth. The child pushed the spoon away and howled "No!"

"Actually, there is something," she said, setting the spoon down.

"Yeah?"

"I'm not very happy," she said.

"Oh?"

"I just don't feel real excited about anything. I just kind of mope around. I'm not real happy about us and our marriage right now."

"You're just tired," he said quickly. He went back to eating. "I get unhappy when I'm tired, too," he said, stuffing a big chunk of roll in his mouth. "Why don't you go to bed early tonight?"

She looked right at him. "It's not being tired, it's us. I don't think we have enough love in our marriage. I don't think we have any love at all."

He looked at her like she was talking Greek. "What are you talking about?" he said. "I love you."

She was going to say, "but I don't love you," but she stopped herself.

"Yes, I know," she said.

"I'll put Tommy to bed tonight. You rest up."

"OK."

She got up and cleared the dishes then poured them both cups of coffee. Danny opened up the newspaper to the sports pages and spread them out on the table. "The Bears beat the Jets last night," he said. He and Marianne were both Bears' fans. "They play Tampa Bay next week. Should be a good game."

"Yeah." He talked on about the football league. She sipped her coffee then got up to wash the dishes and breastfeed Sean. Then she took a long hot shower and climbed into bed at 10:00, the sound of the 10:00 news on TV babbling in the background.

She couldn't sleep.

She hated that man.

Chapter Two

It was after that night that Marianne got bitchy and started picking fights with Danny. She woke up early the next morning, depressed and horrified. She had hoped her hatred would have gone away in the night, like indigestion from a too-rich meal.

But it was still there. She looked at Danny lying next to her, his big bear-like head snuggled in his pillow. She rolled on her back and stared at the ceiling. She felt sick in the pit of her stomach.

Divorce. She would divorce him.

And live on what? Danny pulled in $30,000 a year at the packing plant but she made only $16,000 at Doyen Tool and Power. Her boss, Mr. Merlan, was nice but cheap. She couldn't live and raise two boys on $16,000 a year.

But Danny would give her child support.

That was a joke. Carla Hanson at work was divorced with two small daughters. Her ex-husband left the state and got a new job in Florida, and Carla hadn't received a child-support check in eight weeks. Every time she called his office, his secretary said he was travelling and took a message.

Marianne turned and looked at her husband. Danny wouldn't do that; he wouldn't cut her and the boys off without a dime.

Or would he?

She looked back up at the ceiling again.

No, she couldn't trust Danny. She would have to find another man to support her and her sons.

Sure, she thought, the world is full of men anxious to take on a wife with droopy breasts, a flabby stomach, and two sons by another man. And assuming such a man existed, how would she find him? Could she find him while she was still living with Danny or would she have to divorce her husband first? And how would she support herself while she was looking?

The blanketed hulk next to her began to stir, rolled over, and opened its eyes.

"Good morning, honey," Danny said, snaking his arm under the covers and pulling her in close to him.

"Don't do that," she snapped.

"Come on and be friendly," he said.

"I've got to get up," she said, trying to get out of his grasp.

He nuzzled her on the neck. She felt her skin crawl.

"Give me a kiss first," he said, tweaking one of her nipples.

"Stop it!" she said. She pushed his hands away from her and tried to sit up. "I've got to go feed Sean. I hear him crying."

She made that one up. The baby was sound asleep.

Danny released his grasp. She got up and drew on her robe.

"I don't like it when you paw me like that," she said. "I'm not some piece of meat."

Danny looked at her, bewildered. "You're in a great mood this morning," he mumbled, pulling himself out of bed.

She said nothing and left the room.

She heard him go into the bathroom and turn on the shower.

She passed by the baby's room, went into the kitchen, and started the coffee.

How could she continue to live with a man she detested? She ran her hands through her hair and stared out the window at the wintry dawn. Two cardinals pecked at the sunflower seeds in her birdfeeder.

She just wouldn't think about it. She couldn't do anything about it; she shouldn't brood about it.

She plugged in the coffee percolator.

Maybe she could lose herself in fantasy? She could read romance novels and dream about handsome men with hairy chests sweeping her off her feet. Katie had a lifetime supply of such books.

The percolator started to rumble.

She could get a boyfriend.

She watched the cardinals drop seeds on the snow.

Unfortunately, she couldn't think of a single acquaintance of hers or Danny's who interested her in the least. Maybe she should start hanging out in bars with Danny?

Right. She'd start picking up men right in front of her husband and his friends.

At that moment, Danny walked in, crisp and clean in a heavy wool shirt and blue wash pants. The freezers at the Western Meat-Packing Co. where he worked were cold.

Marianne glared at him as if the plague had walked into her kitchen. She turned the stove on under her frying pan and fished some eggs out of the refrigerator for his breakfast.

She could always poison him.

What good would that do? She'd lose his income.

"Can I have some juice, honey?" Danny said.

"It's coming, it's coming," she said. She pulled two slices of bread out of the bag in the freezer and put them in the toaster.

Danny sat down at the kitchen table, silent and tired in the early-morning light. She turned on the radio. Some man with a professionally cheery voice came on the air and chattered mindlessly.

Danny poured himself a cup of coffee.

Marianne fried up his eggs and dished them out on a chipped blue plate.

He ate quickly and without a word.

She looked at him again. No, she thought. She just didn't like him.

"Tonight's bowling night," he said, getting up from the table. "I'll be home late." He came over to her and she instinctively turned him her cheek. "See you later," he said, pecking her on the cheek.

"Yeah," she said. "Bye."

He pulled his winter coat from the front closet and went out the door. She went to the front window and watched him go down the snowy walk and into the garage. She waved as he backed the car down the driveway and into the street.

Then she went back into the kitchen, poured herself a cup of coffee, and stared out the kitchen window. Three sparrows had joined the cardinals at the birdfeeder. She began to cry.

Danny was a good man. Why didn't she love him? Lots of women would be happy to be married to him. She must be crazy.

She swore she'd be a better wife to him. She'd behave herself. She'd put all these thoughts of hatred and other men out of her mind.

She made herself a piece of raisin toast, sat down at the kitchen table, and contemplated her loveless future with despair.

* * *

And so it went. Marianne would alternate between hating Danny and wanting to escape from him, and feeling that she just wasn't trying hard enough. When she hated Danny, which grew from about 50 percent of the time to a good 85 percent, she was curt and mean to him. She picked fights.

He began to yell at her and avoid her.

She could feel him cutting her out of his life. He stopped calling her "honey," he spent more time with his friends, and he was always taking Tommy and Sean to see his mother — without her. His mother worried about their marriage. Once, after Danny and the boys had gone over there for dinner, she had called Marianne on the phone.

"Danny's here, honey," she said.

"Yes, I know," Marianne said. She didn't care for her mother-in-law, a fat little women with a continuously upbeat disposition.

"He's been telling me that things aren't too happy at home."

Marianne bit her tongue. The meddling bitch.

"Marianne?"

"Yes. I'm still here."

"I've made a little appointment for the both of you at the Chicago Heights Mental Health Center. I know this really marvelous woman there who can help you out. She's helped lots of my friends go through their change of life and other little problems. . ."

"Gloria . . ."

"Now Marianne, don't you worry about it. It will be just fine. You two just need a little straightening out and Mrs. McPherson is just the lady to do it. You just need to learn how to communicate better. That's the problem with lots of marriages today. People don't know how to communicate. . ."

Marianne held the phone away from her ear as her mother-in-law rambled on about suicide, divorce, child abuse, and all the other ills that Mrs. McPherson had been known to cure. "All with just a little talking and a little love," as Gloria put it. "Just accept God's love and love each other and miracles can occur. It's just the miracle of communicating," she said.

Mrs. McPherson sounded like some sort of mystic healer.

Marianne got off the phone after a begrudging agreement to see the woman. If Gloria wanted them to see this woman, they would see this woman. Danny did everything his mother suggested. He held her in awe, like the dumb animals of the field must have adored St. Francis of Assisi. All her children did.

She was a very lucky woman.

Mrs. McPherson turned out to be a big, tall, black woman in a bright-colored dress and with an unusually deep voice. Marianne and Danny were surprised; his mother hadn't mentioned she was black.

Marianne did most of the talking. Danny was a bum, he didn't love her, she was dying at home, she needed love, sometimes she wished she were dead. She went on and on.

Mrs. McPherson said little, only asking for an occasional elaboration. Danny stared at his hands.

Marianne felt relieved, the great burden of pain and frustration lifted from her shoulders for a moment. She looked expectantly at Mrs. McPherson, who was now going to tell her how to solve all her problems.

Mrs. McPherson turned to Danny. "So what do you think, Dan?" she said in her deep voice.

He looked up and shrugged. "I don't know," he said. "I don't think anything's the matter with our marriage."

Marianne's heart sank.

Mrs. McPherson adjusted her glasses and looked at Marianne. "It's often common in marriages to alternately hate and love your spouse. It's nothing to worry about. Essentially, you're just suffering from a lack of communication.

"I think you both are just suffering from overwork and need a vacation. Why don't the two of you go off alone somewhere without the kids and just talk? We can talk about how to open those lines of communication when you come back." She smiled widely, showing a big gold tooth just behind her left canine.

Danny smiled weakly.

Marianne was enraged. How dare this woman trivialize her feelings! She wasn't suffering from overwork; she wanted out of her marriage.

But Danny thought it was a good idea.

So they parked the boys with his mother and he took her to a cheap resort just south of Ft. Wayne. They went snowmobiling, walked in the woods, and ate at the local steakhouse. Danny did his rythmic sex dance on her every night. He gained five pounds from the rich food and spent several hours of each day talking to the groundskeeper who turned out to be an avid deerhunter.

Marianne hated every minute of the trip and counted the hours until she returned home. On the return trip, they had a big fight in the car. Danny always drove too fast; she always complained about it. This time it was snowing heavily and the car fishtailed. She shrieked, he told her to shut up, and she started her litany of complaints.

He blew up and told her she was bitch.

She said he was a fool and a lousy driver.

They drove home in silence, whatever communication necessary made in icy tones.

They hardly talked in civil tones for a week until the reason for the fight faded from current memory and they were tired of being angry.

Then they spoke to each other in flat, toneless voices.

They didn't go back to see Mrs. McPherson.

* * *

The next seven years of their marriage droned on in the same pattern: a tidal wave of a big fight followed by days of flat, calm water and cool indifference. Marianne despaired of love, Danny despaired of domestic tranquility, and Sean and Tommy believed all kids' parents had shrieking fights once a week and then didn't talk to each other. They wondered why mommies and daddies wanted to live together under such circumstances and had several big discussions about it under the covers at night.

They decided adults were crazy.

The dam finally broke just after their ninth wedding anniversary: Marianne had an affair with the vice president of marketing where she worked. Divorced two years after three years of marriage to a stewardess, Jack Dumas liked women, romance, and Marianne – in that order. He viewed Marianne as merely the latest charming specimen in his collection of women. He bought her flowers, took her out when Danny was at his bowling league, and – most importantly – he said he loved her.

She blossomed. She swore she loved him back and was sure he was going to propose marriage.

So – precipitously – one evening in late May she told Danny that she wanted a divorce.

"Fine," he said, his face exhausted. "It's about time." He sounded like a prizefighter relieved to be knocked out after the eighth round.

She used Carla Hanson's attorney to handle the paperwork and negotiations. He was a precise little man who always rushed her through his office. She and Danny endured two months of unsuccessful, court-ordered marriage counseling. Then she filed for divorce.

Jack took her to dinner to celebrate – and to tell her he was being transferred to Atlanta. Thrilled, he looked for her happy congratulations.

She stared at him.

"What's the matter?" he said.

"Well, I thought . . ." she said.

"Yes?"

"I thought we were going to get married," she blurted.

He took her hand in his and looked at her with soft, brown eyes. "Oh, sweetie," he said.

"Well, aren't we?" she said, her voice strained. Tears came to her eyes.

Jack released her hand and turned his coffee cup in its saucer. "Look, honey," he said. "I'm not really the marrying kind of guy. Once is enough. I need my freedom."

Her face fell.

". . . I mean, I can't really call myself a dependable, family kind of guy . . ."

She was screwed. How was she going to pay her bills?

". . . but I still love you. . ."

Marianne looked at him, her eyes cold. "What does that mean?" she said.

He laughed lightly. "It's hearts and flowers, romance and candlelight," he said. "You'll always be my best girl."

She smiled weakly. How many times had he used that line?

"Come on," he said. "Let's go to my house for a little fun."

"No," she said abruptly. "I'd rather go home. I have a headache."

He looked startled then his face hardened. "OK," he said coolly.

He took her home. Two weeks later he left for Atlanta with nary two words spoken between them.

And Marianne went back home to Wanda.

* * *

Danny had been nasty on the property settlement. He wouldn't let Marianne have the house, claiming he could not afford both house payments and child support. So the house was sold and Marianne got half the equity; her share was $7,582.24. She put it in a savings account at the Gilbert Heights State Bank. Often, she took out her savings book and stared at the balance. That money and the $623 in her Christmas Club account were her only assets.

Two months after her divorce, she and the boys were still living with her mother. Wanda finally hit the roof.

"You've got to go," she told Marianne one Saturday morning over breakfast. "You and the kids can't live here anymore. I can't afford it."

"But Mom. . ." Marianne felt a wave of panic.

"No buts. It's time for the three of you to be moving on."

"Mother, I have no place to go."

"Find one. Millions of divorced women are out on their own. Fly on your own wings. I can't support you anymore."

"I'm paying room and board. It's not costing you a dime."

Wanda extended a bony hand and laid it on her daughter's arm. "Marianne, sweetheart," she said softly. "Enough is enough. I'm an old woman. I need peace and quiet. You and the boys have to get on with your lives. You can't just live with me indefinitely in this crummy neighborhood. We can't even let the boys out to play without worrying they'll get killed."

"But I don't have enough money to move," Marianne said quickly. "I can't afford rent."

Wanda shook her head slowly and poured herself another cup of coffee. "That's not my problem, sweetheart. I don't have much money either. When I divorced your father, I had no one to move in

with. Both my parents were dead and my sister was living overseas.
I had to fend for myself. I waited on tables and washed floors. I did
everything and anything to make ends meet.

"And look how good you girls turned out," she said proudly,
looking at Marianne and at Katie, who had just wandered into the
kitchen in her bathrobe.

Marianne thought Wanda was kidding. Katie was a fat,
depressed spinster and Marianne was a bankrupt, divorced mother
of two with no prospects of either a better-paying job or a new
husband. But Wanda looked at them both as if they were
well-adjusted, bright women with great jobs, happy marriages, and
the prospect of wonderful lives ahead.

Marianne heard Tommy and Sean fighting over a toy in the living
room, the sound of Saturday morning cartoons in the background.
She wondered if she was as blind to their faults as her mother was to
hers.

She wondered how many floors she'd have to wash and letters
she'd have to type before her children were grown and on their own
financially. She wished it was sooner rather than later. It was two
months after the divorce and Danny was already a week late on
child-support payments. She would have to get a second job or
they'd really be broke.

A woman and two boys couldn't live on $16,000 a year. Rent on
an inhabitable apartment for the three of them was at least $550 a
month. After taxes, she'd end up with less than $300 a month for
everything else. Plus, her 10-year-old Pontiac was breaking down.
She would either have to patch it up or buy a new clunker.

Wanda went downstairs to do the laundry and Marianne picked
up the morning newspaper off a kitchen chair. She was thumbing
her way to the car ads when her eye caught the headline "mobile
homes."

> Own your own home for less! Forest View Mobile
> Home Park in Sauk Village has new and pre-owned
> mobile homes for you. Prices start at $5500. Off Sauk
> Trail at Shawnee Road.

And there was a phone number.

$5500. She could come up with $5500. She could buy a complete house for what other people put as a downpayment on a dump. That would leave her her salary to live off.

That afternoon she threw the boys into the sputtering Pontiac and headed south to Sauk Village. She drove past chemical plants and warehouses and finally through a series of small cornfields and weedy prairies interspersed with gas stations and small, run-down stores.

Sauk Trail was a busy highway. At Shawnee Road there were gas stations on two corners. On the third was a tired brick building, "The Aronson Water Cistern Company," and on the fourth was a faded blue sign: "Forest View Mobile Home Park: New and Pre-Owned Homes Available."

The "park" looked like a parking lot, with row after row of pastel-colored mobile homes lined up like giant metal bricks standing on their long edges, one next to the other. The bricks came down to nearly the edge of the highway and baked in the late August sun; the only trees were on the far side of the park.

Marianne pulled into the small gravelled parking lot in front of a mobile home with fake wood trim. Another faded blue sign announced it as the "Office and Sales Center."

She expected the trailer to rock when she walked up the small metal steps to the entrance and entered through the flimsy little door. But it didn't. It stood solid and steady. An air conditioner labored in one window. The inside was cool and damp with brown shag carpet and a brown formica desk in one corner. Everything smelled new and like plastic.

A thin man in his late 50s in a yellow golf shirt came up to her from behind the desk and gave her an oozy, friendly-salesman look.

He wanted to show Marianne the latest in his country-estate models: wide-bodied, long trailers painted in baby blue and light gray with bay windows and tiny peaked roofs at one end.

"No," Marianne said. "I'd like to see the used trailers."

"The new models start at only $15,995," the salesman said, ignoring her. He led them down a gravel road a few feet from the sales office. "You get a double stainless-steel sink and built-in dishwasher in the kitchen, wall-to-wall acrilon-500 carpeting made of no-care, polycore-foam, acrylic fiber, textured-marble bath. . ."

"Excuse me," Marianne said, softly, touching the salesman lightly on the arm.

He stopped, annoyed at being interrupted.

"I can't afford that," she said. "I have only $5500 to spend."

"No problem," he said, starting to walk again. "We have special financing arranged with one of the premier consumer-financing companies in the country. Low, monthly payments. You can be in your new home in two weeks. Now let me show you the gorgeous interior of our Sunset Hills Model II here."

He was just opening the door to a lovely, pearl-gray trailer when he noticed Marianne hadn't followed. She was standing at the foot of the metal stairs, flanked by her two boys, all three of them looking up at him.

"Aren't you coming?" the startled salesman said.

She shook her head no.

He closed the door and came back down the stairs. "This model is just what you and the boys . . . "

"I told you I can't afford it," she said angrily. "I have $5500 to spend and that's it."

"But the monthly payments are so low, only $356.87 a month . . ."

"I can't afford monthly payments. I want to own outright." She held up the newspaper ad she held in one hand. "Show me the one you advertised for $5500."

The salesman ran his hands through his hair. "It won't do for you and the boys at all," he said. "It's really quite small."

Marianne smiled stiffly. Sean clung to her hand.

Defeated, the salesman's shoulders slumped.

"It's back here," he said. He walked briskly down the gravelled road toward the corner of the park with the trees. They passed trailers of all conditions. One home's hot-pink finish was streaked with rust; the trailer leaned precariously to one side. In front of it, a diapered two-year-old and an ancient-looking dog sat sleepily in a patch of dirt.

Two doors down was a neat, mint-green trailer with a wide window, a built-on sun porch, and two pink flamingoes on a vividly green little patch of lawn. The car in front of the trailer, a big Chrysler, had Florida plates on it and a big bumper-sticker: "Ask me about my grandchildren."

Most of the trailers were neat and painted in pastels. Some had little sheds behind them to store possessions the owner could not fit in the confines of a house that was only 13 feet wide. All the trailers were very close together with less than 15 feet between them. There was little privacy at Forest View.

The salesman wasn't talking now, he was just walking, impatient to get Marianne and her boys out of the way. He made much smaller commissions on "pre-owned mobile homes."

The $5500 "mobile home" was a true trailer, a silver tin can shaped like a teardrop laying on its side. It rested on four tiny wheels. It was no longer than the living room in Wanda's tiny house.

"This is an antique, a real collector's item," the salesman said. "It's a Happy Wanderer Travel Buggy in perfect condition, over 30-years-old. But as you can see, it's much too small for you and the boys. So why don't we go back to the new models." He started to steer her back to the new merchandise.

But next to the antique, on a weedy lot, was a full-fledged, mobile home with white metal walls, small vented windows that rolled out, and a big window up front. It was square-cornered and roofed and very plain. No peaks or bays on this one.

"How much is that one?" Marianne asked the salesman.

"$7500," he said, his lip curling up in a sneer. "You wouldn't want it. It's 25-years-old."

"Is there something the matter with it?" she asked.

"No. No," he said hurriedly. "It's just that it doesn't have the great features of the newer homes like built-in dishwashers, fine tiled floors, or acrilon super-shag carpetting." He plunged on about the better insulation in the newer models, but she cut him short.

"I'd like to see it," she said.

He glared at her, sighed, and led her up the little metal stairs to the trailer's door.

The trailer was hot and stuffy inside with a damp, musty smell. It had a tiny living room, nice-sized kitchen, and two tiny bedrooms. Every room but the kitchen and bathroom was lined in a dark, plastic paneling designed to look like knotty pine. It made the interior seem dark.

The floor was covered with worn, green carpetting except in the kitchen, where it was covered with cracked white linoleum.

The salesman rolled open the windows. A feeble stream of air wafted through the living room. Marianne could hear the traffic on Shawnee Road. Two children fought over a toy outside; a dog barked.

"Let me see," the salesman said. He fingered his way through his sales book and found the stained page describing the trailer.

"Lot number 36, 25-year-old, Prairie View Home for sale by the estate of Hannah Flavercek," he mumbled. "Where's my other card on this baby?" he mumbled under his breath, sorting through the worn papers and cards in his book.

Marianne and the boys wandered the trailer. The tiny little bedroom could be hers. The boys could sleep in the slightly larger master bedroom. She had enough old rugs to cover the linoleum floor and the worn parts of the carpeting. She could paint the walls a brighter color.

"What do you think boys?" she said to her sons.

"Great, Mommy. It's like camping," six-year-old Sean said, running from one room to another.

"It's a dump, Mom," nine-year-old Tommy said. "Can't we stay with Grandma?"

She looked down at him sadly. "Grandma needs her room. This is the best we can afford," she said.

The boy chewed his lip. With his brown, droopy eyes and slouched stance he looked like a miniature version of his father, Marianne thought. Danny Trabert would haunt her forever in the faces of her sons.

"$7500," the salesman said. "$7500 takes the whole thing, plus the $144-a-month maintenance, utilities, and ground-lease payment."

Marianne looked surprised.

"You lease the ground from us," the salesman said impatiently. "We maintain the roads and lighting and pay the sewer, water, and real estate tax bills."

"Oh," Marianne said, pausing. "I need to talk to my mother about this."

"Fine, fine," the salesman said, snapping his book shut with a thunk.

Marianne brooded all the way back to Gilbert Heights while the boys fought in the backseat. The mobile home was out of the city so the schools were probably better. It was a half-hour commute to her office. She could just afford it if she spent every penny she had.

She discussed it with her mother, who would have agreed with any plan that got Marianne and the boys out of her house.

The next morning Marianne called the salesman and made an offer.

"$6499," she told him.

"Lady," he said, "the price is $7500. You don't make offers on mobile homes." His commission would be even more pitiful on $6499 than on $7500.

"Oh," she said, surprised. "OK."

"Do you want it?" he said.

"Yeah. Yeah, I do."

"It's yours," he said.

She smiled and clapped her hands on the phone.

Two weeks later, she and the boys moved in.

Chapter Three

The first night in the trailer, they nearly suffocated. It had been a 90-degree day; one of the movers had fainted from heat stroke. Marianne and her sons lay on their beds in their dark, hot, little rooms, their sweat soaking the sheets.

The next day she took the last $50 in her savings account and bought two big room fans.

The day after that, a Monday, she took the day off from work and called the local school district. Tommy and Sean would both attend Pottawatomie Trails School, one mile down Shawnee Road. School started the next week; Marianne took the boys in for late registratoin.

A one-story, cinder-block building, "Potty School," as the students called it, spread across a large, treeless field of burned grass, surrounded by cheap tract housing. The building was about 20-years-old and spotless. It smelled of fresh wax and metal polish. The floors gleamed as Marianne and her sons walked through its cool halls to the principal's office.

A friendly woman in a pink dress registered Tommy for the third grade and Sean for the first, then pulled out a map and traced the complexities of the bus route they were on.

"You see, the bus turns west from Shawnee Estates, down Hiawatha Drive, and past the golf course on Route 12," she said, smiling and drawing a stubby pencil around the map. "Then it goes through Hawthorne Acres, jogs down Pickering Road here, and picks up your boys at Shawnee and Route 83 at . . ." She paused, turned to a schedule on the wall, and squinted to read its tiny print. "At 7:48," she said, "southwest corner."

The school also operated an after-school program for children whose parents worked. The kids had milk and cookies at 3:30, played on the playground for 45 minutes, then worked on their homework for half an hour. The bus dropped them off at home at 6:06.

The program was $450 a semester for each child. Marianne sighed and signed up for the monthly payment plan. She was spending all her money before she'd even made it.

Tomorrow was a workday. What could she do with the boys for the next week? She called up Wanda. By promising to clean out her basement and pick up Wanda's sister when she flew into O'Hare from Atlanta the next month, Marianne got her mother to take care of the boys for the week.

The kids were relieved to be back with their grandmother.

"How do you like your new home?" Wanda asked them while Marianne was out at the car getting their suitcases.

"It's aw-ful," they chorused.

"It's so hot we can't sleep at all and we don't know anybody," Tommy said.

"And there's no room for Daddy there," Sean said. "He's got no room for his clothes."

Sean still didn't seem to understand that his parents were divorced, despite his mother's and grandmother's constant lectures to the contrary. Like a heartsick little dog, he would sit in the window around suppertime, waiting for his father until his mother or grandmother would angrily call him to eat.

"I'm waiting for Daddy," he would say.

"He's not coming, sweetheart," Marianne would say. "Daddy doesn't live with us anymore. Mommy and Daddy are divorced."

"But he's coming home soon," Sean would say, ignoring his mother's comments and climbing into his chair at the dinner table. "He just forgot to come home. He'll come home tomorrow."

At first Marianne felt bad for the child, then annoyed. Finally, she just ignored him.

About three months after they had moved to the trailer and five months after she had divorced Danny, Sean stopped sitting in the window. He became quiet and withdrawn. Even Danny's fatherly visits on weekends did not cheer him.

"Why did you leave us, Daddy?" the boy asked for several weeks, his eyes filling with tears.

"We still love you, pal," Danny would say, putting his arm around Marianne. The two of them smiled big, fakey smiles.

"Just because we don't live together anymore doesn't mean we don't love you," Marianne said.

Their divorce was just a friendly misunderstanding. One person had wanted to paint the living room green, the other preferred white. Since they couldn't agree, they got divorced. But they were still friends.

What Sean couldn't understand was if Mommy and Daddy were such pals, why would they stop living together? More than ever he was certain he had done something wrong. He had forced them apart.

For her part, Marianne couldn't understand why Sean wanted her and Danny to be together again. Life was so much more pleasant without Danny: there were no screaming fights. She was enjoying life as a single woman again. She felt a great sense of relief.

She couldn't understand why the boys didn't feel the same.

When Danny came to see them, they jumped all over him, pulling his sleeves, demanding he play ball with them, admire a toy of theirs, or just take them outside to play. Their attention surprised and flattered Danny. They'd never been so excited to see him when and Marianne were married.

"Absence makes the heart grow fonder," he'd commented once to Marianne when he'd come to pick up the boys for the weekend. It was about four months after their divorce.

They stood in the kitchen. She was peeling onions for stew.

"No it doesn't," she said, smiling sweetly and tossing a cleaned onion into the pot.

"I wasn't making a pass at you," he said angrily. Actually he was. He missed being married.

"I know you want me to come back," she said, starting in on a large Bermuda. "But it's no use. This thing won't work."

"Did I say a thing? A single thing?" he said, throwing his hands up in mock horror. He'd once made the mistake of suggesting they get back together, six weeks after their divorce was final. She had looked at him in disbelief and told him he was a fool. She had given him such a withering look, he'd never brought it up again – directly anyway.

"Well, I don't want to hear about it," she said. "I'm tired of fights."

He was going to say that she had started all of them, but he held his tongue.

"I'll see you Sunday night," he said.

"Fine," she said, and kept peeling.

He walked into the living room, gathered up the boys' things, and herded them out to the car.

"Grandma's made pizza for you guys tonight," he said.

They whooped.

* * *

After the divorce, Danny had gone to live with his mother who, unlike Marianne and her mother, was delighted to see him and her grandchildren. If given half a chance, she would have adopted her grandsons.

"A trailer," she'd sniffed when Danny told her of Marianne's new lodgings. "What kind of life is that for Trabert boys?"

She babied her son and grandsons.

"Nothing's too good for a Trabert," she would say, cutting them all extra slices of cake at dinner. Danny had gained 10 pounds since moving back in with his mother.

Tommy and Sean adored her.

"Why can't we have extra cake and ice cream?" they'd whine at Marianne when they came home from their grandmother's. "Grandma lets us have it."

"This isn't Grandma's," Marianne would say. "Eat your green beans."

The boys would mush their canned green beans around their plates and whine more, falling silent under her angry gaze.

They would sulk for two days after their father had gone and start looking forward to his arrival three days before he showed up again.

Boys need their fathers or some male authority figure, Marianne decided.

So she signed them up for Cub Scouts.

And she didn't give the problem another thought.

* * *

Marianne found her freedom exhilarating. She spread out across her double bed at night, enjoying her peaceful sleep undisturbed by masculine snoring.

Each morning she got up and looked contentedly at her clean sink: no tiny shaving hairs glommed together with shaving cream ringed the bowl. No heavy work clothes, stiff with sweat and grime, spread grease stains through her laundry basket.

She particularly liked the quiet. She wasn't yelling at anyone anymore, with the exception of the boys when they misbehaved.

She started reading more. She read an entire book on penguins in the Antarctic, one on sperm whales, and another on the history of Texas. One night, she set down her Texas history book on the coffee table and picked up a trashy romance novel her friend from work, Carla Hanson, had given her.

It had a steamy cover, a steamy plot, and after 10 pages Marianne felt herself wet between the legs.

She needed a man.

She started feeling like a nun. All her friends were women, many of them were divorced, and most of them didn't seem to care much about the male sex.

"Dirtbags, every one of them," Carla was always saying. Her ex-husband was three months behind in child support and Carla was begging money off her widowed mother. Her ex kept telling her to remarry; he had. He'd met some Cuban nurse in Miami, where he had been transferred for his new job, and had married her. She had two little boys. He kept telling Carla he couldn't support two families.

Now he was proving it.

"You should have thought of that before you had them!" she'd shriek at him over the phone.

Marianne heard it all secondhand the next day over coffee at work. It frightened her. What if Danny stopped paying child support? What would she do then?

Danny would never do that. Except for moments of pique, he was too nice a guy.

But then so was Herb Hanson. She never told Carla, but she'd always liked Herb. He was a quiet man with a nice smile and not much hair who sold fittings for sprinkler irrigation systems.

Now Herb had turned into a monster.

Maybe Danny would do the same.

Love wouldn't drive her into remarriage. Economic necessity would. She had to find a man to pay her bills. She and Danny hadn't been rich, but they'd been comfortable.

Now she wasn't even comfortable. The boys were eating more hot dogs and beans than she liked. Every payday her meager paycheck disappeared into a sea of bills.

She was borrowing money from her mother just to pay daily expenses. Her savings were exhausted.

From the gay divorcee, happy to be rid of an unattractive husband, she was now the worried mother, teetering on the edge of poverty and desperate to find a man who would support her and pay her bills.

On top of all that, she was horny.

How could she have ever divorced Danny "for love?" She should have stayed with him and fooled around with men on the side. She could have had her cake and eaten it, too.

She thought of calling him up and telling him it had all been a terrible mistake. She wanted him to come back.

But she couldn't. She didn't want Danny Trabert back. And after what she had done to him, she wasn't so sure he wanted her back either. The boys were now coming home from Grandma Trabert's with talk about Daddy's new girlfriend, Ruth.

He wasn't wasting any time, Marianne fretted. With a doting mother who fed him, no reponsibilities but child support, and lots of free time, Danny could go out and meet other women. He would remarry soon, she knew it.

She pumped the boys for information.

According to them, Ruth was skinnier than her with blonde hair and a bratty little boy, Frank.

Marianne started to panic. Ruth was moving in for the kill. She'd get Danny's paycheck before Marianne could stop her. Marianne and the boys would be cut off, penniless.

At work the next day, she confided in Carla in the coffee room.

"Danny's got a girlfriend," she said.

Carla moaned. "Big trouble, Marianne. That's big trouble. Danny's the marrying kind of guy. He likes having women around." She dumped a heaping spoonful of non-dairy creamer powder in her coffee.

"I don't want to alarm you," she said. "But you'd better be prepared for the worst. Ramona started out as Herb's little friend, too." Ramona was Herb's new wife.

"What should I do?" Marianne blurted.

"Start hustling," Carla said. "I am."

Indeed she was. Carla would interlard her stories of Herb's malfeasance with tales of the dating life. She was having sex with men that Marianne would have called the police on if she'd seen them around her house. They included motorcycle mechanics, bartenders, married men on the prowl, and more than one bored college student, out to sample "older women."

None of them struck Marianne as marriageable material; some made less money than her. But Carla assured her that she had to start at the bottom and work her way up.

"Mr. Money Bags just isn't out there waiting for you with a big sign hung around his neck," she would say. "You've got to find him."

"What if I don't want to?" Marianne would say peevishly.

Carla shrugged. "It's your funeral. You planning on winning the lottery soon?"

Marianne cursed herself under her breath and cursed her children.

Then she planned to go out on a night of bar-hopping with Carla.

She had to find a man.

Chapter Four

She was very nervous when Carla picked her up that Friday night.
They were heading for Sloppy Joe's, the "in" singles bar and night
club of the south suburbs. A former office-furniture warehouse, the
bar spread out like an airplane hangar on the edge of Homewood,
its high ceilings filled with strobe lights and turning glass balls, the
walls lined with tables surrounding the biggest dance floor Marianne
had ever seen.

They arrived around 10. The floor was jammed with dancers of
all ages, mostly young and white, though a group of blacks danced by
themselves in one corner.

Marianne wore her fringed leather top and a pair of tight jeans.
The top was a holdover from her days as a single woman. The jeans
were a product of married life: she couldn't fit into her fringed
leather pants anymore. She'd put on 20 pounds since her marriage.

Carla wore tight jeans and a fluffy little sweater of angora fur.
With her lovely figure, from the neck down she looked like a
teen-ager. From the neck up, she looked like a predator, with
deepening lines around her mouth and black eye makeup.

Carla had brought some friends with her. Susan worked in the
accounting department at work; Pam was Carla's next-door
neighbor. They both wore tight jeans and low-cut tops. Susan had a
better figure than Pam, who was bottom-heavy and had a receding
chin.

They had giggled and laughed all the way to the bar, Pam telling
dirty jokes and Marianne holding her nose close to the window. All
four women wore heavy perfumes. The combined smell of jasmine,
musk, and tuberoses gave Marianne a headache.

At the bar, the four women found a small table just off the dance
floor, ordered a pitcher of beer, and put on their most nonchalant
looks.

Then they waited for the men to find them.

They weren't long in coming. A nice-looking young man in
pressed jeans and a white shirt was soon jiggling on the dance floor
with Susan. Carla went off with a heavy-set fellow with a thick
beard; they seemed to be old friends. Pam excused herself to snort

cocaine in the ladies' room. The bathrooms at Sloppy Joe's were a minor trading station for the south-suburban drug trade.

So Marianne sat alone, smiling hard with her beer set on the table in front of her. For the first five minutes after her arrival at the bar, she felt lightheaded, excited, and ready to party, just as she had years before when she was single.

Now, 15 minutes into her visit and no invitation to dance, her spirits drooped. She felt like the last-place hog at the farm show after the judges had selected the prizewinners and they had trotted off, blue ribbons pinned to their collars.

She tried to keep her spirits up by telling herself she was just at some stupid bar, but her spirits sagged further. Finally, a man in his 40s with a receding hairline, an overhanging gut, and a chest full of gold chains walked up to her and asked her to dance.

She greeted him as if he were Sir Lancelot instead of a middle-aged wreck and went off to the dance floor. He was a terrible dancer and had bad breath. But she was so grateful he'd asked her to dance that she nearly kissed him.

He, on the other hand, ignored her. He stared out into the space on the dance floor as if she weren't there. After the dance, he excused himself and moved on around the edge of the dance floor. Marianne saw him introduce himself to a fat little woman with red hair four tables up the line.

The little pig was making his way through all the women sitting on the sidelines, she fumed. Here, even the ugliest of men could have his own harem. No wonder these bars were popular.

Her spirits sank lower.

Carla came back hanging on the arm of the bearded bear she'd originally gone off with. She held a big glass of beer in her right hand.

"Marianne, honey, I would like to meet a friend of mine," she said in a fakey southern drawl, turning to the man. "This here is Lloyd Fenderly." She smiled at Lloyd adoringly.

Marianne gave the pair a stiff little smile. "Hi, pleased to meet you," she said in her flat midwestern accent.

"Ma'am," Lloyd nodded.

He was about 30, very fat, and wore a blue cowboy-style shirt with piping trim and mother-of-pearl snap buttons. A beat-up Stetson was pushed back on his thick black hair.

Lloyd looked like the kind of man who grew hair everywhere: on his knuckles, on his chest, on his head, on his back. Marianne wondered if he had a furry ass. A tail perhaps?

"Lloyd's into oil and race cars," Carla drawled. "He's from Texas."

Lloyd beamed and Marianne mumbled something about how nice that was. What did Carla see in this idiot?

"Lloyd's daddy owns half of southwest Texas," Carla cooed.

That's what Carla saw in this idiot.

"Lloyd's up north here starting up a little race-car operation for his daddy, watching over all those details," she went on. "He works such long hours, don't you, sweet pea?" She tweaked his beard and smiled. "Isn't he just the cutest thing?"

Lloyd beamed.

Marianne gave him a flat little smile.

"Why don't you come back with us to Lloyd's table and meet some of his friends?" Carla drawled. "He's got the cutest friends."

"I'd love to," Marianne said, alarmed, but tired of sitting by herself. She picked up her purse and followed the couple, Carla's lithe figure swaying gracefully next to Lloyd's huge, denim-clad rump.

They wove through the crowds to the far side of the hall and stopped in front of a table littered with beer glasses and surrounded by five men and two women. The men wore denim jackets and looked like they'd just stepped off an oil rig in the Gulf of Mexico—or some cow ranch in southwest Texas. They were tan and had weathered faces.

A small woman with bleached blonde hair sat against the wall. Two of the men smiled and hunched over a buxom redhead, who was giggling between them.

"Boys, this here is Marianne," Lloyd said, with authority in his voice.

Everyone looked up and smiled at her. You could tell Lloyd was their boss.

"This here is Ralph, Johnny, Pokey, Frank, and Stiff, and I don't know the ladies' names . . ." Lloyd's voice trailed off.

"Rose Marie," the blonde chirped. "Melanie Sue Avrilton," the redhead giggled.

Everyone mumbled hello.

Marianne felt a nearly uncontrollable urge to flee.

Instead, she squeezed in through the chairs and sat down next to one of the men, the little blonde woman on her right.

"You want a beer?" he asked. He had no Texas accent and appeared to be in his late 30s.

"Yes, thank you," she said.

He took one of the dirty glasses on the table, shook out its dregs, and poured her a beer from the half-empty pitcher on the table.

She shuddered and drank, hoping no one had a communicable disease.

The two men on either side of the redhead laughed and tickled her. The redhead squirmed and giggled, "Don't!" and pushed their hands away.

At a small table next to them, Carla and Lloyd held hands and gazed into each other's eyes. It looked like Carla had found her meal ticket.

"Are you in race cars, too?" Marianne asked the man next to her.

"Yep," he said.

"What do you do?"

"I fix 'em." He stared straight ahead, not even looking at her.

"You always done that?"

"Nope."

"What else did you do?"

"I was a plumber."

"Where was that?"

"In Oklahoma."

"You from Oklahoma?"

"Yep."

"I'm from Chicago." She paused, hoping for a response.

He sipped his beer and said nothing.

Oh well, she'd try to jump-start him again.

"Where'd you get that tan?" she said.

"I like to fix cars outside."

"You like the fresh air?"

"That's right."

"You been here long?"

"Nope."

"You came with Lloyd?"

"That's right."

The band on the far end of the dance floor tuned up again. Suddenly, loud rock music filled the hall. Carla and Lloyd got up to dance, but no one moved at Marianne's table. The loud music made conversation impossible. The two men with the redhead continued to tickle her, the blonde leaned drunkenly against a third man's shoulder, and the other two men fingered their beer glasses and said nothing.

Marianne leaned back in her chair and watched the strobe lights flicker over the dancers. An overweight woman in a blue satin jumpsuit gyrated in front of their table.

It was the longest evening of her life.

When she and her girlfriends finally left around 2 the next morning, her ears were ringing from the loud music. Her girlfriends wanted to go to a country-western bar in Calumet City with a 4 am license, but she told them she was too tired.

"Marianne," Carla lectured her, "you're never going to find Mr. Money Bags that way. You've got to get out there and show the goods."

Marianne smiled wanly in the backseat and said she had a headache.

Disgusted, Carla dropped her off at the trailer park and headed for Calumet City.

Marianne dragged herself into her trailer with the profound sense that she'd made a big mistake divorcing Danny Trabert.

* * *

Her sons were up at 6 the next morning to watch the Saturday cartoons. She woke at 7 to the sound of Hereba, Girl Warrior, screaming "Attack! Attack! Here come the Lalutians!"

She cursed Danny. He was supposed to take the kids this weekend but had bowed out on Thursday with some mumbled excuse about other plans.

Marianne guessed he was spending the weekend with his new girlfriend, Ruth.

"Turn that TV down!" she yelled at the boys as she tied her bathrobe and shuffled into the kitchen to make coffee.

Sean stared at her blankly and Tommy hurried to the set. The volume dropped a full decibel.

"Let's play Hulk and Master Death!" Tommy yelled. "Get him, you Congoloids!" He jumped on his younger brother and wrestled him to the ground. They both screeched with excitement.

"Hold it down in there!" Marianne yelled, holding her head. She had a hangover.

"Leave me alone," Sean yelled at Tommy. "Tommy kicked me in the eye, Mom," he howled.

"Stop it, Tommy. Leave your brother alone."

"But he bit me," Tommy whined back.

"I did not!" Sean yelled.

"You did!"

"Did not!"

"Shut up the both of you or you can turn the TV off and go back to bed."

"He bit me on the arm, Mom," Tommy said, pulling up his pajama sleeve and showing his mother a little round bite.

"I did not!" Sean yelled.

"You did!"

"Sean, how many times do I have to tell you to stop biting your brother?" Marianne said, pulling the boy up by his arm and swatting him on the rear end.

"I didn't do it!" Sean yelled.

"Now. . . you. . . stop. . . that," she said, timing her words with each whack.

She released her hold. Sean ran to the bedroom, crying, and slammed the door.

"And you," she said, turning to Tommy, "you stop picking on your little brother."

Tommy gave her his winningest smile. "I didn't do a thing. He just bit me."

Marianne glared at him then headed back to the kitchen. Tommy waited until her back was turned, then quickly pulled up his sleeve and bit his arm. A small, round bite appeared, a perfect match to the first, which was now fading out.

He smiled to himself. It was nice to know he could get his little brother in trouble any time he wanted. He switched the TV to another channel and watched "Combat G.I. " He wished he was at Dad's this weekend. They always watched the cartoons together and ate potato chips. Then Grandma would make them bacon and eggs and cut up a huge coffee cake.

Marianne brewed her coffee, sat at her tiny kitchen table, and lit up a cigarette. Since the divorce, she'd started smoking again and she was always tired. The kids were rowdy.

That damn Danny Trabert.

This was all his fault.

* * *

Mr. Money Bags didn't appear and Marianne got a part-time job as a cashier at the local Jewel. She worked all day Saturday, and Tuesday and Thursday nights for $5 an hour. She worked 16 hours a week. After carfare, baby-sitting, and taxes, she took home $75 a week.

It wasn't worth it. She knew it wasn't worth it. But that $75 paid for food; they couldn't stop eating.

The nights she worked, she'd hurry home from Doyen Tool and Power Bearings Company, slop out something from the crockpot on the boys' dinner plates, and then run off to the Jewel, her pink smock with her name tag shoved under one arm. She'd get home around 11:30, her legs tired and her feet swollen.

She went to singles bars with Carla and her girlfriends for another six months and carried on an affair with a 38-year-old life insurance salesman who had a wife and two kids in Orland Park.

His name was Roger Lucas. Marianne met him at a seminar on money management that he gave at the local high school. She had no money, knew nothing about managing it, but thought if she went to such a seminar she would learn how to make do with what little she had.

Instead, she'd met Roger. A plump man with a receding hairline, he'd sold her a life insurance policy she couldn't afford and asked her out for a drink. Two weeks later he bedded her at the Route 83 Travel Lodge down the road from the tailer park. She had told the boys she was going to a PTA meeting.

"Mom, you don't belong to the PTA," Tommy had said over dinner.

"I'm joining," she had said. She had slipped on her heavy winter coat and boots and left. "You guys go to bed by 10, you hear?"

They nodded.

"Mom's got a boyfriend," Tommy told Sean after she had left.

Sean just stared at him.

They dished out huge bowls of ice cream, turned on the TV, and thought nothing more about it.

Roger met her at the Travel Lodge bar, ostensibly to have a drink and discuss the remainder of her financial affairs. He bought her a whiskey sour, pulled a sheet covered with numbers and columns from his briefcase, and laid it on the table.

"What's that?" she'd said, bewildered.

"It's your financial plan," he said, pointing to a few numbers with the tip of his mechanical pencil. "For only a few dollars a month you can have complete financial security through a fine collection of annuity plans offered by the National Carolina Life Insurance Companies. Build up your nest egg tax-free and provide yourself with a future through these fine programs, which can fund your retirement, the education of your children, and other important family goals."

She looked at him blankly. What in God's name was he talking about? Retirement? Important family goals? Since she had bought the life-insurance policy, she couldn't even afford to hire baby-sitters more than once a week.

Roger droned on. She blocked out his voice.

He bought her another whiskey sour, ordered another bourbon for himself, and launched into tax-free bond funds.

She smiled and sipped her drink. He started on the importance of disability insurance, especially for single mothers who were the main support of their children.

"What would happen if you were to become suddenly ill?" he said, his voice raised in high tension. "Who would take care of your children?"

"Their father," she said immediately. "My mother-in-law would love to have my boys."

That was not the answer Roger wanted. His thick eyebrows knitted together. He changed course.

"But who would take care of you?"

Marianne shrugged. "Nobody."

"Nobody? I can't believe that." He was genuinely shocked. "Doesn't anyone care?"

She smiled weakly, embarrassed.

"That's all the more reason for having disability insurance," he said firmly. "It protects you when your family cannot."

She nodded glumly.

He ordered her a third whiskey sour and began pointing out the details of the deluxe, partial-disability program with the optional life-insurance coverage.

"Hey," he finally noticed. "You're not listening."

"Yes, yes I am," she said, embarrassed at being caught. "I just have a lot on my mind."

"I see," he said. "Well, I think the disability program would really be an asset to you."

"I can't afford it, Roger, honest," she said. "I just don't have that kind of money."

He was quiet a moment. "I see," he said.

"My ex-husband barely makes child-support payments as it is."

"But surely you have other sources of income?"

"Not many." She smiled at him sadly, her eyes filling with tears. "I'm a woman without resources."

"It can't be that bad."

"Oh yes it is," she said, nodding and crying more.

Roger coughed, ordered himself another bourbon, and fingered the glass.

"What you need is someone who really understands you," he said in a deep throaty voice. "My wife doesn't understand me either, you know. I know how you feel."

She nodded, her eyes luminous with tears.

He took her hand.

"I need to be loved," she said, hiccoughing up whiskey fumes. "No one understands my need to be loved."

"I do," he said. "I feel the same way. I'm trapped in a loveless marriage. At least you had the courage to leave."

She smiled again.

He squeezed her hand.

A half-hour and another round of drinks later, they were offering each other mutual consolation on the soft, queen-size bed in Room 312 of the Travel Lodge.

It was the first time she'd had sex since she'd divorced Danny 10 months before. She couldn't believe how much she had missed it, even with someone as homely as Roger.

She got home around midnight, her eyes bleary and her stomach sour.

The kitchen was piled with dirty dishes; toys and the boys' clothes littered the living-room floor. She cleaned up and flopped into bed around 1.

What in God's name was she doing sleeping with a married man?

Chapter Five

Marianne didn't tell Carla and her friends about Roger. Only losers went out with married men, Carla said. Marianne didn't want to seem like a fool. But she liked sleeping with a married man. She got him when he was awake, in a good mood, and horny. His wife had him when he was tired and crabby from work. It seemed like a good deal to her.

Roger was nice to her. He took her to nice restaurants and good motels, bought her a few pieces of jewelry, and didn't talk about his wife.

The nights Marianne saw him she told the boys she was going to PTA meetings. They played along with her although they didn't believe her. Other kids' moms didn't wear glittery eyeshadow, low-cut blouses, and tight skirts to PTA. Nor did they come home after midnight smelling of booze.

Marianne's affair with Roger lasted almost a year. Marianne was his first adultery and he moved on to bigger fish: he took up with his 23-year-old secretary and dropped Marianne. He didn't have the time to keep them both, he explained.

They parted amicably. She never saw him again.

She was upset for several weeks, but then replacements appeared. After Roger, there was Mike, George, "Slim," and Gopal, a quiet astrophysicist who worked at the the Argonne National Laboratory. Gopal's wife was still in New Delhi. He needed someone "to service his masculine needs," as he told Marianne.

She got the contract. Six months later in March, his wife arrived, a bag of brown fat stuffed into a pink sari.

Gopal took Marianne to a good steakhouse, bought her an expensive meal, and gave her $500 for "her loyal service." Then they shook hands.

She never saw Gopal again either.

Her life fell into a pattern. Tuesday and Thursday nights she worked at the Jewel. Wednesday and Friday, she slept with the man of the hour at his house or apartment. And Saturday nights she stayed home with the boys and watched TV, assuming they hadn't gone to their father's for the weekend.

When they did go she pumped them for information on Ruth. She was skinny, they said. She had a wimpy little boy named Frank. She yelled at Frank a lot but not at Daddy.

Daddy seemed to like her.

With the appearance of Ruth, Marianne fretted about her child-support checks, but Danny kept sending them, albeit always two payments behind. But they came, crumpled checks in plain, dirty envelopes, Danny's name an illegible scrawl across the bottom.

Eight months later, Danny married Ruth. But the checks kept coming, as they did when Ruth gave birth to Danny Jr. a year later.

Ruth's ex-husband had stopped paying child support for Frank. So, with the addition of Danny Jr., Danny was now supporting four boys. Marianne was certain he would cut off the money to her sons.

But he didn't. In fact, he seemed happier than ever.

He'd pick her sons up for the weekend late Friday afternoon, whooping Indian yells, grabbing their suitcases, and herding them out to the car.

Marianne resented his happiness but held her tongue. She was getting her checks, Danny was off her back, and the boys seemed to be turning out alright.

Both Tommy and Sean were mediocre students with no disciplinary problems. Sean was unusually quiet and withdrawn, but Tommy had a good dose of animal spirits. A big hulking boy, he was growing into a carbon copy of his father, complete with droopy spaniel eyes.

Sean did little outside school other than attend Cub Scout meetings, where he made birdnests out of twigs and tied ropes full of weird knots.

Tommy, on the other hand, played football, baseball, and started wrestling in junior high. He dropped the Cub Scouts. The scout leaders drove him nuts. Big fat women, they were always lining up the troop, making them sing stupid songs, and checking that they all had clean hankies. From friendly, motherly women they could turn into screaming shrills in 10 seconds.

They reminded him too much of Marianne.

Tommy adored his father. When the boys came back to Marianne's Sunday nights, he chattered on about what they had done with Dad. That continued until Wednesday, when he started talking about what they would do with Dad the coming weekend.

For his part, Sean rarely spoke of his father and was an unenthusiastic participant in the ballgames, roughhousing, and arm-wrestling matches that took up much of the time between Danny and his oldest son.

Danny finally started leaving Sean with his grandmother on weekends. Grandma Trabert let him lay around the house, sleep, and watch TV. She fed him sweets and he gained 10 pounds in as many months.

She also taught him how to knit.

For Christmas that year he knit his mother a scarf. It was a raggy hunk of faded blue yarn lumpy with dropped stitches. Marianne was appalled.

Danny was beside himself. He and his mother had a screaming fight over it Christmas Day when he, Ruth, and all his boys were at her house. After a quick exchange of insults, he picked up the football he'd bought Sean for Christmas and huffed outside with Tommy.

Sean ran to the window and watched them laughing and throwing the ball.

Ruth yelled at Frank to stop hitting the baby. Grandma Trabert sat in a big wing chair and sulked.

Sean could hardly wait until he was old enough to leave home.

* * *

The trouble started when Tommy was 15-years-old.

That spring, he got a girl pregnant.

Lisa Gantz was a stick-thin girl of 15. She didn't tell her parents she was pregnant until she was six months gone and unable to button her jeans. Her mother had been delighted: she thought Lisa was finally filling out. When she found out the real reason, she became hysterical.

Lisa's father called Danny who, in turn, called Marianne.

"That's impossible," Marianne snapped. "The girl's lying. My boy wouldn't do that. She's a slut."

"Put Tommy on."

There was a clatter of dishes, the noise of the TV, and Tommy came on the line.

"Hello, Tommy?"

"Dad?"

"I just talked to Lisa Gantz's father. Is there something you want to tell me?"

Tommy felt himself go cold, but rallied. "No, what?"

"Lisa's father says the girl is pregnant and you're the father. Is that true?"

"Gee, Dad," Tommy said, feigning surprise. "I don't know a thing about it."

Danny coughed. "Did you have sex with her?" he said, his voice strained with embarrassment. He'd never asked Tommy such a direct question about his love life.

"Well, yeah, Dad," Tommy said. "But Lisa goes down on everybody." Actually, Lisa had had only one other boyfriend before Tommy. She was crazy about Tommy, and since she was his first lay, he was fond of her.

But this was survival.

"I don't know where she gets the idea I'm the father," Tommy said. "It could be any number of guys."

"You're sure?" Danny said.

"Yeah."

His father emitted a sigh of relief over the phone. Marianne, who had been leaning over her son's shoulder the whole time, launched another chorus about what a slut Lisa was and how her family had nerve pinning the blame for her pregnancy on a fine boy like Tommy.

"You know, Tommy," Danny continued. "You should use precautions with the girls." He coughed. "You know."

"Yeah Dad, I know," Tommy said. Actually, he didn't know. Lisa had assured him that she was too young to get pregnant; they wouldn't need to use anything. Besides, it was more spontaneous and natural.

What could be the matter with that?

Only that the natural thing happened: Lisa conceived.

"I'll call the girl's father back right away," Danny said hurriedly. "See you Friday. Remember the ballgame."

Tommy and Danny were going to see the White Sox play Detroit on Saturday night.

"Sure, Dad."

They hung up.

Marianne started up as soon as Tommy turned away from the phone.

"You stay away from those girls, Tommy," she said. "They'll only get you in trouble."

"Sure, Mom," he said. A lot of nerve she had telling him to stay away from pussy. She catted around twice a week. Every few months it was a different male voice on the phone, asking for her. Why didn't she get pregnant?

How could Lisa be so stupid?

He went to the refrigerator, fixed himself a ham sandwich, and let waves of relief wash over him. That was close. Lisa was going down with the ship, but he had escaped. He resolved never to see her again.

What a stupid girl.

He bit into his sandwich hungrily, savoring it deeply.

Stupid Lisa.

* * *

Unfortunately for Tommy, the Gantz's were not as gullible as his father.

They hired a lawyer and started legal proceedings against Danny. The lawyer could really do nothing; it was Tommy's word against Lisa's. And Tommy's blood type was so common that blood tests were useless. They dropped the suit.

Lisa went away to some special school for unwed mothers, but not before she tried to kill herself. Her little sister found her early one morning after she had taken all the medications in the family medicine cabinet, including her father's heart pills.

They pumped her stomach, sent her to a psychiatrist, and shipped her off to the Fernwood Public School for Unwed Mothers in DeKalb.

Through the grapevine, Tommy heard she'd given birth to a little girl, whom she had named Elizabeth and given up for adoption. She was back home by August. He saw her on the street one day, on the way to play tennis with one of her girlfriends. She looked right at him, then looked away, as if he weren't there.

He didn't mind. He had a new girlfriend he was banging, Jennifer Lukens. She had big breasts, slim hips, and looked like a model. She made Lisa look like a slab of bacon. How could he have ever fooled around with such an ugly girl?

But secretly, he was proud: 15-years-old and he had already fathered a child.

He was one hell of a potent guy.

If he didn't get caught, he wouldn't mind doing it again.

* * *

Tommy got worse as he got older. Aileen, Caroline, Mary Pat, Susie Closket, Johanna Franklin, Kathy McCormack. The list of his conquests grew and grew. Even Marianne started to get alarmed.

"Don't you get tired of flitting from one girl to the next?" she said one evening over dinner when he was 17. "Can't you just stay with one girl for awhile?"

"You don't stay with one guy," he said, defiantly, looking up from his plate of stew. In the last two years he had put on another 30 pounds. He was starting to look like a linebacker.

"That's different," Marianne said.

"How?"

"I've been married already. I've had my kids."

"I have to get married and have kids before I fool around? Is that when I can sleep with anything that moves?"

She slapped him, hard, across the face. "Don't you speak to me like that!" she yelled.

He sat back, inhaled deeply, and looked at her with the appraising eyes of a man on the hunt. With her lined face, dumpy body, and graying hair cut into a frumpy cap, she was no prize. A man would have to be desperate to make his mother.

"Take that smirk off your face!" she yelled again.

He glared at her, got up from the table, and went to his room.

Marianne stared after him and cursed all teen-agers under her breath. She had given him the best years of her life and this was how he was repaying her? She worked two jobs, kept a roof over their heads, and kept her sex life out of the trailer so she wouldn't scandalize her children. Actually, she had no privacy at home. It was necessary to conduct her love life elsewhere.

She was a good mother. What was the problem with the kid?

She got up wordlessly and started the dishes.

She didn't notice Sean, who still sat at his plate and slowly shoveled peas and carrots into his mouth.

He was used to the lack of attention. He was 15-years-old now, almost as big as his older brother, but much thinner because he rarely ate. Everyone thought of him as part of the wallpaper.

He liked it that way. It made him feel invisible, like no one knew he existed. No one bothered him. As long as he got C's in school and stayed out of trouble, he could do what he wanted.

He was higher than a kite at dinner, having mixed an interesting combination of quaaludes, marijuana, and a party pack of pills a friend of his had given him at school.

No one had noticed a thing.

Tommy knew about Sean's drugs, but didn't care. He viewed him as his convenient, inhouse supplier ready to sell him drugs for the little freshmen girls he loved to seduce. It made it so much easier when they were stoned.

His mother didn't know about Sean's drugs, but then she knew little about him. She was too preoccupied with her own boyfriends, always breaking off with one man and starting up with another.

His father always hung around with Tommy and rarely talked to Sean. And Grandma Trabert just thought he liked to sleep and daydream.

"My little daydreamer," she would say, pinching him lightly on his scrawny arm when he came to her house high on something. It helped that she had inoperable cataracts in both eyes and could hardly see. They would sit in her living room and knit. Grandma rocked in her chair and talked; Sean plugged into his Walkman and ignored her.

He liked to knit while he was on amphetamines or acid. It gave him something to do with his hands while he listened to his music.

And it saved on Christmas presents. Every year, everyone in the family got one of his lopsided, badly knit scarves.

While Sean and Tommy were sinking into drugs and sex respectively, their half brothers were turning into model children. Frank was a member of ROTC and a star student in chemistry at Glenbard West High School. At the age of 6, Danny Jr. could already play Christmas carols on his mother's portable Hammond organ.

Of course Ruth had nothing else to do but take care of her kids, Marianne fumed when Danny casually dropped the information that one of his other sons had won another prize or received a kudo from a teacher.

It wasn't Danny's doing, though he enjoyed basking in the results. It was Ruth: she drove her kids like slaves.

They studied, they took lessons, they went away to summer camp. Sometimes Danny was amazed at the incredible mothering strength of his second wife. She wouldn't let the kids rest. Her beat-up station wagon was always filled with her children and those of her equally ambitious neighbors, bound for the next round of life-improving activities.

Her kids would have all the advantages she never had, so help her God. Frank would be a famous chemist. Danny Jr. would be a doctor or a lawyer.

She didn't like her boys associating with the trashy kids from her husband's first marriage and she didn't like Tommy hanging around on the weekends.

He was a bad influence.

Besides, Danny seemed to like him more than her children. Frank was someone else's son and thought his stepfather a complete fool, but Danny and Danny Jr. were still father and son. Of course, the boy hated to play around and roughhouse. He was more thoughtful than Tommy.

"Your kids are such little monsters," Ruth would complain to Danny over the breakfast table. "Why doesn't Marianne control them more?"

He looked at her blankly. He was used to her complaints about his first brood.

"They're alright," he said.

"They're monsters," she said, serving up eggs and bacon to Frank and Danny Jr., who sat there and ignored their parents' conversation.

"Shut up," Danny said.

"Don't you tell me to shut up," she snapped.

The boys looked up. Mom and Dad's fights often started out with Danny telling her to shut up.

"Keep those monsters away from my boys."

"They're nice kids."

"They'll never go to college."

"So what? Tommy can go to work in the plant next year."

She hrumphed. "Fat chance," she mumbled, turning back to the kitchen.

Frank looked at his stepfather with disdain.

Danny noticed it.

"What are you looking at?" he said sharply.

The boy looked back at his plate with a smirk.

"Don't talk to my son like that, Danny Trabert," Ruth said.

Frank just smiled.

Chapter Six

Danny started to worry that Ruth was right: Sean and Tommy were turning out bad.

So that summer, the summer Tommy was 17, he decided to send his three oldest boys away to summer camp for three weeks. It would be good for them to be out in the woods with each other. Maybe they would all turn out more brotherly.

Maybe some of Frank's "go-get-iveness" would rub off on Sean and Tommy, turning them into more ambitious young men.

In any event, the boys would just have a good time. Play a little touch football, swim, be guys together. It sounded great. He wished someone would send him to summer camp.

Marianne was glad to get rid of the boys for three weeks.

Ruth worried that Tommy and Sean would beat up on Frank. She wanted to just send Frank, but Danny refused.

"They all go, or no one goes," he said.

Actually, none of the boys wanted to go, but Danny insisted.

Tommy said he would be bored in the woods. He was screwing a buxom sophomore and getting it almost daily in her pink-painted bedroom while her parents were at work. Why would he want to give up a great sex life for three weeks of mosquitoes?

Sean wondered how he could get drugs. He'd have to get his allowance well in advance to keep supplied.

And Frank, Frank complained the most. Why would he want to be locked up with a bunch of animals like his half brothers in wooden sheds that leaked when it rained?

His mother urged him to turn his mind to studying the local biology. View it as fieldwork, she told him. Maybe he could make a science project out of it for junior year.

So, one sticky Saturday in mid-July, Danny loaded the three boys in his van and drove them to the camp, a collection of ramshackle buildings on the edge of a weedy lake in central Michigan.

He dropped them off at the main hall, and left them standing there surrounded by their dufflebags, Sean plugged into his Walkman as usual and oblivious to the world around him.

They were fine boys, Danny thought, glancing back at them in his rearview mirror as he drove away. He had done especially well by Frank, even though the boy was not his blood son. And Tommy was going to be a real "man's man."

And they were all brothers.

This summer camp was a good idea.

For their part, the boys waved and smiled as Danny drove away, then checked in with the counselor, a large, brutish-looking young man of about 21.

"Brothers, right?" he said. "You want to bunk together?"

"Are you kidding?" they chorused.

So he put them in separate bunkhouses. For three weeks, they rarely saw each other. Frank worked on memorizing the leaves and forms of all the different trees in the surrounding forest and took notes on their morphology.

Tommy hooked up with a bunch of alcoholic teen-agers and spent much of his time at the local girls' camp on the other side of the lake.

And Sean found a reclusive 14-year-old science-fiction buff who had an unlimited supply of hallucinogenic drugs in his possession. The two of them stayed high for three weeks.

They all had a wonderful time, greeting their father happily when he returned to pick them up.

He wished he had sent them to summer camp sooner.

* * *

Summer camp was as close as the boys ever got to becoming friends. Afterwards they were even more like strangers.

Tommy and Sean still shared their tiny room in Marianne's trailer, but they lived like two migrant workers sharing the same bunkhouse. They rose early, ate breakfast, and went to school, each going their separate ways.

After school, Sean would return home to his room, smoke dope, and listen to music. Tommy would hang around with his friends, chase girls, and play pool. Tommy had a string of part-time jobs with some local merchants and even worked at McDonald's for a week, but the work was too hard. He went back to the poolroom and bummed spending money off his mother and his friends.

Marianne never saw him with a book. He was still getting Cs. She thought he must be naturally intelligent and didn't need to study.

The day of Tommy's graduation, Danny started making noises about having him work down at the plant. He could start out in the warehouse, loading the food lockers of the Western Meat-Packing Company. He could work his way up the ladder. Danny was now foreman in charge of sausage-casing molding on the east side of the huge plant. He thrilled to think that one day his oldest son could be working by his side.

They would be a dynasty of sausage-casing foremen. He saw himself working next to Tommy, introducing him to all his friends. It would be just like when Tommy was younger and they played ball together.

Tommy, for his part, ignored his father's dream. He had no intention of getting up at 5:30 every morning to make the 7:00 shift then coming home every late afternoon reeking of sweat, rancid meat, and the occasional whiff of garlic.

So he did nothing. After graduation, he sat home or went out with his friends all day, funded by the largesse of his mother or his friends' good-natured "loans."

Three weeks after graduation, he still had no job and no leads.

Marianne was the first to come after him.

"So how's the job search?" she asked him one rare evening when he was home for dinner.

"Fine," he said. In reality, he'd done nothing.

"Any leads?"

"A few."

"Like what?"

"You know, a few things here, a few things there." He concentrated on his potatoes.

"I'm not supporting you anymore," she said sharply. "You know that, don't you?"

"Yeah, sure," he said, not looking up.

"You're a grown man now. You can't sit around here doing nothing. You have to go out and make a living, not leave your poor mother dragging home the money from extra part-time jobs."

He said nothing. Marianne's monologues about how hard she worked to support her boys were staples of the evening dinner table.

"So are you listening?" Marianne said.

"Yeah."

"So why don't you have a job yet?"

He stared at his plate.

"Answer me."

"I'm taking a little vacation."

"You've had enough vacation. You've been on vacation since you you were born. I was too nice to you kids growing up. I gave you everything. I worked like an animal to make sure you had everything and now you want to sponge off me the rest of your lives."

Tommy stopped listening.

"Carla's daughters are all going to nursing school," Marianne continued. "They're such nice girls. They know what they want. They'll know how to support themselves and not be a burden to their mother. And what are you doing? Hanging around with a bunch of losers and sponging off your mother."

She went into another chorus of how hard she worked, adding a few lines about how little money they had, and how she worried about how she would live in her old age. She already knew, in her heart of hearts, that her sons would let her die indigent.

"I want you getting a job and paying room and board or I want you out of here, buster," she said.

Tommy stared straight ahead.

"Are you listening?" she snapped.

"Yeah. Yeah, sure."

"I mean it."

"Yeah. Yeah."

"I do. You can go bum off your father."

He sighed deeply.

Marianne glared at him once more, then cut into the pot roast on her plate.

Tommy turned on the small TV at the end of the kitchen counter and watched a rerun of "Gilligan's Island."

Sean just sat there eating his peas and listening to his Walkman. With his gawky neck and headphones and the way he swayed to the music, he looked like some Martian that had just landed for dinner.

* * *

Danny started in on Tommy the next week.

"I talked to Mr. Felsner at the plant," he said when Tommy came over to see him that weekend. "They're hiring a bunch of guys in meat preparation. Work there a few months and I can probably get you down in my neck of the woods.

"It would be great," he said, his eyes lighting up. "We can be together again. Just like the good old days."

He looked at his son expectantly. Tommy smiled and nodded.

"So you going to come down?" Danny said.

Tommy had absolutely no intention of going anywhere near the plant.

"Sure, Dad," he said.

"I'll tell Mr. Felsner you'll be calling him." He gazed at his son happily. "We'll be working side-by-side, son. It will be great."

Tommy couldn't fathom standing next to his father all day watching machinery stretch pig intestine into sausage casings.

He never called Mr. Felsner.

Two weeks later, Danny came after him on the warpath.

"Felsner said you never called him, Tom," he said, his voice perplexed. "Don't you want to work at the plant?"

Tommy shrugged.

"It looks bad, son," he said. "Me telling my boss you're going to call him and then you don't call him at all. You want me to lose my job?"

In Danny's eyes, the thought of not working for Western Meat-Packing was like contemplating hell from the brink. And if Tommy didn't work for Western, where would he work?

It was a mind-boggling thought.

Danny's big spaniel eyes went wide and looked into the matching set belonging to his son.

"So where are you going to get a job, son?" he said.

Tommy shrugged. "I dunno."

"Well you better get on it," Danny said. "You can't be living off your mother and me much longer."

And he went off to mow his lawn without the foggiest clue of how his son would support himself or what would be a suitable job for him.

Imagine, he thought. He never called Mr. Felsner. He doesn't want to work for Western Meat-Packing.

Maybe Tommy should join the army.

* * *

September rolled around, Tommy still lacked a job, and Marianne told him he'd have to pay room and board of $60 a week.

So he moved in with Grandma Trabert.

He mowed her lawn, trimmed the bushes, and promised to shovel her snow in the winter. The old lady was glad to have him around, feed him, and let him sleep in her back bedroom. She even slipped him a few dollars of her social security check.

Danny and Marianne were disgusted.

But then, in November, the old lady had a stroke. Once out of the hospital she needed constant attention. So Danny sold her house and moved her in with him, much to the disgust of Ruth, who found herself waiting on her now-cranky mother-in-law morning and night.

Tommy moved in with Rudolph, a friend of his from the poolroom and a bouncer at one of the big singles bars in the south suburbs. Rudolph got Tommy a job as a bouncer, too.

Tommy liked the work.

The bar, Cindy G's, had an upscale clientele. No guys in hard hats came there. It was all white-collar workers, guys in suits, and their secretaries .

Early in the evening, the well-dressed people entered the bar. The men, fresh from work, wore pressed suits and good ties. The women were flighty and animated in their dresses.

By midnight, the men's ties hung like ropey rags around their necks. Their rumpled suitcoats drooped from their shoulders. The necklines of the women's dresses were askew, their nylons sported runs, and they had trouble staying up on their high heels.

When they hit the crisp, midnight air at the door to the bar, they would stand there and sway a bit, the pounding music of the bar suddenly replaced by the quiet hum of traffic. Then they would compose themselves and walk off, arm-in-arm, with a great sense of self-possession.

Tommy rarely threw anyone out of the bar. Usually, he just opened and closed the door, allowing humanity to flow in and out. He was the doorman at the gates of paradise.

Tommy loved looking at the women. Mostly young and unmarried, they tittered and giggled with each other like flocks of bright-colored birds. The guys in suits were usually older and squired the girls around possessively — puffed-up accountants with their own private harems. The women looked at the men adoringly and laughed at all their jokes.

Those guys never wanted for pussy, he was sure.

The other doormen and bouncers were friendly. They all stood for hours at the door, checking IDs of the younger women, turning away occasional crowds of underage youths, anxious to get their share of the sex and booze inside.

Rudolph was especially brusque with them. A squat, muscular young man, half-German, he liked pushing the young boys away from the door and yelling at them to go home to their mothers. Eighteen himself, Rudolph was only two years older than the boys he bullied, but his size frightened them. After an exchange of obscenities with Rudolph, the packs of boys would slink down the sidewalk back to their cars, muttering and complaining, and leaving all the pussy and booze to the old guys in suits.

Tommy and Rudolph worked until 4 am Tuesday through Saturday. The manager, an enterprising Irishman from the south side, let them have a few beers on the job, but their heavy drinking was saved for after-hours. They'd sit at the bar, bottles of rye whiskey and bourbon in front of them, discussing with the bartender all the "babes" who had come in to the bar that night and wondering who they had left with.

The bartender, Tommy, and Rudolph were all young men. All three of them were obsessed with getting laid.

Sometimes they'd talk about cars. Rudolph had a decrepit Camaro he worked long hours on to keep alive. Tommy had a 1966

Dodge Dart that Danny had given him junior year. He had far less trouble with it than Rudolph with his Camaro, which was 19 years younger than the Dart, but Tommy was embarrassed to drive the Dart. It was an old-man's car.

He was trying to save money from his $300-a-week paycheck to buy a Camaro like Rudolph's, but he wasn't getting too far. By the time all the deductions were taken from his pay and he paid for food, rent, and booze, he was broke.

There was no future in bouncing.

He and Rudolph complained to the owner for more money, but the Irishman just laughed. Rudolph complemented his meager wages by hustling pool and working at his brother-in-law's chop shop in Dolton. He sawed out radiators from stolen cars with a blow torch. The brother-in-law offered Tommy a job, too, but Tommy didn't want to work that hard. He worked all night as a bouncer; he didn't need to work all day, too.

But his salvation was nearer than ever — his own brother.

One evening in the late spring a gang of young men came by the bar. Rudolph started shrieking at them, but they pushed forward one of their members to plead their cause.

It was Sean.

Tommy was surprised to see him.

"What the fuck are you doing here?" he said.

"I'm supposed to have special connections 'cause you're my brother," Sean said.

"Buzz off," Tommy said brusquely. "No minors allowed."

Sean shrugged and turned around. Rudolph drove the boys off with his usual string of epithets.

Tommy stared after them.

Sean looked good. He was wearing an expensive leather jacket, a diamond-stud earring, and cowboy boots. Since Tommy had left home eight months before he'd rarely seen his brother.

Where the hell was a 16-year-old kid getting that kind of money? Mom certainly wasn't giving it to him. The kid had always dealt drugs, but he was a small-time operator — a $5 bag of marijuana here, $10 of pills there.

He was dressing like real prosperity had hit.

Tommy resolved to find out.

Chapter Seven

The next week Tommy stopped by to see Sean.

He hardly recognized the old room. Sean had redone the tiny little closet of a room into a psychedelic den. The walls were covered with big posters of half-naked, overmuscled men and women dressed in animal skins and brandishing swords. They stood in front of mist-shrouded castles.

"The Fantasia series of Golgona," was printed in a medieval script along the bottom of one.

Interspersed with the fantasy posters were posters of mean-looking teen-agers in leather clothes and spiked hair holding electric guitars. Sean had always been a big fan of heavy-metal rock groups. The grunts and shrieks of such a group blared through the expensive speakers hung on the wall.

Sean himself reclined on one of the beds, a huge gold hookah balanced on a silver tray, the soft lights of several huge candles playing over his face.

The place reeked of hashish.

Tommy nearly gagged on the smoke.

"Christ, doesn't Mom give you hell about smoking dope at home?" he said.

Sean smiled a sleepy, lazy smile.

"Mom's cool," he said.

"What's that mean?"

"This is a Jewel night. She won't be home 'til late. I could carve up young girls and burn their bodies and she wouldn't know."

Tommy laughed nervously. "How do you explain all this to Mom?" he said, looking around.

"I told her I work at Burger King," Sean said, taking another draw on his hookah. "She never eats there. How would she know?" He smiled his sleepy, dopey smile.

"So where *do* you get the money?" Tommy said.

"I have my sources."

"What kind of sources?"

"Sources." Sean looked aggravated. "What do you think? I deal, of course."

Tommy plopped down on what used to be his old twin bed, now covered with a rich-colored tapestry cloth. "You always dealt, but this looks like big-time."

Sean shrugged. "I'm expanding."

"Expanding into what?"

"You sure like sticking your nose into other people's business."

"Just curious."

"What are you, a narc?"

Tommy laughed. "I was thinking you might need some help."

"What kind of help?"

Tommy shrugged. "I dunno. Help."

"I thought you had a job."

"I do, but I'd like to branch out. You know, diversify."

Sean folded his arms, lay back in the satin pillows behind him, and stared at his brother. "Let me talk to my partners."

"Partners? You have partners?"

"Yeah, sure I do," Sean said, puffing the hookah once more. "I'm a businessman now, a young entrepreneur." He looked at his brother. "We can always use more new, young talent." He paused. "But you'll have to work your way up from the bottom like everyone else."

"What is this, GM?" Tommy snorted. "I'm your fuckin' brother."

Sean shrugged. "My partners have brothers, too. No favoritism. We decided that long ago."

Tommy stared at him. "How long you been doin' this?"

"Five, six years. I started learning the business in sixth grade." He inhaled from the hookah again. "Even then I knew it had potential." His voice was high and squeaky from talking through the dope smoke. He exhaled. "It's only now that it's starting to pay off for me," he said, indicating the trappings of his room. He leaned forward. "Why should it pay off for you any sooner?" he hissed.

Tommy could see a swath of acne along the lower half of Sean's left jaw. How could this kid treat him like this? Christ, he was three years older than this little nerd.

Tommy looked at his hands and the hole in the knee on his jeans. He needed the money.

"So what could I do for you?" he said, smiling a friendly smile.

"Mules. We're always looking for good mules," Sean said. "Here to Texas, Miami, St. Louis, Detroit. Your car running these days?"

"Yeah."

"Good. We like guys who already have their own wheels in their own names. Keeps overhead down." He coughed and started cleaning out the mouthpiece of the hookah with his fingers. "I'll be in touch," he said.

He set the hookah aside and picked up a textbook lying next to him on the bed.

"I gotta' work on my geometry homework," he said. "Big test tomorrow." He opened the book, pulled out a chewed pencil from between two pages, and started drawing a crooked little triangle on a piece of yellow legal paper.

Tommy stood up and left.

He gently closed the door behind him and looked at the familiar landscape of his mother's trailer.

He felt like he'd just come from a time warp.

***

Sean was as good as his word. A week after his conversation with Tommy, he stopped by at Cindy G's with a group of his friends. Rudolph was about to shag them away when Tommy saw Sean in the back of the crowd. Tommy muscled his way through the kids to his brother.

"Hi," he said. "Any news?"

"You're in," Sean said. "Come by after school Thursday and I'll give you the details." He smiled a crooked little smile and sauntered off with his friends, who Rudolph had started haranguing.

That Thursday Tommy arrived at the trailer early and stood around until Sean came loping down the road, his schoolbooks in a backpack slung over one shoulder.

The kid still took the bus to and from school.

"Where's your car?" Tommy said as Sean approached him.

"At a friend's," he said. "I don't want to be too showy." He opened the door to the trailer.

"Want a Coke?" he said, heading for the refrigerator.

He popped out two cans of Coke and sat at the kitchen table, the cheap oilskin of the tablecloth contrasting with the rich suede of his jacket.

"You're going to St. Louis," he said. "You leave tonight." He handed him a folder. "In here's the name and address of who you're looking for. You call him when you reach the city limits. He'll tell you where to meet him. He'll give you 14 packages, weighing about two pounds each, wrapped in white butcher paper. Put them in your trunk and bring them back to the Chicago address in the folder."

He sipped his Coke. "If you're caught, you don't know me," he said. "Tell them you're running for Jimmy Frencher."

"Who's that?" Tommy asked, bewildered by the stream of directions.

"One of my competitors, of course," Sean said. "We're constantly turning each other in."

"What do I make for this?" Tommy asked.

"$750 plus expenses."

It was more than Tommy made in two weeks at the bar.

"All *right!*" he said, slapping his brother on the back. "I'll see you in a couple days."

"Sure." Sean was always amazed that he could hire someone for $750 to haul $750,000 of drugs.

People had no vision.

Tommy left and Sean went to his room. He turned on his stereo, lit up a joint, and started working on his English grammar homework.

* * *

Tommy told Rudolph that he needed to get away for a few days. "You know how it is. I just got to get away and think."

"Where you going?" Rudolph wanted to know.

"Oh. I don't know. South."

"I'll get Iggy to cover for you."

Rudolph was a real friend.

Tommy was on the road a half hour later. Traffic was heavy initially but soon thinned out. Tommy's old Dart hummed along. He worried it would conk out before he reached St. Louis, but the car ran smoothly all the way. Tommy fiddled with the radio dial and listened to country-western stations while the flat fields of Illinois rolled by in the dark.

What was he going to do with his money?

He decided he'd buy a suede jacket like Sean's. He couldn't have his younger brother upstaging him on clothes, especially now since they were in business together. He grinned. He'd be making lots of money now. He could drive to two or three cities in a week. He could make $2200 a week, just driving around.

He smiled happily and turned up the radio.

He reached St. Louis at 2 in the morning. He stopped at a gas station off the interstate and called the number Sean had given him.

A sleepy woman answered the phone.

Tommy asked for the man listed in the file folder.

"Just a minute," she said.

He heard fumbling in the background.

"Hello?" said a man's voice.

"Hi. I'm from Chicago. I'm here for a pickup?"

"Yeah. Sure." The man gave him a set of directions to an old warehouse on the south side of town and told him he'd meet him there in 45 minutes. "I'll be in a green Chevy Nova," he said.

Tommy got back in his Dart and found the place with no difficulty. It was an old warehouse from the turn of the century with boarded windows and walls covered with graffitti. Not a soul was around.

Tommy locked his car doors and slunk down in his seat.

Five minutes later, a green Nova pulled up next to him. A fat, middle-aged man in a trenchcoat leaned over and rolled down his window.

"Give me a hand with this stuff," he said.

They got out of their cars, popped open their trunks, and transferred the white-wrapped packages to the Dart's trunk.

The man gave Tommy directions back to the interstate. Then he got back in his car and drove away without another word.

Tommy found the interstate and drove out of the city, but was soon so sleepy he found a Ramada Inn and checked in for the night.

He slept a restful, dreamless sleep, happily thinking of how rich he was going to be as a drug runner. He woke at 11 the next morning, got in his car, and drove to the Chicago address without incident. It was an expensive townhouse in Lincoln Park. The Mexican maid who answered the door told him to unload the packages at the back entrance, which he did.

Then he went home to see Sean.

"How'd it go?" Sean said, when he came home from school that day.

"Great. No problem," Tommy said.

"Good. Mark will stop by the bar tonight and pay you. Tell him how much you spent on gas and whatever." He went into the kitchen and poured himself a Coke. "How'd you like it?"

"Great. Super," Tommy enthused.

"Good," Sean said, sipping his Coke. "We can always use good men. I'll have another trip for you soon."

"Great." And Tommy bounded out of the trailer feeling that his future was secure.

Chapter Eight

That night Tommy went to work. Rudolph wanted to know if he felt better after his trip.

"Yeah. I banged a few chicks, smoked a little dope, saw a few friends. It was great," Tommy said.

He could already feel the crisp, dry crinkle of $750 in $20 bills in his fingers. Mark came by about 1 in the morning. A small boy, about 15-years-old, he traveled in a herd of teen-aged boys, approaching Tommy when Rudolph chased the boys off.

"You're Tommy?" he asked in a surprisingly deep voice. He had a clear, transluscent skin with only the first growth of a beard showing.

Tommy nodded.

"This is for you," Mark said, handing him a plain white envelope. "You had expenses?" he added.

"About $100," Tommy said. "Hotel, gas, a stop for a Big Mac."

"No problem." Mark reached into the pocket of his jeans, pulled out a wad of $20 bills, and peeled off five. He handed them to Tommy. "Catch you later," he said. And he walked off.

When Rudolph came back 30 seconds later, huffing and cursing at the kids, Tommy excused himself to the bathroom. He locked himself in a stall and ripped open the envelope. A wad of worn $20 bills and a lone ten were neatly lined up inside. Tommy sat on the stool and counted them: $750 exact.

Add that to his $100 of expenses and he had $850 in his pocket. That was more money than he'd ever held in his hand in his entire life.

He leaned back against the wall, stared happily at the graffitti on the back of the door, and lit a cigarette.

It felt *so good* to have money in his pocket. It was almost as good as fucking. He drew on his cigarette. No, it was better than fucking. You could have a woman anytime, but money was hard to come by.

He closed his eyes, savored his cigarette, and dreamed of the beautiful suede jacket he was going to buy. He'd seen it at a leather store in the big shopping mall, River Oaks. He'd go tomorrow and get it. Maybe he'd get some leather pants to match. It was going to be hot, so hot.

He dragged on his cigarette a few more minutes, savoring his new-found sense of ease, and listening to the flush of urinals.

To think that his father had wanted him to work in the meat-packing plant! He could be working the night shift right this moment, stacking cartons of sausages on pallets in some ancient warehouse, nearly frozen himself from the refrigeration.

He shuddered.

He ground out his cigarette on the floor and went back to Rudolph.

"Where the hell have you been?" Rudolph yelled. "I've been out here for 10 minutes by myself."

"I had to take a dump," Tommy hissed. "Don't they even let you take a dump in this dump?"

Rudolph gave him a dirty look and asked a baby-faced man with a blonde for his ID.

"Shit, man, I'm 29-years-old," the man mumbled, fumbling in his wallet for his driver's license.

Rudolph was a dirtbag, Tommy thought. He looked around the dirty foyer of Cindy G's and shivered in his thin jacket. It was May; it was cold and damp standing in the doorway.

Two drunken couples pushed past him and out into the street. He almost pushed them back.

What was he doing working at this third-rate bar watching the drunks stumble out with their bimbo girlfriends? He was better than this.

As soon as Sean gave him more work, he would be out of here. He glanced at Rudolph, who was chasing away some drunk who had pissed on the front of the building. "Get outta' here, you asshole!" Rudolph yelled.

He was better than Rudolph, Tommy thought.

As soon as he got the money, he was moving out of Rudolph's apartment.

He was starting a new life. He was a man on the rise.

* * *

Two days later, Sean called him with more work.

"Cleveland this time," he said when Tommy stopped by at the trailer after school. "You leave tonight." He eyed Tommy's brown suede jacket and new blue jeans. "Nice clothes," he said, smiling. "It's nice to think you're finally getting some taste."

Tommy was about to punch him when he realized Sean was his boss. His arm dropped listlessly to his side and he smiled.

Sean noticed his restraint and smiled back. "Same deal as last time," he said. "You call from the edge of town, meet the guy, and he gives you the load. This time it's about 20 packages, about five pounds each, and a bale of pot. That's our premium.

"George likes to give us little gifts for doing business with him. You know, like the free gifts you get in Crackerjack boxes." Sean shook his head sadly. "Except his pot is terrible. It's worse than smoking oregano. So when you get out of town, pull over somewhere and dump it. I don't even want to see it."

Tommy nodded.

Sean gave him the folder. "We're giving you a raise. First time we always pay minimum wage. So we'll give you $850 this time, plus expenses."

Actually, Sean was giving him a raise unilaterally. He liked seeing the idiot grin Tommy put on when he gave him money. Tommy obliged by looking nearly dizzy with happiness.

Early that evening, Tommy stopped by the bar and made his excuses to Rudolph. Rudolph was angry he was going off again.

"I can't cover for you all the time," he complained. "Mr. Farley is going to get on my ass." Farley was the south-side Irishman who owned Cindy G's.

"Then I quit," said Tommy, strutting around the foyer in his new suede jacket. "I'll tell that mother to stick it up his ass."

"Then you can do it right now," Rudolph jeered. "Farley's right over there." He nodded toward a small, neatly barbered man standing behind the bar, talking to the bartender.

Tommy's heart jumped. Farley never came down to Cindy G's, yet there he was pouring himself a whiskey and leaning against the bar.

Tommy walked over. He cleared his throat. "Hello, Mr. Farley," he said shyly.

The man looked at him without the faintest glimmer of recognition.

"Tommy Trabert," Tommy said. "One of the doormen?"

"Yes?" Farley said. He still didn't recognize him.

"Well, yes," Tommy said. "Mr. Farley, I've got to leave Cindy G's. I've got another job."

"OK," Farley said, turning back to his drink. "Tell Mike." Mike was the manager.

Tommy hurried to the back room where Mike was busy taking inventory of the remaining liquor stock. Mike was a fat little Irishman with a hooked nose and a clipboard in one hand.

"I'm leaving, Mike," Tommy said.

"Forty-eight, forty-nine," Mike counted. "OK," he said. "I'll tell Maureen tomorrow." Maureen was the bookkeeper. "Fifty, fifty-one, fifty-two." He looked up suddenly and turned to Tommy. "When?" he said.

"Tonight."

Mike dropped his clipboard to his side and looked at Tommy with disgust. "So who do I get to work for you tonight?" he said. "I need two doormen."

"Rudolph can handle it."

"Rudolph will have to handle it," Mike snorted. He looked at Tommy with red-rimmed eyes. "Get out of here," he said. "You're just a bum. I knew it the moment I laid eyes on you."

Tommy glared at him, turned on his heel, and left. On the way out he stopped in front of Rudolph.

"I'm out of here," he told his amazed roommate, his voice angry. "You're running solo now."

"You quit?" Rudolph said, shocked.

"Yeah."

"So what are you going to do?"

"I've got plans."

"Like what?"

"Like it's none of your business."

A cluster of businessmen with their secretaries pushed through the foyer and into the bar.

"I bet you're running drugs," said Rudolph.

"Shut up," Tommy said, his voice anxious.

"Where'd you get that jacket?" Rudolph said.

Four young women in tight jeans walked through the door, their hips swinging as they moved. Rudolph stared at them with such obvious lust that even Tommy was embarrassed.

"The jacket was a gift from my mother," Tommy said.

"Yeah, right," Rudolph said, his eyes still on the rounded little teardrop asses of the young women. He looked back at Tommy. "You're running drugs. I know it. You're going to end up with some beaner sticking a knife in your back."

"Working in a chop shop is such a high-class operation?"

"We pay off the cops. I'll never end up dead."

Tommy looked at him in disgust. "You have no imagination, Rudolph. I'll see you later."

And he walked out of the bar with a confident swagger, scared to death that Rudolph was right.

* * *

The trip to Cleveland was uneventful. He had to get a new water pump for the Dart on the return trip, but the actual pickup was not much different than St. Louis. All drug runners seemed to like to make their transfers in abandoned warehouses at 2 in the morning.

His contact in Cleveland was an Hispanic with a sun-darkened skin and leathery hands. He looked like a migrant farmworker. When Tommy saw him, he nearly started shaking. But the man hardly said two words to him and was gone as soon as the transfer was made.

No one seemed interested in small talk in this business.

The two of them had trouble jamming the bale of marijuana in Tommy's trunk, but Tommy moved his spare tire into the back seat and the damn thing finally fit. The Hispanic had wrapped it in plastic; otherwise, the smell would have been overpowering. Tommy was thankful for this foresight when his radiator overheated near Toledo and he limped into an all-night gas station at 4 in the morning.

All he needed was a car that smelled like the marijuana-mobile.

The mechanic wouldn't show up until 9, so he walked across the bridge over the interstate and checked into the motel on the other side.

The next morning, he was on his way by 10. He got off the interstate in Indiana, drove out on a farm road, and dumped the bale of pot in a roadside ditch. On a whim, he took a little and rolled a joint which he smoked as he drove.

Sean was right: the stuff was terrible.

When he reached Chicago, he dropped his load at an old brick bungalow near Marquette Park. A tall young man, well-built with heavily muscled arms, answered the door. They unloaded the drugs in his garage; again no one spoke.

The next day, Tommy met with Sean at the trailer.

"I need a new car," Tommy said. "The Dart can't handle these long hauls."

"I'll see what I can do," Sean said. "Come back tomorrow."

The next day he gave Tommy $5,000 in cash, told him to buy a dependable, unassuming car with a big trunk and to register it in his own name. "We'll pay for it," he said. "I talked to my partners."

Tommy left the trailer floating on air. He waded through the want ads and bought a three-year-old Buick Skylark from a retired Chicago policeman. It had only 36,000 miles on it.

When Rudolph saw it he gave Tommy a hard time. "Now all you need is a Super-fly hat and some gold chains," he said.

Tommy was so angry he went out and rented a one-bedroom apartment in a new complex near the interstate. He moved his belongings from Rudolph's that weekend, even though the lease ran four more months.

Rudolph was enraged. "I'm going to call the cops and turn you in," he hissed as Tommy lugged his last suitcase out the door to his car.

Tommy set down the case. "Do that and I'll call the district attorney's office on your brother-in-law's chop shop," he said. "You can't pay off everybody. And I'll make sure Oscar knows who did it."

Oscar was Rudolph's brother-in-law.

Rudolph turned white and said nothing. Tommy finished loading his car in silence and drove off.

* * *

Tommy was born to be a mule. He made two or three trips a week, usually to St. Louis, Cleveland, or Detroit. He kept his Buick spotless, wore neat, conservative clothes, and looked prosperous. He told his neighbors he was in sales.

That was no lie. He was.

The business was actually pretty boring: drive 400 miles, call someone in the middle of the night, then go to a desolate part of the city and pick up the drugs.

His contacts remained pretty much the same, but they would constantly switch locations for the pickup. After six months of transporting drugs, Tommy felt like he knew every abandoned warehouse and desolate lot in the three cities he covered. Then his contact in Cleveland started arranging pickups at construction sites in the suburbs. Variety always helped in this business.

For the first six weeks of his new career, Tommy was terrified that someone would stick a knife in his back or that a gang of thugs or police would break up his pickups.

But that never happened. His pickups always went smoothly. It was like transferring bags of sand from one car to another. He started thinking that was all he was carrying.

One morning as he was coming home from St. Louis and was just driving out of the parking lot of his favorite motel, a policeman stopped him. Tommy forced himself to be calm. The policeman told him his left taillight was out. Tommy thanked him, drove to the next gas station, and had it fixed.

He went into the adjacent restaurant and ordered a big cup of coffee. His hand shook as he poured in the cream.

He swore he would always drive carefully, never do any drugs while he was working, and look like Joe College with clean ironed shirts, a neat haircut, and bright eyes. He even bought a Washington University decal for the rear window of his car and a sticker for the bumper: "Have You Hugged Your Kid Today?" The police should like that.

To cut the boredom of driving, he bought some books on tape. He listened to cutdown versions of the *Tale of Two Cities, Carrie,* and *The Maltese Falcon.* He also bought a tape player and started listening to heavy-metal bands. He wished he could watch movies and still drive.

Sean was delighted with his work. Dependable, loyal, clean-cut, Tommy was the best mule he had. A year after he started, Sean let him do a few pickups in New York and Atlanta. It was the same as picking up in the midwest; Tommy just had to drive farther and Sean paid him $1500 a trip. He liked that.

Tommy was now pulling in between $1700 and $2550 a week. He opened four checking accounts in four different suburbs and deposited one week's pay in each once a month. He was saving to buy a house – for cash. Sean and his partners had Swiss bank accounts. Sean promised to set up one for Tommy when he went into the second year of work for them.

"In the meantime, build up a little cash to keep around the house," he told Tommy. "It's nice to know there's $30,000 or $40,000 around for little emergencies."

Marianne and Danny had no idea that Sean was running a major drug ring out of his bedroom. Except for his expensive stereo, his hookah, and some nice-looking clothes, Sean kept his wealth a secret. All his dealings with his Swiss banker went through his lawyer's office in Chicago. He made most of his phone calls through pay phones and billed them to his credit card – also paid by his Chicago lawyer.

To all appearances, he looked like a normal, drugged-out, 18-year-old.

His parents were more suspicious of Tommy.

"Where'd you get that car?" his father asked him when Tommy drove over for dinner one Sunday.

"It's a company car," Tommy said.

"You need a car to bounce people out of a bar?" he said. He was still miffed Tommy had not wanted to work at the meat-packing plant.

"I've got a new job," Tommy said. "I'm in sales."

His father looked at him in surprise.

"I sell medical equipment to nursing homes," Tommy said.

"You're moving up in the world," Danny said, awed. He couldn't imagine his son, at the age of 19, holding down a white-collar job.

"I guess," Tommy said.

Over dinner, Ruth and her brood ignored Tommy, but Danny wanted all the details of his new position. Tommy created an elaborate lie weaving together fictitious customers, a fictitious boss, and an entire product line of adult diapers, bedpans, and hospital linens.

Danny was impressed. His son was going beyond what he had done in his life. He was proud of him.

"Maybe you could get Sean a job in sales," he said over his peas and carrots. "That boy needs some discipline in his life."

Tommy could hardly keep from laughing.

"Sure, Dad," he said. "I'll look into it."

From then on, whenever Danny saw his son he would ask how business was doing.

"Great, Dad," Tommy would say. "Sales are great."

And that was no lie.

* * *

One of the side benefits of having money was that women found Tommy irresistable. Tall, muscular, clean-cut, with a nice car, money, and a sexuality that seemed to come out of his pores, Tommy found he could get laid any day of the week by any of 10 different women.

He took advantage of it fully. He had women in all the cities he traveled to; no point sleeping alone after his 2 am pickups. He was always a little randy and high-strung then. A good fuck did the trick.

He picked up his women at local bars. There was Emmeline in Detroit, Florence in Cleveland, and a cafe-au-lait black in St. Louis named Tesserina. Back in Chicago, he had a string of blondes and redheads in their early 20s, plus a few divorcees in their 30s.

He liked the divorcees. They had a wonderful desperation and intensity the younger women lacked. The most exciting were the ones with children. The children were such a liablity in most men's eyes that the women were thrilled when a man made a pass at them, much less took them to bed. They were wild lovers. He could see why his mother was popular with men.

Chapter Nine

Driving took on a boring regularity that Tommy liked. The days he was going to a pickup, he would sleep all day and leave in the late afternoon, his car filled with books on tape, cassettes of rock music, and bags of pretzels and pop.

He'd pick up the drugs, telephone his local woman, and end up in her bed, where he usually slept until early the next afternoon. With the money he'd saved on the hotel room, he'd take her out to a nice lunch. Then he headed home.

Weekends he took off. He joined a country club and started playing golf with a group of young pharmaceutical salesmen who worked for Baxter-Travenol and lived in Flossmoor. He told them he was a manufacturer's representative for machine tools.

They were a friendly group. In the fall they went to Notre Dame football games. In the winter they went to hockey games, and spring saw them waiting for opening day for the White Sox.

They invited him over to their houses for dinner. Their wives fussed that he wasn't married. Twenty-one years old and he didn't even have a girlfriend. They plotted to fix him up with their sisters and friends. In January, he took one of them to the country-club's Winter Festival Ball.

A fragile blonde woman, Jennifer Franklin had porcelain skin, beautiful shoulders, and one of the loveliest smiles he had ever seen. He fell immediately in love with her.

Jennifer was only 19 and very impressionable. Tommy fawned over her all night and stepped on her feet when they danced. But he was good-looking, wore an expensive tuxedo, and drove a nice big Buick. He also took her to an elegant restaurant after the dance and bought her her first cognac.

She was dazzled.

He asked her out for the next weekend and she accepted.

At secretarial school that week, all she could talk about was what a wonderful guy her sister had introduced her to. For his part, Tommy drove three jobs that week, all of them to Detroit, and practically fucked Emmeline into the ground.

He didn't want to attack Jennifer that weekend, so he decided to spend himself physically on his utility women. A wide-hipped hillbilly with huge breasts, Emmeline didn't mind. Tommy always bought her a good meal afterwards and left her a few dollars for her children.

That Saturday night, Tommy picked up Jennifer at 7 and took her to dinner and the movies. They saw a steamy movie that had Tommy physically restraining himself from grabbing at her soft little breasts. Draped in a loose green sweater, they were just calling to be fondled.

Instead, he grabbed the back of her seat and gritted his teeth. How long was it going to take to get into her body? He stole a sidelong glance at her, her long mascara-ed eyelashes fringing big blue eyes, and wanted to take her right there.

She caught him looking at her and smiled shakily, his look of unadulterated lust taking her by surprise. She shifted nervously in her seat and dug back into her box of popcorn.

She was a virgin, a rarity among many of her friends, who had all lost their virginity at the age of 14 and were now getting married to boys with no future.

But Tommy. Tommy was different. He was well-dressed and had a car. He wasn't working at a gas station or plodding through the night shift at a factory, and he wasn't some poor college kid. He was going somewhere — in whatever it was that he did for a living. What were "machine tools" anyway?

She looked at him again. He was engrossed in the extraordinarily explicit sex scene on the screen. She averted her eyes from the screen in embarrassment and stared at her hands. And he was *so* sexy. She could imagine his arms around her. How jealous her girlfriends would be.

She should claim him right away. She resolved to sleep with him that night.

* * *

After the movie, Tommy took her to a bar and bluffed the doorman to let her in. They took a dark booth in the back and the barmaid bought them beers.

"How did you like the movie?" he asked for the fifth time.

"It was great," she said. Actually, all the sex had embarrassed her.

"I really like you," he said.

She smiled her lovely smile. "I like you, too."

"I didn't think you did."

She just shrugged and smiled, her blonde curls falling forward over her face.

He reached forward and held her hand.

He could feel her shudder with excitement and their eyes met.

"Why don't we get out of here and go for a little ride?" he said softly.

"OK."

He paid for the beers and they left.

He drove her to his apartment.

Tommy had a nice place. He had rented tasteful furniture, hired a cleaning lady, and kept his refrigerator full of beer and junk food.

Jennifer sat on the couch. Tommy turned on some quiet, tinkly music, poured two cognacs, then sat down next to her. She had barely taken one sip from her drink when he put his arm around her and pulled her in close to him, kissing her hard.

She kissed him back hard, surprising and delighting him. He took the drink from her hand, set it on the floor, and laid her out on the couch. Before she knew it, he had a big, cold hand on one of her breasts.

She shuddered.

"Is something the matter?" he murmured into her ear.

"Your hand is freezing," she mumbled.

"I'll have to warm it up," he said, moving his hand quickly from her breast down to her buttocks.

"Tommy," she said, pushing him away.

"It's warmer in the bedroom," he whispered in her ear. "I have a great bed."

"Well. . ."

Before she could say more, he picked her up, carried her in to his bedroom, and laid her out on his bed.

He undid her clothes with expert fingers and admired the beauty of her small white body, the curve of her hip, the clump of blonde curls hanging over her frightened blue eyes.

"I'm a virgin, you know," she said as she watched him undress.

"That's easily remedied," he said. Actually, he was aggravated. Deflowering virgins was not much fun. Maybe this one would catch on quickly.

He got a towel from the bathroom.

"For the blood," he said, pulling it under her.

"Blood?" She looked shocked.

"Don't worry," he mumbled, laying himself on top of her and pushing himself into her.

She bit her lips in pain.

He came almost immediately. Maybe he did like deflowering virgins. It had been quite a long time.

She bled all over the towel and started to cry.

He pulled the covers over her and took her in his arms.

"You'll be alright," he said softly. "It happens to everyone."

"I've got to go," she said, getting up quickly. "My father wants me home by midnight." It was 11:30.

She washed herself off and dressed.

Tommy could hardly pull his clothes on fast enough.

He drove her home. In the driveway, she pulled him to her and kissed him hard, pulling his hand under her sweater and over her breast. He could feel her heart beating fast.

"Now you belong to me," she said quietly, her eyes drilling into his.

He looked at her, small and pale beside him, his hand on her soft, warm skin.

"Yes," he said, surprised. "I suppose I do."

She smiled her magnificent smile.

"I'll see you tomorrow," she whispered.

She slipped out of the car and ran up to the house, turning to wave at him at the door. The porch light went out.

He put the Buick in gear and drove away slowly.

Jennifer was definitely the woman for him.

***

Tommy and Jennifer became an item.

He took her out to a nice restaurant every Saturday night and took her home afterward for sex. He always got her home by midnight to meet her father's curfew.

Sometimes they'd go out with her sister, Martha, and her husband, John. They'd go to the country club and meet the other pharmaceutical salesmen and their wives.

The wives were distinctly colder. Now that he was seeing Jennifer he was no longer "an eligible male," available to be fixed up with their single or divorced girlfriends. The women found him boring.

He rarely saw Jennifer during the week.

"Always on the road," he told her. "The life of a salesman."

He still slept with his girlfriends when he traveled, but when he was home he wanted her — all the time.

So, two months after they met, he proposed.

Ecstatic, she accepted. The wedding was set for June.

Sean hit the ceiling when he heard about it.

"You can't have a wife," he told Tommy. "She'll screw up everything."

Sean was 19 and had graduated from high school. He was still living with his mother, who still thought he worked at Burger King. He had $336,454.36 in his numbered Swiss bank account.

Tommy and Sean argued over Jennifer. Sean almost told Tommy he had to quit.

"Women will be our death," he yelled at his brother. But eventually he gave in. Two of his partners were married. One even had kids. Wives and children were no problem.

The problem was, he thought one day while filling up his hookah, that he wanted Jennifer, too.

* * *

He had first met her at Tommy's, just after Tommy himself had met her. Sean had stopped by that night to straighten out some bookkeeping and there she was, curled up in the corner of the couch, her huge blue eyes peering out from under a fringe of curls.

"Hi," she said softly when Tommy introduced them. "I'm so glad to meet you."

He liked her tininess, her graceful hands, and her smile, though her most radiant looks were saved for Tommy.

He stood there in his jeans and suede jacket and felt the fool next to his brother, who was neatly dressed in chinos and a buttondown shirt. The Joe-College look certainly attracted a a better brand of woman than his expensively attired, high-school drug-addict outfit. He resolved to trim his shaggy hair and shave off his thin beard.

He and Tommy repaired to Tommy's den and straightened out the books. Sean gave him his driving orders for the next week. He wanted to stick around and talk to Jennifer but Tommy hurried him out. Tommy had only two hours to make her and bring her home to her parents.

"Nice to meet you," Sean said to her on the way out. "If you're ever lonely during the week, just give me a call."

Tommy glared at him.

"Brotherly love and concern, you know," he said, smiling at Tommy.

And he left.

* * *

Tommy and Jennifer were married a month after her 20th birthday in a small Lutheran church in Flossmoor. Sean was his brother's best man; one of the bride's giggling, wide-eyed friends was her maid of honor.

The bride was a perfect beauty, her blonde hair done up in French braids and her clear blue eyes brighter than ever. Tommy almost swooned when she came down the aisle, a bouquet of camellias in her hands, her father walking with a stiff formal walk beside her.

Jennifer was the best thing that had ever happened to him.

Her father, Colonel Matthew Franklin (U.S. Army - Retired) had asked Tommy few questions when Tommy asked for her hand. The boy was in machine tools, the colonel knew that. He himself now worked in product development for a paper-goods manufacturer, thinking up new ways to make paper plates.

The colonel found Tommy neat, polite, and well-dressed. He was a fine young man who would take good care of Jennifer. The fourth of four daughters, Jennifer was not the colonel's favorite, though she was certainly prettier than her sisters. He found her not terribly bright and somewhat sullen. He was glad to get her off his hands, even at the young age of 20.

Jennifer's mother had argued Jennifer was too young to marry, but the colonel had dismissed her fears. A quiet woman, Hannah Franklin inevitably followed the colonel's lead in every matter of importance from the choice of Jennifer's mate to the scheduling of her own hysterectomy.

From Marianne and Danny Trabert's point of view, Tommy had made a brilliant match. Jennifer's family had a big house in Flossmoor. The girl herself was a pleasant creature who took her mother-in-law's hard edge and shrewish comments in stride.

The girl even seemed to have a good effect on the wayward Sean. Tall and clean-shaven, he stood next to his brother watching Jennifer come down the aisle. His big bony frame was starting to fill out. He and his brother made a handsome pair of young men at the head of the church.

Marianne looked at them proudly. She hadn't seen her two boys together in one spot in two years. She was surprised to realize that they looked like some of the young men she was picking up at the local bars.

She could be screwing her sons.

She adjusted her blue sheathe dress and smiled. She could still make it with the best of them.

For his part, Tommy was happier than he'd ever been in his life. Sean, on the other hand, was despondent. Jennifer was clearly in love with his brother.

After a noisy reception at the country club, Tommy and Jennifer went on a two-week honeymoon to Hawaii. As docile as her mother, Jennifer came and lay with him whenever he called, the rest of the time remaining a quiet, self-contained creature who never argued or complained and often sat alone, staring out to sea from the terrace of their room. When he asked her something, she would turn her wide blue eyes on him and murmur her responses in quiet, almost musical tones. She relied on him for everything.

He felt powerful around her, almost like a god. He loved her very much. He became protective of her, almost as if she were his young daughter instead of his wife.

When they came back from the honeymoon she was already pregnant with his first child. She was frightened, but he was delighted and his obvious pleasure at her pregnancy calmed her fears.

He had it all — a beautiful and loving wife, good money, and his first son on the way. They planned on moving into their first house in November — a new, $175,000, four-bedroom house on a small lake in Palos Hills. The house was faced with stone in the front and had a tiny cupola on the roof. For some unknown reason it reminded Jennifer of a French chateau pictured in one of her high-school geography books.

They immediately dubbed the house "The Chateau" and bought four rooms of French provincial furniture as a start on furnishing it. Jennifer quit her job as a secretary-receptionist at Levitt Molds and Die-Casting in Harvey and spent her days shopping for draperies, furniture, and baby clothes with her mother.

Tommy started making three pickups a week to meet all his bills.

No one questioned how a 22-year-old man and his young bride could afford such a house, much less furnish it.

Tommy must be doing very well indeed, Colonel Franklin thought as he and Hannah visited the young couple soon after they had moved in. Beer in hand, Tommy showed them the refrigerator with an ice-cube maker in the door, the jacuzzi in the master bathroom, and the wide-screen TV in his den. Jennifer padded behind him, her cheeks blooming, her pregnancy rounding out her stomach, like some medieval painting of a madonna.

Tommy went out to grill steaks for dinner on the gas grill on his patio. He watched the ducks on the lake and the last red leaves falling from the big maple in his backyard. He flipped a steak with a wood-handled fork and his nostrils filled with delicious meaty smoke. He'd come a long way from Marianne's trailer and chasing high-school girls.

Sean was even talking about making him a partner in the business.

He was in heaven.

The next day, a Monday, the drug wars erupted.

Chapter Ten

Tommy never knew exactly what happened. Sean eventually explained that someone in Cleveland named Dominique had decided that the split of existing business wasn't to his liking. He had started making trouble.

The first incidence occurred that Tuesday morning at 2 when Jerry, Tommy's Cleveland contact, didn't make his pickup. Tommy waited for an hour at the rendezvous, a warehouse in a big industrial park just off the interstate.

Then he called Jerry again. There was no answer. In 3-1/2 years of being a mule, he had never had a problem with a pickup.

Confused, he called Sean.

After three or four rings, Sean's sleepy voice came on the phone. When he heard Tommy's voice, he was immediately awake.

"Get out of there," he said, his voice stern. "Now."

"Maybe Jerry had car trouble. He's only an hour late," Tommy said.

"Are you crazy?"

Tommy coughed. He was afraid he wasn't going to get paid because he hadn't made the pickup. With the new baby and everything . . .

Sean read his mind.

"Don't worry," he said. "You'll get your money."

"OK." Tommy hung up quickly, his mind at ease. He went to see Florence, his Cleveland mistress. That night he dreamed of Jennifer and the video camera he had bought the week before. He was going to take pictures of his son's birth.

He could hardly wait for the weekend; this week was off to a bad start.

* * *

The rest of the week went smoothly. He picked up a shipment in St. Louis and another just outside Louisville.

The next week he was off to Cleveland again. This time he had a new contact named "James."

"What happened to Jerry?" Tommy asked Sean when he came to pick up his folder of instructions.

"He retired," Sean said.

"Retired?" Jerry had been his Cleveland contact for two years. A sullen man, he was only about 35-years-old.

Sean smiled. "Yeah," he said. "He went back to school to become an electrician."

Tommy was sure there was more money in drugs than rewiring houses but he didn't say anything. You couldn't acount for people's tastes in work.

"James" turned out to be a flat-faced young man of about 28, thick-set with thinning hair. He was 15 minutes late for the pickup, which was set in an alley behind a warehouse near downtown Cleveland.

It was a cold November night. Tommy pulled his leather jacket around him as James piled the paper-wrapped parcels into the trunk of his car.

Next time, he'd wear a sweater under his jacket. Leather looked good, but it kept you warm for shit.

They had just grunted their good-byes and were heading for their cars when a white Chevrolet appeared. It sped down the alley toward them. Alarmed, they ran for their cars. Tommy got to the door of his new Buick just in time to see someone lean out the window of the Chevrolet and shoot James in the back.

The loud report of the gun bounced off the walls of the adjacent buildings. Tommy ducked behind his Buick just as two shots shattered the side windows in the front seat. Shards of broken glass from the driver's side fell on his head. One gashed his forehead.

The Chevrolet pulled out into the street, turned left, and was gone. Tommy sat trembling in the dirt of the alley, the wetness of the bricks seeping through his pants.

He couldn't stop shaking. This was it: someone was going to kill him over drugs.

He looked down the alley. James lay face down in the filth, not moving. Tommy was sure he was dead. He was about to go look when he heard sirens.

He got up quickly, opened the door to the driver's side, and brushed the glass off the seat. Then he hunkered down in the seat and forced himself to drive slowly to the street. He was sure the Chevrolet would be there, but the street was empty and quiet.

He exhaled deeply, brushed his jacket off, and shifted uncomfortably in his soggy pants. He got on the expressway immediately and headed out of town, swearing to himself that he was getting out of the drug business and shivering as the wind whipped through the broken window.

Florence would have to do without him tonight.

* * *

He drove straight to the trailer park, arriving only minutes after Marianne had left for work. He rang the bell until Sean answered, sleepy and rumpled in his bathrobe.

Sean took one look at Tommy's terrified, gashed face, grabbed him by the arm, and pulled him inside.

"What happened?" he said.

"James is dead," Tommy said.

Sean screwed up his mouth in disgust. "Shit." He twisted the cord of his bathrobe. "Go clean up your face. I've got to make some phone calls."

Tommy went into the bathroom and stared in surprise in the mirror. His face hadn't looked so bad when he'd glanced at it in the dark in the Buick's rearview mirror. Now his forehead had a big, jagged red gash surrounded with purple swelling.

What was he going to tell Jennifer?

He dabbed at the wound with a washcloth and cleaned off the encrusted blood on the edges. He had got off easy; all he had was a rip in his skin. James, on the other hand, was dead.

It had all been so sudden. One moment James was there, the next he was lying in the mud dead. All it took was one shot. It was incredibly easy.

Tommy felt giddy to be alive.

He hung up the washcloth and went back to the living room, where Sean was talking on the phone. Sean's voice was calm and measured, almost as if he were talking to a contractor about reroofing his house instead of a man's death.

"No," he said. "No, we can't move Martinez. He knows too many important people in St. Louis and he doesn't travel well." He paused and laughed. "Try Carrington in Atlanta. And tell him to bring some friends and some firepower. This thing has gone far enough." He paused again. "OK. Talk to you soon." And he hung up.

He turned and stared at Tommy's forehead. "That looks better," he said, smiling.

"So what happens now?" Tommy said.

"We reclaim our market, of course. We're sending in a new contact with some support behind him." He stood up. "You want some coffee? Mom always leaves a pot on for me in the morning."

"But what about James?" Tommy said, following his brother into the kitchen.

"What about him? He's dead. He's not a real important factor right now."

"Yeah. . . Yeah . . .but he's dead."

Sean started pouring. "So?"

"So, what about his wife and kids, and the police?"

"He had no wife and kids, we'll wire $5,000 to his grandmother as an anonymous gift, and the Cleveland police don't know us or James. We don't sell in Cleveland; we just ship through there."

He smiled at Tommy and handed him a cup. "It's just another senseless drug murder. You want cream?"

Tommy took the cup and his hand started shaking. A man had just been murdered and Sean didn't seem to care.

"Don't you care?" he blurted.

Sean turned to him. "Sure I care. James was a good man. But that's part of the business. We have occasional accidents. We try and run a clean ship with no problems with the competitors but sometimes things get out of hand."

He smiled and sipped his coffee. "Ferry is talking to the Cleveland people. Things should calm down soon." Ferry was one of Sean's partners.

Tommy smiled weakly and slumped down into a kitchen chair.

Sean laughed. "Don't worry," he said. "You'll get used to it."

"What if I'm next?" Tommy said.

Sean looked at him steadily. "Everyone's number comes up sometime," he said. "The idea is to have a good time before it does."

Tommy shuddered. "I've got a wife and a kid on the way. What about them?"

Sean smiled again. "Don't worry," he said. "We take care of our own." He sipped his coffee again. "Now let's get back down to business."

He paid him for the Cleveland run — $1,200 in small bills. "We pay extra when you're under fire," he said. "You know, like combat pay." Then he gave Tommy his driving orders for the next week.

Tommy called the local Buick dealer and arranged to bring his car in to have the windows replaced. The dealership would rent him a loaner.

By the time he left the dealer, he felt calm and in control again.

Being a mule was like being in the army. You traveled a lot and people you didn't know occasionally shot at you.

Except drugs paid a lot better.

He told Jennifer he'd been hit in the forehead by some protruding piece of machinery at one of his customer's plants. Then, he'd come out the parking lot and punks had broken into his car.

"Imagine," he told her. "They broke both windows trying to get the stereo, but they didn't get it. Someone must have come by and frightened them away."

She looked at him with her big blue eyes then clucked like a mother hen and dabbed at his wound with a clean cloth. She insisted he rest in his big lounger chair and read the newspaper while she brought him potato chips and beer and sat on the arm of the chair, rubbing the back of his neck.

For a final comfort, she canceled her 2 pm appointment with her mother to shop for a crib and spent the afternoon in bed with him.

He should cut his head more often, he thought, falling into a deep sleep with Jennifer curled up against his side.

He didn't think about James at all.

***

The next week's work went well, with no mishap. He did not go to Cleveland.

However, two weeks later in St. Louis, someone shot at him out of a window of the half-finished factory where he was meeting his pickup, Charley. The two of them hit the dirt and crawled behind a pile of bricks, the bullets zinging off the clay and spattering them with brick dust.

"Who the fuck is that?" Tommy hissed.

"Got me," Charley said. A fat, middle-aged man, he surprised Tommy by pulling a shiny gun from under his heavy sweater. He aimed it at the face in the window and pulled off two rounds. The attacker stopped shooting.

They lay there on the frozen ground, their clothes covered with dust. After two minutes with no returned gunfire, they got up quickly, loaded the drugs in Tommy's car, and left. The entire way home Tommy was sure he was being followed.

He went straight home and called Sean from his den.

"They're shooting at me again," he said.

Sean sighed.

"I could've been one dead mother if Charley hadn't brought a gun," Tommy said.

"Not a bad idea," Sean said. "This St. Louis thing puts a whole new slant on things."

Tommy was alarmed. "What does that mean?" he said.

"The St. Louis people are not known for their flexibility," Sean said. "In fact, they're SOB's. I'd get a gun if I were you."

"What!"

"Maybe you won't have to use it. We'll try to work out the problems in St. Louis. But you wouldn't want to end up dead while we were negotiating, would you?"

Tommy was quiet for a moment. He'd never held or fired a gun in his life.

It was time to leave the drug business.

Unfortunately there were no other jobs he could get that brought in $2400 a week.

"You couldn't give me a desk job or something?" he asked.

Sean laughed. "I've got the whole business on my computer. We don't generate a whole lot of paperwork running drugs."

Tommy felt his heart sink. What could he do? He had to pay for the new wall-to-wall carpeting in his living room, the expensive draperies Jennifer had just bought, and Tommy Trabert, Jr. — all scheduled to arrive in early December.

"Maybe I could deliver in Chicago, something a little less exposed?" he tried.

"We've got plenty of street distribution. Besides, it's no safer. We lost two of our best men just last week. The Latin Kings did them in. You're a good mule; stick with it." He paused. "I tell you what," he said. "I'll give you a raise to $1200 a pickup and $1500 if you get shot at."

That was at least $3600 a week. Jennifer could buy a lot of draperies with that.

"And I'll pay for a gun and a bulletproof vest," he said. "I'll even pay your membership in a gun club so you can learn how to shoot the thing."

It was a tempting offer. He'd be armed; he could fight back. And the vest would protect him from death. The thought that a bullet could strike him in the head or anywhere else, maiming or even killing him, passed briefly through his mind. It was colored over quickly by the thought of all the money he would be making.

"Alright," he said.

"Good. I'll send Luis over right away," Sean said.

"Luis?"

"Our gun man. He'll fix you up."

There was a click on the line.

"I've got another call coming in," Sean said. "Catch you later." And he hung up.

* * *

Luis was a short, nondescript little Mexican with the copper skin and black hair of an Indian. In his cowboy boots and jeans, he looked like a migrant farmworker. He carried a dufflebag slung over one shoulder and a beatup cheap suitcase.

The suitcase was filled with more guns than Tommy had ever seen in his life.

Luis spread them out on the heavy oak desk Jennifer had just bought for Tommy's den.

White and blue-gray steel glinted in the light of his desklamp. The guns were immaculately kept; the smell of lightweight machine oil rose to his nostrils.

Luis advised a revolver; they didn't jam. Of course, if you got in a drawn-out fight, after six shots you would have to reload bullets by hand.

"But you rarely get to that point," he said with a slight Spanish accent. "Three rounds and everything's settled. Everyone's a good shot in this business."

Tommy shuddered.

Luis picked out a long-barrelled revolver in a glistening blue-black steel for Tommy. Good for distance shooting, he told Tommy, handing him the weapon. The gun was remarkably heavy.

Luis rattled off a description of its virtues and specifications. Tommy's eyes glazed over and he stared at the gun.

This thing was supposed to save his life?

It felt like a piece of lead pipe. The idea of something coming out of the barrel and actually hitting and killing what he was pointing at seemed remote at best.

"Don't worry," Luis said, looking at Tommy's dismay. "Even complete losers can learn how to shoot. It just takes practice."

Somehow Tommy wasn't comforted.

Luis then loosened the drawstring on his dufflebag and turned the bag upside down. A collection of shoulder holsters in dark leather tumbled out, followed by a mass of clothing in some blue-black fabric. The clothing fell to the floor with a surprisingly loud thud.

"Bullet-proof vests," Luis said, pawing through the pile on the floor. "I think you're a large to an extra-large, but I brought them all," he said. He turned his brown eyes on Tommy. "I have lots of other calls to make today."

Tommy was a large. Luis strapped him into the vest, then fished out a gun holster from the pile and strapped it under his arm. Tommy felt like a trussed calf.

"You're ready now," Luis said, smiling and stepping back.

"Yeah, all I need to learn is how to shoot this damn thing," Tommy said, waving the gun heavily in one hand.

Luis smiled and scribbled a name on a piece of paper.

"Call this guy," he said. "He's the president of the nearest gun club. Tell him you bought the thing to defend your home and for sport and you want to learn to shoot."

He smiled again. "These gun-club guys are remarkably stupid. They don't want to know more. It sure saves us a bundle on training."

He stuffed the vests and holsters in his dufflebag, snapped the locks shut on his suitcase, and shook Tommy's hand.

"Good luck," he said.

And he was gone.

Chapter Eleven

The Palos Heights Gun Club consisted of two retired policemen from Flossmoor, two insurance salesmen who hunted deer, a steelworker who collected rifles and his girlfriend, a bottom-heavy secretary for a construction company who wore tight jeans and had a remarkable eye.

"Linda is the best damn shot of us all," said Roger, the policeman who was club president.

The club had assorted hangers-on who showed up occasionally for the weekly meetings and some who came once and then disappeared. But the six members — and Tommy — were the core.

They met every Saturday at a public range, each shooting off $30 of ammunition. Afterwards, they repaired to a local bar for a postmortem on their efforts.

Tommy fit right in. He told them he was interested in defending his home and shooting for sport. He showed them the wedding picture of he and Jennifer that he always carried in his wallet. It turned out Linda knew Jennifer's cousin from high school.

And Roger's uncle was also in the machine-tool business.

They were a friendly lot and attentive to their shooting. They had Tommy shooting within minutes. Within two weeks he was a passable shot; within six, he was very good.

Everyone was pleased and told him he was a natural. He thought about buying another gun. He started feeling confident and even cocky about his shooting.

He took his gun home and proudly showed it to Jennifer, who stared at it in boredom. The colonel had hunted deer and had a rack of rifles in the house. In Jennifer's view, all men eventually took up guns, just like all women eventually got pregnant. It was a fact of life.

Within three weeks of getting his gun, Tommy was taking it to pickups, the leather holster warm and comforting under his arm. To his immense relief, he had no reason to use it. Sean and his partners made peace in St. Louis and someone killed the gangleader in Cleveland who was making trouble. Or so Sean said.

Tommy was glad for business as usual. The gun-toting life was not for him. He stopped wearing his bullet-proof vest and almost started leaving his gun at home.

Then one day, four weeks later, he was glad he hadn't.

He was in St. Louis again. This time, he was picking up from Charley on the edge of an abandoned quarry on the south edge of town. It was an inky night and the quarry was unlit.

Suddenly, someone was shooting at them in the dark. Tommy saw the flash of the shots; the sound bounced off the quarry walls.

Without thinking, he pulled out his gun and aimed at where the light had flashed. He pulled off four rounds. Someone screamed and the shots stopped. Tommy and Charley ran for their cars.

Tommy knew he had killed a man; he started to tremble.

"It was either him or me," he told himself all the way back to Chicago. "Him or me. Him or me."

By the time he got home he was calm.

He had done the right thing. It was either the gunman or him. Better the other guy.

He felt a rush of power. He called up Sean.

"You asshole," he said. "I got shot at again in St. Louis."

"You're kidding," Sean said, his voice sleepy but surprised. "I don't get it."

"I think I killed a guy."

"Good, maybe his friends will get the idea we're not too pleased with being shot at," Sean said without missing a beat.

Tommy paused.

"I've never killed anyone before."

"There's always a first time."

There was a pause.

"That's all you have to say?" Tommy said.

"What do you want me to say? You want to die instead? The guy tried to kill you. So he deserved to die. He was scum."

"Yeah. . ."

"Shooting at people is not the polite way to do business."

"What about the police?"

"What about them? They don't know you."

"Yeah . . ."

"Look, enough of this. I've got work to do. I don't want some free-lancer running around shooting at my guys. Go home and relax." He paused. "I'll send you a bonus: $2000 for knocking off one of the opposition. Buy yourself something nice."

There was a clicking noise on the line.

"I'm getting another call. Talk to you later."

And he hung up.

* * *

The St. Louis shooting marked the first of several gunfights Tommy had that winter. Cleveland heated up again; a wiry little black man surprised him at a pickup. He jumped out from behind a garbage can, a knife in one hand, and Tommy shot him. They left him moaning in the alley, clutching at the spreading red spot in his chest.

Tommy wanted to take him to an emergency room. It took all of his new pickup's persuasive power to convince him it wasn't a good idea.

"The guy's nearly dead already," the pickup, whose name was Mark, said. "The police will find him soon."

Tommy felt terrible. He preferred killing people in the dark; he didn't like watching them die.

In February, he shot another man in Cleveland. This one wore a wool stocking cap and ambushed them at a pickup in an old warehouse. The man knicked Mark's arm before Tommy shot him in the leg. Tommy watched the man hobble off in terror. He couldn't bring himself to shoot him in the back, although he knew he should.

Finally, in early March, Tommy and his St. Louis pickup, Charley, skirmished with three men in the back of an abandoned factory. They exchanged five rounds before Tommy and Charley could reach their cars and flee.

Tommy was frightened.

"Just one guy is bad enough," he told Sean later that day. "But three is too much."

"You should get a machine gun," Sean said. "It evens out the odds. I'll send Luis by."

"Now wait a minute. . ."

"It's a mean world out there."

"You don't have to tell me that. You're not the one getting shot at."

"I'm only thinking of your best interests."

"My best interests are that you stop all this damn shooting."

"That's like commanding water to flow up. Guns come with the territory." Sean dropped his voice. "You don't like the heat, stay out of the kitchen."

The phone was silent. Then Tommy gave a long sigh.

"Shit," he said.

And he hung up.

* * *

Two days later, while Jennifer was at the obstetrician's, Luis came by with Tommy's machine gun. A Pakistani copy of a small, snub-nosed Israeli model, the ZN-35 was the size of a lap-dog.

Luis gave him a larger holster. Tommy would have to wear a raincoat to cover it.

"You're moving up in the world," Luis said as he strapped Tommy in. "Most mules only get pistols."

"Most mules aren't going to war zones for their pickups," Tommy snapped.

"You'll love it," Luis said. "You can waste four guys before they move a muscle. I'd take a ZN over a revolver anyday."

He pulled out two clips from his pocket. "Here," he said, sticking them in Tommy's hand. "They've each got 15 rounds." He smiled. "Have a good time."

"How do I learn to use this thing?" Tommy said, fingering the ZN-35. It would be hard to explain to the Palos Hills Gun Club why he needed a machine gun for self-defense.

"It's pretty straightforward," Luis said, taking another clip from his pocket and pushing it into the bottom of the gun. It snapped into place. "Go out in the country pull off a few rounds. You'll love it."

"I'll wonder how I ever did without it?" Tommy said bitterly.

"Something like that."

Luis tied up the neck of his dufflebag and picked up his suitcase.

"Don't get yourself killed," he said. "ZN's are expensive."
And he left.

* * *

The next day Jennifer went into labor.

Thomas Alex Trabert, Jr. was born 24 hours later, a healthy, seven-pound baby who came screaming into the world with a wild shock of black hair on the top of his head.

Jennifer was exhausted. After 18 hours of labor, the obstetrician did a Caesarean, leaving her unable to move without pain and stuck in the hospital for an additional three days.

When Tommy saw her the day after his son's birth, she looked washed out and depressed.

"I've got to go on the road again," he told her softly. "I'll be back in two days."

"Can't you stay?" she said, her eyes pained.

"Sorry," he whispered. "I've my marching orders." He squeezed her hand. Sean had called him that morning and ordered him back to Cleveland. Tommy had argued with him, but Sean said the pickup couldn't wait.

"I'll be back in time to take you home," Tommy told Jennifer. "You just rest."

She gave him her magical smile and laid back in the pillows. He kissed her lightly and swore to himself that he would find another job.

This constant traveling was going to take him away from his family too much.

* * *

Cleveland was cold and damp. Mark had arranged their rendezvous for a farm road 20 miles out in the country. Tommy got there early. He pulled off the road, turned off the engine and lights, and leaned back in his seat.

He looked at the stars and thought of Jennifer and Tommy Jr. He had a wife and son now. They depended on him. Suddenly, he felt old.

A crescent moon came from behind a cloud and reflected off the gray snow on the cornfields. It was so peaceful out here. Maybe he should move to the country? It would be good for the boy to be able to play in fresh air and open fields.

He was wondering how much he could sell his house for in Palos Hills when a pair of car lights appeared over the crest of the railroad crossing about one-quarter mile up the road.

Tommy looked at his watch: 2 am exactly. Mark was getting more punctual.

Or was it Mark?

His heart froze. He picked up the ZN-35 from the floor of the front seat and prayed that it was Mark. With the excitement of Tommy Jr.'s birth, he had not practiced firing the gun. He hoped Luis had loaded it. He fingered the trigger, nervously patted his bullet-proof vest for luck, and waited.

The car slowed down. The moon threw some light on it, but not enough to distinguish how many people were in the car or if it belonged to Mark.

He squinted at it again, but could tell nothing. He rolled down his window and rested the butt of the ZN-35 on the car door.

Suddenly, the car sped up and pulled up next to him.

It wasn't Mark's.

Tommy pulled the trigger.

Nothing happened.

But enough firepower came out of the window of the other car to blow off the top of his head. He was killed instantly, his brains blown all over the nut-brown interior of his new Buick.

The attacking car sped off.

* * *

Mark came by five minutes later and found Tommy's body sprawled across the front seat, his arms akimbo, his mouth agog, and blood seeping from his topless skull.

"Shit!" Mark muttered under his breath. This was the third mule he'd lost in the last six months. He sped off to a pay phone and made several phone calls. Within 20 minutes two men in an old pickup truck appeared at Tommy's car.

One of them drove Tommy's car to a nearby chop shop, whose owners immediately started dismantling it. The other stripped Tommy's body of any identification, his diamond-encrusted wedding ring, and $500 in cash.

Then he stuffed the body in a zippered plastic bag, loaded it into the back of the pickup truck, and drove to a deserted bridge over the Cuyahoga River. He tied an iron weight around the foot of the bag with a chain and dumped it over the bridge.

Tommy and all traces of him had just disappeared.

* * *

Mark called his boss in Cleveland, who placed a call to his contact in Chicago, who called Sean the next morning.

Marianne picked up the phone just as she was leaving for work.

"This is Mr. Hanson at the Burger King," the contact said.

"Just a minute."

"Sean," she called. "It's for you." And she set the phone on the kitchen counter and headed for work without another moment's thought.

Rinsing his mouth of toothpaste, Sean picked up the phone.

"Hello?"

"Sean. Jack here," the man said. "Bad news, I'm afraid."

Sean sat down at the kitchen table.

"Your brother's gone. Blown away in Cleveland."

"Shit."

"Died instantly. An ambush by more free-lancers we think."

"Shit."

"I'm sorry."

"Yeah, well. . . These free-lancers have got to be taken out, Jack. Tommy was one of my best mules. Call Mike. I'll get the guys together here. I've had enough of this shit."

"Yeah. . . OK." There was a pause. "I'm real sorry, Sean."

Sean sighed. "Yeah. . . thanks. He was a good kid."

There was another pause. "Well, I've got to go," Jack said. "Talk to you later."

"Right."

And Jack hung up the phone. Sean set his down slowly.

Shit. Now he had to find another dependable mule for Tommy's route.

They had to come down hard on these free-lance drug runners. They were ruining his distribution system.

He went into the kitchen and poured himself a cup of coffee from the pot his mother had left for him.

Poor Tommy, he thought. He should have known better than to get involved with guns.

Sean had never shot a gun in his life and had no intentions of ever doing so.

Guns were dangerous. They killed people.

* * *

When Tommy didn't come to pick her up at the hospital, Jennifer called his "office phone," an answering service whose operators never knew where he was or when he would return, but who always took detailed messages.

When Tommy didn't call back, Jennifer called her parents, who took her and Tommy Jr. home. Her mother came home with her to help with the baby.

Two nights later, the colonel called the Palos Hills Police Department and reported him missing.

"What business was he in?" the sargeant on duty asked.

"Machine tools. An independent sales rep," the colonel said.

"No vices, no girlfriends, no reason why he would want to disappear?" the sargeant said.

"Of course not!" the colonel thundered. "He was newly married to my daughter and had a fine new son."

"Yes sir," the sargeant said. Faced with debts and family, the man had probably run off with another woman. It happened all the time.

"We'll look right into it, sir," he said. "Someone will stop by and get the details from your daughter."

"Make it quick," the colonel bellowed. "The poor girl is beside herself."

The sargeant marked the top of the form "low priority."

"We'll be by soon, sir," he said, hanging up the phone.

Another wandering husband, the sargeant thought. He wished they had a good murder or two in Palos Hills. It would make the job more interesting.

But nothing interesting ever happened in this dull, upper-middle-class suburb.

Howalski on the swing shift could handle this one.

And he want back to reviewing his parking-ticket rosters for the month.

Volume was up and he was pleased.

* * *

Two days later at 7 in the evening, Officer Howalski stopped by Jennifer's house. The tearful young wife described her husband's devotion to her, his long days on the road selling machine tools, and his delight in his new son.

Howalski took it all down and yawned behind his hand.

"Where was he going when he disappeared?" he said.

"I don't know," Jennifer said. "I never asked him about his business."

"Did you call his office?"

"I don't know where he worked. He said he rented space downtown, but he was never there. He was always on the road."

"What lines of machine tools did he represent."

"I don't know."

Howalski turned to the colonel.

"We never talked about it," the colonel blustered, embarrassed. "We never talked business." He pulled himself up. "We come from a school where gentlemen never discuss business. He was a good provider for his wife and son. That's all I needed to know."

Howalski screwed up his mouth and looked at him. What an idiot. Let's some guy walk off with his daughter without even knowing how he brought home the bacon. His father-in-law would have never let him get away with that when he married Sylvie. The old Polack made him show him the stubs from his paychecks from the police department.

"You could talk to his brother, Sean," Jennifer said. "He might know more."

"Right."

Howalski flipped his notebook shut.

This bozo Trabert had clearly skipped town on his little bride. It happened all the time. The boys get married, knock up their love-doll brides, and leave when the baby arrives on the scene.

His own brother had done it.

He made his farewells and went to see Sean.

* * *

Sean was cleaning out his fish tank when Howalski arrived.

A big, dumb-looking kid who was going nowhere, Howalski surmised.

No, he didn't know who his brother worked for, Sean said. Yeah, Sean himself had a few part-time jobs, but not many. He was going to the local community college at night. He pointed to a small pile of books on the coffee table. He wanted to become an accountant.

This, in fact, was true. Sean had signed up for two classes at Adlai Stevenson Junior College – an entry-level accounting course and business math. He wanted to do a better job keeping the books on his drug business.

What did he think of his brother and his brother's wife? Howalski asked.

Well, Sean said, everyone thought they got along alright, but he thought his brother was seeing another woman.

"Tommy really liked the girls," Sean said. "He knocked up a girl in high school and really spread himself around among the young chicks." He lowered his voice. "I don't think Jennifer knows about that."

Howalski nodded.

"Well, thanks very much," he said, getting up. "If you or anyone hears from your brother, be sure to call us."

"Sure," Sean said.

Howalski flipped his notebook shut and walked out into the cool spring air.

God, this kid lived in a crummy trailer park, he thought, noting the peeling plastic trim on the trailer across the way and the deep ruts in the park's muddy roads.

No wonder his brother was a dirtbag and had run off with a chickie.

He stuck his notebook in his back pocket. He'd pass his information on to the state police. They handled most missing-person searches, badly at best. They were understaffed and too busy chasing speeding truckers on the interstate to concentrate on chasing down guys who wanted to disappear.

For his part, he was glad to go back to his first love — traffic tickets.

Bring in those out-of-town speeders and the people who missed the tiny "no-parking" signs in loading zones. Those cases were dear to Chief Ferguson's heart.

Write up those traffic tickets and you would go far in the department.

He happily went back to the station to get his ticket book.

He was hot tonight. He was going to nail someone from Chicago, he just knew it.

Chapter Twelve

The days dragged into weeks and Tommy did not appear. The colonel called the state police every three days, but they put him off: the officer-in-charge had been reassigned. Someone else was on the case, and had no leads. Yes, they were still looking into it.

The colonel called Tommy's parents for support. He wanted to hire a private investigator.

Marianne was worried about Tommy, but she didn't have the money to pay an investigator. Danny, on the other hand, actually believed the police would find his son.

"He probably just ran off with some friends for a time," he said. "Maybe they went to Arizona or something. Something nutty like that.

"I nearly ran off when he was born," he confided to the colonel. "I can understand the feeling. He'll be back."

The colonel thought he was crazy.

He'd never really talked to his son-in-law's parents before the wedding. Now he was sure Tommy was descended from a line of idiots.

Only Sean seemed to have any sense. Sean called Jennifer every day, brought her flowers, and inquired about his brother. He was the perfect gentlemen and not as dumb as he looked. He was studying to be an accountant.

When the colonel talked about hiring a private investigator, Sean nodded sagely and agreed it was a good idea. But the colonel was not a rich man and he hadn't the foggiest notion about how to find an investigator. He kept talking about it, Sean kept agreeing that it was a great idea, and the colonel kept doing nothing.

But Sean and the colonel had long conversations — politics, football, business. Sean said he had friends on the Board of Trade.

"They're going to let me start trading and learning the business," he told the colonel. "I'm going to really make something of myself."

The colonel thought that was a good idea.

Money started getting tight. Because Tommy was missing and not dead, Jennifer could not collect on his life-insurance policy. And her parents could not support her. The mortgage payment alone on the Chateau was $1400 a month, plus taxes. The young widow was beside herself. The colonel called the bank with the mortgage and described his daughter's grim situation to a cold-voiced loan officer.

She'd have to sell the house, the man said.

When the colonel told Jennifer, she walked the halls of her house with Tommy Jr. in her arms, crying. Sean walked at her side trying to comfort her.

Finally, the day before the payment was due, he gave her a check for $1700.

"Oh, I couldn't take this," she said, hoping he wouldn't believe her.

"But you must," Sean said. "Tommy would want you to."

"But this is so much money," she said.

"I'm doing very well on the Board of Trade," Sean said. "My boss says I'm a natural."

Jennifer's eyes lit up.

A girlfriend of hers had married a man on the Board of Trade. They had an even bigger house than the Chateau and drove BMW's. She noticed Sean's resemblance to his brother. He had the same strong shoulders, only he was thinner and had lighter hair. Tommy had been starting to put on weight; Sean was actually better-looking.

He was certainly more attentive. Tommy was always on the road; then he joined that stupid gun club and was gone all Saturday afternoon.

Traders worked normal hours and came home to their wives.

And she knew Sean was in love with her. She had known it within two weeks of meeting him.

She hoped Tommy *was* gone for good.

Sean would make a good husband.

She blushed and stared at the floor, embarrassed at such a thought.

"A penny for your thoughts," Sean said softly.

"Oh, nothing," she said. "Nothing at all." She turned to him. "I'm just so grateful for the money, I can't thank you enough," she said, aiming her amazing smile at him.

"Oh, don't think of it," he said gently. "You and Tommy Jr. will never want with me around." He took her hand and squeezed it softly.

She trembled with excitement and stared into his deep brown eyes—just like Tommy's.

She hoped Tommy was dead.

* * *

Sean moved out of his mother's trailer and into the guest bedroom at Jennifer's. Jennifer didn't tell her parents and sent her mother home only hours before he was due to arrive.

"You're sure you'll be alright?" her mother had said, eying her grandson fussing in his crib.

"Fine, fine," Jennifer said. "I feel good."

"Well, I'm only a phone call away."

"I know, Mom," she said. "No problem."

And her mother left, turning and waving as she walked down the walk to her car.

Sean arrived two hours later. He introduced his sister-in-law to the joys of daily pot-smoking. By 7 every evening they were stoned and giggling. The first time they got stoned he kissed her. The second time they made love, Tommy Jr. crying in his crib down the hall.

"We're together forever," he told her afterward.

"What about Tommy?" she said.

"He's dead," Sean said with a finality that made her shudder.

"How do you know?" she said.

"Just a feeling," he said. "I know."

She looked thoughtful a moment.

"Are you sad?" Sean said softly.

"Well . . . yes . . . a little." She turned her wide blue eyes on him. "Well, no, not really," she said quickly. "I never would have gotten to know you then."

And she gave him her magic smile. He grabbed her to him and kissed her fiercely.

* * *

The police never figured out what happened to Tommy.

Sean solved his distribution problems and the mules stopped getting killed.

And he kept living with Jennifer. Eighteen months after Tommy's disappearance, she was pregnant by him.

She divorced Tommy in absentia and married him.

Sean Francis Trabert, Jr. was born four months later.

Danny squawked about Tommy's disappearance for at least a year, but never did more than complain. His wife Ruth and her two boys took up most of his time at home and he'd been promoted to management at the meat-packing factory. He was sorry his first-born was gone, but he started thinking of him as having been killed in a war or kidnapped. His memory started to fade.

Marianne took Tommy's disappearance harder. She actually called the police several times, but they easily put her off. One of them finally took pity on her.

"Ma'am," he said, "your son probably ran off with another woman and just wanted to disapper. When he wants to reappear, he'll let you know."

She resigned herself to the wait.

After all, other than Tommy's fling with another woman, Marianne thought her sons had turned out very well indeed. Sean was even giving her money occasionally.

Not bad for a divorced mom.

The End

Fired!

PART ONE

The Act

John Humphreys is a big man.
His blue suit pulls across his chest
    like a wrinkled plastic bag.
He looks at Jim Firthearn
    squirming in front of him.
A worm on a hook, a caterpillar
    hanging from a dead leaf, at the mercy of
        every passing wind.

Humphreys coughs, sits back in his chair
    behind his big, wide desk.
Peaking his hands into a tiny tent
    in front of his face, his lips move.
"Jim," he mouths,
"We've got to let you go."

The knot in Jim's stomach dissolves,
    into the hot slosh of his stomach.
He can feel his stomach rise.
A full system flushout
    like cleaning out a crankcase into the
        dirty oil pan in his garage.

"Reorganization," Humphreys says.
"The new order. Change. Moving the department
    to Washington."
And they have a full staff already.
He rises and sticks out his hand.
"Good luck. You get four months full
    pay."
His hand is clammy hot — a hot-water bottle
    with a loose cork.
And Jim is in the hall.

Five-minute murder. So painless,
    like a guillotine to the neck, a
        chop to the skull, a shot
            to the heart.
And it's over. He's dead.
Throw his body to the dogs.

He throws some pictures in his briefcase,
    a file or two.
Catherine guards his Rolodex.
"Mr. Humphreys says it stays."
They've stripped him of his honor,
    shoved him on the street.
He can't even take his telephone numbers
    home.

Twenty years of loyal service,
Twenty years of travel.
To the office, from the office,
    to and fro, to and fro.
Airports, Holiday Inns.
Exactly one hour for lunch.
Our working hours: 8:30 to 4:45.
Like a clock, like a migrating flock of
    birds leaving their arctic breeding
        ground at the *exact, same time*
          every year
            for a millenia.
Fifty years old.
And now it's over.

Going Home

What will Marti say?
What will Marti say?
The house isn't paid for. Melissa still
    lives at home.

Tommy's got three more years at Michigan State.
The cleaning lady will have to go.
I can sell the Corvette.
I promised Sandy and George
      the downpayment
            on their first house.
Marti will divorce me.
The train is empty, a lonely collection of plastic
      leatherette seats, rocking on the tracks,
            only women and old men rocking their
                way home — and me.

Such a surprise, such a shock, no one
      expected it.
Humphreys was always so nice to me
      to me to me
          to me to me.
Never saw it coming, rumors though.
Should've paid attention to poisonous gases
      floating through the neatly paneled cubicles,
            like mustard gas over the trenches.
Carnage: Johnson, Fiski, Halterdorn, Hershey,
      Panecetti — Firthearn.
Eliminated.
"We've cut our salary costs to the bone"
      by cutting the bones out of living men
            and throwing the flesh on the carpet
                in the conference room.
The cleaning lady will get them.
She can make soup with the bones.

Start a new career!
The opportunity of a lifetime!
A new beginning!
Your chance to start a new life!
You'll look back and laugh at all this
      one day
            if you survive.

Resumes,
Outplacement counseling: They'll teach the
        flesh-picked skeletons how to rattle
                    their bones for new masters who
                            don't mind finding their labor
                                    in the charnal houses
                                            at bargain prices.
Older workers have so much to offer
        in these days of changing
                    demographics.
But not here.
"You're outta' here."

"But I spent all my money,
        all my money," he thinks.
The new boat, the small summer house,
        college for the kids,
Marti's mink coat. The Christmas surprise because
        you had a friend who had a friend
                    who knew someone who had some
                            spare minks.
She looks like a rich lady now.
They were going to start saving when Tommy
        finished school
                    in three years,
And-everything-was-back-under-control.
When-their-finances-were-back-in-order.
Next year, next life, next galaxy.
Marti is going to divorce me.

The Homecoming

Marti stands at the kitchen phone in her pink running suit,
A cup of coffee in her hand.
She sees him in the hallway. Her eyes arch up
        into small gothic vaults, her tiny hand over
                    the phone.

"Are you sick?" she says.
"I was fired," he says.
The phone slides into its holder from her hand.
"Impossible."
"Not at all."
His shoulders droop.
Sorrow drips off their edges, down his sleeves,
        and into a hardening puddle on the carpet.
He's melting on her living-room floor.

Her eyes are wide, frozen, a deer in flight.
Her tiny hand with its thick wedding ring
        is stuck permanently to her mouth.
"I got four months full pay," he says.
Her hand unglues.
"We can get by," he says.
Her frozen eyes nod.
"Don't worry."
They nod more.
"What happened?" her pink-painted mouth asks.
It matches the running suit, a bright, hot pink
        the color of a melted wax crayon.
Cutbacks, repositioning, escalating costs,
The need for fast, quick cuts.
In the end, it was the Japanese who did it.
Competition from the internationalization
        of the domestic American market.
Someone in Tokyo made them fire him.

"What will you do?"
He shrugs, the sharp angles of his shoulders
        rising in a heave,
                like the withers of an old horse.
The smooth-sailing saga of her life
        crashes into a wall.
Her future lies in the hands of this
        stooped, straw-haired, aging man
                melting on her living-room floor.

She is a pawn in a chess game
    between two old broken men
        on the free chessboard in the park.
She is the victim.

The Daughter

Melissa comes home at 4 from Carven Community High School.
Pom-pom queen, tiny like her mother,
    the same rosebud mouth
        perked into a pink
            bow of a kiss.
"Daddy, are you sick?" she says.
Even her voice sounds the same.
His mouth stays glued with shame.
"Your father lost his job, dear," Marti says.
A fact of life, like "the zebras always
    eat grass in the corner
        of their pen."
A fact on animal behavior from trips to the zoo
    every summer
        with the whole family
            so Marti can explain life to her kids.

Melissa stares.
Daddy's become an alien.
He never comes home before 6 at night.
He doesn't exist during weekdays.
Is he the same man?
She looks at him close.
He looks funny in natural light and a suit
    on a weekday,
Like Mr. Herber, the principal,
    his sagging, wrinkled face and blooming jowls
        stuck on top of his shirt collar
            like a gob of ice cream
                on a sugar cone.

"Gotta' run," she says.
The Pom-Poms are practicing at 5 for the
      big game at 7 when the Carven Lions
              take on the Frankville Futuras
                    in basketball action
                        in the main gym.
"Go team!"
Daddy will take care of everything.
"I need new shoes," she says. "And a new
      dress for the winter ball, and
            lab fees were raised for
                chemistry."
Her parents stare at her, their eyes cold.
Her long list of needs and wants
      adds to the growing chain of debts
            that hangs around their necks
                like fetters on a slave.
Each new link brings their necks
      lower to the ground.
When does she start taking care of us?
She bounces off to the bathroom to take
      her second shower of the day,
            use up all the Vita-bath,
                and primp for her boyfriends.
Daddy will provide.

Isn't it nice to have such a lovely daughter?
So clean-cut, so bouncy.
She doesn't use drugs or drink
      that we know of.
He'd like to entwine his fingers
      around her perfect, graceful neck
            and tighten his grip,
                so her voice would spurt out
                    in raspy gasps.
Her last words would be:
      "I want this, I want that."
"*All* the *other* kids at school have one."

The Young Marrieds

Sandy is a sandy young woman
Her hair the color of spun sand from
  Oak Street Beach
Where she met George, and married him
   just one year ago.
The sand flows through her like an hourglass,
   timing the flow of money and goods
     and success and how she and
       George are doing.
They were doing alright until tonight.

"Your father lost his job, dear," says Marti,
   the eternal interpreter.
Jim stares mute, a tiny embarrassed smile
   tickling the corners of his mouth.
He eats his peas with his spoon.
He looks retarded.

Heavy fog descends and glazes everyone's eyes
   except Melissa's.
She's bought a new bracelet and
   clinks it in delight on her
     bird-thin wrist.
"Boy, Dad, what a bad break," George says.
The dutiful number-one son.
He knows all the punches life can give
   a guy.
Like a famous football player
   tackled to the ground,
     his knee twisted to breaking.
He'll never play again. And at the peak
   of his career!
A shame. Happens all the time.

What happens then?

The wounded warrior goes into business — somewhere.
Dragging his gimpy leg behind him to
        his office at the Hammond-McFerguson
                Financial Services Corporation
                        where he does important things
                                that he learned by playing
                                        football his whole life.
George doesn't want to think about it anymore.
He eats his peas and looks retarded, too.

"We've found a wonderful house," Sandy blurts.
"Just $115,000 with the cutest little yard."
She stares at Jim,
        her eyes wide with greed.
She wants, she wants.
Melissa jingles her bracelet
        in the embarrassed silence
                that settles over the table.
The scraping of cutlery on bone china
        sounds like fingernails clawing at
                a blackboard.

"The bitch," Marti thinks.
"Well, my dear," she says, her mouth pouring
        sweetness between its sugar-pink lips,
                "I am sorry, but I think we should
                        wait until next year when our
                                finances are more
                                        settled."
She dollops a glob of mashed potatoes on
        Sandy's plate
                with a plish-plosh splash.

"Yes, of course," Sandy says,
        her voice sweet with
                youthful disappointment,
                        her eyes cast down
                                in near-virginal sorrow.

"The bitch," she thinks.
She could have married the captain of the
     football team at
            Northeastern Arkansas
                 State Teachers College.
Why did she marry George?
She looks at him eating his peas
    with a spoon
        like his father.
They both look retarded.
All the other girls where she works have
    husbands who can buy them houses
        without any help from
            bankrupt in-laws with the
               smell of death about them.
She smashes her peas into her potatoes
    with the back of her fork,
        then pushes the plate away.
She won't come in bed with George
    for a month.

The College Kid

Tommy calls his mother that night.
Pizzas, books, and girls who want to
    fill their bellies with prime rib
        before he fills their bodies
          with sperm,
Are costing him alot of money.
Send more, he tells his mother.
Your father just lost his job, she says.
So send just a little bit more.
Maybe the meat-eating girls will
    settle for lasagna at
        The Pasta Express.
She promises more.
Tommy is her favorite.
She will have no new furniture in her

living room
            this year.
How she sacrifices herself
    for her children.

PART TWO

The Company Helps Out

The Fantick Outplacement Counseling Center is
        next to the Jiffy-Shop Supermarket
                at the Harton Park Shopping Plaza
                        in a grey little suburb with a
                                chirpy cheery name.
Not a prestige location. A bad sign.
Carpets worn like Indian paths
        through the woods.
Tired, fat women on the black, dial
        phones,
Working, working, working in their
        beige metal cubicles
                at their green metal desks
                        finding their clients the
                                dream careers of
                                        tomorrow
Today!
This is life on the cutting edge.

He sits in a chair
        rocky with uneven legs,
                in a cubicle with
                        a too-young man.
"You have many skills to offer," the
        young man says.
He has dandruff.
A soupy spot stares from his tie.
This is all the company
        was willing to spend
                after 20 years
                        of loyal service?
"We need to find where your skills
        are most needed," the young man says.

"Marketing managers are in
      high demand
            all over
                  the greater Chicagoland
                        area."

They will unravel him into a
      ball of old wool
            then reknit him into
                  a stylish new sweater
                        to serve a new lord
                              and master.
Should he find one.

"Not everyone makes it through here,"
      the young man says.
"Some have to take early retirement."
That means they can't find you a job.
Too bad.
You live off your reduced pension
      and work at the hardware store part-time,
            weighing nails and
                  recommending roach killer to
                        busy housewives pushing
                              new baby-strollers.
It's just old Mr. Firthearn,
Lost his job and was never the same.

He has no money.
Instead, he has Melissa's
      new clinky bracelet
            and its charge receipt from
                  Penney's.
And the love and affection of his
      dear family,
            of course.
Marti will divorce him.

He starts to sweat in his medium-good suit,
    the one he used to wear when he visited
        the company's medium-good salesmen,
To make sure they were on the ball,
    towing the line,
        bringing home the bacon,
            doing their best
                for the company.
He could taste their fear,
    a sharp, salty taste
        in the front of his mouth.
It tasted good.
He was the man from
    Central Headquarters,
        walking through their lives with
            hobnailed boots making sure
              they were
                doing their jobs.

He had fired men — men older than him now.
Slackards, drunkards, stupid, unlucky,
They had not met the grade,
    risen to the challenge,
        given it the "old college try."
He had suggested they seek
    "other employment opportunities."
He never saw them again.
One day colleagues,
The next day bums,
Orphans from the corporate family
    up for adoption again.

Their eyes spoke when he fired them,
They glowed with red-hot hatred
    or were foggy with grey sadness
        matching the grey of their
            sharp-creased suits.
It was hard to be a leader.

It would be harder selling roach poison
    to young matrons at the hardware store
        on their way to the supermarket
           to buy their husbands
                pork chops for dinner.

They work on his resume together.
"Most recent position: director of midwest
    sales for well-known supplier
        of chemicals
           to the manufacturers of
                aluminum-based
                    products."
He's really a Caesar without his legions.
A general on the lam.
Someone give him an army
    so he can retake Rome
        and show all the doubters
           what a warrior he
              really is.

The young man writes with pursed lips,
    a cheap pen clenched in his hand
        like a tiny child struggling
           over the alphabet.
Is this his first job out of school?

"We can use more pages if we need them,"
    the young man says.
But his life fits on one sheet
    with a big margin at the bottom.
"Clubs? honors? awards? distinctions?"
"Philanthropic leader in the community?"
Jim shakes his head no.
They paid him.
He gave the money to Marti.
Wasn't that enough?

The young man's lips tighten more.
"Employers like to see well-rounded job
        candidates."
He taps the end of his cheap pen on the
        metal desk.
Tap, tap, tap.
Jim's mind scrambles.
He played in the company bowling
        league for one season
                and was high-scorer at
                        the big championship game
                                against Wambaugh Metal
                                        and Machine Parts.
But his team lost.
The young man couldn't want *that?*
But he seizes it with delight
        and scratches it down
                in the big white margin
                        at the bottom of the
                                page.
Now the page is full.
It *is* the kid's first job out of school.
He will drink with his friends tonight
        and tell them about the
                bowling champ
                        out looking for a job.
Ha, ha, ha.

And that's it.
A resume with bowling glory on the bottom
        and the promise of a phone call
                when the list of sales
                        manager positions
                                gets updated
                                        next week.
The stenographer types his resume on
        a battered computer.
It prints up on a creamy, expensive bond.

Jim walks to his car,
He rips the bond to pieces as he walks.
They flutter behind him,
  spirits dancing in the wind.
They land in the dirty water
  of the parking lot puddles
    and sink
      to the
        bottom.

He'll write his own want ad:
  "Caesar seeks new army to
    cross the Rhine
      and reconquor Gaul."

The Old-Boy Network

Alvin Nagorsky is a mover and shaker
  in the smoky, smelly,
    stinky, gassy
      world of chemicals.
He sells millions every month
He drives a Continental.
He has two handsome, grown sons,
  a big house in a pricey suburb,
    a fashionable wife,
      a slutty mistress,
        and lots and lots
          of money.

Alvin is a success.

Alvin moves and shakes as president
  of the Greater Midwest Council of
    Sales Directors of Chemical
      Distributors and
        Manufacturers.
G.M.C.S.D.C.D.M.
Or the "Chemical Council" to those

in the know.
Alvin is there to help
as are all Jim's
Chem
Council
pals.
What are friends for
if not to help you replace
20 years of seniority,
a $75,000 salary,
and complete medical and
dental insurance?
Friends are a many-splendored thing.

Alvin takes him to lunch
at an expensive restaurant
and buys him a big
steak.
Alvin talks strategy.
"Look your best, stand tall, put
your
best
foot
forward."
"You have experience."
"You have seasoning."
"You have something to offer."
Jim chews his steak.
The soft fibers slide
down his throat in
smooth, little
lumpy gobs,
Washed down by the dregs of
an extra-dry martini,
no olive.
"I'll make some calls for you,"
Alvin says.
He has friends in high places,

low places,
           useful places.
Jim perks up.
The chemical industry is small,
        clannish, and depressed.
Ed Petrenich, Joe Frenaldi,
        and the only black man in the
                group, Al McAllister,
Are all out of jobs.
Al will find one first.
He fills EEOC quotas for black employees.
Jim, Ed, and Joe do nothing but work.
Jim thinks of taking up party tricks.
He can entertain top management at
        their annual corporate retreat
                in West Palm Beach every
                        winter.
Sales strategies and projections, anyone?
A few card tricks?
He feels like a fat salmon
        with a hook through its cheek.
Yanked from cold clear water,
        he flounders helpless on the
                bank until he dies.
He tightens his fingers around the
        stem of his pink crystal
                martini glass,
And orders another.
They talk about golf.

He eats 10 pounds of steak in two weeks,
He drinks 14 martinis,
He gains five pounds.
His friends are out there
        looking and calling and
                talking and doing
                        the best they can
                                for him.

Harry finds him a good lead
    in Akron.
But Marti refuses to move.
It would traumatize Melissa,
    who is now president of
        drama club, head cheerleader,
           and the favorite lay of
             the captain of the
               football team.
A sales job shows up downtown.
They'd take a chance on a fossil like him —
    for $20,000 a year plus commissions.
"Commissions can reach $15,000
    a year," the sales manager says.
His voice is awed.
He's 20 years younger than Jim
    and twice as stupid.
$35,000 is nothing.
Where does the money go?
Marti throws it in the toilet and flushes.
The green bills swirl,
    then disappear down the
        porcelain throat
           with a satisfied
             gurgle.

PART THREE

The Grind

Jim interviews, he talks,
He starts reading the want ads
    in the Sunday paper
        when he thinks no one is looking.
He goes into the city twice a week
    "to confer" with his friends.
He calls the young man at outplacement
    but the young man doesn't remember telling him
        about there being any jobs for
            50-year-old regional sales
                managers of chemical companies.
"I've got jobs in women's apparel,
    toys, farm equipment, and textile
        machinery
            in the Sun Belt."
"None of them would suit you," he says,
    dismissing 20 years of loyal service
        to the leading supplier of chemicals to
            the aluminum industry with a nod.
"Sorry."
He hangs up.

Jim and Marti watch money slip
    through their fingers,
Penny by penny, bill by bill.
He begrudges his children the meat they
    put in their mouths.
Melissa helps out by buying a cheaper
    brand of tampons.
Marti helps out by getting a job
    selling fish to their neighbors
        in the gourmet deli section
            of the big, new supermarket

on the highway.
She wears a big name tag on her
    cheap, striped uniform:
        "Hi! My name is Marti.
          "Can I help you?"
She smells like cod all the time now.
The oil seeps into her hands
    and becomes part
        of her papery,
           pink-white skin.
She laughs.
She calls herself a "fishmongress."
She tries to make the best
    of a
        difficult
          situation.
But she starts to hate him.
He can tell by the way she sets his
    bowl of soup down before him for
        lunch.
It slops over the rim of the bowl
    into the cracked plate
        beneath it.
The creases around her eyes deepen into
    tighter, steeper canyons.
They are filled with venomous snakes
    and scorpions with
        arched, stinging
          tails.
The creases in his pants are no longer perfect.
She irons his shirts leaving
    wrinkles in the sleeves.
He's a failure, she thinks.
A failure.
Her father was right 30 years ago
    when he said Jim would
        never amount to
          much.

See.

He can't help it.
Interviewers don't like him.
He hasn't done this stuff for 20 years.
And he looks old,
Older than his 50 years.
The midwest winters and summer suns
        have turned his fine, porous skin
                into leatherette,
Like the plastic seats of
        cheap, old
                kitchen chairs.
He abandons chemicals.
He stops lunching with Alvin and friends.
They understand.
You have to pull up and move the wagon
        train farther down the trail
                when you can't find water
                        and pasture nearby.
You got young'uns to worry about.
The fields are greener over there
        in financial services or
                food processing
                        or marketing to the
                                Chinese.

He actually talks with someone
        marketing to the Chinese.
A small Italian with drab
        olive skin and his
                fat, white partner
                        from the Bronx.
They sell ladies' purses.
500 million purseless
        Chinese women
                are waiting
                        for bags of

American cowhide.
The Italian and his fat white partner
    will be rich.

Deodorant would be next.
Two billion armpits.
After a hard day in the fields at the
    Lotus Bud Communal Rice and Hog Farm
        there was nothing better than
            a quick shower and a dab
                of Old Spice under the
                    arms.
It was progress.
Next it would be frozen turnovers to pop in
    the microwave oven before breakfast
        while the middle son
            toted nightsoil to the rice paddies
                in a battered zinc
                    bucket.
They were the original organic farmers,
    those Chinese.
We'd be more like that in this country
    if we weren't all
        so
            terribly busy
                and
                    stressed out.

They were both quite mad.
They offered Jim a job.
He could sell to the provincial council of
    Nanking through the national
        consumables directorate
            in the central party
                headquarters in
                  Peking.
The directors would like Jim.
They liked old men.

The Americans who came to them
        were much too young.
Old men were wise men.
All the directors
        were 75-years-old.
Jim would almost be a spring
        chicken
                to them.
They would like dealing with a man
        who had been a master of
                chemicals.
He must have been a
        very important man
                in America.
They would be so honored.

He was tempted.
He would travel to China
        meet strange people
                eat different food
                        learn to use chopsticks.
He took Marti to the local
        chop-suey joint
                to practice.
Over the pork chow mein she
        shot him down.
"At your age. The very idea!
        "It's so risky.
                "Stick to what you know.
                        "You're going to retire
                                in 15 years
                                        anyway."
She made it sound like next week.
He told them no.
They made a fortune
        without him.

He watched his four months of full

severance pay melt away into
    food and phone bills
        before his very
           eyes.

All was silence.
The phone lay dead in its
    cradle.
The mail brought only
    bills and mail-order
        catalogues.
His 500 resumes had disappeared.
Eaten by birds?
Lost in the mail?
He had carried each one to the
    mailbox on the corner,
        tenderly slipping
           it into the waiting
              lip of blue-painted
                metal,
Praying that the perfect company
    would respond: "You're hired.
        "You can do exactly
           what you've been doing for the
              last 20 years at
                twice the pay."
Plus a company car.
He would work in his old office,
    with his old people,
        and the same, old,
           manageable problems.
He'd get the old seat on the 4:58
    and rock his way home like a baby
        rocked to sleep in a hand
           cradle.
He'd nuzzle his mouth up to the corporate
    teat and suck on it until
        he fell into a

                contented sleep.
Then he would retire.

But no one wrote back.

The Solution

The Atkinson Real Estate Agency
      is looking for staff.
A white placard sits
      in their window.
"Classes begin soon: join our
      expanding new firm
            as a sales consultant."
Your career in real estate.
Make a great fortune.
Be rich.
Maybe he could learn enough
      to sell enough
            and buy enough
                  to make enough
                        just to live on
And then retire when he's 65
With just enough to
      live in a modest section
            of Tucson and play golf
               all winter.
His game would improve.
Marti would get a tan.
Her white skin would turn
      a dry crinkly brown and peel
            off in papery layers
                 to the sun-bleached bones
                    below.
She'd like that.

Real estate would save him.
He was at the bottom

of the well of his financial
resources and
starting to come up
dry.
He signed up for the next class
and hoped there was enough
water left to last
through a
small drought.
Marti stopped talking to him.
He was just too stupid to
get a real job.
She always knew
it would turn out
like this.
She put her face in her
cod-smelling hands
and cried.

Age was no limit
at Atkinson Realty.
A 74-year-old grandmother of
eight had once been
their leading producer.
She was very peppy,
a ball of fire,
a real go-getter,
Selling real estate to the gas-station attendant
pumping high octane
into her pink
Cadillac.
"Say, young man, I bet you
and your best girl are
out looking
for a house."
"Am I right?"
She always was.
She had had a stroke

and died one year ago.
Harold Atkinson
    wanted to have her stuffed,
Her pink brocade briefcase in one hand,
Her listing book in the other,
The tarty little red felt hat
    she always wore perched
        on her blue-gray hair,
The hat's whiff of veil
    pinned back to its crown with
        a diamond stick pin
           the size of a small
              screwdriver.
They settled for a plaque on
    the wall.
"In memory of Selma Gatch Hatterly:
    real estate saleswoman
        extraordinaire
        1975 - 1989."
Harold Atkinson believed
    in the elderly.
They had made him
    a lot of
        money.

Jim studied hard,
    his thick workbook
        spread out on the kitchen
           table among Marti's
              cooking and complaints.
He finally moved to Melissa's room
    his long legs curled under the
        curlicues and gold trim
           of her tiny, girl-like
              desk.
Contracts, sales agreements, escrow accounts,
Listings, closing statements, commissions,
Pro-rata taxes, water, sewer, and gas.

He passed with flying colors.
Now he had to make a buck.

PART FOUR

Hustling for a Buck

"The sky's the limit!"
    reads the sign in
           Harold Atkinson's office.
"Go for it!"
    reads the sign
           in the men's room.
But Jim had been "going for it"
    for years and
        his sky has
           developed a particularly
                low cloud cover.
It hovers a few feet
    above the bottoms
        of his pant legs.
He sold nothing for four months.
Not even a nibble.
Not even a polite
    "we'll call you back
        if we're
           ever
               interested."
Marti was frantic.
His bed now smelled like a
    fishing boat on the North
        Banks of Labrador.
Dead cod lay everywhere.
Marti's eyes stared at him
    at night with the cloudy
        lustre of a rotting
           mackeral's.
She was a dead mackeral in a flowered
    flannel nightgown.
They borrowed money on their credit cards

just to live.
"Things will get better,"she said.
"We'll pay it off after your
        first
                    big
                            sale."
Wives were supposed to be
        cheery through
                    "difficult times."
It said that in the
        wives' handbook.
But they didn't have to
        mean it.
It said that, too.
She hated him for real
        now.

He worked nights.
He worked weekends.
He walked through more
        ranch houses with
                    family rooms,
                            working fireplaces,
                                and ice-cube-making
                                    refrigerators
Than he thought existed in
        the entire world.
Buyers were lemon yellow fish,
        swimming through a sea of
                    split-levels,
Nibbling at one,
        eying another,
                    then swimming off to
                            another corner of
                                the ocean,
Leaving him in a barren waste
        with a few stingrays playing tag
                    on the dead, sandy bottom.

Then.
One day.
He sold a house.
What joy! What bliss!
He made $2400.
It was not enough for a wife,
        a girl in high school,
                a boy in college,
                        payments on two, late-model cars,
His mortgage, real estate taxes,
Income taxes, heat, telephone, electricity,
Sewer and water and a nice two-week vacation to
        a warm, uncrowded resort of good quality
                once a year.
His bills stood up and roared.
They ate his $2400 before
        it made it to the bank.
They chewed off its neat corners,
        and snapped it in half with
                powerful jaws,
Tossing the ragged carcass
        bleeding on the bank's
                steps.
Marti said he had to get
        another job.
He needed two jobs to fund
        his one life,
                and the lives and needs of
                        his near and dear
                                ones,
Who, of course, were
        too-young,
                too-needed-at-home,
                too-unskilled,
To work long hours at something
        they detested
                to bring

home

the

bacon.

They did agree to
     stop eating steak,
               not renew their health-club memberships,
               and not buy new winter coats
                         next year.
How they suffered!
Christmas would not be a big holiday
     this year.

He got a second job
     as a night security guard.
He walked deserted aisles
     in a metal-walled warehouse,
Miles of cardboard boxes
     stretching along either side,
The path to nowhere,
A maze.
He was the ball in a giant
     pinball machine,
               bouncing off miles of cardboard.
They paid him next to nothing.
He and his thoughts
     wandered the barren corridors,
               exhausted and rattling
                    like the ring of keys he jingled
                         in one hand.
He came home at dawn,
     slept until lunch,
               and went back to work.
He was the living dead.

The New Customer

Mr. Johnson was a big square man
     with a short, short haircut

buzzed up the sides and
        ending in a plateau
                across the top
                        of his head.
A flat-top.
It was a landing field for
        tiny little airplanes
                whose tiny little stomachs
                        would be tickled by the
                                stiff
                                        black
                                                hairs.
He was a sausage in a suit.
A hot big man
        with muscles
                like a horse.
They strained against his clothes.
A constant sweat beaded
        his forehead,
                rolled into his eyes,
                        made his skin glow
                                red.
He was looking for a house in
        a good neighborhood,
                with good schools,
                        good transportation,
                                in good condition,
                                        price was no object.
He had picked it out already.
He showed Jim a photo.
It was Jim's house,
        with Jim and Marti
                and Melissa and Tommy
                        and George and Sandy
                                and Fluff the cat
                                        standing in front
                                                looking stiff and
                                                        formal.

"That's my house," Jim gasped.
"Keep the cat," Mr. Johnson said.
"I have enough cats."
But he wanted everyone else.
Especially Marti.
"She's my kind of
        woman," he leered.

He was very business-like.
He had a contract in hand.
It promised Jim
        "eternal rest,
                "eternal happiness,"
                        and "eternal golf.
"At the courses of your choice, of course."
The guy was clearly mad.

How to get him out of here?
Don't want to make a scene.
Humor him.
Play along.
Maybe he'll leave on his own.
Jim smiled a wide flat smile
        that stretched the ends of
                his mouth out
                        to his ears.
"OK," he said. "It sounds good to me."
He signed.
Grace the secretary notarized it.
"Good choice," Mr. Johnson said.
"I'll call next week about closing."
And he left.

Jim sat down,
Another loony out the door.
Suddenly he started sweating.
He had a sharp pain in his chest,
He leaned against his desk,

He barely cried out,
     a muffled mumble like
          a wounded rabbit
               attacked by a dog pack
                    along the
                         railroad
                              tracks.

He slumped over in his chair,
     dead.
Grace the secretary called an ambulance.
Mr. Atkinson called Marti.
She cried.
She was relieved.
No more bumbling husband
     to embarrass her
          with his poverty
               and grief.
All his money stayed.
He had $800,000 in life insurance.
She would be a
     very
          merry
               widow
                    indeed.

Eternal Retirement

Jim woke to the gentle rocking of
     the train.
It was the 7:26.
He looked around.
He was dead.
He had been judged,
God had looked preoccupied.
This was eternity?
It looked like commuters
     on their way
          to work.

He recognized faces from
    20 years of rocking
        back and forth
            to and from
                Chicago.
The conductor smiled hello,
And nodded at his monthly pass
    stuck under a plastic
        flange on the seat
            in front of him.
Where was he?
He was on his way to work!
Not selling real estate,
Not guarding cardboard,
He was a chemical man again,
Selling to the leading users of
    chemicals in the
        aluminum industry.
He was wearing his best suit.
He felt great.

At the station he walked to his
    office with a zingy step,
        swinging his briefcase.
Everyone was there.
Humphreys. Catherine.
The pukey little salesmen
    who would never be as good
        as he.
His office was filled with
    crepe paper and balloons.
Oh bliss! Oh joy!
It was his retirement day!
Catherine brought him a big
    cup of coffee.
"We're going to miss you," she said.
A tear pooled in the corner
    of one blue-eyeshadowed eye.

"You're the best boss
     I
          ever
               had."
There, there.

Humphreys congratulated him
     on his latest coup:
Every manufacturer of aluminum in the
     midwest had ordered
          enough chemicals to keep the
               company's plants chugging
                    and spewing at full
                         capacity
For the next 30 years.
"Not bad, Jim," Humphreys said.
"Are you sure you won't stay?
"They want to make you C.E.O."
Jim shakes his head no.
His family needs and wants him.
He looks at the photo of Marti
     and the kids on his desk.
She looks friendlier.
The children smile with eternal gratitude
     for the privilege of
          bearing his name.

The party is very nice.
The chairman begs him to stay.
He offers him a lifetime
     consulting contract
          whenever he's in the area
               and wants to stop by
                    and just talk.
They hang a plaque with his name
     on the mahogany-panelled
          walls of the board of
               directors' room.

They buy him a gold-handled golf club,
    with his name inscribed on its shaft.
He chokes.
They give him a standing ovation.
They shake hands with him
    with pumping, grateful
        enthusiasm,
They adore him.

He leaves on the 3:54,
A full hour early!
Marti is waiting at home.
She is young.
Her face is kind and good.
The crevasses on her face have
    turned to gentle valleys
        smiling with the freshness
           of spring.
She asks about everything,
    listens enraptured,
        and kisses him
           with youthful
              passion.
"I want you," she says.
He smiles with pleasure.
This isn't Marti.
She looks like Marti,
    sort of.
But he doesn't care.
The Marti look-alike takes
    him to bed for
        two hours of sexual ecstacy
           like he hasn't felt since he
              was 19 and in the army
                in West Germany.
Then she makes him a sandwich
    with Polish ham on
        good white bread from

                    the bakery.
This *really* isn't Marti.
He's glad.

The children are all gone.
Their photos sit on the piano.
They're all geniuses with
        well-developed personalities
                and brilliant careers ahead
                    of them.
They write him adoring letters,
Thanking him for everything he's done,
Promising they'll come
        to see him soon
                next time they're in town
                        delivering a paper at the
                            international convention of
                                nuclear astro-physicists.
To think they were once
        little rug-rats
                happy to bounce on his
                    knee.
Now, so close to winning the Nobel Prize!

The fake Marti is all packed.
The house is to be closed for winter.
The next morning they're off to Tucson!
Flying first-class,
        the fake Marti by his side,
                he feels truly alive,
                    now that he is dead.

Their house in Tucson is adobe
        with bright red tiles for a roof,
                and a Mexican maid,
                        who cooks wonderful
                            meals over the mesquite
                                grill.

He is surrounded by wonderful, dear friends
    whom he has just met but
        who feel dear, and close,
           and sweet, and who love to
              listen to whatever
                he has
                  to say.
He plays golf with them
    all the time.
The courses are warm and green,
    the air dry and clean,
        and the views are
           forever.
He shoots par today,
Two under the next.
He and his new close friends
    plan a golf tour
        of the West Coast.
They'll stay in all the best hotels,
Eat all the best food,
After all, the company gave
    him $2 million of stock
        when he retired.
The fake Marti is delighted.
She loves to watch him
    do everything.

Over a moonlit dinner on their
    little patio,
His eyes on his beautiful wife,
He wonders,
    a small tweak
        in the back
           of his head,
Where the real Marti is.
But he doesn't wonder long.
He's dead and
    his golf game is improving.

On Earth

The real Marti irons Mr. Johnson's shorts,
    big black boxer shorts
        with extra room in the
            front for his amazingly
                big dick.
It has a hook on the end
    that drives
        Marti mad
            during sex.
She's hot for Mr. Johnson.
Hotter for him
    than for any man
        she ever knew,
            even the encylopedia salesman
                she once had a fling with
                    when the children
                      were little.

She hasn't washed in weeks.
Her blonde hair is dull
    and raggy.
The house fills with grime
    and old newspapers.
Bugs appear.

The children adore him.
Melissa develops herpes,
Tommy flunks out of school,
And George and Sandy's
    house burned down
        last week.
Mr. Johnson has brought
    them all such
        good luck.

Mr. Johnson sits home all day

Mr. Johnson sits home all day
    in his boxer shorts
        watching TV,
            drinking beer,
                smoking dope,
                    and screwing her.

Four times a day,
Five on weekends.
In between she irons his shorts
    and sends out for Chinese food.
He likes chicken with cashews,
Hold the MSG.

The heat is off.
Her arms are covered
    with scabby sores.
They have no money.
Mr. Johnson gave it away to
    a Jehovah's Witness who
        came door-to-door
            preaching the Lord's word.
It was such a nice gesture.

She's happier than she's ever been.
She doesn't miss
    old Jim
        at all.

Mr. Johnson likes that.

The End